D1795823

Reluctant Phoenix

Reluctant Phoenix

Helen Parker

Captain's Inkwell  2018

First Printing: 2018

ISBN 978-0-244-41233-3

Captain's Inkwell
c/o 40, Captain's Road
Edinburgh, Scotland EH17 8QF

For Sanne

Acknowledgements

With gratitude to tutors and fellow students
at Manchester Metropolitan University.

Many thanks also to Mike, Joanna and Stephen,
and to Brian, Jane, Georgina and Sheila.

Heather

Cairo

January 2011

It was the smell that first alerted Heather. What was it? Fire crackers? Stink bombs? Poisonous gas? She knew something was different as soon as she stepped off the metro. Crowds were normal in Nasser metro station, people's paths criss-crossed to and from the multiple entrances and exits, but tonight's crowds were more agitated than usual. Faces were strained, footsteps quicker. And there was that smell.

Her exit was the one that led over the Nile and into Zamalek suburb. The stairway was uncannily deserted. She soon discovered why: at the top was a column of police, lined up with unaccustomed precision, rifles at the ready. The shock took her breath away for a moment, but at least they were facing outwards, away from her. No exit that way, then.

Back in the station she stepped alongside two comfortable-looking women. 'Ana aiza aroh Zamalek. Fein, min fadlik?' *I want to go to Zamalek. Where, please?*

The first woman tugged on the sleeve of her companion, who asked Heather, 'What you need? Can I help?' Silently, Heather cursed her inadequate Arabic.

She exited in a different place and paused to get her bearings, while the familiar crowds swirled round her. The smell was much stronger here, snatching at her eyes and throat. Covering her nose and mouth with a corner of her cotton scarf, she made her way to the main road. Why was the traffic so light? Where was the customary gridlock? It was 10pm. Usually the pace would just be hotting up.

Across the main road, she headed towards the bridge. This was her route, but there were *no cars*! Instead, there were small pieces of debris and broken glass strewn across the road, yet the shops and cafes were open. Men sat in the coffee shops smoking and sipping strong sweet coffee with cardamom. A teenage boy with glasses of tea on a tray glided along the pavement from shop to shop. She couldn't see any women, but that wasn't unusual here. They'd be at home by now, attending to their families' needs. Mostly, people would ignore Heather, a lone western foreigner walking unusually fast.

Nevertheless, all her senses were bristling. She'd hear an occasional distant burst of laughter from inside a coffee shop and smell the pungent aroma of shisha as a door opened and closed. She gasped as a bold rat shuffled among the rich pickings in the gutter. Again she paused, trying to figure out a different route back to her flat. There wasn't one. At least, not on foot, alone, in the later evening, and with no taxis available. She had to cross the Nile. She'd have to follow where the road led.

There was no panic on the street, nothing to avoid. Whatever the incident, maybe it was over now, forgotten. Someone would clear up the glass in the morning. Furtively, keeping close to the shop fronts, away from the open road, she scurried the half mile towards the river. Here, the pavement was so narrow, just a kerb really, that she could easily be clipped on the arm by a passing wing mirror. Usually, that was the scary part, but it was different tonight.

At the beginning of the bridge, she stopped and held her breath. Something was going on. But there were a few pedestrians, including young couples. The presence of young women out and about here gave her courage momentarily, but peering down at the dark corniche she could make out groups of young men, gangs, throwing missiles up on to the bridge. Something landed at her feet and she was enveloped in a cloud of choking smoke.

Instantly she was blinded. Her eyes were burning and sealed, impossible to open. The sound and feel of bodies hurtling past her in both directions vied with the pounding of her heart in her throat. People were shouting, canisters clanging. She clung to the railings on the bridge and hoped she was as invisible as she felt, a female Scottish student with no axe to grind in the political morass happening around her. A merciful breeze, ever present along the Nile, brought partial relief, like escaping into the garden in the middle of peeling onions.

So this was tear gas.

Two more minutes, and she was able to feel her way along the railings to the far side of the bridge, open her eyes a slit and take the steps down into Zamalek suburb and towards her flat. There, below the bridge, was a different world. The working day had ended, the evening had begun, and talking, shopping, sauntering, eating, living, dying, fighting, loving, hoping and despairing were continuing as normal in Cairo's customary organised chaos.

Beth

Edinburgh

June 2012

Rain like hailstones beat a tattoo on the car roof. Two days and two nights without respite, a true Scottish summer. Soul was whimpering and restless, his wet fur making the car reek. Keeping the window open to dilute the smell of wet dog only intensified the noise and chill.

Beth shivered.

Homeless. It was a word with a certain aura of horror, of mystique. She'd learned that most homeless people hadn't become homeless because of drugs or alcohol. An addiction may have resulted from their homelessness, not the other way around. They may have been competent, successful people, fallen on hard times. They were without family support, had no financial resources, nowhere to go, hungry, dirty, degraded. How did she rate against the check list? Only one out of six. Because of the car and the money.

And The Wall.

Her morning routine included building The Wall. Meditation, some might call it. Brick by brick, or stone by stone, she built a mental wall of protection. Those solid, immovable rocks held back the past, obliterating memories of the treacherous house - the stairs with their perfidious banisters - and rendering the future undecipherable. Who knew? Who cared? Now, in the middle of the night, the wall might have been made of polystyrene.

Beth struggled into her waterproof, still damp after hanging uselessly over the back of the passenger seat, and pulled her umbrella from under the driver's seat. 'C'mon Soul. Walk.'

They skirted the supermarket car park, keeping away from the shop itself. Beth heard no one. Saw no one. She and Soul might have been the only living beings on the planet. She remembered thinking the same previously, on night shifts in the hospital, but never for long. There had always been a coughing patient, a summoning buzzer, some minor crisis to break the monotony and help her to stay awake in those ghostly small hours.

She had no problem staying awake now. Soul was wearing his collar, but Beth had found she didn't need the leash. He stayed close or returned when she whistled.

They came to the canal. The water level was high, and Beth shuddered, but at least there was no danger from traffic here, and no one to see her and wonder. The towpath was tarmac, so not muddy, despite the recent downpours. Soul trotted along, nose to the ground, tail high. At last the steady rain had reduced to a drizzle and despite the darkness, the path was visible when a faint apologetic moon peeked through the clouds from time to time. Beth could clearly see the patch of white on Soul's rump, never far ahead. She was still shivering, even though it was June, but with The Wall in place she was absolved from planning for the winter. She thought of coffee, and how she couldn't use the camping gas in the rain.

The damp cold of the dark canal towpath seeped, not only into her bones, but into her very spirit. If it was true that we all love ourselves, that we look after number one, then why was she here, walking alone in the early hours? There was a road bridge over the canal up ahead. Underneath, it would afford some shelter from the drizzle, but Soul had stopped. 'C'mon,' she urged him. 'It'll be drier.' But Soul was adamant. His heckles rose and he gave a low growl.

Longing, now, to be out of the rain, Beth stomped under the bridge, regardless. Instantly she heard a rustle and a sighing breath. The blackness was absolute, paralysing. Over her shoulder she looked for Soul, but he had gone. Like mute sirens, the oil slicks on the water beckoned, enticed. Beth expected to be strangled, drowned, raped or, at the very least, robbed. She wondered dully where the attack would come from, and was taken by surprise when a gentle rough voice spoke quietly from the deepest shadow: 'Ye've nae business bein' here, lassie. Awa' hame the noo.'

The human voice broke the spell and Beth turned and ran, her feet slapping on the wet path, her umbrella bumping her shoulder. Fear made her unnaturally breathless, and she slowed, panting, trying to restore her heartbeat, and it was then she spotted Soul, fifty metres in front of her, standing and looking, not at her, but at a tree growing beside the towpath.

As she watched, a figure, tall but whippet thin, that she had taken to be part of the tree, detached itself from the trunk and stood in front of her. It was a boy, a young man of undeterminable age, in an inadequate jacket and soaked jeans, rain trickling off his straggly hair.

'Evening,' he grinned. 'Reckon the rain's easing off.' He looked up at the sky, like an old man on an afternoon stroll. 'They call me The Wire. Pleased to meet you.'

Beth said nothing.

'It isn't polite not to introduce yourself when some says hello,' he announced.

'It isn't polite to interrupt a quiet evening walk…'

'Evening? It's two o'clock in the morning!'

'You were the one who said good evening!' Beth retorted, with a hysterical urge to giggle. How surreal. This couldn't be happening. If push came to shove, or worse, could she outrun him? She cleared her throat. 'Good morning. My name's Elizabeth.'

'Now that's better, Elizabeth.' Was he mocking her? 'Now what, may I ask, are you doing along this walkway at two o'clock on a wet morning?'

'I might ask you the same question.'

'Ah, that's easy. I live here. Here, and there,' he pointed towards the bridge, 'and everywhere,' his pointing hand swung round elegantly in an all-encompassing arc, like an aristocrat, a lord of the manor. 'But you sleep in your car. You were here three nights ago, but the dog – that's a new acquisition.'

Beth's heart began thundering again. How did he know? She'd been so cautious, so careful to be unobtrusive, to remain anonymous. She'd varied the car parks in which she'd spent the nights, the twenty-four-hour supermarkets with facilities. She hadn't parked in the same places or frequented any location at the same time each day. She had wanted a black car, but Dad had said yellow was safer, easier to see. She should have been adamant, over-ridden him.

'You heard what Scottie said under the bridge – *you've no business here, go home.*'

'I haven't got a home,' Beth said, but she felt a fraud.

'Well, let's see. You've got an umbrella that's not broken. You're only a bit damp, so you've not been outside consistently for the last two days. Your hair's clean and so are your finger nails.'

Self-consciously Beth looked at the hand that was holding her umbrella.

'Your skin's clear, so you're eating a good diet. The dog's wearing a new collar. You've got money. Your clothes fit you and they're clean. They're your own. I bet you've even got a mobile phone…'

'What are you, a spy? MI5?' Beth laughed, an uncontrolled explosive burst.

The Wire smiled serenely. 'No, merely observant. But when you go to buy breakfast at that supermarket in the morning you can get me a chocolate croissant.'

Beth was speechless. The Wire reached forward a hand and stroked the side of her face. She jerked back, but not before noticing that his nails were severely bitten and he wore a signet ring, a tiger's eye stone apparently set in gold. She turned haughtily and stalked back towards the car park, Soul trotting contentedly beside her.

Back in the car, the dog settled down immediately on the passenger seat while she turned the ignition urgently, yanked the car into gear and roared out of the car park, straight to the motorway, the skin of her cheek burning where The Wire had touched her, and already aware of a gaping gash in her Wall.

Heather

Cairo

January 2011

Heather's concentration was waning. She looked round to see if the other four students were feeling the same. Yep, she recognised the signs. Andrea was wrapping her blond hair round her fingers, her blue eyes glazed over. Rosa had a none-too-surreptitious handbag mirror inside her text book, and she was trying to re-stick one of her false eyelashes. Tarantula legs, Tony called them. Ryan was stretching his long legs under the desk which was much too small for him, and trying to supress a yawn.

Only Martin the Geek was listening to the teacher with rapt attention. He pushed his glasses up on his nose and tried a question. *'Ostez Samir,'* he began, *'ana aiza arif fein…'* but Heather gave up trying to follow his question, because she had spotted Tony's blond head. He was bobbing up and down in the corridor outside the classroom.

What was he doing there? Had his class finished already? She glanced at her watch. Another fifteen minutes to go. There was a brief knock on the classroom door and the director stepped smartly into the room. He was a big man, balding and clean-shaven, always smartly dressed, but aloof. In Heather's limited experience, Egyptian men were confident, outgoing, eager that you should love their country. Like Ostez Samir. He was a good teacher, mostly, and always up for a laugh. But with the best will in the world, it was hard to keep going on grammar in the second half of the afternoon.

Heather and her four fellow-students looked up, and Ostez Samir paused by the whiteboard, marker in hand.

After a short exchange in Arabic between him and the director, too fast for Heather to grasp, the director exited, but as he opened the door again, Heather glimpsed Tony gesticulating incomprehensibly to her.

'Okay, we finish now,' Samir announced, already picking up his book and papers. 'Early today because there is some trouble in street. Is better you to go now.'

'What kind of trouble?' Heather asked.

'Oh, you know,' Samir said, waving his arms ineffectually. Heather didn't know.

'Neighbourhood dispute?' Martin suggested.

'Cost of stupid tomatoes?' Rosa giggled, trying to translate the Arabic idiom they'd learned the previous day.

The other four students were gathering their belongings in haste, and Heather followed suit. Samir said goodbye and strode out. In the corridor, Tony was still waiting impatiently. He gave her a peck on the cheek. 'Hurry up! If we leave now we might see some action!'

'What sort of action?'

'Some of the locals are protesting about the president sitting on millions of dollars while they can't afford bread. Sounds like Marie Antoinette. *Let them eat cake.*'

'But *yesterday* was demonstration day,' Heather said, the memory of tear gas still vivid, 'not today.'

Tony guffawed and Heather, her own foolish words echoing in her head, felt embarrassed. He said, 'Demonstrations don't obey any rules! Like everything else in this country. That's what makes it so exciting.'

'Wait! I left my scarf.' Heather hurried back down the corridor into the classroom and retrieved her light cotton scarf from the back of her chair. It seemed that her class was the last to be dismissed. Everyone had left the building. As she and Tony ran down the stairs, they were met by the other four coming back up.

'About turn,' Martin told them. 'The bowab won't let us out yet. Says there's an angry crowd gathered round the gate. Told us to wait a while.'

'What's it got to do with him?' Tony remonstrated. 'Bowabs are supposed to guard the outside of the door, not legislate for those inside. He's getting above his station.'

'That's not fair,' Heather began, picturing the kindly old man with a creased, leathery face who sat night and day outside the language school, nodding to the students as they arrived and left, gratefully accepting tips and little gifts of food, while doing odd jobs in exchange.

'Well, he's only a servant!' Tony grumbled.

'He understands more of the situation than we do,' Ryan said. 'Let's give him the benefit of the doubt.' Heather couldn't help warming to Ryan. He was tall and broad-shouldered with a lazy Texan accent. And he was always reasonable. Tony scowled and said nothing.

Rosa linked arms with Andrea. 'So, no homework. Very good. I very thirsty. I go to drinks machine.' The two girls marched off together to the student common room and Martin and Ryan followed.

Tony grabbed Heather's arm and pulled her aside. 'Let's go up to the roof! We'll be able to see from there without being seen.'

It was true. Their school building was a traditionally-styled Middle Eastern edifice with a flat roof and access from the central staircase. Tony took the steps two at a time, and Heather trudged up after him. From up there, above the fifth floor, they had a bird's eye view of the street, the Nile and the Qasr-El-Nil Bridge. The bridge must be closed to traffic: there were thousands of pedestrians moving slowly towards the city centre.

'Looks like they're heading to Tahrir Square,' Heather remarked. She and Tony sat down and leaned their backs against the brickwork, warmed by the afternoon sun. Her four classmates looked upon her and Tony as a couple. It was true that she went to events with him, that they did things together, and she appreciated his companionship, especially in Egypt. But they wouldn't have been a couple if they'd met in the UK.

'What did your teacher tell you about what's going on?' she asked him.

'Not much. I don't think he knew very much. Anyway, he said it in Arabic. I'll have to brush up on my political vocabulary.'

'Huh! You're a natural. You don't even have to study. Bet you passed your school exams with flying colours every time.'

'Ha! I wish!' Tony laughed a brief, rueful laugh. 'The only way I was ever able to pass exams was by cheating. Not that I wasn't clever enough. I was.' Heather smirked. Modesty wasn't one of his attributes.

Tony ignored her and went on, 'But I never studied, and when it came to revision, I didn't have explicit enough notes or a background of knowledge about any of my subjects. Except maths. I found maths easy, and it didn't need revision. It was like doing puzzles.'

'Huh. Maths,' Heather muttered. 'I had to pass because I wanted to do physiotherapy, but I hated it.'

'Ah, but I was in love with my teacher. She was

young, blond and funny, and when she stretched to write step-by-step working on the board, her short skirt used to ride up...'

'Stop it!' Heather thumped him. 'But what did your parents think?'

'What about?'

'About your school performance? Or lack of it.'

'My dad used to say *You'll never get a good job, son, if you don't go to college. And you'll not get to college if you don't pass your exams.* My dad imagined a good job was one where you wore a suit and left for the office on the 7 o'clock bus every day. Thing is, I don't respect them or their opinions.' He snorted. 'Their lives are just little suburban time-fillers, an endless dreary round of breakfast, work, dinner, television and bed. Then, at the weekend, a brief session in the pub after mowing the lawn. A tiny square lawn. In the summer they go to Rhyll or Morecambe for a week. And once, they had a week in Lanzarote, where Mum was too hot and Dad complained about the crowds.'

He stopped and flicked little bits of masonry over the parapet. Heather got up and leaned on the railing to watch the protesters. Most were young, about the same age as herself and Tony, people with their whole lives ahead of them. Far from being an angry crowd, they looked like holiday-makers on an outing. The guys were chatting loudly, gesticulating generously. The girls, headscarves colour-co-ordinated with their jumpers or shoes, were laughing and enjoying themselves.

But Tony was continuing, 'Anyway, I've visited more countries than my dad's had hot dinners, I've picked more varieties of fruit than you'd find in Tesco's, I've slept under a lot of mosquito nets or under the stars, I've met a lot of girls, had a few amphetamine trips and now… and now I've decided to stay put for a bit and learn Arabic. It's easy. Like maths puzzles.'

He paused, and Heather realised her mind had snagged on the bit about a lot of girls and a few amphetamine trips. He'd been looking outwards, at the slowly moving crowds. Now he turned to her. 'How about you? Bet you did it all by the book. Bet your parents were dead chuffed.'

'Well, they were chuffed when I qualified, yes.'

'But then you moved here and they miss you like hell and want you to go back home…? Wait a minute, you said they're…'

'Divorced.'

'Yeah. Er… sorry.'

'I guess you could say it was all hunky dory until the arrival of the Cat Woman.'

'What?' She had Tony's full attention now, though she wasn't sure she wanted it.

'Yep. Pa went after the Cat Woman.'

'*Pa?*' Tony was smirking.

'Yes! Father. Dad. I call him *Pa*. All right?' It came out more aggressively than she'd intended.

'Yeah. All right. Chill.'

'Well, Pa left Ma – my *mother*…' Heather paused but Tony said nothing, '… for some woman he met at the vet's because her cat was sick, and our dog - *Pa's dog* - had swallowed the front door key. We used to go to Israel when I was small, and I loved it, so I was going to go back there and learn Hebrew and work as a physio on a kibbutz or something. But I went off the idea and swapped sides and opted for Arabic instead.'

14

'You didn't need to fall out with your *pa* so comprehensively. Most people's parents are divorced nowadays.'

'But it wasn't just that...' Heather stood up and leaned over the railing at the edge of the roof. She wafted her hand in front of her face. 'The mozzies are out. Let's go inside.'

Gregor

Edinburgh

June 2012

Darling Heather,

It's mid-summer here in the Scottish capital, but not so as you'd know it! We've had torrential rain for several days this week, though that UFO did put in an appearance for a couple of hours yesterday. You've caught me writing about the weather. How boringly Scottish. If you're still in Egypt I guess you're sweltering. I expect you'd love a bit of drizzle!

Of course, you know how I spend most of my time. You never were turned on by history at school, though I wonder if anything has changed now that you've lived through an Egyptian uprising. You'll have heard the one about 'History repeats itself. It has to. No one listens'. So true. Of course, for me, history continues to be riveting, so it consumes my days – that and walking Nero on Arthur's Seat.

Gregor leans back from the computer and stretches his long arms and legs. He rereads *you've lived through* and feels that familiar panic-induced bile rising in his throat. Surely, if she'd been killed, he would have heard. Somehow.

Arthur's View, Gregor's unpretentious detached house, is perfectly situated between the traditional tenements of the Old City and the extensive hilly wilderness of Holyrood Park, the Queen's back garden. From his study window he can see the iconic shape of Arthur's Seat. *The same shape as the sphinx,* Heather had remarked. Sparkling memories of sunny, laughter-filled family picnics flit through his mind like chick-flic promos. Today, clouds create patterns of light and shade dancing across the sheer cliffs of Salisbury Crags, highlighting bright patches of gorse and occasional clumps of heather.

Suddenly Gregor longs to be up there. The hillside welcomes him like the house never does. It embraces him, forgives him, demands nothing except his presence. He doesn't feel alone up there – not because of the ubiquitous ramblers – sight-seers, regular dog-walkers, fitness-freaks, even sketchers, their paper secured by a dozen bulldog clips from the chilly, cleansing wind – but because of the age-old volcanic rock. Its permanence. Its immutability. The 360 degree view can mirror his moods. Dark clouds blacken the water of the estuary, whipping up little white horses, heralding storm and high tide. On bright days the sunshine seeks out every winking window, every silver dome, every dazzling metal surface of the multi-faceted city. What dramas, domestic or international, Arthur must have witnessed from his seat above Holyrood Palace, watching kings and queens come and go, succeed or fail, live and die.

Nero thumps his heavy black tail twice. That dog's a mind-reader.

How could anyone ever get tired of this place? Hill walking on your doorstep, just metres from all the attractions that a capital city has to offer. An environment to suit young or old and everything in between. How could Heather turn her back on it? He knows, of course: not it – him.

What's the point of writing?

Yesterday, when I was walking the dog,

He pauses and his eyes drift to the window again, hypnotised by the hill. He knows why he's writing – it brings her nearer, though he imagines she'll ignore the email. She'll flounce off defiantly with her pretty little chin in the air to put some music on as if to drown out his voice. Funny things, emails. You can't quite delete even the spam without glancing at it. Promotional snail mail is different. You can bin it unopened, or return to sender. Of course, she may have put a filter on emails from him, but something keeps him writing. Better keep it brief, in case she just gives it a couple of seconds. He deletes the second paragraph, but in the first he's aiming to show her that he's putting himself in her shoes. Or trying to.

Tearing his gaze from the red-jacketed ramblers, pinpricks on the hillside, the constant but ever-changing view, he concentrates on the screen again.

Yesterday on the hill I met

No, not met. How to describe it? He'd been walking a few metres behind a girl who looked so much like Heather that his breath caught in his throat. Same height and slight build, same long dark brown hair. If she hadn't slipped and fallen, he'd have quickened his pace and overtaken her, just in order to catch a glimpse of her face. Maybe he's getting a bit paranoid, if every slim, be-jeaned female between the ages of eighteen and thirty might be Heather. He begins paragraph two again.

Yesterday Arthur's Seat was particularly muddy and slippery after all the rain we've had. A girl walking her dog in front of me slipped and hurt her ankle. Probably a sprain. Definitely not a break, *though **you**'d have known for certain. Anyway, I ended up helping her down the hill…*

Gregor stops again. How can he tell her that the daughter-look-alike had been very reluctant to accept assistance? That he himself had so wanted to help, but shrank from the physical contact? That she worried all the time that she was too heavy, leaning on him, whereas she was as light as Feather Heather, a skinny girl who looked as though a puff of wind might derail her. Gregor never lets that look deceive him. Girls like that can have wills of steel, can look sixteen while being world-weary, or having the wisdom and life-experience of a thirty-year-old. Of course, face-to-face, she didn't look at all like Heather. Her fair skin didn't have that warm Mediterranean glow that must stand Heather in good stead in Egypt. She didn't have Heather's dark eyes, either. Her eyes were alarmingly blue.

…but she was very upset. Irrationally, I'd say. Any adult with a sprained ankle will put on a brave face after the initial 'ouch'. I took her back to the house and she sat on the front doorstep. She cried harder after I made her a cup of good coffee and I insisted she ate something sweet. (I still make oatmeal cookies!) I was trying to treat for shock. Wish you'd been there.

Wish you'd been there? No, that's no good. Makes him sound pathetic, when all he means is he would have valued medical input.

You should've been there.

No, that's worse. Sounds judgmental. Condemnatory.

Her dog was a spaniel. She called it Soul. Said it wasn't really hers, but it had attached itself to her. She'd been to the police station to report finding it but she was hoping no one would claim it. Found myself hoping the same. She seemed to need it. Anyway, after a while she recovered a bit. I gave her a tubigrip. She accepted a couple of pain-killers, then I gave her a lift back to her car in a supermarket car park. Said it wasn't far to drive home, and she was confident her ankle would hold up.

Finally Gregor revises his email and sends a brief, sanitised, totally emotion-free version and, given that he doesn't really believe Heather will read it, can't resist adding his usual postscript.

Miss you. I'm innocent. Please believe me.

And he hits *send* before cold feet kick in.

Heather

Cairo

January 2011

Heather and Tony went into the student common room. The now empty space, usually alive with chattering international students milling around the drinks machine, was uninviting. The garish orange plastic seats, cold in winter, but stickily sweaty in summer, were stacked in a corner. A couple of ageing sofas faced each other across a stained coffee table. Three non-matching easy chairs, probably donated by students moving on, faced a small bookshelf of dictionaries, grammar books and language-learning resources.

Heather's four classmates were drinking cola bought from the drinks machine. Andrea and Rosa were sharing a sofa. They stopped talking and looked up as she and Tony went in and Rosa tugged her skirt down. It showed just an inch or so of slim, tanned thigh. She probably wore her skirts much shorter in Italy, but this was Egypt. Andrea held the cool can against her forehead and stared ahead.

Ryan, relaxed and dependable, set his meaty knees apart and rested his hands comfortably on them.

In the stillness they could hear shouting in the street. 'Wonder what they're saying?' Martin mused. 'Wish my Arabic was better. Can you hear it Tony?'

Tony would like that - Martin was deferring to him.

'It's about money,' Tony said. 'The injustice of taxes and the rise in the cost of living.' Heather didn't know whether to believe him. Was he making it up in order not to lose face?

'I sure as hell don't blame them,' Ryan muttered. 'Ain't no justice in this whole region.'

'But is so – so - colourful. So different. You can do - something, er, anything!' Rosa's sparkly dark eyes scanned the room. Tony grinned. Heather groaned inwardly. Tony was so susceptible to a pretty face. Rosa's exotic Italian accent merely added to the attraction. All respect due to Rosa for learning Arabic through English, though her English wasn't that good. It must be a rigorous mental exercise.

But just now Heather disagreed with Rosa's view of Egypt. You could do anything? Heather had found, rather, that you could do very little. She felt constrained by wearing long skirts, long sleeves and high necks in the oppressive heat. She'd got used to walking around keeping her eyes on the ground to avoid unwanted attention, even though her dark hair and olive skin were an advantage. Thankfully, she didn't get the hassle that Andrea had to put up with, being blond. Heather had never held feminist views, but the situations of some of the downtrodden women nudged her towards a belligerent discontent.

Just then there was a commotion in the street. The volume increased exponentially and then there followed a series of sharp cracks. 'Was that gun shots?' Andrea squeaked, running to the window. Her hands flew to her face. 'I've never heard gun shots up close!'

'Away from the window,' Ryan said quietly, getting up quickly to take her elbow and pull her away. 'You don't know what kind of mood they're in. Might take a shot at anything movin'.'

Andrea allowed herself to be led, and stood with her back to the wall, panting a little.

'Or they might just be shooting in the air,' Ryan

added. 'You know how it is when they get excited.'

Was he right, or just trying to console Andrea? Heather wiped her sweaty palms on her jeans.

Tony crept to the side of the window, squinting at a forty-five degree angle. 'There are definitely two opposing factions,' he stated.

'Yep. Pro-Moubarak and anti-Moubarak,' Ryan said sardonically.

'They say he was a good leader at the beginning, but he got greedy,' Martin said.

'Yes. Someone once said, *Power corrupts and absolute power corrupts absolutely*,' Tony quoted.

'Yeah. That'd be Lord Acton, one of your nineteenth century politicians,' Ryan told them. Heather's toes curled. Tony would take that as a gauntlet. She knew Ryan. He was her classmate, after all, so she knew he was merely stating a fact, not scoring points, but Tony was scowling. He began to pick at some flaking paintwork on the window frame, like a bull in a bullring pawing the ground. If the six of them had to spend a long time cooped up together, ill-feeling would be the last thing they'd need. Why did men have to observe this pecking order all the time? What a waste of energy. Why couldn't they just – *be?* But Tony had chosen to settle down and apply his capable mind to Arabic and Heather felt honour-bound to support him and to keep the peace.

'Is anyone injured? Can you see?' she asked, standing beside Tony and taking his arm.

'Looks like they're heading to Tahrir Square. That follows. It means liberation!'

'Yeah. Liberation from the British,' Ryan said with a wry smile.

Oh, no, Ryan, Heather thought, not again. Don't get

him started.

'Well, what about the fall of Saddam Hussein and what's happened to Iraq?' Tony bristled. Ryan merely nodded.

'Why to Tahrir Square?' Rosa asked.

'It's the centre of bureaucracy,' Martin said, '...and corruption. The Mugammaa.' They all nodded. They'd all had to queue, frustratingly, for hours in that chaotic municipality building to renew their visas, only to be told to come back tomorrow with different documents. 'There are five-star casino hotels pandering to the rich and famous,' Martin continued, 'while Egypt's finest historical treasures are crammed into an inadequate, neglected space with the infrastructure crumbling all around it. All the tourists who ever come to Cairo go there. They have to pass through Tahrir Square. If I was the president, I'd want...'

'If I ruled the world...' Tony sang. Everyone ignored him.

'If I was president,' Martin repeated, 'I'd want to be proud of my capital city. I'd plant grass or a garden in the middle of the Square, with benches so that those tourists could sit and admire it. I'd erect a statue or monument or something of one of Egypt's Nobel prize winners – Ahmed Zawail, or...'

'Naguib Mahfouz,' Andrea supplied.

'I wonder if that guy, Mohamed Bouazizi, had any idea what he'd started,' Heather said.

'That Tunisian guy?' Rosa asked.

'Yes, the one who set himself on fire because the authorities wouldn't let him have a street vendor's license.'

'Seems a bit of a radical protest, just for a street vendor's license,' Tony said.

'Exactly!' Martin almost spat. 'After so many years – decades – *centuries* - of bureaucratic rubbish, corruption, military dictatorship…' He was spluttering now. 'It had to be something radical. It was crazy, but I admire him!'

Heather had never heard Martin hold forth like that. He was blushing, now, taking off his glasses to polish them on his T-shirt, but she'd been impressed by his impassioned political stance and she wanted to say something to encourage him. 'Right…' she began.

'Ooh, take a chill pill,' said Tony, grinning.

'If I was an Egyptian, or an Arab, even, I'd want change,' Martin urged, unabashed this time. 'If I had a wife I'd want her to be able to go to university and to get a job. I'd want a president who was seen and respected by the people, not one who stole billions of dollars from them and owned palaces plastered with gold while there are villages with no clean water, no schools, no *food!*'

'Maybe it's because it's such an enormous country,' Ryan said, 'an unmanageable size to organise and legislate for.'

'But look at the US!' Martin argued. 'It's just as big. I know the rural areas are different from the cities, and I know there are a lot of problems in the cities, but at least the people have shoes…'

There was a pause while they listened to occasional shouts from the street.

'Is too warm in here,' Rosa complained. 'Tony, please to open the window.'

'The mozzies are out,' Heather said, and reached for the switch to the ceiling fan. Nothing happened. She sighed. 'The fan's not working.'

Rosa moved over to stand beside Heather. 'Is correct

switch?' she asked, trying it as Heather moved aside, then going over to try the light switch instead. Nothing.

'There's a power cut,' Tony groaned.

'Ah. That explains why I can't get any Internet access,' Martin said.

'Wonder if it's just our building?' Tony peered from the window at the other buildings down the street and Heather went to join him.

Andrea was sitting near the drinks machine, huddled over her phone. She sighed, put it away in her pocket and folded her arms around herself. Rosa sat down beside her. 'Is true,' she exclaimed. 'Now my flat-mates not know where am I.'

'No one will know if we're safe,' Andrea added. 'I mean – after the gunshots – they might think...'

'Let's just hope...'

'Useless infrastructure.'

'Par for the course.'

'Could be a government scam to prevent flash mobs.'

They lapsed into silence. Tony sprawled on the other sofa and took his shoes off. 'Coming to join me, babe?' he said to Heather. He patted the seat next to him. Excitement, tension and a long day had taken its toll. He needed a fresh shirt. Heather stayed at the window.

Dusk in Egypt never ceased to take her by surprise, even now. It seemed that one minute the sun was shining, even in January, and the next, night had fallen. Outside, undeterred, the crowd moved in a phalanx towards Tahrir. Against the fading sunset Heather could make out silhouettes of young adults. Here and there, pinpricks of light suggested torches or an occasional match. Was this protest justifiable? Was there a righteous cause to be fought over? Were there human rights violations to object to, claims to make, tubs to thump? Was she morally obliged to raise her voice with others'? If so, better to be out there…

But this was not a foreigners' dispute.

Inside, the common room was in darkness.

'If we're going to be here a long time, maybe we should play a game?' That was Martin's voice.

'What, like I spy?' Tony mocked. 'I spy with my little eye, something beginning with F.'

Beth

Edinburgh

June 2012

Saturday afternoon and the library was closed. No chance to charge her phone or laptop, then, but what was the point, anyway? Now that the term had finished, Beth's uni classmates would assume she was just staying on in Edinburgh for the summer. After ten days or so, any hope of Uncle Bob or Aunty Nessa getting in touch was fading. And Paul? Her only cousin was beginning to be a distant memory. She hadn't seen him for, what? Two years? He'd probably changed – grown a beard, put on weight, developed muscles. Did he ever think of her? Or were his infrequent brief emails merely duty?

As for national or international news, she could get that on the car radio. If she wanted.

Beth decided to vary her walk with Soul and drive to Cramond. There was plenty of space along the waterfront there for a dog to run safely with no danger of cars and little risk of his getting lost, especially since he never seemed to stray far from her, as if his very survival depended upon her - a comfortable, reciprocal arrangement. But was he being short-changed, now, because her sore ankle was holding her back? Cramond would be easy and besides, she used to love to go there as a child.

The warm sun had enticed weekend strollers along the riverside, together with small children learning to cycle on the wide, traffic-free promenade, while skate-boarders and roller-bladers darted expertly in and out. There were people sitting at riverside tables outside the café, and there was a queue at a nearby ice cream van. The sea-salt tang mingled with the inviting aroma of coffee. Beth paused to watch the swans that always gathered, hoping for scraps, at the point where the narrow River Almond flowed into the wide, majestic Forth.

At the head of the causeway leading to Cramond Island, she stopped to study the tide times. The tide was at its lowest, but Beth's natural caution had always discouraged her from walking across. Childhood tales of people who got stranded all night on the island, or who incurred the wrath of coastguards by needing to be rescued, curbed her curiosity, although crowds of people made it there and back safely every low tide. The very thought of the returning tide catching up with her, swirling round her ankles, cutting off her route to safety, sent waves of terror though her.

Soul was already off along the beach, nose to the ground as usual. Beth walked eastward towards the place where the Firth of Forth, already so wide she could hardly see the opposite shore, opened out into the North Sea. She paused to watch a metallic grey Royal Navy ship progress up-river towards the naval base at Rosyth, along the deep channel beyond Cramond Island.

She was so engrossed in the glittering vista, she failed to notice that someone had stopped beside her.

'We can't go on meeting like this! How's the ankle?'

Alarmed, she turned. It was the man from Arthur's Seat. Her knight in shining armour. George... Graham... Gregor? Yes, Gregor. Soul ran up to greet him like a long lost friend. 'Oh, getting better, thanks.' She was disconcertingly glad to see his familiar face. Their only meeting had been significant for her. His kindness was like an oasis of warmth in a season of bitter loneliness. He'd given her a tubigrip and fed her with cookies and good coffee. He was wearing jeans and an old tartan shirt with the sleeves rolled up, instead of a bulky waterproof, and she could see he was older than she'd originally thought, but quite wiry and strong. His hair was grey but still thick. 'Just enjoying the view.'

'Yes, it's lovely, isn't it?' He stood beside her, looking out. 'We used to come here as a family. Very safe for dogs and young kids.' She nodded. She felt strangely at ease with him. Despite childhood training of not talking to strangers, and her own recent determination to keep The Wall firmly intact, she didn't feel at all threatened.

'Soul can run around here while I just amble. Easier on the ankle,' she said.

'Mind if I amble with you? Old Nero, here, is better at ambling than sprinting these days.' He patted the black Labrador.

'Of course.' They continued on down the path.

'Soul - unusual name for a dog?'

She laughed momentarily, embarrassed. 'Yeah. Remember I told you he kind of adopted me? He looked lost and I tried to find his owner. Finally I said to him, *There's nobody here, not a soul.* He pricked up his ears every time I said *soul*, as if it really was his name, so it became his name.'

'He seems perfectly content with you.' They watched the two dogs, tails in the air, trotting along the beach.

'Magnificent view of the estuary from the train going to Inverkeithing,' she said, changing the subject. 'Have you been?'

'Yes. But once my daughter learned at school about the Tay Bridge disaster...' Gregor interrupted himself to add,

'D'you know the story? Sir Thomas Bouch was a nineteenth century engineer, and he designed the Tay Railway Bridge. Queen Victoria travelled over it in June 1879 and she was so impressed she gave him a knighthood for it, but it turned out to be premature because the bridge collapsed during a storm the following December, and Sir Thomas was blamed for cheap workmanship.'

The account rang distant bells and Beth remembered school history lessons. 'Sorry. I'm boring you,' he said. 'It's just my passion for history.'

'No, no, I'm interested in history, too,' Beth assured him, 'at least if it's relevant, like, local, or something.'

'Seventy-five people died,' Gregor continued, 'and Sir Tom himself died a few months later. The poor guy must have been broken-hearted. His health was already poor and people think this was the last straw.'

Broken-hearted. The last straw. The world swayed around Beth and in the dark recesses of her mind, memories and hallucinations began to swirl in a devilish dance. She held on to the wall for support.

'Oh!' Gregor gasped. He reached out as if to take her elbow, but stopped short, his hand in the air. 'Is your ankle very sore, or…'

He had given her a cast iron excuse for faltering, but suddenly she couldn't lie to this sensitive man. She wanted to tell someone. She needed to peep through a tiny gap in The Wall. 'Yes, it is a bit sore,' she conceded, 'but it's just that, that, my father died recently, and talking about people dying still…'

'Oh, I'm so sorry. So sorry.' Now she felt embarrassed about distressing him. 'Let's head back,' he suggested.

She nodded, they turned round and she forced

conversation again. 'So, you have a daughter?'

'Yes. Must be about the same age as you. Maybe a bit older. She's in Egypt learning Arabic. Thinks she might work there.' He paused. 'Not the safest place to be, but she was adamant. Funny, when it comes to travelling to the Middle East, she's quite fearless, but she doesn't like confined spaces and she never liked the train journey over the Forth Bridge. Maybe it was because of the Tay disaster, or the fate of Thomas Bouch. When she learned the story, she thought he had been unjustly blamed. She's not particularly politically astute, but once she gets the bit between her teeth... Sorry, I'm going on again.'

Beth's ankle was, indeed, beginning to ache.

'Sore foot?' Gregor asked again. She nodded. His empathy was disconcerting. 'How about a coffee at the café?'

'Great minds think alike.'

'And fools never differ,' he agreed.

She smiled, relaxing among safe, bland clichés.

At the café they found a table outside and Beth sat with the dogs while Gregor ordered coffees. The café had clearly been busy all day and the bin outside was already overflowing. After a minute or two, Nero left her chair and ambled to the bin, enticed by the smell of the day's litter - the half-eaten buns, the sandwich crusts, paper napkins smelling of burgers. Gregor reappeared with coffees on a tray, but at that moment Beth saw Nero had a problem. He was heaving, choking, trying to vomit. Regardless of her sore ankle, Beth dashed across to him, straddled him from behind and lifted him to stand on his hind legs. With her arms round his torso she squeezed quickly and suddenly once – twice. Something shot out of his mouth. 'A bottle top!' Gregor and Beth said together. Beth lowered the dog, which now stood four square, head down, drooling. Silence had fallen at the café tables. Beth looked round, embarrassed. Everyone was watching.

'Where did you learn to do that? You must be our guardian angel!' Gregor was looking at her quizzically.

'Look, the café provides bowls of water for dogs,' she said. 'Canine equivalent of hot sweet tea. For shock!' She led Nero to the bowl where he lapped, slowly at first, then enthusiastically. The crisis was over, and gradually conversation resumed, with a gentle clatter of cutlery.

Gregor was still looking askance. 'Where did you learn to do that?' he said again.

'Oh, that's just basic first aid training,' Beth said. 'Works on humans, so I thought it might work on dogs, too.'

'Come on, the coffee will be getting cold.' They sat down and pulled Nero and Soul beside their table.

'So you're passionate about history?' Beth began.

'Yes. Immeasurably! Every period in every country and especially family trees. Just nosy, I guess.' He laughed briefly. 'I just love finding out who people are and where they came from. What they did and why they did it. It can lead to so many surprises.' He rubbed a hand over his stubbly beard. He looked younger when he smiled.

'So it's your favourite hobby?'

'Hobby, job – well, it's my life, really. History. And my daughter. And the dog.' He reached down to pat him.

'Job? What sort of job?'

'Teaching… but I'm doing research at the moment. And what about you? What's your line?'

'Medical student.'

Where? Here in Edinburgh?'

'No. Dundee.'

'Ah, so you're just home for a wee break – to see your... mother.'

'It's... the summer holiday. Vacation.'

'Ah. Brothers and sisters?'

'No, just me,' Beth said, but, eager to divert attention away from herself lest The Wall should crumble, she added hastily, 'You just got the one daughter?'

'Yep. Just the one.'

An uncomfortable silence. Their first. This relationship – what was it about? Gregor was old enough to be her father. She searched for something to say. 'Does your wife share your passion for history?'

Gregor paused. 'No, I'm afraid not. In fact, she left me.' He looked down. Beth took a breath to try to say something sympathetic, but he continued quickly, 'It was my fault. I strayed. My daughter hasn't forgiven me. I can't blame her.'

Time to change the subject again. 'You said you're doing research?'

'Yes. I'm studying the famous people whose statues are in Edinburgh. I've spent days wandering around like a tourist, photographing them all. Did you know, Edinburgh seems to be unique as a city for so many statues of philanthropists, philosophers, scientists who've made breakthroughs significant for the good of mankind. Makes me feel proud of my city! There was Dr Thomas Guthrie...'

'Oh, yes! The Ragged Schools.'

'Yes, that's right. And Sir Joseph Lister, as in Listerine mouthwash.'

'Discovered germs, or at least, how to minimise infection.'

'Absolutely. And Sir James Young Simpson.'

'Chloroform and anaesthesia!'

'Right! You know more of our city's history than you were letting on!'

'But those last two are connected with medicine, so I...'

'Of course. Then there was Sir David Brewster.'

'Ah, you've got me there. What did he do?'

'He was a physicist, mathematician and astronomer. He invented the kaleidoscope and studied light – reflection and refraction and that sort of thing - useful for lighthouses.' Gregor frowned a little. 'His statue's outside one of the university buildings, and I've got a photo of him, too. But on my fridge there's a wonderful illustration of light - a postcard of Mount Hood reflected in Mirror Lake. Perfect reflection. It's aptly named. It's absolutely beautiful.'

'Mount Hood?'

'Yes. It's in Oregon, USA.'

'Have you been?'

'No, more's the pity. But I've become quite philosophical about David Brewster. At first, when I started to study his life, I formed the opinion that his work on refraction and light – he was a keen photographer – was much more important than inventing the kaleidoscope, which is just a toy.'

'Yeah, I used to have one. Used to like it.'

'Yes. Sometimes I think about the fact that however you rearrange the little shapes, by shaking the thing and holding it up to the light, you change the patterns, but never the pieces. Like life, really. Fragmented, but just the same.'

He had stopped looking at her as he spoke, and was gazing into the distance, beyond the car park, towards the silhouettes of the Pentland Hills. 'Mount Hood reflected in

Mirror Lake is the polar opposite of those fragmented pieces: calm, peaceful stability.'

The Labrador shifted his position with a canine harrumph.

Gregor leaned over to pat him, and chuckled. 'I've made my hallway at the house into a gallery – mounted all my photos, chronologically, to try to pinpoint areas of development that affected life in the city. But I've added a few for light relief, like Nero lifting his leg against the plinth where David Hume is sitting, dressed like a Roman in a toga, or a seagull perched on top of Adam Smith outside St Giles Cathedral. Then there are festival revellers kissing John Knox – all a bit irreverent actually.'

'Yeah, I vaguely remember noticing that your hallway was a gallery!'

'Of course – when you hurt your ankle.'

She remembered sitting on his front doorstep, and that he had left the front door open while he made coffee for her. He continued, 'We have a smattering of war memorials, and of course, that's good and right – young guys who have given their lives for Scotland. But we don't have many warlike generals or finger-wagging politicians. The philanthropists are mostly people you learn about in history at school because they have improved the lot of the Scottish people.'

'Mmm.'

'Sorry. I'm going on again.'

'No, no. It's interesting.' What was really interesting was how Gregor came alive as soon as he started to talk about history. His eyes crinkled with enthusiasm and he used his hands as he spoke, like a Frenchman. She wished she'd had *him* as a history teacher. She bet he used to read

36

bedtime stories with lots of different voices, like her...

'Yeah,' she said, bringing her train of thought under control. 'It's true. About statues, I mean. Edinburgh certainly has a lot. When I was at school we had an exchange student from Germany. She was terribly intellectual, and when we showed her around the city, she asked about every statue – who it was, and what he did. I didn't know any of it. She showed up my ignorance! Wish you'd been my history teacher. I might've got a better grade!'

The weather, unpredictable as ever, changed abruptly. The sun clouded over, the café tables were swiftly vacated and a stiff breeze persuaded Beth and Gregor back to their cars. Beth was careful to let Gregor leave first, and spent several minutes checking some imagined message on her phone before driving slowly out of the car park.

Puzzled, she reran the conversation in her mind. He'd said he was researching at the moment, not teaching. Did schools give career breaks to teachers? She'd never heard of teachers taking career breaks. Sounded like *gardening leave*. Isn't that the term they used for stress or mental illness? But Gregor didn't seem depressed or unhinged in any way. That was her own prerogative.

Heather

Cairo

January 2011

Heather heard the familiar knock on the door of her flat: three raps, pause, two raps, so she would always know it was Tony. She opened the door. 'Get any sleep?' he asked.

'Eventually. You?'

'Ditto.'

'I cannae sleep when it's so noisy, and I think I'm still catching up from last Wednesday.' She yawned. 'What time was it when we left the common room? Four?'

'Nah, later. It was getting light already. But there's no school today, either.'

'No school today? How do you know?'

'Been there already. Met the receptionist guy... Ahmed? Mahmood...?'

'Hammed. Was anyone else there? From my class?'

'Nah. Not that I saw. There were two girls from the elementary class, but there were big notices in Arabic and English: no classes until further notice.'

'Boring.'

'Bet you never thought you'd say that having no classes was boring!' Tony laughed. 'Memories of school.'

'Och, I quite enjoyed school.'

'Swot. Anyway, there's more news.'

'More news?'

'There's a curfew.'

'A curfew?'

'Yes, Miss McParrot, a curfew. Stop repeating

everything I say. We have to be in by four.'

'But it's not even dusk at four!'

'Well, I guess no one will stick to that rule, like all the other rules in Egypt.'

'Oh. But *we* should. It's nothing to do with us foreigners, remember. No point in exacerbating the problem.'

'But the locals are already flouting the rules. Have you seen the TV?'

'No. Only been up a few minutes. Why?'

'There are still thousands in Tahrir. Camping. Refusing to move until there's a resolution.'

'Camping in the Square? Wow.' Heather stood, taking this in. 'So if we go out we ought to avoid the city centre and be back by mid-afternoon. I shouldn't have slept in. But I need breakfast. Cuppa tea?' He nodded and they headed for the kitchen.

Without warning, the place was filled with a thundering, ear-splitting roar, and Heather found herself on the floor, crouched, cowering in a corner against the wall. A bomb? Automatic weapons? Armageddon?

The racket lessened as suddenly as it had started. She let out the breath she had been holding, and took her hands from her ears, but neither of them said anything for a long moment. She lifted her head and looked around. Tony, stooping and bending at the knees, crept to the window. The sound could still be heard, but more faintly.

'Planes. Fighter jets,' he said, straightening up.

'What for? Are they going to bomb the city?'

'Their own city? No chance. I reckon they're just there to intimidate the crowds. Persuade them to leave Tahrir.' The end of his sentence was almost lost in the renewed roar of the returning planes.

Heather sat on the floor, and waited for her heart to stop hammering. Tony could always recover his cool so quickly.

'Let's go up on the roof and watch!' He was already moving towards the door. 'C'mon.'

Heather hauled herself on to unwilling legs and followed him to the stairway. They weren't the only ones with the idea. The stairs rang with quick steps and excited chatter as everyone made for the exit above the tenth floor. Roofs in Cairo tended to be rubbish-dumping areas. Where else could you put that broken chair, that ripped mattress with the springs poking through? But someone in the block had shovelled the rubbish to one side and tried to make a seating area. There were a few struggling pot plants, a couple of wooden benches and the inevitable wall painted with the Egyptian flag.

A crowd leaned against the balustrade. The view was stunning. They could see the Marriott Hotel, its new blocks forming a square around the older building, a former palace, its swimming pool glinting in the sun. Next to it was the new Episcopal Cathedral, shaped like a Bedouin tent. It reminded Heather of the Roman Catholic Cathedral in Liverpool, but Tony called it a pineapple. Beyond it was a maze of narrow streets, poorly lit and scary at night, except for little shops selling everything from mobile phones to hummus and flat bread, open until the early hours of the morning. Each cluster of buildings was flanked by a mosque, each minaret seeming to outdo its neighbours in height and brilliance. Banned from their usual route today, cars revved and honked, exasperated by the gridlock, the noise amplified by the tall buildings. The Qasr-El-Nil Bridge leading to Tahrir Square still had queues of pedestrians, six or eight abreast, shuffling along it.

Circling above the Square was the news helicopter, but then the fighter planes returned, carving a huge arc over the city centre. Their roar shook the whole building again and several people ducked.

'It's not scary when you know what's happening,' Tony said as the noise died away once again. 'It's stupid. What's the point? Everyone in the Square knows they're not going to *do* anything. It's just a big racket.' Objectively, Heather had to agree. Anyone living in Cairo quickly became inured to noise, even of this magnitude. So why were her knees so shaky and her breathing so irregular? Tony lowered his voice a little. 'What a waste of government money! Bet they're laughing in the Square, mocking the establishment that thought they could scare people back home that easy. Bet it's a party down there. Let's go!'

'What, to Tahrir?'

'Yeah! How can we be here in a revolution and not join in? It'd be a terrible missed opportunity!'

'But all the Embassy warnings tell us to stay away from protests, and, if there's a curfew, we're supposed to observe it.'

'We can still observe the curfew. It'll only take us half an hour to walk to the Square, and the curfew doesn't start till four o'clock. We could be down there by one o'clock and leave at half three.'

'Oh, I dunno…'

'Fu… flipping heck, Little Miss McPerfect! Where's your sense of adventure?'

He was making an effort for her because she didn't like it when he swore. She wanted to encourage him, but the tear gas experience and an edgy night spent in the school common room were enough adventure for her just now. But Tony would despise that argument. She needed a better one. 'But it's nothing to do with us. They haven't got anything against foreigners. It's an Egyptian problem, Moubarak against the rest, as far as I can see.'

'Exactly!' Tony was almost hopping with enthusiasm and impatience. '*Since* it's not a foreigners' problem, there's no harm in going to have a look. Imagine going back to the UK after this and saying, *We didn't see anything. We stayed in the flat and read a book like obedient little children.* Everyone'd take the micky. They'd think, *What a wasted opportunity. What a pair of wimps.* Anyway, the people in the Square are so bent on their political ideals, they won't even notice us.'

Despite herself, Heather was almost persuaded. His words rang true. They had both come, individually, to Cairo to enhance their world view, to escape the status quo, to equip themselves to become citizens of the world. What better moment to broaden their horizons?

'Come *on* Heather. We can buy a coffee on the way. Don't be a fossil. You sound like my parents.'

Heather had never met Tony's parents, but whenever he mentioned them, it was always with negative connotations. She didn't want to be equated with them.

'Okay.'

Out on the bridge it was hot – hotter than a Scottish summer, anyway, and, as usual, Heather cursed the cover-up clothes she felt obliged to wear. At the same time, she was glad to blend in with the crowds, her dark hair and long sleeves marking her out, if not as an Egyptian, at least as someone in keeping with the Middle East. She wished Tony's hair was a bit darker, but at least he'd given up wearing those tights jeans that showed off his Calvin Klein boxers. That kind of gear just wasn't acceptable here.

The atmosphere was positive, almost jovial. With his better Arabic, Tony was able to chat to a few locals. As he had predicted, the people in the Square were not at all cowed by the fighter planes. The crowds on the bridge had moved slowly. Once they reached the Square, it was almost standing room only, though in the middle there was the camp site Tony said he'd seen on the television – new home of the brave die-hards who were determined to stay there until they brought about genuine political change.

Heather looked around. All ages were there, from the very young to the really decrepit. Journalists reported that a baby had even been born in the Square. But the majority were young adults, like themselves, people with their lives still ahead of them, wanting democracy, freedom from a dictatorship which, according to Martin, had started well but become oppressive. Young Egyptians had watched their parents hammered into the ground by excessive hard work, low pay and a severely restricted lifestyle.

'Wow,' Tony breathed. 'Your friend Martin should be here. This is *real* democracy! Look, there are all levels of society, judging from the clothes – and the teeth, or lack of dental work! But look how many women there are!'

It was true. There were young and old, veiled and unveiled, traditional dresses and denim jeans. One woman held her baby aloft. On his bib, in Arabic, was the word *leave*. Heather gazed around and saw the same word inscribed on every available surface. Moubarak couldn't miss that message.

They stopped to listen to a boy, surely no more than fourteen, hoisted on a young man's shoulders, proclaiming at the top of his voice in simple Arabic, 'Our flag is red, white and black: red is the blood of the martyrs; white is the soul of the people; black is the anger of Egypt.'

'I got it!' Heather said, grabbing Tony's arm with delight. 'I actually understood what he said!'

Despite the tightly-packed crowds, there were people wandering around dispensing sandwiches and cups of water. Heather and Tony were glad of the bottled water they had brought with them, but Heather declined a sandwich because there were people hungrier than her, more in need than she was. One or two optimistic salesmen were peddling T-shirts with slogans across the front. In a cramped corner against a wall, a young woman was painting faces with the Egyptian flag.

'Look,' Tony said, pointing. 'That woman's poster. It's a line from the Qu'ran: *God's victory is surely near*. They really believe God is on their side. But some of the claims are ridiculous.' It was true that almost everyone bore a slogan - on a poster, their T-shirt, their hat, forehead... One young man held high a large soft toy donkey with the name *Moubarak*.

'Very rude,' Heather commented. 'But how do you mean, ridiculous?'

'Well, they're claiming Moubarak is in league with Hamas, Mossad, Hezbollah – you name it!'

Tony wandered over to chat to a group of young men. They were well enough dressed, probably well enough educated to help Tony out if his Arabic wasn't up to it. Perhaps they were equally keen to practise their English.

Heather looked around at the people enjoying the holiday atmosphere. Small children waved flags and danced in a circle. Flags and slogans hung from every ledge and window flanking the Square. People were smiling, chanting, singing, making the victory sign, united in a joyous certainty that freedom was just around the corner.

There were sudden gasps, and a palpable ripple of consternation affected the crowd. Friendly faces became worried. Smiles turned to frowns. People began to shift, despite the tens of thousands pressed into the limited space of the Square. A gentle rumble, like Chinese whispers, but increasing rapidly in volume, passed through the crowds. Heather strained her ears to hear what people were saying. It sounded like *gamelle* – camel. Couldn't be. Heather cursed her inability. Arabic was such an obdurate language, so dense, so intractable. People had told her that lots of English words came from Arabic: take coffee, for example, they said; but when the Arabic for coffee was pronounced, no way did it relate to anything familiar. Even numerals, which Heather had understood to be of Arabic origin, weren't used. Instead, they used 'Arabic-Indic' numerals, no help at all to confused language learners.

But the crowd was shifting more while Heather was day-dreaming, and suddenly, with a corporate frightened intake of breath, people squashed against each other to open up a pathway. She found herself pulled, pushed, bundled into a bunch of women telling her something urgently. Heather turned. She had heard correctly. A train of unsaddled camels, driven from behind by men yelling and brandishing sticks and the ubiquitous Egyptian flags were trotting briskly towards them. Those huge beasts, so haughtily regal in the desert, were so ungainly, so out of place in the city centre. How did they get here? *Why were they here?*

But they were running straight at them!

'Tony!' Heather screamed. He was standing in the pathway of the approaching camels. He turned – the wrong way – towards her and stepped forward, and the clip-clopping of the camels' feet on the cobbles was muffled by the sudden incomprehensible shouts of the pushing, shoving crowd surrounding them.

Tony turned too late. He was struck by the lead camel and somehow spun round, knocked down, hitting his head on the cobbles. The other camels trotted on, some missing him with their hooves, some trampling his body in the dust. Afterwards Heather seemed to hear the echo of that dull thud, his head on the stone, distinct from the sharper sound of the camels' feet. Instantly his body became a sack, a lifeless bundle, so different from the cheeky, young, vigorous enthusiast of a moment ago.

Heather's senses froze. Overcome by horror and disbelief, she watched while a bunch of young men picked up Tony's mangled body. As they did so, his head lolled to one side and she saw the back of his skull, a red mush. She remembered being supported by several women, and helped, or dragged, into the makeshift hospital at Qasr' El Dobara church beside the Square. On the way she caught a glimpse of the spot where he had fallen, a red splodge on the ground, quickly gathering grey dust. The crowd reconverged over the place, even as she watched.

Inside the cavernous building it was cool, and her eyes took a moment to get used to the dim light after the bright sun. There was a general bustle of activity, urgent low voices, quick movements. Heather felt locked down. Kind hands seated her on a chair and a young woman knelt beside her, while Tony was taken further, into another room.

'Hello. My name is Amira. Your husband? Your

46

brother?'

'Friend,' Heather managed to whisper. Her gaze was riveted on the door where they had taken Tony. His eyes had been slightly open and Heather knew instinctively that he was dead. She began to shiver uncontrollably and Amira produced a blanket to put round her shoulders, then held on to her hand. Heather sat, inert, while people moved around her and some would stop, momentarily, to speak in Arabic to Amira, then to move off again. They would sometimes look towards Heather and nod sympathetically, while Amira stayed beside her, occasionally muttering banalities gently, but not expecting a reply. Someone handed Heather a fresh bottle of drinking water. Amira unscrewed the top for her and encouraged her to drink.

Eventually two men came out of the room where Tony had been taken and stopped beside Heather's chair. One had a stethoscope around his neck. He was long and lean and he folded up his limbs like a grasshopper to squat down and speak to her as she sat. Heather fixed her eyes on his shoes, newish trainers, but already grey and smudged from the dust and crowds. Why would anyone wear white trainers in Cairo?

'My name is Mohamed,' he said, 'and this is Ashraf. We are doctors.' Heather dragged her eyes up to his face. He was young, with lustrous dark curly hair, but his face wore an expression of weary sadness far beyond his years. 'I am so sorry,' he was saying, 'your friend has passed away.' Heather stared at him. She knew this. Why was he telling her now? He glanced towards Amira, who tightened her grip on Heather's hand. 'I think he was killed instantly. He knew nothing. He felt no pain.' His words meant nothing to Heather. What was she supposed to do?

47

The other man, the one called Ashraf, had produced a chair and a clip-board. He sat down beside Heather and remained silent for a long moment. Then, 'I'm so sorry. Very sad. So sorry.' His voice was gentle and rich, and Heather looked into his face. He had the usual dark Egyptian hair, but his skin was much paler than Mohamed's and his eyes - his tragic eyes - were blue! He pulled a pen from his pocket and started to take notes. It was only when she had to spell her name that Heather realised they were speaking English. In an uncomprehending daze, she gave details – her name and Tony's - their language school and their principal's name, though she didn't know Tony's UK address.

'And you?' Mohamed said, 'Are you from the same town?'

'No,' Heather said. She thought for a moment. 'We met here. He's from England, I'm from Scotland.'

'Scotland? From Edinburgh?' Ashraf asked.

'Yes.'

'Ah! I studied medicine in Edinburgh. Very fine city. You must miss your city, I think.'

Heather said nothing.

'So you don't know his family?'

'No.' Suddenly Heather returned as if from a long distance. His parents! She gasped. 'Mr and Mrs Long - his parents! How can we tell them? What should we do? What will happen to him... to... to his body?'

'He will be taken to the hospital – to the morgue. We will inform the language school. They will have his contact details.'

'Yes.' There didn't seem anything else to do or say. 'Er, thank you. I'd like to go home now... back to my flat.'

'You are sure you are feeling well?' Ashraf asked.

'Yes, yes… thank you.' She looked again into those sad light eyes.

'Then Amira will take you. She will accompany you to your home.'

'Where you live?' Amira asked.

'Zamalek.'

'Okay. We come with you.' She stood up and beckoned to another young man whom Heather hadn't noticed before, standing by the wall. 'This my brother, Fikri.'

'No, no, it's okay…'

'No, we come with you. Is past curfew. I have paper.' She produced a form that seemed to give her some sort of immunity for breaking the curfew. With a last look over her shoulder at Ashraf, Heather allowed herself to be led away.

Despite the curfew, tens of thousands remained in the Square and there were still hundreds on the bridge. More continued to head into the Square, some were leaving, most were just hanging around. Heather glanced back at the building they had left. 'A church? But there were doctors, and… Mohamed…?'

'Now, for the revolution, it is a hospital.' It was the first time Fikri had spoken. 'For everyone. For Muslims and Christians. This revolution is not about religion. Is about justice.'

It was dark now, but the strong searchlight from the helicopter would occasionally pick them out before sweeping along the river and back towards the city centre. Amira and Fikri didn't try to make conversation, but Amira linked arms firmly with Heather and steered her past groups of people, sometimes greeting them, sometimes giving what might have been a brief explanation.

As they left the main road for one of the small back

streets of Zamalek, Heather became aware of a little group of young men standing on the corner. These back streets were always badly lit, and Heather had often felt glad of Tony's blustering presence as they walked in the dark. Suddenly she shied away from two guys leaning against a wall. They were carrying baseball bats.

'Is okay,' Fikri assured her. 'Is for protection. They protect their families. And you. TV news say prisoners out. Coming to Cairo along Alexandria road.'

Vigilante groups. Tony would have joined one. It would have been another story to tell when they got home.

They had arrived at her flat. 'This is where I live. I'll be okay now. Thank you Amira.' She paused. 'But, why are you…?'

'You are welcome. Our pleasure to serve you. We are members of the church – Qasr' El Dobara. We make military hospital during the *thawra* – er – revolution. I pray for you.' Smiling sadly, she stood back while Heather found her key and unlocked the outer door. Turning as she went inside, she watched Amira and Fikri retreat down the dark vacant street.

Heather trudged up to the third floor and unlocked her empty flat. She stood for a moment in the gloomy hallway. It was eerily quiet. There were no voices from the street, no cars revving and honking. She went into the kitchen and switched on the light. The kettle was on the floor. She must have been holding it when the first fighter jets went over, a lifetime ago. She realised she'd eaten almost nothing all day, then turned hastily and vomited into the sink.

50

Beth aged 5

Edinburgh

January 1997

'Is it the right sort of snow, Daddy? Is it? Is it?' Beth pressed her nose against the sitting room window. Her breath misted the glass as she called out. Her father turned and straightened up from clearing the front path. Thumbs up. Yes! They could go sledging! Beth squealed with joy and bounced up and down on the sofa.

Her dad propped his shovel against the front porch and stamped the snow off his boots on the step. He opened and closed the door quickly and went into the sitting room. He took off his glasses to wipe them and pretended to grope his way across the room. Beth reached up and put her warm hands on his cold red cheeks. 'Daddy, you're freezing!'

'Only my face, sweetheart. My heart's warm, and so is the rest of me. Come on, Fizzy Lizzy, let's get your coat and boots.' Beth loved that name. It was much more exciting than Beth. It made her feel light and springy, bubbling in the sunshine.

In double quick time Beth was togged up in her warmest gear and Daddy had put the sledge in the boot of the car. They drove to 'their hill'. Beth felt it belonged to her personally, because usually there was no one else there. Daddy said that other sledgers preferred the steeper, faster hill nearby. He said this hill was fast enough – for now. The snow had a thin crust of ice on top, and Beth's slight weight didn't even dent it.

She was proud of the sledge. Daddy had made it

himself and it had shiny, polished runners. The snow was always crisp and clean, she remembered later, a shimmering white landscape, created specially for their enjoyment. The sun, reflected off the snow, was dazzling. She screwed up her eyes.

The sledge was big enough to take both of them downhill, Beth sitting between Daddy's knees as they flew over the unspoilt surface, leaving their mark, but compressing the snow for a faster run next time. At the bottom of the hill, Dad guided the sledge up a little hump so they could fall off safely sideways into a snowdrift, breathless and laughing.

'Again, Daddy? Pull me up the hill?'

'You're getting too big for that. C'mon, we've got to stomp up the hill.' Beth made a face. 'Giants and fairies?' he cajoled.

'Okay,' she conceded, grinning. Giants meant that Dad could take giant strides but he wasn't allowed to run, only walk. Beth could run with small steps, fairy feet. Of course, she reached the top first, and Dad arrived moments later, panting dramatically with effort. 'Hurry up, Daddy. Let's go again!'

On repeated downhill rides the sledge became a racing car, an off-road motor bike, a go-cart, a jet-ski, a speed boat, a glider, an Olympic gold medal-winning cycle, a bob-sleigh and a runaway horse. They sledged until their tracks had impacted the snow and made the course smoother. They sledged until they were hot and sweaty and their noses ran. They sledged until the sun dipped in a fiery ball over the far side of the hill, turning the white hill rosy pink, and then they trudged back to the car.

'We'll just go and see Mummy on our way home,'

Daddy told her as he fastened her seat belt.

'Oh, Daddy, do we have to? I'm hungry. Isn't it tea time?'

'We won't stay long.'

'Couldn't I go to Granny's while you go to see Mummy?'

'You haven't seen Mummy for a while. I think she'd like to see you.'

Beth pouted. Daddy had taken the special shine off the wonderful afternoon. 'How do you know she wants to see me? She's always asleep,' Beth retorted.

'We can't be sure she isn't listening. She might be dreaming about you. She might be thinking, *I wonder how my Beth is doing? I hope she'll come to see me soon and tell me all about the snow.*'

Beth remained silent, unconvinced.

The snow had been cleared from the hospital car park and it stood in dirty grey heaps around the edges. A cold wind had sprung up and Beth pulled her woolly hat firmly over her ears. Daddy held her hand and walked too fast, so she had to trot to keep up. The lights in the corridor were bright, and made her blink a bit after the badly-lit car park. Mummy's room smelled the same as always. A stinky hospital pong. Beth had never smelled this smell anywhere else. She hated it. She breathed through her mouth.

She kept her eyes fixed on Daddy, on his heavy shoes which already had a line round, where the snow had begun to dry. She looked at her own wellies. They were shiny clean. 'Shut the door, pet,' Daddy said, and reluctantly Beth came in from the doorway and closed the door behind her. He moved a chair and sat on it. Beth kept looking down. She didn't let her eyes stray to the motionless figure on the bed.

Dad began to speak to Mummy. His voice was low and gentle as he described home and the snow and a nice friendly new person at work. He didn't say how he had dropped a jar of jam in the kitchen and made a big mess and cut his finger and said bad words. He didn't say that he'd been very tired the day he had to show the nice new person how to do everything at work. He didn't say how the car had skidded in the snow in the driveway and scraped against the gate post. But Beth knew.

Then he began to talk about Beth herself, how clever she was, how well she was doing at school, how many friends she'd made. Beth didn't know if she was doing well, and she could only think of one friend, Annabelle. Then came the moment she'd been dreading. 'Beth, come and sit beside your mum, sweetheart. Here...' Dad moved another chair to the other side, and patted the seat. Beth didn't move. Dad came to stand beside her and gently but ever so firmly he took her hand and walked her to the chair next to Mummy's face. Gently but ever so firmly, he sat her down. 'Now, hold your mum's hand, pet. There, like that.' He folded Mummy's hand around Beth's hand and held them both clasped together.

'Here's Beth, Abi,' he said to Mummy. He was the only one who was allowed to call her Abi. Everyone else had to call her Abigail. 'We've been out sledging, love. The air was freezing, but the exercise warmed us up.' It was true. Their hands were warm, clammy, sweaty. Were all their hands hot, or was hers making Mummy's hand hot or was Mummy's sticky hand dampening hers? Dad took his hand away and went round the other side of the bed to sit on his chair. Beth didn't dare move her hand, but she did bring her gaze up to rest on Mummy's face. There was a scary tube thing sticking in her mouth. Daddy said it was to help her breathe. Her eyes were closed. They were always closed. Her hair was short. It used to be long, and she used to grumble about the tangles. The room was hot and Beth was uncomfortable in her coat, her boots and her scratchy woolly hat, but she couldn't take her coat off with one hand.

'Tell Mummy what you've been doing, Beth,' Dad tried to coax her. It sounded like she'd been doing something wrong. Beth racked her brain, but she thought she'd been good all day. She'd tried to be specially good so they could go sledging.

'Tell her about sledging,' he suggested. Oh, not something bad, then. But he'd just told her, hadn't he?

'We went sledging,' Beth said, but Mummy didn't reply. Beth looked back at their hands. Could she move hers yet? She looked at Daddy. His cheeks were no longer red, as they had been out on the snowy hill. Now they were white and his eyes were very serious. His face looked dragged downwards, like when she sat on his knee and pulled his skin to make funny faces until they both giggled. Maybe she *had* done something naughty after all.

Now Dad took Mummy's other hand and put his face close to hers. 'We miss you so much, love. Hurry up and get well. We're looking forward to having you back home with us.'

What? Was Mummy coming home? With that thing in her mouth? Beth kept very still. If she didn't move, if she closed her eyes, maybe she'd be back home in her bedroom, and this would all be a bad dream. Maybe she and Daddy would be sitting at the kitchen table eating toast and listening to Daddy's favourite music. It had gone quiet. Dad wasn't speaking any more. The only sound was the beep-

beep-beep of the machine behind the bed. Beth opened her eyes just enough to peep through her eyelashes, but she closed them again hastily. Dad had taken his glasses off and he was crying. Daddy was crying! Not sobbing. He didn't make a noise, but big fat tears were running down his cheeks.

Beth tried to keep quiet, but suddenly the room was filled with wails and shouts and her voice wouldn't obey her. 'Let's go home now Daddy. *Please!* Now, Daddy! I want to go home!' Immediately there were two nurses in Mummy's room, and one of them was taking her by the hand and leading her out while Daddy kissed Mummy on the cheek and whispered something in her ear. Was he telling Mummy that Beth was naughty? Beth screamed and tried to pull her clammy hand away from the nurse's cool dry one, and Dad was speaking quickly to the other nurse, and the corridor was echoing with screams.

Then, 'C'mon, kiddo,' Dad said, scooping her up and carrying her swiftly back to the car, where he fastened her seat belt and she wasn't screaming any more.

'What do we always have after playing in the snow?' he asked.

Was it a trick question? But Daddy never tricked her. 'Warm blackcurrant?' Beth replied hopefully, sniffing and hiccupping.

'Absolutely!' he replied. 'And what else?'

'Toast and butter!'

'Right on.'

'And can we have honey?'

'Definitely.'

The house was warm when they opened the front door. Warm, but not too hot. Daddy pulled off her boots, and

Beth took her coat and hat off and ran into the kitchen. The house always smelt the same. It smelt of home.

Heather

Cairo

January 2011

Heather lay in bed and stared at the ceiling. If she kept very still, maybe her surroundings would re-order themselves. This incomprehensible nightmare, this volcanic eruption of non-reality would fade into oblivion. If she moved her eyes, the outlines of furniture, visible in the moonlight through her thin curtains, wobbled with her fatigue. If she froze her mind in the moments before the incident… The incident? A word to explain a triviality. This was no incident. This was an earthquake, a catastrophe of cataclysmic proportions. An eclipse. The end of a life. The end of her own life as she knew it – had known it - up to this point. What would happen now? How would she explain to those legendary people back home, whose opinions Tony had been so concerned about? What would her life in Cairo be like now?

Soon, the sky would turn dark blue, then mauve. Dawn would bring the need to make decisions. At different points in the night she had tossed and turned, sweated and shivered and dropped asleep momentarily several times only to wake trembling with horror. She had wandered round the flat, switched on the television, stood at the window looking towards Tahrir, then gone back to bed. She must make one final attempt at sleep.

She was woken suddenly by an insistent ring on the doorbell

of her flat. In a daze she got up and stood with her ear to the door. 'Meen hinaik? *Who's there?'*

'It's me, Ryan,' came the familiar drawl, and Heather opened the door, fell into his arms and began to sob.

'Oh, Ryan, it's you! I'm sorry, sorry…it's Tony, he's…'

'I know.'

'You know?'

'I went to the language school.'

'The language school. Oh.' Heather drew back suddenly. Was it so late? Had she slept after all? She was only wearing yesterday's T-shirt and pants. She hadn't washed since… She must smell. 'Could you wait five minutes? I should put some clothes on.'

'Sure. There are still no classes, so I've got all day.'

'Thanks. Er, make some tea. The kitchen's there.' She pointed.

'Ah, the British cup of tea,' he muttered, and headed for the kitchen.

Heather took a shower in record time, brushed her teeth and pulled on clean jeans and T-shirt. Back in the sitting room, she said, 'You went to the school?'

'Uhuh.' He handed her a mug of tea.

'They said there's still no classes?'

'No classes till further notice. Because of the curfew.'

'What else did they say?'

'Well, the principal was there – because of what had happened – because of Tony. I believe the hospital had got in touch with them. He wanted to inform Tony's class and ours, because you and Tony…' She nodded. 'He said you had been there too, but that someone took you home and they knew you were safe.'

'Yeah. Amira and her brother. They were very kind.

Everyone at the hospital - the church - was kind. There were doctors, young guys, Ashraf and Mohamed. But I was useless, Ryan.' Heather began to sob again. He took her mug from her and put it on the coffee table. 'We shouldn't have gone to Tahrir in the first place. I let Tony persuade me. Didn't want to be a wimp. I'm the practical one. He's the adventurous one. Was. I just didn't want to be the boring one. Then, when I thought I heard the camels were coming, I should have warned him. I heard the word, you know, *gamelle*... but I thought I couldn't't've heard right. I should've told him to watch out. I was too late. Then I didn't even know his parents' names or their address.'

Ryan waited while she cried.

'It was horrible. I saw his head. It was - he had - there was this patch on the paving stone...'

He moved across to put his arm round her shoulders, and she buried her face in his shirt until the sobs subsided and left her limp. She drew upright and blew her nose.

'You had any breakfast?'

She looked at him dumbly.

'I figured not.' He picked up a paper bag he'd left on the chair next to him. Heather hadn't noticed it. 'Can I get a plate?' She nodded and he went to the kitchen, coming back a moment later with a fresh Egyptian breakfast of flat bread, hard-boiled eggs, tomatoes, bananas and a little pot of beans, 'foule', the traditional way to start the day.

'Thanks Ryan. You're very thoughtful.'

He waved aside the compliment. 'Eat your breakfast.' Heather did so, chewing mechanically, while Ryan leaned back and drank his tea. He stretched out his long legs and seemed to fill the little sitting room with his comfortable large presence. 'At school they said they expect Tony's family will want to fly his body back. They guess someone might want to come over and accompany it. Him.'

'But how did they get in touch? The Internet's down. No mobiles.'

'Landlines. They're still workin'. Dontcha got one?' He looked briefly round the room.

Heather shook her head. 'Only a useless mobile.'

'What's more, your Embassy is gettin' involved.'

'The British Embassy?'

'Of course. They'll help you. Each area of Cairo has a rep – they call him a warden. Him or her. A regional warden. Didya know?' Heather shook her head. 'This is yours.' He passed her a slip of paper with a name and address scribbled on it. 'It's a woman. She's not far from here. I looked it up on the map. I guess she'd give you some advice. They said at the school that they expected we'd all want to go home – to our countries – but…'

'What? Not finish the course?'

'Well, at the moment there's no course, so – I reckon so.' Heather was silent for a moment, as this new information sank in.

'The curfew's still on, so we can still go out and about in the mornings,' he continued, 'but we have to stay in our accommodation in the afternoons and evenings. Just for a few days. To see how it pans out. They reckon Zamalek is safe, but they warn us against going anywhere near the protests.' Heather pulled a face. 'Sorry,' he said. 'Silly comment.'

There was a silence, while she mentally faced an afternoon, evening and then another night alone. Ryan must have read her thoughts. He said, 'I share an apartment with Martin. It's only five minutes from here. We've got some cool

DVDs. And food. We know the guys with the weapons at the end of our street – the vigilantes. I've been practising my Arabic on them, and if I spin them a little yarn, they'll turn a blind eye to me walking you home later this evening. Wanna come?'

So Heather took her jacket, stuffed some apples and a carton of milk into her bag and set off to while away the day with Ryan and Martin.

'You're in luck! The elevator's working today. Just as well. We're on the seventh floor.' Ryan, ever the discreet gentleman, heaved open the heavy gate to the lift, and stood aside to usher her in.

Heather had long since stopped herself getting nervous in the rickety old contraptions that shuddered and grumbled and sometimes stuck between floors. But today those niggly nerves were bobbing just below the surface. Enclosed spaces and heights. Knowing there was a big drop below. When the lift ground to a halt right outside Ryan and Martin's door, she let out a pent-up sigh of relief.

Ryan unlocked the door and led her into the living room. She could see Martin standing on the balcony, gazing towards Tahrir.

'Hey, that's some view!' Heather said, moving out to join him.

'Heather!' Martin said, stepping back.

'Sorry, didn't he tell you?' She nodded towards Ryan.

'Yes, but... I'm so sorry, so sorry about Tony.' He pushed his glasses up.

'Yeah. Thanks.'

'I heard. We went to the language school.'

'Yeah. Ryan told me.'

'I'm amazed that they let you go back to your flat on your own.'

'No, but they didn't. This sister and brother went with me. Amira and...'

'No, I mean, to be on your own in the flat,' Martin insisted.

'They didn't realise, most like,' Ryan interrupted. 'In Egypt no one lives alone. Everyone lives in families or shared apartments. What about Tony's room-mates?'

'They're Egyptian,' Heather told him. 'Probably with their own families, or even in the Square.'

'So, what will you do now?' Martin took his glasses off and wiped them on his T-shirt.

'Now,' Ryan said with emphasis, 'she'll have coffee. In fact we'll all have coffee, then we'll walk to the supermarket before curfew, then we'll entertain one another with sparkling wit and talent.'

Heather smiled and relaxed a little. She went back inside and looked round the flat. It was comfortable enough, a little larger than her own, with several customary coloured rugs on the tiled floor, and dark, elaborately-carved, dust-trap furniture. Ryan went into the kitchen and she followed him. It was pretty good as student flats went. They were usually sparse. Fitted kitchens were rare in Egypt – just a cooker, a sink and couple of cupboards. Not even a fridge was mandatory. She looked round appreciatively at the home comforts – a coffee machine, with a grinder beside it for the beans, a shiny electric kettle, mugs with cartoon characters from American television shows and dozens of photos stuck to the fridge with magnets.

'Your family?'

'Yep, that's the gang,' Ryan said. 'They didn't want

me to leave them behind. That's Mom and Pop, my brother Seb, my baby sister Mary-Beth, and that's Cosmo – he's an Irish wolf hound.'

'Ah. My father's got a dog – Nero.'

'The emperor?'

'No. Black. A black Labrador.'

'Of course – Italian for black – nero.'

'He should probably be Gris or Grigio or something now. He's getting old, but Pa still walks him for miles every day.'

'You haven't mentioned your mom...?'

'Oh yes, she likes dogs as well, but she and my father aren't together any more. Divorced. And Ma's new bloke is allergic to dogs. But Pa would've wanted to keep Nero anyway. He even chose our house to be near Arthur's Seat for walking the dog.'

'Who's Arthur?'

Heather smiled. 'No one really knows.' She laughed out loud when Ryan looked so confused. 'It's the name of a hill in Edinburgh. A hill with two peaks – well – humps. The shape of a lion lying down. Almost shaped like the Sphinx but much bigger. But it's right beside the city centre, and it's territory owned by the Queen. It's her back garden, just behind Holyrood Palace, her Scottish residence.'

'Ah, the Queen.' Ryan stood to attention. 'Sounds like *some back yard*! But I'm guessin' you like your city.'

'I do.'

Ryan busied himself making coffee, while Heather looked at the photos. His father was tall and athletic-looking, his mother smaller and elegant, an archetypal American couple. Mary-Beth, the *baby sister*, must be at least sixteen, with long auburn hair and an impish grin, while Seb could have been Ryan's twin. All had even white teeth and bright smiles. 'Do you miss them?'

'Would that make me a Mommy's boy if I said I do?'

'Of course not,' Heather said, though she realised with a jolt why she had asked. If she had brothers and sisters, a family who smiled together for photos, and a big goofy dog to complete the picture, she'd miss them to the moon and back. As it was, she had no siblings, a father who lived alone and who had let the side down big-time, a mother whose attention was now on husband number two and her awkward teenaged step-sons, and now Heather herself found her career plans crumbling round her ears. But she missed her city.

Martin tore himself away from the balcony view and sat to have coffee. 'It's all changed,' he said enigmatically.

'What has?'

'What they're demanding. In 1948 it was pan-Arabism – one of the results of *western* domination and the establishment of the State of Israel. Stupid move, that. Now it's because there's no democracy, no freedom to express opinions, and absolutely no equality in wealth distribution across the whole Arab world.'

'Yes, prof, if you say so.'

'But it is,' Martin insisted, rattled by Ryan's brush-off. 'They used to blame westernisation for the ills of society, but it's all changed now. Now, everyone's beginning to realise that it's freedom from - from fear or oppression that helps people build better societies – and - and a new definition of human dignity.'

Heather liked to listen to Martin, even though Tony used to call him a geek. He was informed and thoughtful and, she felt sure, well on the way to realising his ambition of working in international relations. Now he rocked his mug, watching the coffee dregs swirling round.

'That's why it's not a foreigners' problem,' he went on. 'They have no bone of contention with *us* any more, just with the injustice of their own system. A thirty-year-old injustice. It's even more maddening for Egyptians that they see their leaders being humiliatingly subservient to foreign powers, but tyrannical towards their own people. So many people in the villages are grindingly poor, but have you seen Moubarak's palace here in Cairo?'

Heather nodded. 'But isn't it true in many countries that the rich get richer and the poor get poorer?'

'I suppose so, but not to this extent.' Clearly agitated, Martin stood up, put down his mug and went out to the balcony again.

'The guys in the street told me a joke that's going round,' Ryan said. 'It goes like this: Nasser: death by poison; Sadat: death by shooting; Moubarak: death by Facebook!'

Heather smiled, and Martin, listening from the balcony, commented, 'Yeah. That's why they took the Internet down. So here we are, cooped up like chickens, not allowed to join in the fun and games down in the Square – sorry Heather.' Martin was staring at her. She'd probably gone pale. From time to time she felt her throat was closing up. Fun and games...

'Were y'all close? You and Tony?' Ryan ventured gently.

'No, not really. That's just it! Now I feel guilty for not being closer, for not taking care of him. I was supposed to be the sensible one. He was the adventurous one. But I should have insisted that we...'

'Like a naggin' wife, you mean?'

At first Heather was shocked, but a hint of a smile played at one corner of Ryan's mouth. 'Know what I reckon?' She shook her head. 'It may be a little early to say this, and you'll most likely disagree at this point.' Heather sat up and put her mug down. 'I reckon Tony's parents will be fixing on coming over. I think it would be real nice if you could be the person to meet them. *If* they come. You were the one who knew him best – the only one who really knew him – and if they haven't been to Cairo before, they're gonna need a minder. And, as you said, you're the sensible one.'

'Oh, but I'd be useless. I'd probably cry. My Arabic is hopeless…'

'But you know how things are done in Cairo. Most things. You know how to get to the airport, how to take a taxi, how to be polite and fit in culturally. And as for crying – I believe that would be quite appropriate - under the circumstances.' He smiled, and she allowed herself to smile, too. 'At the hospital they probably need someone to identify the body and…'

'Oh, there's no doubt about it. I was *there*,' Heather remonstrated, tears springing to her eyes again.

'Yeah, yeah, I know. No, what I mean is – probably someone from his family needs to be here. For legal reasons. But we're foreigners. Who knows how they do things round here?' He sighed and ran a big hand through his sandy hair. 'It's like driving through fog. Actually, I don't believe even the Egyptians know how it's done. 'Cos it's never been done before.' He drank his coffee again and stared into the distance. 'Helping his family might absolve your guilt a little. Not that you have any guilt to absolve,' he added hastily. 'Promise me you'll think about it?'

'Okay. I'll think about it.'

Beth aged 10

Edinburgh

April 2002

'How many?' Dad called out of the kitchen window.

'Seven,' Beth replied, counting the chocolate eggs in her small yellow basket. She loved Easter at Granny's, even though she knew, now that she had reached *double figures,* all the intriguing places in Granny's garden where Easter eggs could be hidden. But Granny would have made jelly for her dessert – blackcurrant jelly with tinned mandarin oranges, so that the little orange segments took on a pinky-purple hue, and their shape made her think of shrimps floating in an inky sea. Dad never made jelly. Jelly was a granny-treat, and Beth didn't plan to grow out of it any time soon. The others would have simnel cake. Beth wasn't keen on that spicy cinnamon taste, though she knew Dad would give her the marzipan ball from the top of his slice.

Aunty Nessa and Uncle Bob hadn't arrived yet. She probably wouldn't have to share the egg hunt with Paul. At thirteen, he was far too grown up, though he was still good for climbing with her in the apple tree, or watching Granny's old video of *Home Alone* over and over until each of them had memorised almost every word.

When her egg collection reached ten, Beth went indoors. That was the full total, and it was chilly outside, anyway, despite the bright sun. 'Can I eat a little one now, Dad? I promise I'll eat my lunch!'

'Okay, just one then.'

Beth chose a small egg in pure gold foil and

unwrapped it very carefully, so she could smooth out the foil to use in an art collage later. She popped the egg into her mouth.

'Beth? Come here, Sweetie, and stir this custard for me please,' Granny said. Beth put her basket on the kitchen table and went to the cooker. 'What're you going to be when you grow up?' Granny continued. 'You could be a chef in one of those posh hotels.'

'She's going to be a doctor,' Dad announced. 'Aren't you, love?'

'Yes. So I can help people like mum to get better.' She'd told Granny lots of times, but Granny seemed to keep forgetting. Anyway, Dad had said it lots of times, too.

'Of course,' said Granny. 'Maybe Aidan or…'

'Or Paul,' Dad said too loudly. 'Paul likes cooking. He thought of becoming a chef.' He turned to Beth. 'You've got chocolate on your face, love. Go in the cloakroom and wash it off before Paul and Aunty Nessa and Uncle Bob come.'

Beth went, but she was puzzled to hear Dad talking too loudly to Granny. Like telling her off. Poor Granny. She was getting a bit old. She couldn't help forgetting things sometimes.

'I can hear a car,' Beth announced, coming out of the cloakroom and looking out of the hall window to see their car pulling into the drive. 'Here they are!'

'Beth, love, go and put a napkin in each glass on the dining table,' Dad said, handing her a packet of yellow napkins with rabbit pictures on them. 'Do it neatly. Make sure they're all facing the same way.'

'But Dad, Paul's just…'

'Do it, love,' Dad said. Beth knew that look and didn't argue. He pulled the door to behind him, and after the initial greetings, Beth could just hear him speaking urgently in a low voice, before Uncle Bob came into the dining room. He lifted Beth up and swung her round.

'Oof, you're getting too big for me to do that, young lady!'

'What do you think, Uncle Bob?'

'What about?'

'The table. The way I've done the napkins.'

'Oh. Yeah. Beautiful.'

'Where's Paul?'

'In the kitchen, helping Granny. Go and see him.'

So Beth ran into the kitchen and flung her arms around Paul. He was skinny, and taller than her, so she fitted neatly under his arms. She knew they didn't look alike, because of her dark hair and his light mop, but she knew his face like her own, the freckles over his nose, the pale birthmark below his ear and the way his eyes screwed up when he smiled. He returned the hug, then continued stirring a pot. 'Granny made custard,' he whispered. 'Should've made gravy! You don't have custard with simnel cake, but you need gravy with roast lamb.'

Beth considered this for a moment. 'Do you want to be a chef when you grow up?'

'Dunno. Could be. Is that what Granny said?'

'Yes.'

'She gets ideas, you know. Maybe I'll be a chef, or an engineer, or an accountant.'

'Don't you want to be a footballer? All the boys in my class want to be footballers.'

'Nah. Not good enough. I like playing, sure, but it'd be obvious by now if I had potential.'

Beth didn't know what potential was, and engineer or

accountant didn't sound as interesting as chef or footballer. 'I'm going to be a doctor,' she announced.

'I know. You've said that before. Or your dad has.' Paul stopped stirring and turned to face her. 'You don't have to be what your dad chooses, you know. You can choose for yourself when you're older.'

'But I want to be able to make people better, so they don't die, like my mum,' Beth objected. 'Dad says that doctors are getting cleverer all the time. They'll be able to cure loads more diseases by the time I'm a doctor!'

Paul was standing still and staring at her. 'Rats! I've let the custard go lumpy,' he hissed. 'Granny'll have a pop at me.'

Easter Sunday lunch didn't seem as much fun as usual, even though Uncle Bob told a few jokes and Aunty Nessa had made up a quiz for Paul and Beth. Beth even knew some answers that Paul didn't know, but she suspected Aunty Nessa had put those questions in specially, like, *Who does Tom meet in the midnight garden?* 'Hatty!' Beth had answered promptly because that was her favourite book that spring.

But Dad was a bit grumpy and Granny was flustered, probably because she'd made custard instead of gravy and Paul forgot to stir it so it went lumpy. Granny had made jelly for Beth, but it was lemon jelly and it didn't have any mandarins in. Beth didn't say anything because she didn't want to upset Granny any more, and anyway, she thought that if she complained, Dad might be cross.

She and Paul watched part of *Home Alone*, but Dad dragged her away before the end, and told her to get in the car, so she and Dad left Granny, Uncle Bob, Aunty Nessa and Paul to have tea without them.

'I wanted to stay longer,' Beth grumbled as they arrived home.

'Granny was feeling a bit tired. I don't think she was very well, so it was better to leave early.'

Beth frowned. Granny had seemed okay to her. Then she said 'Can we have honey sandwiches for tea?'

'I think we're run out of honey. Have to be peanut butter.'

Heather

Cairo

January 2011

The plane was two hours late – two hours in which Heather went over the events of the past few days a thousand times. Unable to sit still, she prowled around the airport, returning every few minutes to reread the arrivals board, to check the progress of BA Flight 155.

The airport was a choppy sea of shifting humanity, waiting impatiently. Fashion-conscious young women, their outfits colour-coordinated, their headscarves pinned with a milliner's precision, walked together, arm in arm, giggling, their weary plump mothers in floor-length galabeyas puffing anxiously behind them. Children ran haphazardly, sometimes worming their way through eager crowds pressing against the barrier. Skinny smiling boys carried suitcases with apparent ease, then held out a hand for baksheesh. The vaulted chamber echoed with the urgent commands of parents, incomprehensible announcements over the paging system, the trundling of luggage trolleys, the occasional shriek of excited welcome. The air quivered with the smell of sweat and cigarette smoke. It was too early in the season for air conditioning.

What would Tony's parents be like? Would she recognise them? Tony hadn't even carried a photo of them. What was it like to lose your son? Children were meant to outlive their parents. This couple might be hysterical with grief. What if they made a scene in this very public place, in a culture that was not at all averse to staring? Dark questions continued to swoop like bats around her head. What would she say? What could she do? How would she spot them – an average middle-aged white western couple? There had been plenty of those arriving during the time she'd been at the airport.

Some women, unprimed in cultural mores, wore inappropriately short skirts and sleeveless tops, their toe-nails newly varnished for their strappy shoes, while their male counterparts wore shorts, polo shirts and sandals. Others looked like something out of *Death on the Nile*, their obtrusive sun-hats and smart white cotton shirts and slacks declaring to all that they were On Holiday.

Not all those couples were British. Planes came from every capital city. It wasn't difficult to distinguish the well-cut, tailored, supercilious French, or the Americans with their straightened, whitened teeth and nose-jobs. Italians had dark curly hair, sparkling eyes and beautiful soft leather shoes. Nationality-spotting was a welcome diversion.

Heather knew that facially, she herself could pass for Italian, but her jeans, T-shirts and trainers quickly marked her out as British, except that today, for such an occasion, she was wearing an ankle-length navy skirt and a pale blue linen jacket. She'd even borrowed an iron for the jacket. Her formal clothes exacerbated the wholly alien situation. When she tried to think of what to say, her throat closed up. Her heart thumped until she felt she needed to sit down. She found a wall to lean against instead, her breathing ragged and her palms clammy.

The door into the arrivals hall opened suddenly and the choppy sea became a fully-fledged tornado as a deluge of the newly-arrived gushed out. Heather's caricatures came to an abrupt halt. Most of these looked like returning

Egyptians. Crowds of welcoming uncles, aunts, grand-parents, children, brothers and sisters flooded past the No Entry sign, totally ignoring the ineffectual instructions of an official who, presumably, was telling them to back off and wait patiently.

The decibels increased with the clamour of excited welcome, of hugs and kisses, for this was a culture where men kissed men and women kissed women. The eager heaving crowds in the arrivals hall suddenly looked like the New Year sales. It seemed everyone took *all* their possessions on *every* trip; there were families returning with seven or eight suitcases and a couple of blankets rolled up.

In all the hyperactivity and uproar, she spotted the reunion of an elderly couple – the woman had arrived, the man limped forward eagerly to greet her. They held each others' arms and stared for a long moment into each others' eyes. How strange was this exuberant, restrictive culture, where married couples shouldn't hold hands or show affection publicly. They stood in a private, transparent bubble, oblivious of everyone else. Their obvious longing to hold one another made Heather's throat ache. She turned away, swallowing the lump and brushing away rogue tears.

Gradually, slowly, the swaying, laughing crowd made its way through the bottle-neck of the exit, the slow emptying exacerbated by the lack of queuing. But no matter. Families were reunited and the party, presumably, was just beginning. A measure of calm and quiet was restored to the arrivals hall, but the lull merely brought her dreaded moment nearer. Each heart-stopping memory of Tony's last days made her sweat or shiver. She realised she hadn't even liked him all that much – it was just that company was valuable in a place like Cairo. She knew Tony had valued her companionship. Sight-seeing, trying out local restaurants, travelling on the metro or buses – everything was easier if there were two of you – someone to laugh with at the strangeness of local customs – someone to chat to when you couldn't understand the conversation going on around you. Heather knew she and Tony would never have been together if they were back home. In fact, she had planned to bring the relationship to a close as soon as circumstances changed – if Tony didn't do so first.

She longed vehemently for this encounter to be over, or, better still, never to happen at all. Her mind danced around the innumerable *if-onlies*. If only she had persuaded Tony not to join the crowds in Tahrir; if only she herself had refused to accompany him, he might not have gone. If only they had heeded the Embassy warnings. If only they'd eaten that ubiquitous street salad with its insufficiently washed lettuce, and spent the day vomiting! How ridiculous could you get?

A worse thought was scratching at the corners of her mind. She'd been trying to ignore it all day, but now it confronted her head-on. What if they blamed her? No need, she'd tell them, she was already doing that job for them.

At last the arrivals board announced *Landed* and then began the serious wait and search. In her fidgety hands she held the now damp paper with *Mr and Mrs Long* written in black felt tip. She tried to edge nearer to the barrier, in the hope of spotting them before they spotted her, though she didn't know what difference that might make.

Suddenly there was a commotion beyond the barrier, in the baggage reclaim area. Voices were raised and everyone waiting surged forward. Heather's heart thumped in her throat. She imagined Mrs Long fainting, Mr Long bellowing at unsuspecting officials who had allowed his son to confront such danger. Then the doors opened again, and the passengers from Heathrow began to trickle out. Heather spotted them immediately: an average, grey-haired couple of average height, with an average-sized suitcase with wheels and a neat carry-on bag, he in dark trousers and a beige anorak, she in a black jacket, low-heeled court shoes and grey pleated skirt. As Heather approached them diffidently, her eyes fixed, somehow, on that pleated skirt, she murmured 'Mr and Mrs Long? I'm so sorry, so sorry…'

Heather studied the little map on the hotel brochure that Mr Long handed to her. It didn't offer many clues, but the address was there, and Heather knew that when you gave instructions to a taxi driver, you had to start with the general district, then narrow it down.

'Taxi? Taxi?' Eager obsequious drivers pressed around them, smiling and bowing solicitously.

'No, no. La'a shukran,' Heather said, looking straight forward and striding past them. She urged the Longs to do the same. 'They charge too much directly from the airport, and it's not that far to Heliopolis. It's better if we go out on to the road, if you're okay with that.'

The Longs nodded and Heather, carrying their cabin bag, thrust ahead of them, brushing aside every urgent offer of help.

'Heliopolis, min fadlak?' she asked the first taxi that stopped.

'Na'am, na'am.' The driver nodded, got out, opened the boot and stowed the bags inside.

'Saba-een?' she asked, opening her wallet. '*Seventy*?'

He looked shocked. 'Mia wa khamseen!' '*A hundred and fifty!*'

And so began the inevitable game of bartering, Heather allowing her suggestion to be pushed up a little, while he allowed his to drop, until they came to a firm agreement of one hundred. Mr and Mrs Long looked lost and forlorn, and Heather, at last, felt of some use. 'Would you mind sitting in the front, Mr Long?' she asked, 'while Mrs Long and I sit in the back? Men sit beside men. It's the culture, you know.' Clearly they didn't, but they were passively willing to go along with anything she suggested. Mr Long sat at the front and put on his seat belt. Heather knew it would leave a dusty diagonal stripe across his anorak. He'd be the only one in years to wear it.

'I'm George,' said Mr Long, 'and this is Eileen. Please use our first names, it's less formal.'

'Yes, please... like 'e says, less formal,' Mrs Long repeated like an automaton. Heather wondered if they were always like this, so bland, so accommodating, or whether bereavement had emptied them of assertion, of decision-making, even of feelings.

'All right. Thank you,' she said, and tried to concentrate on the route. On the way, Mr Long – George – sat rigid, flinching a little at every junction, clearing his throat nervously every time they sailed though a red light. It might have been better to be counter-cultural, for Heather to sit in the front. The driver clearly sensed that conversation wasn't going to be possible, and contented himself with lighting a cigarette and blowing the smoke ineffectually towards the open window. He was racing, squeezing at top speed past every possible car on the inside or outside, and turning left from the right-hand lane.

'Don't worry,' she told the Longs. 'It's always like this, but actually the drivers are very skilful.' Eileen, clearly unconvinced, clung on to the arm rest.

Once Heather recognised the outskirts of Heliopolis, she told the driver the name of the street and hotel. Winding the window right down, he leaned out and repeated the names to nearby drivers until he seemed to have received adequate directions.

To Heather's huge relief, they arrived at the hotel named on the brochure, and the driver helped with the luggage. George brandished a wallet full of Egyptian notes, and Heather cringed. This was a fortune to the average Cairo taxi driver. But she selected a one hundred denomination note, and added a twenty of her own as a tip, and the driver left, satisfied.

The hotel was pleasingly clean and organised, the receptionist spoke a little English, and Eileen, ashen and staring, relaxed a little. 'Please come up to our room with us, 'eather,' she said. 'We've not 'ardly 'ad chance to speak to you.'

'Aye, come on up, lass,' George added. So Heather, carrying the cabin bag again, trailed along the corridor with them, squeezed into the lift with them, and then stood back as they unlocked their room and surveyed the scene.

The room was adequate – an average twin-bedded hotel room with stiff sheets, a neat little en suite and a card with information and meal times in Arabic and English.

'Ooh, isn't it *lovely*, George,' said Eileen, shrugging off her jacket and sitting on the edge of one of the beds.

'Aye, it'll do,' he agreed, slinging the suitcase on the other bed. 'Sit yourself down lass,' he said to Heather, indicating the only armchair in the room. Heather sat.

'We're very grateful to you for meeting us like this,' George began.

'Aye, very grateful,' Eileen echoed.

'Don't know as how we woulda managed without you.'

'No,' Eileen agreed, 'we wouldn'ta managed.'

'We've never been abroad before, see, 'cept for Lanzarote...'

'An' it were much too hot.'

'Aye, too hot,' George agreed.

Heather had been nodding sympathetically, trying not to grin. She cleared her throat and bent down, ostensibly to adjust her sandal strap. *Oh, Tony, now I know why you wanted to get away.*

'We're happy in England, see,'

'Happy in England...'

'But our Tony, he always wanted to go away and have adventures.'

'Adventures!'

'Said as how it were borin' at home,'

'How could it be borin'? He had friends down the pub. He could meet them every night...' George looked affronted.

'Every night.'

Heather felt an irresistible giggle rising. Her diaphragm started to shake and she cleared her throat again. If only she could think of something innocuous to say, to change the subject, but Eileen saw and misunderstood. 'You poor dear. We're *so* sorry. We were delighted when Tony told us he'd met a nice girl. We knew you was a nice girl, 'cos our Tony, he wouldn't go with any old riff-raff...'

'No, he wouldn't. Told us as how you're a qualified medico an'all…'

'Physiotherapist. I'm not a doctor,' Heather put in quickly, her breathing unsteady.

'Aye, lass, that's lovely,' George continued. 'You were so good for our Tony. He wrote us postcards bout you, so he did.'

'Aye, postcards. Never used to write before. Not till he met you,' Eileen added. 'We could tell then that he were going to be happy to settle down at last. That's why we're so sorry, cos it's your loss as much as ours.'

'More, even,' George emphasised. 'You two had your whole lives ahead of you.'

'You'd've made our lad so happy,' Eileen sniffed, pulling a lace-edged handkerchief out of her handbag. 'We were so looking forward to the announcement.' And Eileen got up, bent over Heather and gave her a hug. She smelled of powder, cheap scent and something else – mothballs?

Announcement! The scarcely-controlled giggle and sudden misapprehension proved too much, and this new development heaped guilt upon Heather exponentially. When the giggle surfaced, it came as a tragic moan and a flood of tears. Was this hysteria? Heather had read about it, but never experienced it. It took her a horribly long moment to react and hug Eileen back. How could this have happened? How could they have the idea that she and Tony had been almost engaged? What had he said? She'd been under the impression he hardly communicated with his parents. She couldn't let them continue under this illusion. How was she supposed to react?

'I don't know what to say…' she began.

'No, it's all right, chuck,' George said. 'We

understand. You're young. You'll find another handsome lad.'

'Now's not the time to say that, George,' Eileen scolded.

How was it that *she* was the one deemed in need of sympathy? What if these bereaved parents knew her real feelings for Tony? Did they need to know the truth? What harm would it do to let them imagine she shared their grief in equal measure?

'No, you're right pet,' George agreed. 'There aren't any more like our Tony. Maybe we should talk about plans for tomorrow.'

Heather arrived promptly by arrangement at the hotel at nine the next morning, and the Longs were waiting beside the reception desk. They were each wearing black. That, at least, was cultural, Heather thought, except for Eileen's felt hat with a black feather, like something from Agatha Christie's *Miss Marple*.

With a repeat of the previous evening's taxi journey, they arrived at the hospital where Tony had been taken. Unorganised crowds hung around the entrance outside, their voices raised in concern or anger – Heather wasn't sure which. She had never been in an Egyptian hospital, and feared the worst, but she was impressed. The corridors were white and gleaming, and notices were in English as well as Arabic. Better still, as soon as they approached the reception desk, a slim woman in a mauve suit joined them. Heather gauged her to be about the same age as her mother. 'Good morning. I'm Marian Braithwaite. From the British Embassy.'

She turned to George and Eileen. 'You must be Mr and Mrs Long?' She shook hands with each of them. 'I'm so very sorry about Tony,' she said. 'I'd like to take you to see him.'

Heather was immensely relieved. She hadn't imagined how she would manage this part. She hovered. 'Please come as well, Heather,' Marian said. 'I understand you were a good friend of Tony's?'

'Oh yes,' Eileen affirmed. 'They must've made a lovely couple.'

Heather shook Marian's hand but said nothing.

Marian must have been here before, or else she was just quicker off the mark at reading and following the signs. The morgue was in the basement, and as they went downstairs they left the crowds behind, and the atmosphere became more tense. George and Eileen clung on to each other, and she was aware of her own shoulders stiffening. Marian's Arabic was fluent, and as she had a word with the doctor in charge, Heather remained at what she hoped was a respectful distance. But eventually, as they were ushered in to the room where Tony's body lay, Eileen grasped Heather's arm firmly so she had no choice, and they trooped in together.

Tony's face and hair had been cleaned and he was covered up to the neck by a clean white sheet. What had she expected? The mangled, dusty body she had last seen? The sightless eyes half open? His eyes were closed now and he looked at peace. The mortal wound on the back of his head wasn't visible. He used to tease her with what he called his *good boy* expression. That's how he looked now. That's how he might have been, if she…

Despite paramedical training, Heather had never seen a body in a morgue before. She was having trouble breathing out.

Eileen was weeping silently, letting tears course down her face unheeded. 'Come on, Mother,' George urged her. 'Let's say our goodbyes.' Keeping hold of Eileen with his left hand, he touched Tony's shoulder through the sheet with the other. 'Goodbye son. We're gonna miss you.'

He stepped back a little and gently pushed Eileen forward. 'Gonna miss you, son,' she said, and stooped to kiss Tony's forehead, though her lips didn't quite touch.

Heather reached behind for the door frame. The air around had begun to hum and spots of black marred her vision. 'Heather, do you want to...' Marian began, then the next thing Heather knew, she was sitting on the floor, her back against the wall, her head between her knees and Marian holding her shoulders.

Memories of the next hour were indistinct. Marian, it seemed, had called for Embassy reinforcements, who took the Longs away to do paperwork and then to return to the hotel for a late lunch. Heather was conveyed with Marian in an Embassy car to Marian's home, where she was ensconced in a puffy armchair and fed cheese on toast and sweet tea while Marian went off to make phone calls.

What a flat! Heather surveyed her surroundings with awe. It was a palace. In common with most Egyptian homes, it had multiple seating areas. Egyptian families could be huge. The horizontal blinds were partly open, casting stripes of sunlight across the cream rug. Cream rug! But it was clean and wonderfully soft on Heather's bare feet. Were her feet clean enough for the rug?

The dark oak corner cabinet was well-stocked with red and white wines, gin and even a single malt. Inside the glass-fronted sideboard was a bone china dinner and tea

84

service and a silver teapot, milk jug and sugar basin. The coffee table was two-tier, glass on top, oak underneath, but it was carved in the shape of the map of Africa. On the glass top stood a set of coasters of Middle Eastern art, and on the lower level were various art books, and one on Egyptian architecture, which purported to span 5000 years.

But the walls - it was a veritable art gallery. There were classical prints – Rembrandt, Vermeer, Botticelli and so many more that Heather didn't recognise, then there was a collection of Impressionists, which she had loved ever since going on a school trip to Paris in the sixth year. She recognised Monet and Gaugin, Renoir and Cezanne. But there were also originals – oils and pastels and a collection of sketched portraits. Was Marian herself an artist?

Relaxed and well fed, Heather burrowed into the armchair. The cushions were elegant – embroidery on silk – but one was covered in a fleecy material with a picture of a cute puppy – decoration quite out of keeping with the rest of the room. Heather picked up this cushion and clasped it to her. Her eyelids were heavy and she had no idea what the time was when Marian reappeared with her own cup of tea and another one for Heather.

'So sorry to wake you my dear. I imagine you're needing to catch up on sleep at this stage.'

Guiltily, Heather put the cushion to one side and sat up straighter.

'So you found Ozzie! My daughter bought me that cushion. She has a puppy called Ozzie that looks exactly like that – apparently. I haven't seen it. She lives in the US. She's British-Egyptian, but her husband is American. She's phoned me a dozen times since it all went pear-shaped here, urging me to fly over there, but I keep telling her I have a job to do here. Anyway, how are you feeling, my dear?'

'Much better, thanks. Thank you for looking after me – and Mr and Mrs Long. I suppose I'd better be getting back.' She put her cup and saucer on the coffee table and started to get up, but the four walls threatened to shift around her, and the floor didn't seem to be flat.

Marian stood up and gently pulled her elbow. 'Sit down, Heather. I've got some suggestions to make.' Heather did as she was told. She didn't have the energy or will power to resist. 'I think it would be a good idea for you to stay here with me tonight. I understand you don't share your flat? You live alone, is that right?' Heather nodded. It had never been an issue before, but now it seemed significant. 'Well, I have a guest room, and you are very welcome to stay there. We'll get a taxi back to your flat so you can collect a few things.'

'Thanks, that's kind, but what about the Longs?'

'Someone will take care of them. Don't worry. One of my colleagues is helping them to make arrangements to repatriate Tony. His parents will accompany him of course. But once their paper work is completed there'll be no reason for them to hang around. And I'm sure they won't want to. The only question is, whether you want to fly with them?'

Heather gasped. Since Tony's death she hadn't thought beyond trying to get through the next few hours. 'I'm on a course. I'm learning Arabic…' Even as she said it, any ambition she'd had seemed to blur around the edges, and the future looked like a gaping hole.

Beth aged 15

Edinburgh

June 2007

'All set?' Dad called through Beth's bedroom door.

'Yep. Just coming.' Beth opened her door and stepped on to the landing. She had put on black trousers and her favourite long lacy white shirt. Should she wear all black? Granny herself would have chosen yellow or red for her own funeral, something jolly. 'What do you think?'

But Dad was already downstairs. He glanced up cursorily. 'About what?'

'About my outfit. Should I wear my black shirt or is this one all right?'

'That one's fine.'

He hadn't even looked. If she'd worn purple with orange spots, he wouldn't have noticed or, if he had, he wouldn't have cared. 'What would Mum have worn?' That stopped him in his tracks. She knew it would.

He froze, his hand half way to the hall table to pick up the car keys. 'Dunno,' he said finally, though Beth knew he had a clear mental picture of Mum in some lovely outfit – a lemon-yellow evening dress, maybe, or a smart burgundy suit with a short skirt. These were the living room photos that were familiar to Beth. It was only the photos, now, no longer the person, that she saw in her mind's eye.

Dad himself looked smart in his black suit. It was a classic cut and would never go out of fashion. He had worn it for Mum's funeral, and now he was wearing it for Granny's. She wondered vaguely whose would be next, though he would need braces as well as a belt if he lost any more weight. His dark hair was slate grey these days, too, though he didn't like Beth to mention it, even when she said he looked distinguished.

'They used to say pneumonia was the old man's friend,' Dad had told Beth when they'd received the phone call about Granny's death. 'In her case, I think it was true.' Beth hadn't understood, but he explained it was better, in his opinion, for Granny to die quite suddenly, after a mere week's illness, than to undergo a further slow, ignominious decline into dementia. In Beth's opinion, it would have been better for Granny if they had visited her more often, if Beth herself had been allowed to go and play snakes and ladders, or Scrabble, even if Granny couldn't remember some of the words. But Dad had always tried to shield her. How was she going to become a good doctor if she wasn't allowed to visit sick people?

The funeral was small. Beth and Dad, Aunty Nessa and Uncle Bob, Granny's next-door-neighbours and a few friends from her book group. Dad said that these friends were particularly loyal and charitable. They had put up with Granny even when dementia had robbed her of the ability to retain the characters or plots she read about, but she enjoyed the warm, familiar ambience, the friendly faces of the participants, and the cup of tea.

Beth was the only young person at the crematorium. She felt mildly annoyed with Paul for taking a gap year in Australia, working on a sheep farm. She had thought the worst thing about the funeral would be his absence, but, in the event, it was the spooky moment when the curtains closed, as if drawn by a ghostly, unseen hand, around the coffin, which was borne by magic into the furnace, hidden from view but not from a fertile imagination. It was a moment so horrific, so final. It was the end of Easter egg hunts or hide and seek in Granny's big garden, the end of old videos, of playing with Paul, of listening to Granny's funny stories about when Dad and Uncle Bob were small, of lessons in jam-making and the healing properties of lavender. Beth glanced from Uncle Bob to Dad and back. They were uncannily similar to look at, but as different as two brothers could be. Chalk and cheese, Granny used to say. Uncle Bob, so chatty, blustery and full of jokes and teasing. Dad, so melancholy and increasingly silent.

'Wonder who'll be next?' Uncle Bob muttered with uncharacteristic gloom as they left the little chapel.

'Me,' Dad replied.

Beth's huge effort to be grown up deserted her, then, and hot tears of panic and anger spilled over. Aunty Nessa instantly linked arms with her and marched her away along the neat path flanked by well-tended flower beds and shiny new plaques. Their jaunty, vibrant colours mocked her. *Cheer up*, they goaded callously. The path led out of the back entrance of the crematorium into the edge of the town.

At the first coffee shop, Nessa sat Beth at a table outside in the sun and ordered two cups of hot chocolate. 'Your dad can be tactless at times, Beth.' She gave Beth's shoulders a quick squeeze and planted a kiss on her cheek. 'It must seem there is too much dying and not enough living in your young life.' She dug in her bag and produced a packet of tissues. 'But you'll be the one to change this family's fortunes. You'll meet a gorgeous young guy and have six kids and make your dad proud of you!'

'Dad will only be proud of me if I become a doctor.'

'Hmm.' Aunty Nessa paused. 'Do you *want* to become a doctor?'

'Well, yes, I guess so. But even if I save the lives of people who get hurt like Mum did, it'll still be too late for Mum, and therefore also for Dad.'

'That's very perceptive, young lady. But you must do what you enjoy doing, and what you're good at. That's how to make headway in this life.'

'I can hardly remember Mum any more,' Beth said, with a fresh rush of tears. 'But I know he thinks of her all the time. Sometimes I want to remind him…'

'What?'

'I want to remind him that…' There was a buzzing sound, and Aunty Nessa fished in her bag again and brought out a shiny new mobile phone. She studied the screen for a moment. 'It's a text from Uncle Bob. He wants to know where we are. I'll just text back and tell him we'll be there in a few minutes.'

'Can I see?' Beth asked after she had finished. She handled the little phone with respect. 'Next Christmas…' she said.

'Absolutely! When I was at university, we had to queue up to use the pay phone in the hall of residence, and as for getting an incoming call – I think carrier pigeons might have been more efficient. By the time you go to uni – *if* you go… Anyway, what were you saying?'

But Beth had regained her equilibrium and had donned her grown up mask once again. It was too selfish to say, 'I want to remind him that *I'm* still here.' Instead she said, 'But Granny was Uncle Bob's mum as well. I'm so sorry…'

Aunty Nessa squeezed her hand. 'Yes, and we'll all miss her terribly. But you know, she had a good life. She'd had her time, and somehow, since the dementia, she wasn't the same mum or granny any longer. We'll all prefer to remember picnics on the beach with her…'

'… and Paul and me climbing the apple trees in her garden…'

'Yes, and her scones with cream and jam…'

'… and those bedtime stories that she could just make up as she went along. I can even remember some of them. And Paul said he once wrote one up for an English composition at school!'

'Did he? He never told me that. Granny would have been tickled pink.'

'Maybe he told her.'

'I hope he did. He's so sorry he couldn't be here to say goodbye today.'

'Yeah. I miss him. Is he enjoying it? In Australia?'

'You bet! I reckon he's becoming a regular Digger! He likes the outside life-style, and he says that, with Australians, what you see is what you get. He says they get bad press for being too blunt, too in-yer-face. But Paul likes that. He never liked it when people would pussy-foot around an issue without saying what they really meant.' Aunty Nessa clamped her lips together and stared at her cup as if she were angry with it. Beth felt momentarily like an intruder.

'I'm glad he's having a good time,' she said lamely.

Aunty Nessa shivered, seemed to shake herself back to the present. 'Yes, it's proving a great move for him. Of course, we miss him horribly, but he's young, too, like you. Time to live your lives.' She paused. 'It's been a very hard time here for you and your dad – for all of us – but especially for him, after your mum… Come on, let's go and be polite and eat sandwiches with the book group.'

Heather

Edinburgh

June 2012

The morning had seemed interminable, and a brief lunch break beckoned invitingly. Working in July always made Heather feel cheated. Even at twenty-five, she looked upon those school and university summer holidays as hers by right, somehow, though she was well aware that the rest of the world took only two weeks' holiday. She consoled herself with the fact that the wind was chilly, so she wasn't missing much, even though the sun was bright.

'Just going to Coffee Plus,' she told Marjorie, grabbing her jacket from the hook inside the little staff room.

'Our coffee not good enough for you, hen?' Marjorie called after her, leaning her ample, cardigan-clad bosom across the reception desk. Actually, it wasn't, and Marjorie knew that, but she was laughing and she held no grudges. Tomorrow Heather would make sure it was Marjorie's turn to escape for half an hour.

As she reached the outer door, Heather bumped into a lost-looking young woman hovering on the doorstep.

'Er, I wonder if you could help me? Can I make a physio appointment or do I have to have a referral from my GP or something?'

She should have zipped up her jacket over her uniform tunic. If she hadn't looked official, the girl might have taken her for a patient and not stopped her. But there was something about this girl. Something intense, but more than that, Heather felt as if she was looking at the sister she didn't have. Same height and build. Same colour and length of hair, except that this girl had electric blue eyes.

'I'm sorry,' the girl said. 'Is it your lunch break? Maybe I should come back later?'

Absolutely. But something made Heather break all the rules. She should just have pointed her to Marjorie at the desk, but instead she said, 'I'm just going across the road for a coffee. Do you want to come?' Instantly she regretted it. What sort of professional would this girl think she was? She started to backtrack. 'Of course, there's reception...'

But at the same time, the girl looked relieved and responded, 'That would be great. I was just thinking about coffee.' They both tittered nervously. 'My name's Beth - Elizabeth Gomersall. I hurt my ankle last week.'

'Heather McLuskie. I'm a physio here – well, of course, you can see that. Come on, let's go to Coffee Plus.'

In the café Heather ordered a filter coffee and a tuna-filled croissant. 'Make that two please,' Beth told the barista. She turned to Heather. 'D'you want to get a table? I'll bring the coffees.'

Heather slung her jacket across two chairs, but by the time she returned to help carry the trays, Beth had paid. 'Oh, but you shouldn't do that,' Heather remonstrated. 'I can pay for mine.'

'No, no, it's no problem. Anyway, I'm interrupting your break. It's the least I can do.'

Wrong-footed but curious, Heather led Beth to their table and took a seat. How should she play this? Was this a first appointment with a new patient, or coffee with a new friend?

'So sorry,' Beth said again. 'I should've...'

'You said you injured your ankle? Did you go to A

and E?'

'Er, no. Someone helped me, then I bound it up myself, but I actually expected it to be better before now. I've got a dog, you see. I have to walk him.'

'A dog? What sort? We always had a dog when I was growing up. A Labrador. They're so soft and sloppy...' Sharp memories of Nero brought a rogue lump to Heather's throat.

'Mine's a spaniel. I've not had him very long. He kind of latched on to me. He's very affectionate and amazingly obedient.'

'Look, I can't really ask you to take your shoe and sock off in here,' Heather smiled apologetically, 'but I'm pretty sure I've got a gap after my next patient. Can you come across to the clinic at, say, 2.30?'

Dog chat broke the remaining ice, and Heather felt refreshed as she hurried back to the clinic. She didn't know whether to expect Elizabeth to turn up at 2.30, but there she was, in the waiting room on time. Had she just been hanging around outside all that time?

In the treatment room, Heather manipulated Beth's foot gently back and forth, left and right. It was certainly a bit swollen and bruised, but nothing too serious. 'How did you say you did it?'

'I was walking my dog on Arthur's Seat last week. Remember all that rain we had? It made the ground slippery, and I wasn't sticking to the well-trodden path. Anyway, I slipped. Must have put my foot down a rabbit hole or something. My ankle was agony. At first I thought I might even have broken something. But there was a man there – older man, but very fit-looking. He was walking his dog too. He helped me down the hill and took me to his house because it was nearby. Gave me a tubigrip. Actually he gave me coffee and cookies as well!'

Immediate warning bells rang in Heather's mind. What was it Pa had written in that email she'd glanced at? Something about a girl who'd injured her ankle on the hill and been overly upset about it, and he'd helped because she'd looked like Heather herself? She cleared her throat and asked as casually as she could, 'What sort of dog did he have?'

'A black Labrador. A very friendly ploddy dog!' She smiled.

It couldn't be. Could it? 'Yeah, Labradors are very popular,' Heather said, then sat very still, willing her renegade heart to calm down. After a moment she added, as lightly as she could, 'You wanna be careful about meeting old men on the hill.'

'Oh, he was harmless, I'm sure of it. He was very polite and... and... reluctant. I kept imagining I was too heavy for him.'

'Oh no, he...' Heather caught herself, almost too late. 'I mean, you're not very heavy. Well, I don't think you've done anything too serious, and the ankle is making progress.' Heather showed Beth some exercises for her foot and ankle and gave her a printed copy of simple instructions. Then she accompanied her to the reception desk. 'See how you go, and make another appointment if you feel you need it. Okay?'

'Okay. And thanks.'

Heather slipped alone into the staff room and poured herself a glass of water. Beth had met her father. It had to be. There were too many similarities. She'd always skimmed through Pa's emails, pretending to herself that she was deleting them unread, but not being able to ignore them completely. He'd always protested his innocence, even though he'd been obliged to leave his school because of the accusations of inappropriate conduct with an under-age student. She had wanted to believe him, but now, here he was, looking after young girls and taking them home.

Peering through the window blind, she watched Beth leave, walking with a slight limp, but with something else: with stiff shoulders, a diffidence, a heaviness that a young, fit twenty-year-old shouldn't have. And the girl was so formal.

Heather leaned against the wall and continued to peer between the slats of the blind. If only she'd asked Beth if she knew the name of the 'older man' with the friendly black Labrador. Or even the name of the dog. Then she would have been sure.

She always relished the brief respite in the middle of a working day – as well as the good coffee – but she'd often felt awkward, eating a quick lunch alone, when the rest of the world seemed to be in twos or threes. She had enjoyed the brief encounter with Beth – someone nearer her own age to chat with. She thought of Ryan – faithful emails and phone calls – but a continent away. Other girls had local boyfriends or pals, people to talk with about their aims and goals, their successes or frustrations. Sometimes Heather would look at herself in the mirror to check whether she had two heads.

Marjorie bust into the room. 'Oh! There you are!' She paused. 'Are you all right?'

Heather stood upright and smiled briskly. 'Yep. Fine.'

'Only, Mrs Thingummy is here again.' Marjorie pulled a face.

'Okay. Please tell her I'm just coming.' Marjorie backed out of the door and Heather put her glass in the little sink. Mrs Snell. There was a hypochondriac if ever there was one. Or possibly just a lonely lady who needed some personal attention.

Personal attention! Maybe that was what Beth needed more than ankle exercises. Didn't we all!

Beth

Edinburgh

July 2012

A week later in Coffee Plus, Beth ordered a juice, but decided not to get anything to eat yet. She sat at the table that she and Heather had occupied last time and glanced at her watch. Twelve-thirty. That was the time Heather took her break last week. Twice, Beth almost got up to leave. What would Heather think of her? Too eager? Too pushy? She had done her exercises assiduously, and her ankle certainly felt much better. Maybe time was the healer, but she had admired Heather's professionalism mixed with friendliness – the sort of medic she used to dream of becoming.

The door was opening. Beth craned her neck, hopeful but embarrassed. It was Heather. She stood up and gave a small wave. 'Hello. I wondered whether this was your regular haunt. I hope you don't mind. I fancied a juice before the appointment.'

'Course I don't,' Heather smiled. 'Good to see you again. It's my turn. What would you like?'

'No, no, I don't need anything more, thanks.'

Beth waited while Heather went to order, soon reappearing with two tuna croissants and coffees. 'Oh, you shouldn't have…' Beth began.

'Nae probs. It was my turn. Juice is full of vitamins, but…'

'…but no protein or fats,' Beth finished.

'And as for caffeine…'

'It keeps us going.' They both laughed.

'Anyway, how's the ankle? Or should I wait for the appointment to ask you?'

'Much better, thanks. I've done the exercises to the best of my ability.'

'To the best of your ability! Sounds like a high school report! Well done. You get a gold star.'

Beth smiled and looked down. She could feel herself blushing. It was an apt joke. She felt a mere schoolgirl, while Heather was a qualified professional.

'Er, I didn't know what you like, except I know you like tuna,' Heather said, "cos of last time.'

'No, that's great. Really. Anyway, I like everything.'

'You said you're a student, right? My mother always says students can't afford to be fussy!'

'Yes, that's right.' She laughed briefly. 'And what about you? Have you worked in this clinic since you qualified?'

'No. I went abroad for a while. I've only been here six months. Not sure if I want to stay for ever.'

'Abroad? Where did you go?'

'Egypt.'

'What, during the revolution? The Arab Spring, or whatever they called it?'

'Yep. The uprising.'

'Wow! Funny, the guy I met on Arthur's Seat, when I did this...' Beth pointed to her ankle, '...said he had a daughter working in Egypt!'

'Really? Maybe he... I wasn't actually...' Heather looked down and fiddled with her napkin and Beth wondered whether to change the subject. But Heather continued, 'I was learning Arabic, but the school had to close, so there was no point in staying on.'

'Learning Arabic? I imagine that was hard.'

'Yes, it was. I wasnae very good at it. I thought I'd be able to get a grasp of it, 'cos I was quite good at French at school, and also with living there, hearing it all around me, you know.'

'But the script is so different isn't it?'

'Yep. Impossible. And they speak so fast.'

'Were you hoping to work there? As a physio?'

'Yeah. Wanted to do something useful. Thought I might be able to *help people*. Ha ha! Sounds so pathetic, doesn't it? Who was I to think I could be of any use? Ethnocentricity is the name of the game.' She scowled and cradled her coffee cup in both hands.

Beth was silent. She had obviously touched a nerve, and she wasn't familiar with the ethno-word. But that phrase, that treacherous, meaningless phrase, *help people*, sent warning bells clanging through her own bruised mind.

'Sorry,' Heather said after a moment. 'Anyway, I came back and got a job. Like normal people do.'

'So, do you live with your parents?'

'No. Got a wee flat. I stayed with my ma when I first came back. My parents are divorced. Ma has a new bloke. He's okay, but I felt a bit like an optional extra. Anyway, soon as I got a job I found a flat. I really like it. It's a new build, quite near the city centre, so very convenient. My own little pad.'

Heather returned to her croissant and Beth finished her coffee.

'Anyway, what about you?'

Beth took a deep breath. Here we go…

'Oh, I meant to say,' Heather added, 'and I know it's not very professional and all that, but I know that an appointment at the clinic isn't cheap, and students aren't usually rolling in dosh, so if you like, I could call in to see you at home, so you wouldn't have to come to the clinic. If you don't live out in the Styx, that is. Where *do* you live?'

'Oh, you don't need to do that,' Beth said hastily. 'Shouldn't you be making a profit for the practice?' She grinned.

'Maybe the Middle East is rubbing off on me. Some things are much less formal there, but people do know how to look after each other. At least...'

With a sudden jolt, Beth realised Heather's lip was trembling, though she was lifting her coffee cup and bowing her head over it to hide it. How had she upset Heather? Had she offended her? What had she said? Beth busied herself stacking her plate and cup, folding her napkin. Heather pulled out a tissue, sniffed and grinned. 'Sorry, I...'

'No, *I'm* sorry. I didn't mean to...'

'No, it wasn't you. Talking about it just brought it all back.'

'Not doing well at learning Arabic?' Beth was floundering.

'No, well, yes, but there was so much more. Looking after people. It all went wrong. I met this guy, Tony...'

So while tables were vacated and refilled around them, the coffee machine hissed, and friends met, ate, chatted and parted, Beth heard about the beginnings of the uprising, Tony's death, the arrival of his parents and Heather's meeting Marian.

'In the end, I stayed with Marian for almost a week,' Heather said, swigging the dregs of her coffee, though it was certainly cold by now.

'So you didn't fly home with Tony's parents?'

'No. They only stayed another twenty-four hours. I guess the Egyptians were glad to get rid of an inconvenient foreign body,' she smiled ruefully, 'sorry, no pun intended. Anyway, I wasn't anywhere near ready to make any big decisions. But I did go to their hotel to see them again before they left, and I promised to visit them at home in Manchester. And I have. Once.' She pulled a face. 'They're nice people, but it wasn't an easy visit. They thought Tony and I were about to get engaged! But it wasn't really like that at all.'

'Did you, um, undeceive them?'

'No. I decided a half-truth was kinder. I let them think that Tony and I were much closer than we were.' She leaned back and sighed. 'I told them about all the fun things we did, like riding a camel in the desert, watching the Whirling Dervishes, running through the water jets at Al Azhar Park...'

'What?'

'Al Azhar Park. It's a lovely place. You have to pay to go in, but not much. It's a big area, and the amazing thing is that it never seems to get crowded. Imagine that! An area of Cairo that's not crowded. And there are several restaurants at various points. The first bit is cultivated – beautiful walkways and flower gardens – then there's a hill, which is just that – a hill. You can walk around it at the top. It's a bit like Arthur's Seat. A view in all four directions. At sunset you can see the lights twinkle on all over the city and you can hear the call to prayer from all the mosques – if they get their timing right, that is.'

Beth's imagination was struggling to keep up. Like Arthur's Seat but with tended flower beds and restaurants? But Heather's eyes were dancing.

'On the lower part, before the hill becomes steep, they've made this area with water jets that spout up from the ground. Of course, elegant Egyptians walk around them and admire them, and sometimes allow their toddlers to stand at the edge to cool them down. But Tony and I, we skipped right through them, much to everyone's shocked disgust. It was such a relief to get cool that day. But then these guys in uniform appeared from the ticket office and I assume they were about to tick us off, or even throw us out, but we ran off up the hill, and Tony called *Sorry* in Arabic over his shoulder. At least, I think that's what he said. Knowing Tony, it could've been *F off!* Egyptians don't run. It's undignified. So no one caught up with us, but on our way up we saw some school girls splitting their sides giggling!' Heather was laughing as she recounted it, and it made Beth smile, though her mind was still fixed on Tony's parents' bereavement.

'Anyway, staying with Marian was fantastic. Just what I needed. She's an art teacher at the university, and she holds these get-togethers – soirées, she calls them – for colleagues and friends. They wear all sorts of weird gear, as you might expect from artists, but not to draw attention - just to be individual and creative. Marian was only wearing a conventional suit in her British Embassy role. The rest of the time she wore swirly skirts and silky tops and flimsy scarves – and those colours. It was like living with an exotic bird!

'She's a widow. Her husband was Egyptian – quite a bit older than her, but Egyptian husbands often are – and he came from a wealthy family, hence the gorgeous flat. Her daughter's married to an American and lives in the States. She wanted Marian to go over there to avoid the troubles, but Marian's life is clearly in Cairo. At first, I thought, why is it such a big deal that I live alone, when she herself lives alone in this enormous mansion? I think it's different because she's a widow. But she's *so* hospitable. I reckon I wasn't the first student in distress to stay there, and I won't be the last. I worked out she was the same age as my mother, but she didn't *tell* me what to do, you know? But she gave me lots of time and asked me questions that helped me realise I was barking up the wrong tree.'

'The wrong tree?'

'Yeah. I had this supposedly altruistic motive to be useful. I'm a qualified physio, but there are lots of us here in Scotland. But you see all those poor people in the Middle East, clearly in need of all sorts of medical help. Don't get me wrong. In an emergency, the services are pretty good, but if you could see the people with no limbs, or half a limb, or twisted backs – and the malformed children who'd obviously never had any therapy…' Her eyes filmed over again.

'But Marian helped me to see that I was on the wrong track. I felt sorry for the people, but I hated the culture that had allowed this to happen to them. I didn't *embrace* the culture. She kept using that word. What's more, my Arabic was pretty poor, and my progress was painfully slow. Tony was brilliant at it. I think he sometimes pretended he could understand, just to impress people, but you should have heard him actually speaking. Sounded really natural and fluent. I don't think I'd ever have been able to reach the professional standard I'd need – all that medical vocabulary. In the end, as Marian predicted, lessons at the language school were cancelled for the foreseeable future, so I had nothing to do, and no one to do it with, except stay out of harm's way.'

'So you came home?'

'Yeah. Marian helped me to pack up and book a flight. I stayed with my mother for a couple of weeks, then got this job and found a flat. On my own!'

'So you feel settled?'

'Yeah. Sort of. For the time being. I love the flat.'

'And the job?'

'Well, it's okay. The colleagues are nice, though a fair bit older than me. Conversations seem to revolve around families, children and grandchildren, football training and swimming lessons. Don't know whether I'll do this for the rest of my life, though. Just need time to regroup.'

Heather sat up and looked at her watch. 'Oh no! Look at the time! I had no idea, rabbiting on...' She shot up, grabbed her jacket and bag. 'Look. Phone me. Or come again next week. Let's do something together. Make a plan. Okay?'

'Okay,' Beth agreed, 'and thanks for lunch.'

Heather

Edinburgh

July 2012

'Look at us! Like a pair of predictable middle-aged biddies, set in our ways!' Beth said, grinning.

Heather laughed, mostly at Beth's old-fashioned turn of phrase. It was true, though. She had begun to look forward to finding Beth having lunch at the same coffee shop even once her ankle was better. Same table, same choice of food. But it was much better than sitting at a table alone.

'So you reckon your ankle's quite better?'

'Yes. Strong as an ox. Thanks to you.'

Heather smiled. She had occasionally wondered if Beth hadn't prolonged the physiotherapy treatment longer than necessary. That in itself intrigued her. The clinic wasn't cheap, but Beth never complained.

'In that case, let's go out somewhere. Let's see a film, or take in a gig. I know! Let's go to a club. There's lots to choose from. There's Espionage, or Revolution, or the Liquid Room or...' She stopped. Beth had gone pale and started biting her thumbnail.

'What's up?'

There was a pause, then Beth said, 'Ach! I don't have anything to wear.'

Heather laughed outright. 'That's every girl's prerogative. Nothing to wear. Chance for a new wardrobe – or at least a trip to Primark!'

'But I don't, I mean I've never...'

Heather stopped laughing. Beth really did look

scared. 'How old are you?'

Beth's pallor turned into a blush. 'Twenty.'

'Twenty! And you've never been clubbing? It's time to remedy that. Have you honestly got nothing suitable to wear?'

Beth was staring at the table. 'No, honestly. But...' she looked up. 'Would you come shopping with me and help me choose something?'

In the fitting room, Heather and Beth, each with their statutory allowance of five garments, commandeered adjacent cubicles. Taking it in turns to view and comment on each other's choices, and to return individual items for a different size or colour if necessary, they giggled their way through outfit after outfit, to the annoyance of the moody attendant. 'She's just jealous,' Heather whispered. She stepped back to appraise Beth's choice of skirt and top. 'You look good. No, you really do.'

Beth was pulling a face. She seemed so reluctant to receive compliments, not only about her clothes just now, but about anything. Better boost the self-confidence.

'You're very slim, not skinny, just right. And you've got nice legs. You ought to wear a skirt more often with legs like those. And that cerise really suits you. Gives you a splash of colour.' She needed the colour, Heather had noticed. She was always pale, but now a slight blush was creeping up from her neck. Good. Must have hit the spot.

'Now, how about shoes? You'll have to have something comfy enough to dance in, or do you usually take your shoes off to dance?' Too late, Heather remembered there was no *usually*. This was a first. 'Let's pay for these, then hit the shoe shop - get something sparkly but comfy.'

Heather steered Beth to the cashier, and allowed Beth to persuade her into buying a sleeveless top. Beth had no trouble paying, and Heather controlled her customary grimace at digging out her card from her bag, while words like rent, heating, council tax and grocery bills threatened to punch holes in her peace of mind.

In the shoes department, Heather sat back while Beth set aside her trainers and tried pair after pair of shoes with a small heel. 'I haven't – I mean – it's ages since I... What do you think of these?'

Heather nodded approvingly. The sassy pink shoes with a sparkly bow sat well with the cerise top.

Like the proverbial shopaholics, laden with purchases, they were disgorged with other shoppers from the over-warm store and into the wind funnel that was Princes Street on a breezy Friday afternoon. 'Maybe this is what it means to throw caution to the wind,' Beth laughed, trying to gather her carrier bags around her and zip up her jacket at the same time.

'Sounds like your mum's turn of phrase,' Heather said. 'Or even your gran's!'

'Yeah, it was probably my gran's.'

'You, um, you haven't got your gran any more?'

Beth paused. 'No. She died when I was fifteen. You?'

'Not my father's mum. She died when I was tiny. But my mother's mum is still alive, but she's in Kent. We don't see her very often.'

'And you said you don't have any brothers or sisters?'

'That's right. You too?'

'No brothers or sisters but I've got a cousin, Paul. He's

as good as any brother. He's always been my best pal, really.'

'Lives nearby?'

'Yes, well, no. I mean, he used to, but he's in Australia at the moment. It all started when he had a gap year there and loved it. He graduated as a water engineer and he's working there now. You got cousins?'

'Yes, but they're in Kent as well. Anyway, they're older than me. Married, both of them. My parents met down south. My mother is half Portuguese. My pa is Scottish. We moved back to Scotland when I was a baby, but my parents are divorced now. Of course, I told you.'

'Yes. I'm sorry. But you went abroad...'

'I guess it was partly because of their divorce. I was so angry with them – with Pa, anyway, 'cos it was all his fault. But as I said before, Scotland has lots of medics and para-medics and the Middle East needs more, especially nurses and therapists. So I went abroad with all these big ideas of how I could change the world, or at least my little bit of it, but it turned out that all I did was fail to protect the one person I could have influenced.'

'Tony?'

'Yeah.'

They made their way with the summer visitors who kept stopping to take photos of Edinburgh Castle or Princes Street Gardens and with the disgruntled locals who paused to stand and complain about how long it was taking to complete the proposed tramway. Amid the chatting, shoving, sightseeing crowds, Heather talked again about Tony, how annoying he could be, how much fun he could be, how he made her mad and made her laugh but, most importantly, how he had worked so hard at Arabic and was proud of his own success. They'd seen a lot of Cairo together but, in between times, he had expressed some well-thought-out opinions. She knew she was going over old ground, but Beth always seemed content to listen.

'For all his blustering, I think he was actually not very confident,' she said. 'He always felt he had to compete with everyone, especially the other guys. With Martin 'cos he was such an intellectual – so switched on politically – with Ryan because – well, I don't know why, really. Maybe just 'cos Ryan was taller!' They laughed, then, but Heather added, 'Everyone said I was the settled one, the sensible one, the one with my head screwed on right. But actually, I didn't have a clue what I was doing. My Arabic wasn't very good and I basically just tagged along. I knew full well we shouldn't have gone to Tahrir. I should have persuaded him not to go. Ach! I've been over it a hundred times in my mind.'

They had arrived at Heather's bus stop. 'Anyway, thanks for listening. See you at ten tomorrow evening outside the Tron. Don't be late – I'll feel like a lemon standing around on my own. Come on the bus. You won't be able to drive home after a few drinks. Oh, and don't wear your best jacket. You'll be taking it off as soon as we start dancing.'

Beth

Edinburgh

July 2012

Beth looked around the club and shut her mouth. She'd been gaping. She stuck close to Heather in the swaying, jostling crowd of bodies. Heather had been right about the jacket. The room felt tropical. A rotation of coloured lights lit up Heather's smile.

'Let's get a drink first. What're you having?'

Beth hesitated. 'Whatever you have, but let me pay.'

'No, we go Dutch here. My contribution was the suggestion; yours was agreeing to come with me. No other debts. How about rum and coke?'

With their drinks they found a couple of stools to perch on and surveyed the scene. The music was loud and the beat persuasive. Beth was glad of the new clothes. There were girls in shorts, girls in miniscule skirts, girls in leopard print skinny jeans, girls in Korean yoga pants and every colour and style of pretty, sparkly, shimmery, strappy top. Better still, Beth didn't feel out of place, though many of the girls were much more heavily made up than she was, and carried themselves with confidence and… and with a certain anticipation of having a good time. There was no other way to define it.

Sipping her drink, she turned her attention to the guys. She remembered those long ago high school discos, when the boys stood nervously in one corner, and the girls twittered in another, and eventually some brash boy would swagger to the girls' corner and ask the prettiest girl to dance. The ice would be broken, and they'd revert to young people with friends, who could talk about sport, TV programmes and the latest celebrity scandal, or about their longing for world peace and their aims and ambitions beyond school exams.

'C'mon, drink up and let's get out there,' Heather urged.

Beth finished her drink more quickly than she would have liked, and followed Heather into the middle of the dance floor. Suddenly nervous, she giggled, 'Can you do ceilidh dances to club music?'

Heather scrutinised her for a moment, then said, 'Just let the music take you.'

It was true. The music took them. At one with the surrounding, tightly-packed dancers, jigging to a beat that shook the walls and the floor, Beth kept looking round to check what others were doing, to blend in and notice without being noticed. She was surrounded by laughter and smiles, hugs and shouted chat, pulsating rhythm – and people enjoying themselves. This was all her Christmases and birthdays rolled into one. This is what she had always imagined life should be like, filled with excitement, joy and carefree togetherness.

She was suddenly aware of grinning stupidly, and of Heather smiling at her, amused. Then Heather said something that Beth couldn't catch, but she nodded in the direction of a guy who had been dancing near to them for a while. Beth glanced surreptitiously. He wasn't particularly tall, but he had broad shoulders – swimmers' shoulders – and dimples and cutely crooked teeth. Heather was nudging her elbow, flashing her a look. What did that look mean? Gorgeous, eh? Or watch out?

At the same time, she heard him shout above the music, 'What're you drinking?'

'I, er...'

'We're together,' Heather warned him.

'Okay. The more the merrier.' He grinned. 'I'm Jem, by the way. Jeremy – but they call me Jem.'

Heather introduced herself and Beth. They went to queue at the bar. 'You both from round here?' he asked.

'Yeah,' Heather said. 'You?'

'Nah. I come in from Penicuik every Friday. Not much to do there. More happening here.'

'Right,' Heather said. 'But how do you get back there after this finishes?'

'I dinnae. I kip at my mum's. Her latest bloke doesn't like it, but he works on a Sunday morning anyway, so he can't grumble about me sleeping on the sofa for a few hours. I'm always gone by the time he comes back.'

'Ah,' Heather said.

Beth said nothing.

'How about you?' The boy aimed his question at Beth.

'I'm a student in Dundee, so I'm not down here very often either.'

'So, just for the weekend, like?'

'Well, I'm taking a break just now.' Beth's heart began to thump. All these questions. The Wall felt suddenly fragile. Change the subject. 'You got brothers and sisters?' The question came out fast and breathlessly.

'Me? Yeah. One brother. Don't see him very often though.'

'Oh? Has he moved away then?'

'Aye.'

'Far away?'

'Dinnae ken. Our mum's bloke doesn't like him, either. I reckon he's just taken off. Probably sleeping rough somewhere.'

'Ah, that's hard,' Heather sympathised.

'How about you?' Jem asked Beth. 'Brothers and sisters?'

'No. Just me.'

'Parents live in Edinburgh?'

'Yes. Er, no.' Now the room was beginning to blur. Beth bit her tongue. The happy exhilaration had caught her off her guard. She'd concentrated for so long on dodging people, so she could avoid questions, decisions, social workers, psychiatrists, asylums, the nut house…

'Must be good booze,' Jem laughed and looked from Beth to Heather. 'She's forgotten!'

Suddenly the ground beneath Beth started to lurch. The music turned to loud clamour, the unfamiliarity became overwhelming. How could making friends, going out on a Saturday evening, behaving like other people, ever become *normal*? Chatting about her gran with Heather, mentioning Paul and his love of Australia – it had felt so natural. Now she was back to square one, trying to preserve anonymity, hiding behind her Wall – how long could she go on doing it? And what would happen if… when…

'Hey, Beth! What's up? You've gone a funny colour, even in these lights.'

'It's hot in here,' Jem said. 'Come on. I know where the back door is. She needs some fresh air.'

Beth followed Heather as she pushed her way through the mass of bodies, keeping hold of her arm. The room was swimming and Beth felt sweat prickle her face and trickle down her spine. Her mouth filled with saliva and she groaned 'Heather...'

Jem pushed a door and they were outside where three metal steps led down to a gloomy alley. Beth just had time to grab the railing and lean over before vomiting. Heather put an arm round her shoulder and handed her tissues. Beth leaned heavily on the railing. She longed to lie down, but the ground was wet from a recent shower and the car... the car... Beth's knees buckled suddenly, and Heather caught her, propped her against the wall and supported her. Safely wedged, Beth tried to slow her breathing and regain control. She closed her eyes for a moment, but when she opened them again her head swam and she thought she'd faint.

'Your admirer has pushed off,' Heather observed, looking round. 'Obviously the squeamish kind.'

The fresh cool air made Beth shiver, but it was welcome. Her heart rate was slowing and she risked opening her eyes momentarily. The door opened and Jem emerged, holding a paper cup of water in one hand and an old metal chair in the other. He carried the chair down the three steps and set it against the wall in the alley, beckoning Beth and Heather with his chin. 'Hmm, I take it back,' Heather muttered.

With Heather's help, Beth staggered down the steps and sank on to the chair. He thrust the cup towards her. His hands were strong, clean but rough. She accepted the water and sipped slowly. Finally she stole a glance at Jem. He was probably about the same age as her, early twenties, anyway. He was studying her anxiously. She looked away.

'You feeling any better?'

'Yes thanks,' Beth lied, and added, 'As you said, it was a bit hot in there.' What was wrong with her? It was true she wasn't used to alcohol, but she suspected she wasn't drunk.

There was something about the music, the colour and movement, the normality of people enjoying themselves and the fear... the crippling fear of being found out, of having to make decisions, to face the future, of being *referred*...

Heather looked at her watch. 'Time to split. Beth needs her beauty sleep.'

'You're not *going?*' Jem protested. 'It's only one o'clock. The night's young!'

'It's old enough for us,' Heather stated. 'C'mon Beth. We'll have to go back in and get our jackets, then we can go out the front and get the night bus home.'

Heather made her way back through the gyrating bodies, Beth clinging dizzily to her arm, claimed her jacket and Beth's and made for the door. Beth struggled to follow. As they burst once more into the cool night air, Jem was right behind.

'Um, it's been great to meet you. I was just thinking, um, wondering, here's my mobile number.' He thrust a slip of paper at Beth. 'It'd be nice to catch up with you sometime.' Dumbly, Beth pushed the paper into her jacket pocket.

'In your dreams...' Heather retorted, but quietly. She took Beth's arm and marched her towards the bus stop. Jem didn't follow. Beth managed a glance over her shoulder. He was standing alone, looking young and crestfallen.

'I don't think he meant any harm,' she stammered.

'Maybe not. Better safe than sorry. Which bus stop? You live in the Cramond direction, right?'

Beth shivered. Her head ached, and for a moment she couldn't remember which car park she had left the car in. 'Er, no, not Cramond... south. Liberton, Peebles...'

'Well, which? 'Cos I'm not leaving you till I've seen you safely inside your own front door.'

'No! I'll be fine,' Beth declared. 'You've got to get home, too.' She was shaking uncontrollably and struggling to hold back tears.

'Don't be daft, Beth. What sort of friend would I be if I abandoned you at this point? This evening was my idea. Thought you'd enjoy a bit of fun, but...'

'I did!' Beth interrupted. 'I *did* enjoy it. It was just, well, the drink and...'

'But you only had one glass!'

'But I... sorry... I don't usually...'

'You don't usually have *one* glass?'

Heather was staring at her. Beth knew she was a hopeless liar, but she didn't want to lose Heather. Heather was a friend. She was *normal.*

'Actually, I don't really drink at all.' It sounded so stupid. Such a bald statement. 'My dad...'

'Ah, I see. Your dad drinks too much and you disapprove. You don't want to go the same way. Is he actually an alcoholic?'

Now the tears spilled over and Beth sobbed. They were standing fifty metres from the night club door. Other couples or groups of revellers were staring at them or giving them a wide berth. Heather steered Beth across the road and away from the eerie street light. 'Come on, you'll feel better after a warm night's sleep. Tell me your address. *Please.*'

'I'm not going home,' Beth sobbed, able, eventually, to get the words out. 'I'm just going to my car.' She fought to get a grip. 'I just need to get to my car. Then I'll be fine.' She blew her nose and tried to stop shaking.

Heather stared at her for what seemed like ages. 'Well, come and stay at my place. I've got a big comfy sofa and you can borrow a T-shirt to sleep in.' She began to steer Beth in a different direction.

'No, no, I can't!'

'Course you can. You *have* to. You're in no state to drive anywhere and you need a bed.'

'I can't! There's Soul.'

Heather looked around. 'No one's looking at us. Anyway, they're going back in to the club now.'

'No! I mean my dog! Soul! He's in the car.'

For the first time, Heather looked deflated. Beth stammered, 'But it's all right, I can… I can…'

'Right, listen,' Heather said at last. 'Here's what we'll do. We'll get the bus together to your car and I'll drive it to my flat, let the dog out and give him some water and find him a rug to lie on and then we can both get some sleep.'

'But the car's only insured for me. Anyway, you've been drinking as well. You've had more than me!'

'You are so maddeningly *correct!* I'll drive carefully and no one will ever know.'

The bus did nothing to help Beth's nausea. They had to get off one stop early for her to vomit into the gutter. Heather said nothing, but hung on to Beth's arm as they walked the last couple of hundred metres and staggered into the car park.

There was Soul, overjoyed to see them. He leapt out of the car and trotted smartly to find a lamppost. Beth managed to open the car boot to get out his bowl and a bottle of water and to shut the boot smartly before Heather could see its contents.

Soul finished drinking, found another lamppost and

was then persuaded to get back into the car. 'I feel better now. I reckon I could drive,' Beth said.

'No way. If we have to stop for you to throw up, I'd rather it was me driving. Give me the keys.'

Heather's flat was on the third floor of a new, modern block, with a few parking spaces for visiting cars. She parked in one of those and instructed Beth to get whatever she needed from the boot. Beth grabbed a bag with a change of clothes and her wash things and, as an afterthought, Soul's bowl. 'Is it okay to bring him?' she asked.

'Course. Better be quiet on the stairs though. We're not *really* supposed to have pets here, but no one's going to know.' Beth glanced nervously at each closed door, and cringed at the clickety-clack of Soul's claws on the stairs.

The sitting room was small, and one wall of it was the kitchen, but Beth's bleary first impression was that it was comfortable and friendly. Heather produced a sheet and a duvet, and hastily put a pillow case on a cushion on the sofa. She spread an old towel on the floor. 'That's Soul's bed. That's the bathroom and that's my room.' Heather pointed to the only other two doors. 'D'you think he'll settle there?'

Beth took Soul's collar and showed him the bed. She made him sit, then lie down. With a grunt he did as he was told, eyeing her suspiciously.

'D'you need anything? I'm gonna hit the hay now. It's catching up on me.' Heather yawned hugely then smiled and hugged Beth briefly. 'You gonna be OK?'

'Yes, thanks to you. You're very kind.'

'You're very kind,' Heather repeated with a posh

accent and a chuckle. 'Night. Sweet dreams.'

Beth lay cosily in the dark, alone apart from Soul. Equilibrium returned, fragile but welcome. She stared at the ceiling, still visible in the light of street lamps shining through the thin curtains. She thought about the club, its colour and music. Its joyous life.

She thought about Edinburgh. It must be one of the world's smallest capital cities. It wasn't even Scotland's biggest city. But it must be one of the quietest. It was remarkable, if what Heather had told her about Cairo was true, that the city never slept, that the noise rarely abated. Even on a summery Saturday night, here, so near to the city centre, the solid old metropolis could rest peacefully under the weight of its secrets.

Beth slept.

Next, she was drowning in water that was gushing down the stairs and flooding the hall. The very ground she was standing on was unstable. She shouted to Dad, but he was turned away, couldn't hear her, wouldn't look at her. She couldn't move against the weight of the water, and as she lunged for the banisters, they became seaweed and there were tentacles grabbing and shaking her and someone was screaming, screaming and a dog was barking…

Heather

Edinburgh

July 2012

Heather woke to a commotion very close by. Someone was screaming and a dog was barking. The neighbours must... Beth! The events of the previous evening came back in a rush. She threw off her duvet, snatched her dressing gown and dashed into the lounge.

'Beth, are you okay? What's wrong? What happened?'

All along, Heather had known that something wasn't right. Beth had had one drink. *One drink!* Maybe she had a medical condition that prevented alcohol consumption. Or she was on medication and she hadn't let on.

Now here they were in the middle of the night – what was the time? Beth was sitting up on the sofa sobbing, her eyes staring but unseeing. Soul was pushing his nose into her knee. Heather took hold of her shoulders gently but firmly. 'Beth, Beth! It's okay. It was just a nightmare. Everything's okay.' Heather knelt on the floor beside her, but kept her hand firmly on one shoulder. Gradually Beth's breathing calmed, she stopped sobbing and ran her hand across her face. She turned towards Heather and her eyes focused.

'Sorry,' she gasped, 'sorry, I, um, I must have been dreaming. Sorry I woke you.' She put one hand on Soul's head.

'A nightmare. You were having a nightmare. What were you dreaming about? They say if you recount your dreams, they fade away.'

'My dad, um, he...' She was gasping again,

hyperventilating.

'Okay. Bad idea. Never mind. Don't speak. Breathe.' Heather herself was breathing deeply, willing Beth to do it. 'Breathe in through your nose, out through your mouth. That's right. Again. Deeply. In – out - yes, that's it.' They sat for several minutes until Beth was breathing normally again. 'So your dad - he drinks, he can be violent, you are afraid to go home?'

Beth shook her head.

'You don't drink because of something your dad did?'

Nods this time.

'He hit someone when he was drunk?'

Beth shook her head, and with what looked like a huge effort, she said, 'He wasn't really drunk. But he'd had a couple of drinks. Said he was just a bit sleepy. There was a car accident. My mum…'

'Your mum was killed?'

'No. Hurt. Badly hurt.'

'It took her a long time to recover?'

No response.

'She didn't recover? She was permanently disabled?'

Nods. With a juddering sigh, Beth said, 'She was in a PVS, a persistent…'

'I know. Paramedic, remember?'

'Sorry. She never recovered.'

'Oh, I'm so sorry. She died?'

Nods.

'Recently?'

'No. When I was small.'

'And you were having a nightmare about that?'

Beth made no response, but just stared. The clock ticked. Soul lay down beside the sofa, yawned and settled his head on his paws. Heather wanted desperately to go back to bed, but Beth clearly wasn't ready. What was more, Heather knew she hadn't got to the bottom of it, and she felt mildly resentful that Beth was holding out on her. Where was her father in all this? She'd go with that physios' cliché, *no pain, no gain.*

'So, your dad has always told you not to drink because it's dangerous? Right?'

'Yes.'

'Well, that seems wise. But this happened when you were small. And your dad doesn't drink at all now, right?'

'My dad - he died.'

'Oh!' Heather gasped. 'Um, when?'

'Last month.'

'Only last month? Oh, Beth, I'm so sorry.' Heather felt way out of her depth. So Beth had no parents, no brothers and no sisters. How to pursue this line of conversation? Heather sat on the sofa next to Beth and hugged her. Now Heather was the one floundering, casting around for something to say, an approach to take. The implications of this new information threatened like a tsunami.

Finally, she said, 'But your home... You're camping in your car because you don't have a home?'

'No. The house is still there. My dad had made a will. He left the house to me. It's just that – that - I can't...'

'Can't face the empty house?'

Beth nodded again. Her tears had dried now, but her face was white and gaunt. They sat in silence until at last the hint of a tiny smile played on Beth's lips. 'When I was a child I had a nightmare, once, that I fell over the banisters, but before I hit the floor I woke up and found everything was all right. So then, whenever I was in a tight spot in a dream, I'd somehow run to the banisters and *jump* over them, and wake up and everything would be okay. Stupid, right?'

'Well, unusual.'

'But now, I can't face the house, and the banisters are…' The tears came again, but she brushed them aside impatiently.

Heather abandoned all hope of any more sleep. Most people's approach to helping bereaved friends was misdirected: instead of veering away from talking about the dead person, it was better to keep channels of communication open.

'Was your dad very sick?'

Beth's face became even whiter and the tears resumed unchecked. Wrong question, then. Heather tried again. 'What job did he do?'

Beth was weaving the edge of the blanket around her fingers. 'When I was little he worked for an insurance company. It sounded desperately boring. He never really talked about the job itself, just about his colleagues.' She paused and sniffed. 'He used to do accents, you know? There was this guy called Angus who was overweight and loved American gangster movies. Apparently, when he talked about the movies, he'd slip into a bad drawl and Dad would imitate him. I never met him, but I feel as if I did. Dad was such a brilliant mimic.'

The tears had stopped, and Beth was gazing somewhere into the distant past. 'He could mimic anybody, even singers. He liked the Spice Girls!' She laughed, briefly, and Soul lifted his head. 'But before that, he used to fancy himself as Benny Andersson. From Abba? There was a photo of Dad as a teenager with hair and beard just like Benny Andersson. Actually, he really did look like him – soft floppy brown hair and nice eyes. But when he started to go grey he shaved his beard off and had his hair cut very short.'

Heather couldn't think what Benny Andersson looked like, but Beth's face was becoming animated. 'He had all these Abba cassette tapes. We used to sing them together. We'd always end up laughing.'

More tears, then after a minute Beth continued, 'A while after Mum died he changed jobs and became a freelance gardener, so he could arrange his times around me. Sometimes I went with him and we played in other people's gardens.'

Her features drooped now, and Heather said quickly, 'He sounded like a lot of fun.'

'He was. At least, when I was little he was. But then he became more serious. And more grumpy. I think that when I was small, he was always trying to compensate, you know, trying to be two parents rolled into one. I reckon he played with me more than most dads did, because Mum couldn't. And then when she died he thought, well, he thought it was his fault.'

'And was it?'

'Well, he was driving the car when they had the accident, but I was only five and I wasn't in the car at the time. We used to go and visit Mum in hospital. At least, he did, and usually he took me to Gran's while he went. I didn't go very often. But that's when I started to want to study medicine.'

'When you were so young?'

'Yes. At any rate… it's when we used to talk about it, me and Dad. He used to say, *When you grow up, you could be a doctor, and help people like Mum to get better.* As I grew up, he kept pointing out how medical science was developing so fast, that diseases were being eradicated, that damage to the brain and nervous system could be reversed...'

'But I think we're still quite a long way off that,' Heather remonstrated. Her mind drifted to some of the patients she'd treated.

'Yeah, I know. But he was so set on it that it made me more determined not to let him down. Him or Mum.'

A question was beginning to wriggle in Heather's mind. Whose choice was her course of study, really? Instead, she tried a different tack. 'What did your school friends do after school? Did any of them go in for medicine?'

'School friends?' Beth fondled Soul's ears, and stared at him for a long time. 'Well, Annabelle went to Newcastle Uni to study archaeology.'

'Was she your best friend?'

'I guess so. But Dad used to say *What use is archaeology? It doesn't help mankind.* So I didn't tell him much about her. Anyway, then she had this boyfriend, Robert, Robin, or something, so we didn't...'

'Did you have a boyfriend?'

'No. Had to study. Anyway, Dad would've been lonely if I'd gone out a lot. Somehow, he didn't really make any friends after Mum died. He worked alone, no colleagues or golf buddies, so the times we spent listening to music together and hiking and stuff were important to him.'

'Hiking?'

'Yes. We used to be aspiring Munro baggers.'

This was new. 'Munros? How many did you bag?'

'Oh, only about ten. We still had a long way to go. We did Ben Vorlich, Ben Lawers, Lomond of course, Schiehallion...'

'Just you and your dad?'

'Yes. He used to say it was what kept him fit. He certainly never put any weight on. He was thin as a rake, even though I tried to feed him up. I enjoyed cooking, but sometimes I think he just ate the food because it was there. Or else we'd eat in front of the TV and he'd get so engrossed that he'd forget to eat, so the food was cold, then he wouldn't want to finish it.

'He used to like documentaries. Said he might learn something. Didn't like fiction, for some reason. I always wanted to watch films or dramas, but if I did, he'd wander away, and he clearly didn't know what to do with himself, so I gave up trying.'

'So did you watch his programmes with him?'

'Not really. I used sit with him in the sitting room, but I'd wear ear phones while I studied. If I listened to classical music it didn't disturb my study. No words. If I studied in my room he used to get lonely.'

Lonely. That was the second time Beth had used that word. Heather began to feel angry with this man who had restricted his daughter's life so comprehensively. Besides, she was tired now. Very tired. 'Maybe if I came with you to the house? Maybe you could face it then?'

'Maybe. Um, thank you. Sorry to burden you with all this. Sorry to wake you. Time to get some more sleep.' She moved back to horizontal on the sofa, and Heather, guiltily grateful, nodded, gave her another hug, and went back to bed.

Where did the rest of Beth's family fit in? She'd heard about Cousin Paul. What about aunts and uncles? She planned to ask in the morning.

Beth

Edinburgh

July 2012

Beth lay for a long time staring at the grey rectangle of window. In the summer in Scotland, the nights never got really dark, especially after a sunny day. She had always loved the short light nights. They made her feel less alone. It was easier to imagine people out and about, getting back from night shift, setting off early to work, pacing around the house with a colicky baby or studying at the computer all night. Or just walking along the beach into the dawn. If she hadn't been with Heather, she might have done that now. Soul was sleeping – not on the towel-bed Heather had put down for him, but right beside the sofa, as close as he could get. He'd spring up if she moved.

Her daily Wall was beginning to crumble. She knew that now. She'd always known she couldn't keep building it for ever – couldn't keep living in her car and imagining reality would leave her alone. Maybe she'd been hoping that her wounded heart would heal up, like a grazed knee or a cut finger, if she kept it protected and didn't use it for a while. Talking about Dad had been cathartic. She felt a swoop of affection towards Heather, who owed her nothing, but who had been such a friend. And now Heather had offered to go with her to the house. She would accept the offer. Maybe if she painted a couple of rooms – she'd always wanted to paint her room orange, colour of sunshine, Mediterranean fruit, warmth – but Dad said it was unsuitable. Her room was magnolia. If the worst came to the worst, she could have the banisters ripped out and something quite different put in – something more open-plan in light pine.

With a glimmer of a possible future, Beth fell asleep again just as the grey light turned to pale blue then yellow.

Something was touching her cheek. Beth tried to brush it away and turned over, revelling in being able to stretch out fully, after so many nights curled up on the back seat of her car. But then she was awake. Soul was licking her face, his tail thumping hopefully against the sofa. 'Sorry, I think I woke him up,' Heather said softly, emerging from the bathroom. 'I'll just get dressed then I'll take him out. Make yourself some tea.' She disappeared back into her room.

Beth felt curiously relaxed. She put the kettle on then went into the bathroom. She heard Heather moving about, talking to Soul, and finally leaving the flat with him. She took a luxurious hot shower, then pulled on jeans and a T-shirt, roughly folded up the bedding she had used, and made a pot of tea. She found a yellow check table cloth, and laid the little table with cloth, plates, bowls and cutlery. She found a toaster, the heel of a loaf of bread, pots of honey and marmalade and a packet of muesli. Then she poured a mug of tea and set herself to take in her surroundings.

First, she opened the curtains. They were delicate and cream with a border of yellow rosebuds. The morning sun streamed in. Beth stood at the window and looked out on the communal parking space flanked by shrubs, and punctuated with a triangle of flower beds. Someone had made an effort. Dad would've…

Then she stood facing into the room, letting the sun warm the back of her neck. Heather had certainly put her own stamp on the place. The walls were painted a fresh lemon yellow. One wall bore several prints of Middle Eastern life: traditional village scenes, with farmers working beside the river, scything, or herding goats; camel riders in flowing robes; palm trees and bougainvillea.

Blue-tacked to the cupboards were photos of people: a mum and dad and a small girl on the beach; a black Labrador, tongue lolling in a smile; a group of paramedics in uniform; a young guy grinning at the camera but pointing at a city spread out below him as far as the eye could see. Tony?

There was a small bookcase with some study-type files, a mixture of novels, classical and modern, and two or three coffee table books – heavy tomes with magnificent photos – of Cairo, of all of Egypt, and of the Middle East in general.

The sofa she had slept on was long and saggy, old, but covered in a stripy cotton throw in yellows and reds, like the awning of an old sweet shop. The carpet was worn, but mostly covered by a multi-coloured loose-weave rug. Beth smiled as she looked around. It was homey, welcoming. She picked up the big book about Cairo and sat down to admire the beautiful photos.

When Heather returned with Soul, she looked appreciatively at the breakfast table. 'Oh, that's nice. Thank you. The bread's nearly all gone. I bought us some fresh rolls.' She put them on the table along with a net of peaches, and she stowed a carton of milk in the fridge.

Beth poured some water into Soul's bowl and gave him a handful of dog biscuits. 'Did anyone see you with him?'

'No. It's Sunday morning. They're all still asleep!' She sat down at the table, topped up Beth's mug of tea and poured one for herself. 'There's a question I've been meaning to ask.' Beth looked up warily. 'Don't you have other relatives? Apart from your cousin Paul, that is. Other cousins, uncles, aunts?'

'There's Uncle Bob and Aunty Nessa, Paul's parents.'

'And where do they live?'

'They're in Livingston, not so far. I went round to Aunty Nessa's first, after I left the house, but a neighbour told me they'd gone to Australia to visit Paul. Said they'd only left the week before, but that they'd be gone a couple of months. They don't seem to be replying to emails or texts. Anyway, Dad and Uncle Bob seemed to have had some sort of argument. It's ages since we saw them and they don't phone any more. I never really found out what it was about.'

Heather was silent while she sipped her tea. Then, 'So. After we've finished breakfast, we'll go to your house. Don't stay there. Come back here. You can collect some more things – if you need to, that is – and bring them back here.'

'Okay.'

Heather was looking at her hard. Perhaps she'd been expecting her to refuse, or to kick up a fuss. Beth felt herself blush at the memory of the night just past. She busied herself spreading honey on her roll. Maybe the house wouldn't be so bad. It was a lovely sunny morning. Houses looked better in the sunshine.

'I suggest we go in two cars,' Heather said after breakfast, 'in case you want to bring extra things back, and because I want to call in the supermarket on the way back.'

Beth drove slowly, checking her mirror at each junction or set of lights to make sure that Heather was following. At one point she stopped for pedestrian lights for a young man loaded with shopping bags to cross. Just as he got to the other side, one of the bags burst, and he stood for a moment, forlornly, surrounded by a broken coffee jar, rolling apples, a loaf of bread and some packets and tins.

'Oh! It's Jem!' Beth exclaimed, and Soul sat up and fixed his nose to the back window. Beth pulled over, wound her window down and gesticulated to Heather, before jumping out of the car to help.

'Hi Jem!' she said breathlessly.

'Beth!'

'Let me give you a hand. I've got a spare bag in the car.' She reached into the car to get it and began quickly shoving Jem's shopping into it. Heather pulled in behind her.

'Thanks. You feeling better?'

'Yes,' she said, embarrassed now. 'Yeah, sorry about last night. I wasn't... I was just...'

'As long as you're okay. I didn't want to...'

'Really. I'm fine. Pity about your coffee.'

'It's stuff for my mum. She's sleeping late.'

He was picking up the pieces of the broken jar carefully.

'Here,' Beth suggested, 'wrap them in the burst polythene bag and give them to me. I'll put them in a bin.'

'Well, if you're sure. Thanks.'

Heather came to stand beside them. 'Hi.'

'Oh, er, hi. You taking good care of her, then?' He nodded towards Beth.

'Trying to.'

'Aye, well.' He turned to Beth. 'You still got my number?'

'Um…'

'Here it is, in case you…' He pulled a simple business card from his pocket. 'I keep them for work. People need to call me. I'm a carpenter. If you ever need shelves put up, cupboards fixed on to the wall – any household job, I'm a dab hand with a few tools. I can paint and paper, too, fix fences, chop trees down, prune bushes. Anything, really.'

'Anything but get your shopping home successfully,' Heather said, but she was grinning, now, and he grinned back good-humouredly.

'C'mon, Beth. We better go.'

So Beth pocketed Jem's phone number and got back into the car, smiling and waving to him as she pulled away.

Why was Heather so wary of him? Because of Tony? Once bitten, twice shy?

They'd reached her own road and Beth wished desperately that Heather was beside her, not behind in a different car. There were the MacKenzie toddlers at number 6 riding tricycles in the front garden. Someone at number 10 was cutting the grass. That deceptive sun made the air sparkle, encouraging Sunday Scots out for some fresh air and to dredge up the worn clichés about not blinking in case you missed the sunshine, or summer came on a Sunday this year.

When they arrived at the house, Beth turned into the front drive and pulled all the way up the side to the garage, to leave room for Heather's car behind her.

The front lawn was horribly overgrown. How long since it was cut? At least a month, and of course, this was its primary growing season. Beth felt mildly ashamed of it. Groping in her bag for her key, she paused to take in the front of the house. The paint on the window ledges was peeling. She and Dad had not done much to modernise the house. Nothing in fact. The interior decorations had been Mum's idea. Dad – and latterly Beth – had tried to keep the house clean, but she knew the kitchen sink was showing its age, and the bathroom – avocado – could do with renovation. Beth had no interest in house fashion, but now she felt self-conscious.

Tentatively, she turned the key in the lock. It would be okay. Heather was right beside her. Together they stepped into the hall. The door had pushed aside a stack of mail. An unwelcome smell hit them. What was it? Nothing definable – just a fusty, closed-in, unloved smell. A shaft of sunlight through the open front door picked out a thin film of dust on the hall table.

Averting her eyes from the banisters, Beth made for the kitchen, Heather following. There were two mugs in the sink. Why? Ah, yes. She had made coffee for the lawyer, Mr - something Italian. Riccardo? Ranelli? Ravello! That was it – Marc Ravello. His mug had a hard dried stain in the bottom. Her own coffee had remained undrunk. It had evaporated an inch or so, leaving an ugly brown rim, then congealed milk at the top. Beth turned away. Otherwise, the kitchen was tidy. The formica work tops were worn down, but the old gas stove was clean and the tiled floor swept clear of crumbs.

They went through to the sitting room. A desolate vase of dead tulips stood on the mantelpiece, the stalks bent right over, most of the petals lying around the base of the vase in a dusting of yellow pollen. Abandoned. Forgotten. Beth swallowed with difficulty and tried to remember Heather's breathing exercises - in through her nose, out through her mouth. There was Dad's chair, with the cushion she had inexpertly sewn for him when she was about thirteen. It still had a dent in it, the shape of his back. Just visible under the side of the chair were Dad's old tartan slippers with holes in the toes. Breathe. She fixed her features, trying to reconstruct The Wall even as she moved.

'Well, it all looks okay,' Heather said. Beth stared at her. 'I mean, I wondered whether someone would have broken in – with it standing empty for a while. Like, I mean, burglars...'

Burglars. Unimaginable. Breathe. It all looks okay...

'D'you want to go upstairs? Maybe collect some of your things?'

Upstairs. Past the banisters. Beth led the way, trailing her hand along the wall to keep her balance. The bedroom doors were closed. She pushed the door of her own bedroom. She'd left the bed neatly made. Good. There was all her stuff - her childhood books, her pink fluffy soft toys heaped mournfully on a shelf, a curling Green Day poster on the back of her door.

She opened her wardrobe. There were her clothes from another life – smart black trousers for ward rounds, a casual denim skirt, a couple of pairs of jeans, and the dress Dad had bought her for Paul's graduation, never worn, because they hadn't gone. There it hung resplendent: a pale turquoise silky material, shaped flatteringly in at the waist, then flowing softly just to the knee. There were matching, elegant, impractical shoes that pinched.

'Wow! Gorgeous!' Heather exclaimed, picking up the shoes. 'You should've worn these last night!'

Last night? Ah yes, the club. It seemed so long ago.

'Know what? We left Soul in the car!' Heather said suddenly. 'I'll go and let him out. Did you leave the car door

136

unlocked? You don't mind if he comes in, do you?' And she was off downstairs while Beth stared numbly at the detritus of her life.

Soon there came the sound of scrabbling feet on the stairs, and Soul burst in, all smiles and wagging tail. How could she have forgotten him, left him all alone?

'Look, he's so pleased to see you. Is there a back garden? Can I take him out there? C'mon, boy,' Heather ran down the stairs with Soul following. Beth sat on the edge of her bed. From there she could see Dad's closed bedroom door. How had he left the room? Had she even been in? She couldn't remember. She knew the weather was warm but she was shivering, icy, her teeth chattering. She pictured a neatly-made bed, his old-fashioned striped pyjamas, his glass of water on the bedside cabinet. In her mind she opened the wardrobe door – his two really smart suits, the black and the blue, his shirts, the pullover Mum had knitted for him before Beth was even born, and that he never wore but always kept. Then the cupboard – socks and underwear, ties, belts, seldom-worn cuff links. The drawer on Mum's side of the bed, the one he never opened.

Black spots threatened Beth's vision and there was a roaring in her ears. She gripped the headboard and leaned her head on her knees. She stayed like that for a few minutes, trying to blank her mind. Gradually she felt able to stand up. She was sweating now, a cold, clammy sweat that left her hands slippery and her clothes uncomfortable. Slowly she made her way downstairs, hand on the wall more firmly this time, pausing to stare at the scuffed banisters, where the paint was rubbed off and the wood was splintered.

'Hi!' said Heather, bursting in with Soul from the back garden. Her face was red and shiny from running around with him. 'Did you choose anything you want to bring?'

Breathe. Smile. Look normal. 'Um, I ought to do a bit of sorting. Why don't you go on home and I'll join you later this afternoon?'

'Well. If you're sure? I mean, do you want me to help you sort? Put things in boxes, or whatever?'

'No. It's okay thanks. I just need to think out what to take. It'll need some decisions, you know?'

'Oh. All right. If you're sure?' Heather said again.

'Yes, sure,' Beth said, putting a hand on the hall table to steady herself.

'Well, I'll leave Soul with you then, shall I? To keep you company? See you later then.' And she went out of the front door, closing it with a sharp click behind her.

Beth heard Heather's car reversing out of the drive, then heading off down the road. She waited a moment, Soul standing expectantly in front of her, panting and beating his tail against the leg of the hall table. She went out of the back door into the garden. There was Mum's rose bush, *In loving memory*, a few petals knocked off its blooms, where Soul must have dashed past it. The back lawn, like the front, was shamefully overgrown and the borders full of weeds. When it came to their own garden, Dad used to say *Weeds are only flowers in the wrong place*. She sat on the old wrought-iron bench mounted on a couple of mossy slabs at the edge of the lawn.

How ridiculous to think she could begin again. How alien of Dad to imagine she could make a new start – a better start – without him. How could an ember burn alone on a cold hearth? Or plants survive without roots? They were as doomed as that vase of tulips in the lounge.

The words of that letter Marc Ravello had shown her

swam in front of her eyes. Anger consumed her suddenly, bringing her out in a sweat again, making her head pound. Far from merely breathing with difficulty, now she was panting, gasping, as if she'd been running.

She went back inside, with Soul following, and stood for minutes staring defiantly, dry-eyed, at the banisters, then forced herself to look away. What was it Marc Ravello had said? Something about Mum's photo album in the cupboard under the stairs? Dad had wanted her to have it. She brought her breathing under control and opened the cupboard.

They'd kept a small torch on the shelf just inside the door. The battery was fading and it took Beth a couple of minutes to negotiate the Christmas decorations and years of National Geographical magazines, to find an inauspicious-looking box, battered and dusty, containing an old photo album. She switched off the torch and put it neatly back on its shelf. She carried the box reverently into the sitting room and shut the door to keep the banisters out of sight.

Photos. They could trigger happy memories, sweet nostalgia, unbearable sadness. She and Dad hadn't taken any photos for years as far as she could remember. Anyway, this was Mum's photo album, and Marc had mentioned it specifically. Because Dad had wanted her to have it. Her pulse quickened.

She could no longer conjure up Mum's face, but memories of time spent with her were warm: songs, stories, dancing and giggling – tricycle rides round the garden; sausages for lunch with creamy mashed potato.

Orange blossom perfume. Dad had bought the same for her. It was in her toiletries bag now, at Heather's.

Was there a *reason* Dad had mentioned the photo album rather than anything else?

139

Slowly she opened the box, lifted out an old black album and stared at the first page. Her mother and father, aged about twenty, sat on a rock at some sunny beach. Her mother's long, thick dark hair covered her shoulders. Her dad had a beard and a moustache. They were both wearing brightly-coloured shorts and T-shirts and laughing and squinting into the sun.

They were happy. Carefree.

Now, by dying, they had both, one after the other, heaped their insurmountable tragedies on to her, given her no say in the matter, no casting vote. Anger threatened to constrict her breathing again. Her heart was thundering in her ears, her fingers leaving sweaty marks on the photo. She slammed the book shut, rammed it back into its box, stalked out into the hall and hurled the box back into the cupboard. With a roar of rage, she slammed the cupboard door and stood, panting.

After some minutes, she moved slowly, deliberately, across the hall. She closed the kitchen door to prevent a through-draft banging the doors shut, then went out to the car. She chose several packets of dog food and took them into the kitchen. She opened them all up, tipping them into a stainless steel bowl, and placing them on the kitchen floor. She filled another large bowl with water and put it beside the food. Soul, clearly delighted, started straight in. Beth wedged the back door open for him, then, while he was eating, went back upstairs. She changed into the turquoise dress and the smart shoes, hanging her jeans and T-shirt neatly in her wardrobe and going back downstairs.

She left by the front door, closing it behind her. She opened the car and got into the passenger seat, smoothing her skirt underneath her as she sat down.

She locked the car, then reached for her bottle of water and rummaged in her bag for the packets of paracetamol she'd bought on previous supermarket trips.

Heather

Edinburgh

July 2012

When Heather went out of the front door, she'd closed it behind her so that Soul didn't stray out on to the road. Beth would probably be glad to have a bit of time to herself. Thinking time. She'd looked pretty pale, but she was very calm and quiet. Amazingly brave. It was a nice enough house. Just needed a bit of TLC.

Heather thought of her own flat, then of Pa's house – home, as it used to be. She and her mother had painted her room there while she was a student – lemon yellow. Maybe she was a bit fixated on yellow. But it wasn't little-girly pink, and she'd never had that teenage rebellious phase that demanded that you paint your bedroom black or deep purple. Her bed used to have her patchwork quilt on it, the one Mum made for her twenty-first. Some of the favourite novels of her teen years were on her bookshelves: the *Tillerman* series by Cynthia Voigt and several of the *Chronicles of Narnia*. She'd like to see her old room, but that would mean visiting Pa, and she wasn't ready to forgive him or trust him yet.

She stopped at the supermarket for mince, tinned tomatoes and kidney beans. There was chilli powder and rice in the flat, some frozen sweetcorn and plenty of fresh fruit. She was tempted to buy a ready-meal, but if Beth had been eating off-the-shelf supermarket stuff for a while, she'd surely enjoy home-cooked food.

Back at the flat Heather washed the breakfast dishes,

made a peanut butter sandwich and replied to a text from a university friend. She took in some news from the Internet and spent a while on Facebook. Should she borrow a camp bed for Beth for another night? There was space for it in her own bedroom. But if Beth was going to have nightmares, and if Soul was going to sleep beside her, then Heather would rather have her room to herself. The sofa was long, and Beth had said she was comfortable. No need for a camp bed.

The thought of bed and the late, interrupted night reminded Heather of how sleepy she was. No harm in having a horizontal half hour.

Heather woke suddenly, disorientated and a bit cold. The day had clouded over. It was six o'clock! She hadn't intended to sleep for so long. She didn't expect Beth to be this late. She must have been at the house for hours. Maybe she'd got thoroughly immersed in the job and wanted to finish it. Heather put the kettle on for a cup of tea and made a start on cooking the mince for chilli con carne. It would be good to have a welcoming meal ready and smelling delicious. Half an hour later, Beth still hadn't appeared, so Heather phoned her mobile. It was switched off. She should try the landline. Surely she could find the phone number on Google. Gomersall was an unusual name, after all, and she knew the address now, so it shouldn't be too difficult. But it was. Her search proved fruitless. There was nothing for it. She would have to drive over there again and tell Beth to take a break and come and have some dinner.

The traffic had built up and Heather felt irritated. She switched on Radio 2, hoping for its lightheartedness, its inconsequential chat. She must keep herself in check for

Beth's sake, Beth who had been so calm and organised, and who must feel exhausted by now. She turned in to Beth's drive. Her car was still there. At least she hadn't left yet. Heather got out quickly and ran up to the front door. It was closed – locked. She rang the doorbell. Inside, Soul set up a frenzied barking, but there was no answer to her ring. She tried again. Nothing. She waited a moment, and heard Soul's feet scrabbling in the hall. Then she heard him outside in the back garden. Maybe Beth was outside and couldn't hear the doorbell. Heather made her way round the side towards the gate that led to the back garden, past Beth's car.

Then she saw.

Beth was sitting in her car with the windows closed. She was wearing her beautiful turquoise dress, and she was asleep. Wait! She was leaning at a strange angle. She didn't look at all comfortable. Heather tried the car door. Locked. She rapped on the window, first with her knuckle, then sharply, with her car key. Nothing. Heather's knees turned to water and her heart thumped in her throat. Wildly, she looked around. No one was about, now. The gardens were empty. She didn't know anyone around here. Who should she ask for help?

She made herself stop and breathe deeply for a moment, then she phoned 999 and asked for an ambulance, describing the situation breathlessly and not very coherently. Then she waited. She went round to the back garden and received an ecstatic welcome from Soul. Briefly, she went in through the open back door and saw his food and water bowls, half empty. Then she returned to Beth's car, taking Soul with her. She worried that he would run into the road, but it was a quiet road, and anyway, he stuck close.

The ten minutes waiting for the ambulance were

interminable. She phoned her mother's landline. No answer. The mobile was switched off. She phoned her university friend, but the ringtone went straight to voicemail.

Then she dialled home. Pa. As soon as he answered she rang off. She dialled again and this time she listened to his voice, 'Hello? Hello?'

He wouldn't recognise her number. She had changed it after returning from Egypt. Of course, he didn't know it was her. 'Hello?' Then he switched off.

'Pa! Pa!' Too late. He'd gone. If she dialled again, he'd ignore it, think it was a nuisance call. Please. One more time. She dialled. 'Pa?'

'Heather?' The voice was hesitant, incredulous. 'Is that you?'

'Oh, Pa!' and she burst into tears.

'What's happened, pet? Are you all right? Where are you calling from?'

'I'm home. I'm in Edinburgh. Only, I need some help. I need you to come over. Now.' In two inadequate sentences she managed to explain where she was and what had happened.

'Sit tight. I'll be there in a jiffy.'

The ambulance came, and with calm expertise they made a neat hole in a quarter light in Beth's car to unlock it, lifted her out smoothly and efficiently and whisked her away to the Royal Infirmary. Because of Soul, and because of her father, Heather opted not to ride in the ambulance, but said she would follow shortly to the hospital, and as the ambulance rounded the corner at the end of the road, Pa's familiar old silver Fiesta arrived.

Heather had planned to stand aloof and to explain guardedly what had happened. After all, she hadn't yet

145

forgiven Pa for cheating on Ma, and as for the other thing…
It didn't bear thinking about.

How long was it? Two years? Eighteen months, at
least, but Pa looked just the same. Same brown cord trousers
and green check shirt, same long lean figure, maybe a bit
thinner with hair a little longer, but the same sensitive dark
eyes. Initially, she stood with her arms stiffly by her sides as
Pa pulled her into a hug, but her eyes closed and she smelt
that familiar smell of Lynx, good coffee and Nero.
Involuntarily her arms crept round his middle and she
remembered that long-lost feeling of being protected,
supported and relieved of ultimate responsibility. They
stood like that for minutes and she felt Pa's stubbly chin on
the top of her head.

Finally, she began to pull away a little, and he
murmured, 'I've missed you so much… so much. I didn't
even know you were back here. Thought you were still in
Egypt. Worried about you every day, every time the Middle
East was on the news, wrote you emails…' A wave of guilt
washed over Heather. Why had she sworn Ma to secrecy?
Why had she been so determined to live her life apart from
him?

Beside them, Soul began to run round in circles and to
bark. 'Wait a minute! I recognise this dog!' Pa said, squatting
down to fondle Soul's floppy ears. 'This is Beth's dog. At
least, the one that adopted her. What's up, fella? What are
you doing here?' He looked up at Heather. 'What's he doing
here?'

Heather couldn't begin. Why had she held out on him
for so long? Did she really not trust him, her own father?

'The girl – the one you found in her car – your friend –
was it Beth?'

Still Heather paused, then finally, 'Yes. I didn't realise you...' Wait a minute. That was a lie. She had realised. She stepped back. 'Yes, it was Beth. What were you doing, becoming friendly with a young girl, a girl young enough to be... to be *me*? A young girl in a vulnerable situation. And you invited her into our... your home. For goodness sake, Pa. She's young and pretty, like...like...'

Pa stepped forward, reached out. 'Heather, sweetheart, I only helped Beth. She didn't come in. She sat on the front doorstep. And I didn't touch that girl at school. I'm innocent. She had it in for me, wanted better grades, she and her sister... She threatened me, blackmailed me, and when I wouldn't cheat on her behalf, she accused me of...of inappropriate conduct. You have to believe me...'

'How can I, after what you did to Ma? They say there's no smoke without fire. If you wanted me to trust you, you should have proved yourself trust*worthy!* But instead of that, you smashed up the family, threw away what we all had, went against what you used to teach me, to be loyal and to tell the truth...' She was raising her voice, but she couldn't stop herself. All the anger of the past two years was erupting like a volcano threatening to engulf both of them. '*How* could I be sure?'

'I admit I cheated on your mother. Once. And I've paid for it over and over. I lost her... and you...' His arms dropped to his sides, his shoulders slumped. He looked so much thinner and older. Pa, old? How could that be? They used to race each other to the stone compass at the top of Arthur's Seat, arriving gasping, sweating and laughing, with Nero, just a puppy, running rings around them, barking, and Ma following more slowly, claiming to be dignified. They used to take a picnic to the beach at Aberdour, and challenge each other as to who would be the first to brave the freezing sea. And when she was much smaller, they'd stand on the bridge above the rail track near Dalmeny Station and wave to the train drivers, who would wave back and sound the whistle, Bee-Bop, specially for them.

Pa's misdemeanour had sullied these memories. Childhood nostalgia that should have brought joy and laughter now only brought her bitterness. He had cheated her as well as Ma. Now Ma had a new life, a new partner, a new family, even, whereas she, Heather, what did she have? Tears of self-pity pricked the backs of her eyes. Then, in a sudden moment of stabbing clarity, Heather saw her own unhappiness for what it was, saw the selfishness that had been totally unaware of what Pa, too, had lost through a moment of foolish wrongdoing. It brought back the awful guilt of Tony's death, her stupid heedlessness, her attention to projecting her precious image. Pa stood motionless, his features sagging, his familiar clothes hanging on him, too big nowadays.

'I'm sorry...' Her voice had dropped to a whisper. It was an invitation, and again they were hugging, squeezing each other fiercely, expelling the mistrust, making up for lost time. Heather's tears were running freely now, but they were such mixed up tears: fears and sadness for Beth, the tragedy of her parents' divorce, horrible regret over her own self-centredness and deception. But they were also tears of huge relief.

A passerby on the pavement glanced at them furtively, and Heather pulled away at last.

'Beth...?' Pa said.

'She was still alive. They reckoned she'll pull through. Eventually.'

148

'Where did they take her? To the Royal?'

Heather nodded.

'Shall we go? Maybe they'll let us see her? Or at least give us some news. Let's leave your car here for the time being. What about Soul? D'you think he'll come in my car?' He bent down again to stroke the dog.

'I'll get his blanket from Beth's car. I'll have to lock the house, too. I'll go through the back garden and come out through the front door. What should we do about Beth's car? They had to smash the window to unlock the car and get her out.' Heather's knees weakened again at the memory.

'We'll have to leave it for now. It's right up against the house, away from the road. This doesn't look like a rough neighbourhood. Anyway, the broken window might be enough to discourage potential thieves. If there are any of her things in the car, it might be an idea to leave them in the house.'

Heather opened the boot and stepped back.

'What is it, pet?'

'Come and look.'

Pa moved to stand beside her. There was a camping gas, a Tupperware with a couple of apples in it, a tin of powdered milk, and some cereal bars. She moved aside a sleeping bag and a small pillow to reveal a melamine plate, bowl and mug and some cutlery. There was a toilet bag full of wash things, a bowl big enough to do your laundry in, a packet of dog food, a bucket, a six-litre water container and a pile of books. Finally there was a sports bag full of clothes – jeans, T-shirts, underwear and a couple of warm sweaters.

'Where was she planning to go?' Pa breathed.

Heather stared. It took a moment for the light to dawn. 'I only got a glimpse of it before. I don't think she was going anywhere. She was just living in her car.'

'*Living* in it?'

'I reckon so.'

'Why?'

''Cos she can't face the house now her dad's no longer there.'

Heather pushed a few things into one of Beth's bags – wash things, a change of clothes and a book or two and carried the rest into the hall. In the house she retrieved Beth's laptop and purse from the kitchen counter. She locked the back door, took house keys from the hall table and Beth's car keys. She checked that the house was secure while Pa settled Soul on the back seat of his car, and they were off.

At Accident and Emergency it took them a long time to extract news of Beth. The receptionist was smart and efficient, her lipstick newly applied, her streaked blond hair carefully tied back into a sophisticated roll. Small sparkly earrings glinted officiously. No, Gregor and Heather weren't Beth's next of kin, or even distant relatives. Eventually, Pa pulled her away and the receptionist resumed typing.

They sat in the waiting room, any potential conversation of their own stunted by the distress around them. An old couple sat with their shoulders pressed together. They were staring vacantly at the floor. A middle-aged woman in a wheelchair shifted awkwardly. A small child whimpered and a teenage girl threw up periodically into a cardboard bowl. From time to time a nurse came and announced a name, then someone would limp, stagger or trudge after her, while everyone else in the room sighed and settled back to resigned waiting.

Eventually Pa leaned close to Heather's ear and whispered, 'Change of shift. Come with me.' A new, older receptionist had replaced the original one. Her name badge read *Connie*. She had a comfortable figure and a glowing round black face full of friendly compassion. 'Good evening,' Pa began. 'We've just come to enquire about Elizabeth Gomersall. She was brought in by ambulance this afternoon. My daughter here,' he put his arm round Heather's shoulders, 'was the one who phoned the emergency services.'

Connie smiled kindly from Pa to Heather. 'Are you family?'

'No,' Heather said, 'but she's my best friend.' Tears threatened again.

'Okay. Please tell me your names, and take a seat again, and I'll see what I can find out.' Another staff member came, while Connie disappeared down a corridor, returning within a couple of minutes. She beckoned them back to the desk. 'I tracked her down. She's sleeping peacefully now, and the doctor says she's going to be okay. She'll sleep for quite a while, so I suggest you both go home and get some rest, and come at visiting time tomorrow afternoon. She'll have been taken up to the ward by then.' Connie gave Heather a card with a map of the hospital and a list of visiting hours. She marked the ward where Beth would be taken. They thanked her and wandered outside.

'Where are you...?' Pa hesitated. 'Are you staying with Ma?'

How strange that her own father didn't know where she lived. Heather felt ashamed. She had read his emails, never replied, willingly deceived him. 'No. I've got a little flat.' She told him the address.

'Maybe you'd like to... to come and stay at home tonight, so we can go and visit Beth tomorrow. It wouldn't take long to make up your bed. You could sleep in a T-shirt, and I've got a couple of new tooth brushes in a packet.'

Heather had worried that Pa had kept her room like a shrine, exactly as she had left it, with the waste paper bin unemptied and the old sheets on her bed. But instead, she found the room clean and tidy. The patchwork quilt was neatly folded on the bed. Pa dug clean sheets, a duvet and duvet cover from the airing cupboard and they quickly made up the bed together. He pulled her into a goodnight hug, kissed her temple lightly, and left her.

Alone in her old bedroom, Heather buried her face in the pillow case with a rainbow design which Ma had bought her when she was ten and remembered those heady days when the future lay bright and promising in front of her, when she was going to change the world with her brilliant professionalism and her tireless, competent hard work. So much for helping people. Instead, people around her died, or nearly died, and it was her fault. *Her fault.* She was supposed to be grown up. What happened to the wisdom and sensitivity of the mature? Or the expertise of the trained paramedic? Stupid, *stupid* girl. She was so angry she wanted to howl, to rage against all the injustice and harshness that the world had a habit of heaping upon the unsuspecting. It was only the presence of Pa the other side of the wall that kept her quiet. Instead, she twisted the corner of the duvet round and round, then bit it until she was biting her own hand and drawing blood.

Finally the small shot of brandy Dad had given her lulled her to sleep for what remained of the night. She woke to a sunny Monday and turned away from the window, burying her head under the duvet. What right had the day to be bright and positive when she felt so groggy and adrift?

Pa knocked quietly on her bedroom door, and when she grunted, he entered and set a cup of tea down on her bedside cabinet. 'Better phone in to work when you've had your tea, pet, and come and have some breakfast.'

After a phone call to Marjorie at the clinic, she settled down to toast and coffee and a very long conversation with Pa.

Beth

Edinburgh

July 2012

Beth drifted in and out of sleep. Sometimes, when she was barely awake, she was aware of the sun outside, but the blinds were tilted away from her, so that her room was delightfully cool and shady. Butterfly thoughts floated prettily in her head, and just as she turned to take in their shapes and colours, they would flutter away indistinctly. Her bed was crisp, white and clean and she could stretch right out in it. There were people outside her room, but their existence drifted in and out with her consciousness. They weren't her responsibility and they didn't demand anything of her except to take medication and to eat and drink a little occasionally.

Those times mingled with sensations of carefree days, standing with Mum and Dad on the waterfront at South Queensferry, throwing bread to the birds. How clever they were at catching it in mid air! She would spot the greedy ones and the young, slow ones and try to distribute the bread fairly.

Or she would go with Dad into the city centre during the Festival, and watch jugglers in the street, or monocyclists balancing spinning plates on poles. Street artists would draw wonderful pictures on the pavement. Once Beth asked someone if he was sad when it rained and washed away his beautiful work, but he replied that he could have just as much fun painting a different picture the next day.

Other times, she would force her unwilling eyes open

and see the window blinds in stripes, like the banisters, and she'd remember patches of what had happened to her. Her abdomen and throat were sore and she remembered vomiting a lot. Memories like malicious bats would swoop around her, threatening to tangle in her hair. Then she would slide, out of control, into shouting at Mum, trying to wake her, to get her attention, but unsuccessfully, while Dad would sigh a lot and sometimes cry and not listen to her when she was trying to tell him something important, so that in the end she stopped trying.

Eventually she'd started writing letters, then emails, to Paul. She never told him how unhappy she was. She just wanted to be part of his exciting, boyish world of science experiments, dissecting frogs or visiting the trenches and war graves in France and Belgium. Then Paul left for Australia, and she would wake bereft and sweating, her bedding in a tangle, while a quiet, gentle nurse held her hand and measured her heart rate, prior to administering some medication that restored peace.

Sometimes she was vaguely aware of someone sitting in her room, beside her bed, but she didn't want to remember who it could be, nor what she ought to say, so she kept her eyes closed and waited for sleep to return.

Then came a time when she was thoroughly awake, and a nurse was speaking to her. 'Come on, Elizabeth. Time for a shower. I'll help you.'

The shower was wonderful. The nurse remained tactfully just outside the curtain while Beth shampooed her hair and tilted her face gratefully to the cleansing stream. Back in bed, she felt exhausted, but able to eat the ham and salad that appeared with tea and a scone at five o'clock. Food restored her energy a little and she sat up in bed, propped against pillows. From this vantage point she could see through the window into the corridor. Her room was right opposite the nurses' station, and her door was always open, but now she could see other people, without uniforms, wandering along the corridor. Visitors. Someone paused and knocked on her open door.

Heather stood hesitantly in the doorway. 'Hi. How are you doing? Can I come in?'

'Heather, I'm sorry!' Instant awareness, like a sharp knife, brought tears that slid unchecked down Beth's cheeks. 'So sorry... I didn't mean for you to...'

'No, I'm the one who should be sorry,' Heather interrupted. 'I should have realised. Shouldn't have left you at the house on your own. It's just that you were so calm, I had no idea...'

There was another knock. Another figure hovered in the doorway. 'Gregor? What are you...? How did you...?' Embarrassed, Beth dashed her tears away with the back of her hand and sat up straighter.

'Beth, this is my father,' Heather said, and went to stand beside him.

Beth was confused. She looked from one to the other. Finally, she said, 'I didn't know. Didn't know Gregor was your father.'

'I know. I'm so sorry,' Heather began again.

'I didn't know you'd met Heather,' Gregor said now, stepping further into the little room. 'Even when you said you'd been for physiotherapy, I didn't put two and two together.'

'You couldn't have. You thought I was still in Egypt,' Heather told him.

Beth was looking at Heather now. 'I told you I'd met a

man who helped me. Said I'd even been to his house. I even told you about Nero. You must have realised. You just… you just…' She looked from Heather to Gregor and back. 'Why didn't you tell me? Why?'

Instead, Heather had tried to warn her about trusting people too much. Trusting men too much. But she had trusted Heather, thought Heather was her friend. Now the tears came with uncontrolled sobs, and Beth slid down the bed, wishing she could disappear, willing unconsciousness to take her.

'I'm so sorry,' Heather was saying again, but a nurse came in and spoke quietly to Heather and Gregor, who nodded, turned to Beth, blew kisses and promised to return soon. Then they left, holding on to each other.

The same nurse stayed with Beth for a few moments until another came with tablets and a glass of water, and Beth swallowed the tablets obediently, and, turning away from the corridor, closed her eyes and went to sleep.

Next time she woke it must have been the middle of the night. Her room was dark, but there was a nurse at the desk in the corridor, her peaceful face illuminated by a desk lamp. Beth was reassured to see her there, without needing to speak. She closed her eyes once more, but remained very much awake.

Why hadn't Heather admitted that Gregor was her father? Why had she warned her against him, or men like him. Of course, some men preyed on young girls, but Beth went over everything Gregor had said and done. He'd been kind and careful. They had sat outside at the Cramond café. He left doors open, like an escape route. She had sat on his front doorstep when she sprained her ankle, and he had left his own front door open. She had noticed his lovely photos of the Edinburgh philanthropists. He couldn't be – couldn't be grooming her. He'd admitted that he was divorced, that it was his fault, that he regretted it. If anything, it was she who had been hoping to bump into him again, yearning for his kindness and friendship. Looking, yes, looking for a father-figure. Was Heather jealous? But she already had his attention and affection. Whatever was she thinking?

Beth kept coming back to the subject of trust. Heather had seemed trustworthy. Friends didn't hold out on one another. Did they? They didn't keep secrets from each other. She realised with a sudden jolt how much she had been holding out on Heather and Gregor, how she had told them as little as possible about her past, about Dad. Secrets. Unmanageable, unprocessed half-truths. Now she was following in his despicable footsteps. How desperately he had let her down, and she had taken on board his evil role model. How ridiculous that he should think that now she was grown up, she didn't need him.

Had she pushed him into his drastic action? She couldn't be all he needed. God knows, she'd tried. She'd kept the house clean, she'd learned to cook really well. She'd appreciated the same music as him, watched the same films. She'd taken up tennis because he'd loved it. Latterly, she'd even beaten him! She'd gained a place at medical school, and fulfilled his long-held aims for her. She'd been the dutiful daughter and yet, and yet - it hadn't been enough. He'd held out against her. How was she expected to know that he had lost all hope?

The only people she had were Heather and Gregor, and she'd scared them off, driven them away by her accusations. Where were Uncle Bob and Aunty Nessa when she needed them? Where was Paul?

Beth

Edinburgh

July 2012

The following evening, before Heather and Gregor arrived, Beth dressed in the clothes Heather had left for her and sat in a chair beside her bed, waiting. At six o'clock Heather peeped round the door, came in and bent over to hug her briefly.

Gregor followed her in. 'You're looking better.'

'Thanks. Feeling better, too. Listen, I'm so sorry about – '

'No, it's we who are sorry,' Heather insisted. 'Sorry for not being open with you. We're pals, eh?' Beth nodded. 'And pals don't hold out on one another. Our fault.'

'Okay,' Beth said slowly.

'Let's leave aside the recriminations,' Gregor said. 'We're all sorry, but let's just see where we can go from here.' He stooped to kiss the top of her head lightly, then went to take two chairs from a small stack in the corridor.

'He thinks you're his other daughter,' Heather whispered.

Beth smiled. 'He once said you and I look just the same from the back.'

'Yeah. That's probably true.'

Gregor set down chairs for himself and Heather then he explained the agreement the two of them had reached the previous evening. 'We recognise you aren't ready to sort the house just yet, and we don't think it's a good idea for you to continue living in your car, so we'd like you to come and live with us – with Heather and me.' Beth felt herself blushing as he mentioned the car. 'We got your window fixed. It was only the quarterlight.'

'The window?'

'Pa!' Heather interrupted, 'She won't remember.'

He stopped.

What was it she wouldn't remember? There were certainly things she couldn't remember, didn't want to remember. Heather took her hand. 'We can bring your car to our house as soon as you like. You've seen the house. Soul thinks it's his home already, anyway.' She grinned.

'Soul!' Beth gasped. How could she have forgotten?

'He's fine,' Gregor assured her. 'Nero likes his company. Heather is back in her old room for the time being, and we've got the guest bedroom all ready for you.'

'I've got money. I can pay.'

'Oh, our rates are quite reasonable,' Gregor said with a grin. 'Just dish-washing twice a day and an occasional pile of ironing.'

Beth relaxed. 'Thank you. I'd like that.'

'So when can you come? Will they discharge you today?'

'Funny,' Beth said as they left by the main entrance. 'I used to like hospitals. Felt at home. Thought medicine was my vocation.'

'It could still be,' Heather said. 'There's no reason why not.'

'I even used to like dissection,' Beth continued. 'I was

in a dissection class when the Dean of Studies – when I got the news. About Dad. Dad's lawyer came. Poor man, he was so nervous. And kind. Offered to have me stay with him and his wife at their house. Used to be a friend of Dad's in their student days.'

She remembered the dean's office, the thrumming sound in her ears as the lawyer delivered his news. The situation had been surreal, like a film set. She'd noticed the clock ticking and a burst of distant laughter from the corridor.

'Dean of Studies? Wow!' Heather breathed. 'Dundee, you said. So your training hospital must've been Ninewells?' Beth nodded. 'It's famous, isn't it? Pioneered laser surgery, or something?'

'Yes. That's right. It's – it's a really good place. It's just that…'

'Ah,' Gregor said suddenly. 'It's where your dad died.'

'But her dad lived in Edinburgh,' Heather corrected him. She turned to Beth. 'So it must've been the Western General, or, or here?' She turned to look back at the Royal Infirmary as Gregor unlocked the car.

'No,' Beth said. 'He didn't die in hospital. He died at home. He took his own life.'

Heather

Edinburgh

July 2012

Beth said no more, but merely stared out of the car window. Pa didn't question her further, and Heather, for once, took his lead and remained silent.

Installing Beth into the guest room was a straightforward job. She was uncannily acquiescent. Heather had expected apologies, explanations and guilt. She showed Beth where her other belongings were, the ones she and Pa had brought from her car and the house. 'You can put stuff in these drawers,' Heather told her. 'The wardrobe's empty as well.'

'Thanks.' Beth began to unpack silently, though tears were leaking periodically from the corners of her eyes.

'Bethie,' Heather began, 'after you got the news, I mean after the lawyer's visit, did you - did you cry?'

Beth turned to her, surprised, and stood still. 'I don't think so. No.' Heather's whole being was shouting *Why not?* But she said no more. Beth didn't seem to realise she was crying now. Trauma. It was a steep learning curve.

The next few days were filled with frequent short dog walks, small nourishing meals and only as much conversation as Beth was able to manage. She slept a lot and she said her energy was returning, but she had yet to sustain any sort of long activity. Heather was bursting with questions, but she held back with difficulty, especially while Beth's tears continued to leak unheeded.

Heather cut down her work hours to spend more time with Beth. Sometimes she thought wistfully of her own little flat sitting empty, but being at home with Pa and Beth was more important just now. One afternoon, at Beth's request, they walked together to the corner shop and bought baking ingredients. Then Beth shut herself in the kitchen for an hour and produced a wonderful selection of tray bakes.

'Do you have any other hidden talents, Beth?' Pa asked jovially.

'I'm pretty good at housekeeping. Had to be I suppose.'

Silly question, Pa. Heather glanced at him. He grimaced.

'Sport?' she asked. 'D'you play badminton, or swim?'

'Watch football? Play golf?' Pa asked with a grin.

'No football or golf, I'm afraid, though I have played badminton. Can't stand swimming. Oh, I can swim – Dad made me go to lessons, made sure I learnt, but I just hate water. Boat trips, even walking over bridges!' She shuddered.

'Music?' Heather asked, 'apart from dance music, that is!' She and Beth shared a smile.

'That music was quite, um, special, but I suppose I'm more of a classical girl. Learned the flute at school.'

'The flute?' Pa said, delighted. 'You must give us a rendering.'

'My flute's…'

'…in the house?' Heather finished for her.

'Yes.'

'The house, Bethie,' Heather hesitated. How to word it? 'I mean, if we all went together for a short time, would it help you to get some things? I mean, we wouldn't need to go in your dad's room. And did the lawyer make any suggestions? You know – about the house? The bills, the deeds, all the legal stuff…'

'Heather,' Pa warned. 'All in good time.'

'Marc – that's Dad's lawyer – he took care of everything. All the finance and stuff. He said he would be available to me anytime. He came to visit me in the house. Even bought me some flowers. But he had to come back to fill me in on – on the rest. I hadn't asked how Dad died.'

'But you told us, he took his own life.'

Beth looked away, out of the window for a long time, until Soul pushed his nose enquiringly against her knee. 'I think I should take him out,' she said, standing up.

'But is that what happened, Bethie?' Heather insisted.

Beth took a deep breath. 'I thought he'd, you know, he'd taken tablets. An overdose…'

'But, um, he didn't?'

'No. He hanged himself from the banisters.'

Heather gasped 'Oh no!' and Pa groaned.

Beth looked down, her hand on Soul's head. 'When Marc told me, I went to look at the banisters. They're all scratched and chipped. Don't know why I hadn't noticed before. After that I couldn't – couldn't look at them.'

Heather remembered opening the front door of Beth's house with her that first time, when the sun had picked out the dust particles and she, Heather, had so insensitively played with Soul, then left Beth to…

'But how did Marc know?' Heather demanded.

'Dad wrote him a letter and asked him to go to the house.'

'Bloody hell,' Pa groaned. 'How could anyone – any

164

friend – cope with seeing that?'

'He was protecting *me* from seeing – that!' Beth said, and Heather recognised defensiveness, willed Pa to rein in his imagination.

'C'mon, let's all go out and take Nero as well,' she said quickly.

'Marc had said he thought it would be better if I was the one to contact Aunty Nessa and Uncle Bob,' Beth continued as they walked, three abreast, up the now deserted stony path. 'Or maybe it was Dad who had written that. I've forgotten. Anyway, that's where I headed, and I guess I was hoping I'd get a welcome and an invitation to stay with them – at least for the time being. Even though the two branches of our family had sort of slipped out of contact, we were, after all, a *family*. I reckon that, in the back of my mind, the camping stuff was just a fall-back idea.'

They'd reached the top of Arthur's Seat. Just as well Scotland never really got dark in July. There was a brisk breeze, as always, but Heather was sweating and slightly out of breath, glad to pause and take in the view. The street lights were on now, and the lit-up windows of houses and flats looked homely. Edinburgh itself seemed to welcome her back in a way she hadn't experienced since returning from Egypt, but it made Beth's story of assumed homelessness increasingly poignant.

'But Bethie,' she said finally, 'how did you manage the loneliness day by day? I mean, not just the practicalities of daily living, but... but *life itself*?'

'I built a mental wall every morning, a protective wall, to keep myself in and others out. It went something like this:

' Dad had left me plenty of money.

'I was young, healthy and not stupid.

'The body and mind have a great capacity for healing.

'No one was asking anything of me.

'I had no current responsibilities.

'All paperwork was taken care of.

'I knew how to keep safe, clean and nourished, unlike some of the patients I've treated.' She was reeling off her points dully, like a list of facts learned by rote for an exam.

'I told myself I was an independent, competent adult.

'I could contact Marc whenever I needed to.

'I had all necessary contact with the outside world through my laptop and phone.' She shivered. 'I thought that a broken heart would eventually heal, like a broken leg or a cut finger.' She was shaking uncontrollably now.

'Come on,' Pa said. 'The breeze is getting up. Let's go back down.'

'Ach! Look at the time!' Heather exclaimed, 'And we haven't even had dinner.'

'We fared rather well on Beth's baking,' he reminded her.

'But were you planning to keep living in your car for *ever*?' Heather said. She couldn't let it go now. She had to know.

Beth was silent for minutes as they turned and made their way down the darkening hill. Then, 'I thought I would see this thing out, and return to the house and to university as soon as I felt ready. The Dean had said there was no rush, and then it was the end of the academic year anyway.

'I felt that as long as I kept this wall of protection intact, I could remain aloof, hold my head high and – and - keep living. That was all that mattered.'

Heather linked arms with Beth on one side and Pa on the other and the three of them made their way home with Soul and Nero plodding contentedly beside them.

Beth

Edinburgh

August 2012

Walking became a panacea for Beth. She chose less populous routes. Sometimes she took a bus to the Pentland Hills. Gregor gave her a map, and she and Soul, with a bottle of water and a bar of chocolate, would walk for hours, drinking in Scotland's beauty and the vicissitudes of its summer season. Arthur's Seat was near, untainted with old memories, but much too frequented in the summer. So Beth chose to walk there only in the rain, when the population thinned out, but the newly-washed foliage shone and the panorama offered wispy clouds over the city and storm clouds over Fife, the Forth and out to sea. She was physically strong, now, and what did it matter if she arrived back at Arthur's View soaked? She had no need to look smartly professional, nor even as cool as a student, and Gregor kept an old towel by the back door for drying off wet dogs.

Little by little Beth found she could remove a small part, temporarily, from her protective wall. She could tease out a brick from the middle, like playing Jenga, so she could peer through it, peruse the view, understand it for what it was, then, if necessary, replace the brick.

Sometimes through the gap she'd see herself and Mum sitting at the kitchen table, painting over a doily on to play paper, then peeling off the doily carefully to reveal an intricate pattern like the stonework of a cathedral. Or she'd see Dad pruning trees, then advancing upon her stealthily behind a branch, murmuring portentously, *till Burnham Wood shall come to Dunsinane!* Then she felt no need to replace the brick. She was happy to allow that space to become permanent. Rarely did she see Mum and Dad together, and if she did, Mum was lying unconscious and Dad was sitting beside her, weeping. On those occasions the air was cold, and it quivered with unspecified threats, so she would replace the brick hastily and run after Soul, laughing, chasing him and pretending to growl, making him bark playfully. Then she would concentrate on the distant horizons - the fishing villages of Fife or the arable countryside of East Lothian.

Some days, she'd peep tentatively through a gap in her wall and imagine bodies of water – the turgid canal on the night when she encountered The Wire, or the Water of Leith after a downpour, tumbling, brown and noisy, like the lives of people around her while she, balanced precariously on a rock beside the water, would try to avoid their curious glances. Sometimes a sea, travel-brochure blue, would turn suddenly grey, and life's unpredictable twists, like a sudden squall, would send sea birds seeking the protection of cliffs or outcrops of rock.

Occasionally she'd relive those television clips taken during the 2004 tsunami – cars, furniture, buildings, surging inland like icecream wrappers on a breeze, while animals and people were swept to their deaths amid the flotsam and jetsam of that unprecedented disaster. It had terrified her irrationally at the time, and in unguarded moments she would imagine herself carried along, like so much discarded litter, unnoticed and out of control. On those days she'd run with Soul back to Arthur's View where Gregor would put the coffee on and pull out a chair for her at the kitchen table, and talk light-heartedly about the kind of history she'd learnt from the Angry Aztecs or Incredible Incas. How did he know what she needed? She used to imagine he had a sixth sense until she caught a glimpse of her own ghostly face in the mirror.

Mostly she opted for unfrequented country routes, but occasionally she stayed in town. One day, when it was overcast, she didn't fancy getting a soaking in the hills, so when Soul became restless, she set off along the local streets. She clipped the leash to his collar as they approached the main road. It was more for her own peace of mind than his safety. His nose was often glued to her heel, with or without her bidding. But she shortened the leash as they approached an elderly woman with a tripod walking stick. Her progress was slow, her appearance unremarkable, but Soul began uncharacteristically to strain at the leash and to thrust his nose at the woman as they passed. 'No, boy. C'mon,' Beth hissed, embarrassed. But the woman stopped and looked, shocked, from her to the dog and back again. Beth smiled hesitantly.

'Sol?' the woman said, leaning one hand on her stick, and fondling the spaniel's ears with the other. 'Solly?' Soul leaned proprietorially into her coat and closed his eyes.

The woman looked at Beth again. 'Did you...? How did you...?' She seemed to sway a little, and Beth stepped smartly nearer to hold her arm.

'What's wrong?'

'This is Sol. My dog. I lost him.' A single tear found its way down a crease in her cheek.

It was Beth's turn to be shocked. 'Your dog? When...?

How...?'

'I fell. Broke my hip. It took a while for the ambulance to come. Mrs Squires – that's my neighbour – heard me calling and she must have left my back door open. I didn't use to keep Sol's collar on him at night. When Mrs Squires came back and locked up the house for me, he was gone. She said she looked for him for days. I was in hospital quite a while.'

Beth's heart was thumping. She looked around. 'Do you live near here?' She looked at the stick. Stupid question.

'Yes, dear. Just down the road.' She pointed vaguely.

'I found Soul – Sol – in the supermarket car park. Actually he found me.' Beth blinked hard. Was she going to have to relinquish Soul now? 'Of course, his name... I looked for an owner, but when I told him *There's nobody, not a soul...* He pricked up his ears. Whenever I said *soul* he seemed to respond. Now I know why. It sounds the same.'

'My husband Ralph – he named the dog when he was just a pup. Sol had this way of looking at you with his eyelids half closed, as if he was thinking hard. Ralph said he looked wise. Like Solomon. So he became Sol.'

It was logical. 'What should we,' Beth began, then faltered. 'Um, do you want to take him... to take him home?' The word came out strangled.

Now the woman looked at Beth properly. She drew herself up straight. She wasn't *so* old – seventy something – but a broken hip could add on ten years. 'Have you been looking after him, dear?'

'Yes.'

'He's a good boy, isn't he?'

'Yes.'

'Ralph trained him. He was so patient, was Ralph, and

171

he adored that dog. After Ralph died, I didn't walk the dog as much as I should have. Too achey. I guess I already had osteoporosis and arthritis by then. And now…'

'Do you want me to continue walking him? We could share him. I could bring him to visit you. I could come every day, or he could sleep at your house and I could come and walk him.' She was spraffing, but she couldn't stop. Couldn't bear to hear the answer. 'I could buy his food for you – he's been having a varied diet, a balanced diet, sometimes I give him fresh meat and other times he has those pouches that they…'

The woman was smiling. It took years off her. Her kind eyes were dancing. 'You love him, don't you dear?'

'Yes!'

'You wouldn't like to lose him now.'

'No.'

'Why don't you come to my house for a cup of tea. It's not far. Sol knows it well. I'm forgetting my manners.' She thrust out a hand. 'Penelope Tyler. Call me Penny.'

'Thank you, Mrs Tyler - Penny.' Beth said, shaking the proffered hand. 'Elizabeth Gomersall. Beth. And I'd love to come to your house for a cup of tea.'

In the short time it took for Beth and Penny to saunter back to Penny's house, Beth had constructed a mental picture of an elderly person's home: flowery wallpaper, patterned carpets and heavy oak furniture. It was an undeserved caricature. In fact, Penny became younger all the time. She stowed her stick in the hall and hung her coat on a peg and glanced towards Beth. 'Now, will you have coffee, or tea, or I think I've got some juice in the fridge. My grandchildren were here last week.'

Beth went into the sitting room and sank into the black leather sofa. Sol trotted contentedly after her and stood beside the radiator under the window. 'Come here, boy,' Beth encouraged him, patting the carpet beside her, but he turned a circle and remained standing, confused. Beth looked round. There were some family photos, but none of those blue jugs with *Souvenir from Little Puddlewick-in-the-Marsh* that she had expected. There were two brightly coloured abstract prints that she felt she should recognise.

Penny came in with tea and scones on a tray, and followed her gaze. 'Lovely, aren't they? They're Klimt, you know. I bought that one,' she put the tray on the coffee table and pointed, 'for Ralph for his sixtieth, and he bought that one,' she pointed again, 'for mine.'

'I love them,' Beth enthused. 'They're so vibrant.'

'Oh, Sol, I'm sorry!' Penny said suddenly. She turned to Beth. 'I moved his basket. It used to sit there, under the radiator, but I couldn't bear to be reminded all the time that I'd lost him. I thought he'd been run over, you know. Come over here, boy.' Sol looked from Penny to Beth, then turned round twice and lay down where he was.

'What a diplomat!' Penny laughed. 'I think it was fortuitous that you found him, or that he found you. I can't walk him enough, and anyway, I'm hoping to move into sheltered accommodation. I need to sell this house, but there's some work to be done on it first. The window frames need a lick of paint, and the garden...' She looked out of the window to the back garden. It was distinctly overgrown. 'There's a gardener that comes every so often, but he's over-subscribed. When it doesn't rain, everyone wants him. Naturally. And the trouble with painters and decorators is that they want a big job. Can't be bothered with a few window frames. I can pay – there's no problem there. But estate agents say that first impressions count for a lot. I wouldn't sell it for what it's worth if I can't give it a make-over first.'

Aware that Penny was starved of company, Beth stayed a little longer. She assured her that she had plenty of time and agreed to return and meet Mrs Squires next door. 'She's struggling to walk her own dog these days,' Penny said. 'We're none of us getting any younger. But she – you know – she carries too much weight!' She smiled conspiratorially.

Sol was content to leave with Beth eventually, and by the time they arrived back at Arthur's View, Beth had hatched a plot. Heather's car was just pulling into the drive. 'Hey,' Beth greeted her, 'you'll never guess who I've met!'

'Good afternoon to you, too. Have you had a good day?' Heather said sardonically.

Beth grinned. 'Sorry. Have you had a good day?' She didn't wait for a reply. 'I met Penny Tyler. She's Sol's owner.' Heather stopped with one hand on the car door.

'Sol's owner? *Soul's* owner?'

'Yes. She lost him when she fell and broke her hip. Her neighbour left the door open.'

'Does she want him back?'

So Beth recounted the conversation to Heather, and included Penny's need for work to be done on the house. 'So I was wondering… You remember that Jem said he could help with any practical jobs we needed?'

'Jem? But he meant he was willing to help *you*. He was being kind – polite - and he wanted to repay you for helping him. Anyway, he fancies you.'

'*Fancies* me? No chance. Maybe he was being polite, but I think he really was willing to help. Anyway, Penny is a very deserving cause.'

'And you've known her – what? Ten minutes? Bethie, you're so gullible.'

After dinner Heather got up to clear the dishes. 'I'll do it tonight, love,' Gregor said. 'I know it's your turn, but I've concentrated long enough on writing today. Need to do something practical. You go and do Twitter, or whatever. Anyway, Beth will dry up, won't you Beth?' Surprised, Beth nodded. So Heather disappeared into her room without arguing.

'You were quiet during the meal,' Gregor observed. 'Not that you're usually noisy, of course...' He smiled apologetically. 'Remember the maxim?' He nodded towards the postcard on the fridge. Beth glanced at Mount Hood reflected in Mirror Lake – the transparency of it.

'Come on, out with it,' he insisted.

She smiled then, not sorry to be so easily readable. 'You're being just as devious. You banished Heather on purpose!' They both smiled.

'Yes. So?' Gregor smiled.

'I had an idea.'

'About Sol's owner?'

'Yes, but it's not just that. As I said at dinner, she needs some help to bring the house up to scratch before she puts it on the market.'

'Do you think she's going to be able to cope with house selling and all that?'

'Oh, I think so. Got all her marbles. It's just that she's

175

got arthritis and she's been diagnosed with osteoporosis.' Gregor grimaced. 'No, it's just the painting and gardening. Do you remember us telling you about Jem, the guy we met at the club?' Gregor frowned. 'And we met him later by chance. His shopping had spilled on the street. It was the day I...'

'Jem?'

'Yes. Jeremy. Anyway, he gave me his card. I've still got it. It sounds posh, doesn't it? – his card. But it's just a card with his work number, and he said he's a painter and decorator, a joiner... He said he was good at practical things. Offered to help. I thought I might phone him and tell him about Mrs Tyler – Penny.'

'Hmm. And you didn't mention this at dinner because...?'

'Heather doesn't think it's a good idea.'

'Why not?'

'She thinks he was just being polite, or that it's only me - us – that he was offering to help. And she's being protective. Of me. Because I'm gullible.' Seventy-five per cent on the honesty scale. No need to repeat Heather's every word.

Gregor laughed, then scratched his chin thoughtfully. 'Hmm. Heather still has a few chips on her shoulder, understandably. But don't let her hang-ups become yours. I think there's no harm in trying. Let Heather sleep on it and tell her in the morning that you're going to give him a call.'

Beth

Edinburgh

August 2012

'Hello, Jem?'

'Yeah?'

'Hi. It's me, Beth – from the club, and the shopping bags.'

'Oh! *Beth*! How're you doing?

'I'm fine thanks.' Of course, she'd been sick. He'd been kind. 'Fine *now*, thanks. It was just…'

'It's great to hear you. What're you up to these days? You're a student. You back at uni?'

'No, not yet. It's the summer holidays.'

'Ah. Summer holidays.'

'Jem, I was remembering you said you could do all sorts of jobs – like, practical stuff, if ever we needed.'

'Yeah! Nae probs.'

'It's not actually for me, but, d'you remember I have a dog? At least, it's not really mine, but…'

'A dog?'

'Yes. It's a long story. I look after it because its owner can't walk it any more. She's not that old, but she's not very fit. She needs some decorating done at her house so she can sell it.'

'She wants to sell the dog?'

'*No! The house!*' She laughed. 'Look, could we maybe meet up and I could explain?'

'You bet!'

Beth took a deep breath. Better be careful here. 'You

coming to Edinburgh at the weekend?'

'Yep. Tomorrow. Meet me at Costa on the corner of Princes Street and Hanover Street? About six o'clock? My bus gets in around then.'

Beth arrived in town early. Festival season had festooned the solid, old city with colour, humour and noisy bustle. Comfortably anonymous among the crowds, Beth wandered through Princes Street Gardens on to the cobbled area between the art galleries. The excited holiday atmosphere was almost palpable. She took in the stalls of hand-crafted goods from every continent, the icecream and candyfloss sellers and finally the street performers who had capitalized on every available square metre. She stood still to watch monocyclists, fire-eaters, knife-jugglers, contortionists, conjurors, acrobats and musicians of every type. Audiences had certainly imbibed the holiday spirit. They cheered, clapped, ooh-ed and ahh-ed as required. They willingly tossed coins into performers' hats and moved on chatting and laughing.

Just before six, Beth went into the coffee shop. It was on the first floor, and its corner location gave a 180 degree view. She bought a coffee and sat by the window. The pavements were packed with visitors, and there was no sense of rush hour or a weekend push. Instead holiday makers strolled in leisurely fashion enjoying the capital city's world-acclaimed August attractions.

Beth saw Jem arriving. He glanced at his phone before pocketing it and entering the building. She saw him arrive at the top of the stairs and look around until he spotted her. He had a scrubbed-up look, and self-consciously she smoothed her shirt down and tucked her hair behind her ear.

'Hi,' he said, 'you look great.' She smiled, unsure what to say. This wasn't a date, just a... What was it? A business meeting? A friend asking another friend for a helping hand? Any confidence Beth had absorbed from the festival goers melted away. Was she being presumptuous? Why would Jem, whom she really didn't know at all, want to help Mrs Tyler, whom she also didn't know at all? 'Sit tight,' he said. 'I'll just get myself a coffee. Can I get you anything else?'

'No, no thanks.'

It gave Beth a moment to gather her thoughts. She fixed on the postcard in Gregor's kitchen. Light and simplicity. No airs and graces. Huh! As if she had any.

'So, what are you doing with your long student holiday?' Jem asked, sitting down and shrugging off his jacket.

Momentarily, Beth imagined the students on her course travelling to exotic places, climbing Mount Kilimanjaro, undertaking voluntary placements in Third World clinics, planning electives in Kathmandu, Mumbai, Santiago... 'Well, I've done a lot of walking, sometimes in the Pentlands.'

'Yeah, I guess you have to do that. With a dog, I mean. But you said it's not really your dog?'

So Beth launched into the tale of being adopted by Sol, and then, so much later, of meeting Penny Tyler by chance. 'I feel I owe Mrs Tyler something, because she's kind of *lent* me her dog all this time, and he's been, well, he's been a good friend.'

'Aye, but I reckon you and Mrs Tyler are quits. You've looked after him for her, and she's lent you a friend. You dinnae owe her anything.'

Did she feel under obligation? But Jem was grinning. 'Wonder if the dog can hear the difference between his two names? So what d'you call him now? Soul or Sol?'

'Oh, he'll probably always be Soul to me, and Sol to Mrs Tyler. But I have to admit, people can look at me peculiarly when I call *Soul!*' They chuckled, and Beth went on to explain what sort of work Mrs Tyler needed on her house. 'She insisted she could pay for it. She's not looking for any sort of hand-out.'

'Yeah, that's wise,' Jem said. 'That way, she'll get a proper, professional job, with some guarantees. I'd be glad to do it. I'm an experienced painter and decorator, you know.' Beth nodded. 'Plumbing, too. I've done lots of carpentry and joinery jobs. Nothing electrical, I'm afraid. That's my brother's department.'

'But you've got a job in Penicuik?'

'Sort of, but there's often not enough work and Callum – that's my boss – takes the more secure jobs. Well, obviously. It's his business, after all. But he's very fair. Says I can take other jobs if I can get them, and he'll arrange my time accordingly. I'd really like to move up to Edinburgh if I can. There's more going on here – jobs and everything else.'

'Like clubs?' Beth said with a grin.

'You bet! You and me should go again sometime. Yeah?'

Beth smiled. She found she *would* consider going again, partly to lay some ghosts, but also because Jem was so easy-going, quite relaxing to be with. They bought more coffee and chatted until the hot-dog-eating festival visitors in shorts and T-shirts were replaced by smartly-dressed restaurant-diners and theatre-goers, out for the evening. Beth and Jem made arrangements to meet the next day at Mrs Tyler's house after Beth had phoned her.

'So where will you stay tonight? At your mum's?'

'Aye. I'll go to the cinema now so as to arrive late. I'll sleep on the sofa and her bloke won't even notice me.'

'Will your brother be there?'

'Might be, but I doubt it. I'll have to make a concerted effort to track him down one of these days.' He paused and looked down at his hands. Beth looked at them, too. They were strong hands, with short finger nails and callused thumbs. Competent hands. He wore a signet ring on his right hand.

'I don't suppose you'd like to come to the cinema with me *now*?' he said. When he looked up, he was blushing. Momentarily, Beth was going to accept. This guy didn't trot out chat-up lines. His face was open and a little shy. But what did she know about guys? She wanted to ask Heather's opinion.

'Thank you,' she said, 'but I ought to...'

'...walk the dog?'

'Yeah! But I'll see you tomorrow.'

'Ah, so this is the laddie!' Jem said, squatting down to pat Sol. 'He's a beauty.'

Beth smiled. She wanted everyone to like Sol.

'A typical Lothian day,' he remarked as he and Beth opened Mrs Tyler's gate. 'Haar as bad as a November fog until eleven, then it'll become a scorcher!' He stood for a moment surveying the front of the house. 'Aye, I see what she means. The house faces south. Gets the best and the worst of the weather.'

Beth looked around. How did he know which way the house faced, if the sun wasn't out?

'She'll get some nice sun in the front room in the winter, though. Bet the house will go like hot cakes once it's fixed up.'

Mrs Tyler – Penny - was not having a good day. 'It's the damp,' she explained. 'Rain or mist, it gets into my bones. I'll be all right later, once I've got moving.'

'Oh, are we too early?' Beth asked, concerned. She glanced at her watch.

'Not at all, dear. You mustn't mind me.' Painfully, she walked round the house, showing Jem the work that needed to be done. Then she insisted on offering them coffee and biscuits before they left.

Arrangements were made, finances discussed, dates and times fixed. Jem had brought his professional credentials for Penny's perusal.

'Don't come to the door. We can see ourselves out,' Beth said, taking the cups through to the kitchen.

'All right, dear. And thank you for bringing Sol. It's always so good to see him.'

'Would you… would you like me to leave him? For a short while?'

Penny paused. 'I'm tempted. The house never used to feel so empty when he was around. But, no. He needs to be out and about. And he's clearly very at home with you.' In fact, Sol had stood up and gone to the front door. 'But I really appreciate you bringing him.'

Jem was bending down to pat Sol, and Penny turned conspiratorially to Beth. 'There's Mrs Squires - next door – you remember?' Beth nodded, though she hadn't. 'She's got work that needs done, too. But we'll tackle that one later.'

Beth nodded again. So she wasn't the only one to put Jem on trial. Fair enough. She didn't know whether Jem was a good worker or not, so why did she feel protective of him all of a sudden?

Once Penny had closed the front door, and Beth and Jem had shut the gate behind them, Jem said, 'I've got a free evening. How would you feel about going to the club? Of course, bring Heather, too, if she wants to come…'

'Thank you. I think that'd be good.' She grabbed a get-out clause. 'I just need to make sure Heather and Gregor haven't planned anything.'

'Yeah, sure. Give me a call?

'Yeah. Will do.'

'But you don't even know him!' Heather expostulated.

Gregor paused. He was standing at the kitchen work top behind Heather, making cheese on toast for lunch. 'He might be a chancer, just after a pretty face. A gullible pretty face. Bet he can spot them a mile off.'

'Spot what? Pretty faces?'

'Naïve girls who aren't at all street-wise.'

'Well, at this rate, I'll always be naïve and gullible!' Behind Heather, Gregor grinned and gave Beth a thumbs up.

'How would you get back home? Back here.'

'Bus, I suppose.'

'I could fetch you as long as you're not excessively late,' Gregor offered.

'Pa! Clubs go on all night! People stay till dawn,' Heather said.

'I couldn't possibly ask you to do that, Gregor,' Beth began.

Gregor put his knife down and turned round. 'I think I should be the arbiter, here. Beth's right. She'll never get to know people and make friends if she doesn't try.'

'But how can she...' Heather began. Gregor put a firm hand on her shoulder.

'Just chill a moment, pet. Jem isn't a total stranger, so it's a start. You've met him, haven't you, love?' Heather nodded. 'And he didn't have horns or a tail?' Heather smiled. 'So, Beth, I reckon it would be a great idea for you to have an evening out with him as long as you keep your phone with you at all times, don't let your drink out of your sight, and let me pick you up at one o'clock.'

'One o'clock, Pa? But that's ridiculous! No one goes to a ...'

'Have you changed sides, pet? A minute ago, you didn't think Beth should go. Now you're saying one o'clock is too early to leave. I'm talking compromise here. What do you think, Beth?'

For an answer, Beth put her arms round his neck and gave his cheek a peck. She stood back and watched a blush creep up from his neck. Heather giggled with glee and pulled Beth's hand. 'C'mon, Bethie. Let's decide what you should wear!'

Beth

Edinburgh

August 2012

'Now remember, Beth: start with a soft drink, so you can down it fast if he suggests dancing straight away. Then you won't have to leave it unattended. Arrive a few minutes late then, with any luck, Jem will have got there before you, and you won't have to stand around alone outside. Don't take money. Well, only your entrance fee and enough for a drink.'

'Yes, aunty,' Beth said.

Heather pulled a face at her. 'You know I'm right, don't you?' Beth smiled and nodded. 'And your phone. How are you going to carry your phone if you don't take a bag?'

'Here,' Beth said, her hand on her bra.

'Right,' Heather said, smiling. 'Good job it's a small one. Your phone, I mean!'

They both doubled up with laughter just as Gregor arrived in the hall. 'I'm missing out on something here. Share the joke?'

'No way, Pa,' Heather hiccupped finally.

'Come on then, Princess,' Gregor said, offering an Austenesque arm to Beth. So, wearing an understated short black skirt with Heather's shimmery blue top, and armed with Heather's advice, Beth took Gregor's arm and walked to his car with him.

'Dad, don't forget to drop her around the corner, out of sight, so that no one…'

Gregor gave a salute, and he and Beth got into the car.

Heather was right. Jem was already there, waiting for

Beth, and they went in to the club together. He wanted to pay for her, but she insisted on paying for herself. No obligation, that way, Heather had told her. 'All right,' Jem agreed, 'as long as you let me buy you a drink.'

'The music's not as loud as I remember,' Beth said as they perched on bar stools with their drinks.

'It starts a bit quieter and builds up later.'

'You remember I have to leave at one?'

'Aye, Cinderella. Nae probs. It's okay for me, too. I got a job to do tomorrow.'

'A job?'

'Aye. My mum's neighbour wants a shelf put up in her bathroom. Mum's bloke could do that, easy, but he's too lazy to lift a finger for other folk.'

'What's his job - your mum's boyfriend?'

'He's in construction work as well. Brickie, mainly, but he knows a thing or two. If he'd pulled his finger out I reckon he could've been an architect. As it is, he can't always get work, so it's just as well my mum's got a job at the hospital.'

'At the hospital? What does she do?'

'She's a receptionist in dermatology.'

'Ah. Dermatology.'

Not A and E, then. She wouldn't have been the one who admitted Beth. She smiled.

'Wha'?'

'We used to call it derma-holiday.'

'Holiday?' Why, like?'

'Dermatology. Derma-holiday. It was a slightly easier placement. Very few emergencies or anti-social hours.'

'For doctors, aye.'

They paused, sipped their drinks and watched as the

dance floor filled up slowly.

'So – you're on your long summer break, and then you'll go back to Dundee and be a doctor, then, is it?'

'Well, to be honest, Jem, I don't think I will.'

'Don't think you will? Why not, like? Exams too difficult. I know I wouldnae be…'

'No, it's not that. I quite liked the study. I just don't think I want to do that sort of work all my life. It's not a job where you can chop and change, you know. Statistics say that nowadays adults are likely to change jobs – even career paths – at least four times in their working lives. But not doctors.'

'Aye, I reckon that's about right. My dad's on his third, and he's not even our generation.'

'Your dad? What does he do?'

'He's a bursar in a private school now. But he used to work in the bank, and before that he worked in a hotel. On the management side. He said there's always jobs for skilled craftsmen in a hotel. That's why he encouraged me and Josh to get apprenticeships.'

'But, he and your mum…'

'Divorced. Ten years ago now. Me and Josh were early teens. Dad's married again. Mum and her bloke didn't bother. She always says *Been there, done that, got the T-shirt.* Doesn't want to get married again. Just as well, I say. Her blokes don't stick around long enough. Doesn't say a lot for her taste in men.'

'Your brother, Josh. You said he's an electrician?'

'Yeah. Like I said, Dad advised us to do a practical training. Apprenticeships and college courses. Certificates and diplomas. The works. Said we'd never be out of work. But Josh – he's really bright. He got all his certificates double quick time. He's a wizard with a computer, too. He set up a website for the first firm he worked with. He could do anything.'

'But now?'

'Dinnae ken. He took off. Summat went really wrong. He's an awkward sod to be around. Can't get on with anyone for more than five minutes. Maybe it was drugs or – his girlfriend left him, Mum's bloke didn't like having him around…'

'Couldn't he live with your dad?'

'Dad's new wife has a teenage girl. Didn't want our Josh to rock the boat. Anyway. Enough about my lot. What about your family? You don't have brothers and sisters, you said. Your dad a doctor, too?'

Beth picked up her glass and drank again. She thought of Gregor's postcard. It seemed like Jem was being pretty honest. It was her turn. No need to spill *all* the beans. 'My dad died. It was him, really, not me, that wanted me to be a doctor.'

'Ah. Sorry to hear that. Long time ago, was it?'

'Well, no. Just a couple of months ago. Initially, that's why I left uni. Then the summer term finished and I stayed here.'

'Needed to help your mum, like.'

Beth looked out across the girating, twisting bodies, the flashing lights, the laughter and exuberance.

'Let's dance, Jem,' she said, and she took him by the hand into the middle of the dance floor.

'You should be asleep by now,' Beth scolded, as Heather

opened the front door.

'Too excited,' Heather said. 'Did you have a good time? What was it like? What was *he* like?'

'Tomorrow,' Gregor urged. 'Tomorrow is another day…'

'Good, and yes, good,' Beth said, trying to be enigmatic. 'But I'm bushed. Thanks for waiting up, Heather. Really. Brunch at eleven? I'll go to the bakery.'

'Or I will. Goodnight both,' Gregor said, and went upstairs, turning off the hall light and leaving them in darkness.

Beth didn't sleep as late as she had intended. She went into the bathroom, and when she returned to her room, Heather was there with two cups of tea.

'Come on,' Heather said, 'dish the dirt!'

'You're such a teenager!' Beth scolded, but took the tea gratefully. 'I had a nice evening. Really. The dancing was good fun.' She told Heather about the conversation, how she'd admitted to Jem that her parents were both dead, that she wasn't planning to return to university, that she was staying at Arthur's View while decisions were made about her family house, that she herself had suffered a form of depression.

Heather listened carefully, nodding from time to time, approving the degree of honesty without unnecessary details. 'But what about Jem? Did you, you know, did you *like* him?'

'He's really nice.'

'Nice! My English teacher said it was such a limp word. Something has to be tolerable, or acceptable, or amazing, or fantastic, or incredible, or…'

'Or enjoyable and pleasant.'

'Was that all?'

'Isn't it enough?'

'No chemistry?'

'What?'

'Chemistry. It was Marian's word. Remember I told you about Marian, the British Embassy warden who looked after me so well after Tony died?'

Beth nodded, tugged her duvet round her knees and wrapped her hands round her tea mug.

'She was great. More than nice!' Heather grinned mischievously. 'She was a friend and a mum rolled into one. She said any boy-girl relationship had to have kindness, sincerity, selflessness… and chemistry. Fireworks! So did you really *fancy* him? I know that's a schoolgirl word, but… did it do something to your gut, being with Jem?'

Beth sipped her tea. She'd no need to think about whether she fancied Jem. She didn't. He was kind, friendly and sincere as far as she could tell, but she didn't fancy him. But how could she tell Heather that she felt a million miles away from taking the step – steps – giant leaps - needed to move close to someone. Anyone. Trusting herself to Heather and Gregor had been like climbing Everest, despite their unmitigated generosity. Boyfriend and girlfriend relationships stank of impermanence; look at Heather and Tony; look at Josh and his girlfriend. Look at older adults – Jem's parents, Heather's parents, her own parents. And where were Uncle Bob, Aunty Nessa and Paul?

'No,' she said. 'No chemistry.'

Heather looked so disappointed, that Beth searched for something else to say. 'Was that what it was like for you with Tony – chemistry?'

'Huh! No. Not really. Not at all, in fact. He was a good companion – good fun. Outrageous sometimes, even embarrassing, but no chemistry.'

'How would you recognise it – this chemistry?'

'Oh, you'd recognise it.'

Beth

Edinburgh

September 2012

'He's a good worker, your young man. Mrs Squires thinks so, too,' Penny declared, threading her fingers into Sol's glossy coat.

'Good. I'm glad. But he's not my young man, I mean, he's just a good friend.'

'Well, dear, he's the sort of friend you need to cultivate: hard-working, polite, reliable. He did an excellent job for me, and I've had a much better quote from the estate agent after your... I mean, after young Jem gave the place such a face lift. The house goes on the market next week. Look out for the board next time you come.'

'I'm so glad,' Beth said again. 'And it sounds like the work that Mrs Squires needs is a much bigger job.'

'Yes, I think that's right. Reflooring, fitted cupboards, washing machine plumbing in differently. You've made such a good start on the garden, and she's very grateful for you walking her dog. You ought to set up in business, the two of you. Call it something like *Helping Hands!*'

Beth laughed. 'It's certainly what Jem would like to do – set up in business, I mean. But I'm not sure I'd have any skills to offer.'

'I must beg to differ, my dear. Being friendly is definitely a skill. Caring for dogs – and people, knowing about garden plants, all sorts of housekeeping skills – spotting what needs done and doing it before being asked – well, that's a rare attribute. You say,' she paused. '...you say you're not going to return to your studies?'

'Yes, I think I've decided. The university say they'll hold my place for a year, in case I change my mind, but I don't think I'm cut out to be a doctor.'

'But, my dear, making people better is the biggest service anyone could ever do!'

'Yes, I know, and that was why I opted for medicine.' It was true. She'd always wanted *to help people.* But now it seemed a nebulous aim. No need to tell Penny that medicine was her father's choice. 'But you know, you don't actually get to spend *time* with people. GPs are constrained to ten minutes max, often with people with dozens of problems. Surgeons don't often get to see their patients *awake!* Problems within the NHS never seem to be far from the headlines.'

'That's true, but you don't seem to me to be the type to duck out of problems.'

Beth felt herself blushing. Here was this sweet lady paying her the highest of compliments, with no idea of her total inability to confront even her own problems, never mind anyone else's. 'I didn't give Sol a drink after our walk. Is there a dish I could use for him somewhere?'

'Yes, of course. You'll find his old water bowl in the cupboard under the sink.' Beth found the bowl, filled it, and called Sol. She opened the back door and put the bowl down. She watched him lapping joyfully, then shaking and spraying her with drops. She glanced next door, in time to see Jem lean out of the bedroom window and give her a thumbs up, then tap his watch. She waved and nodded and went back inside.

'I've made sandwiches for Jem and myself, Penny. Is it okay if we eat them in your back garden? Can I make something for you, too?'

'There's some soup in the fridge, thank you. I only need to reheat it. But you and Jem are welcome to come inside.'

'Thanks, but he's a bit manky. Anyway, it's sunny, and I think he'd rather be outside.'

Jem washed his hands at Penny's garden tap, and they sat on the grass in the sun. Sol joined them for a short while, then took himself off to flop in the shade of the shed. 'It's not the weather for a fur coat,' Beth remarked.

'You're right. It's not the weather to be the size of Mrs Squires, either. She's been sweating like a pig all morning!'

'She can't help it.'

'Sorry. Not meaning to be rude. I mean, so have I, of course, but I've been working hard. No, what I mean is, I reckon she eats for summat to do. She's bored, like. She ought to walk the dog, but she knows she'll get out of breath. If you was to walk *with* her and the dog, or to go shopping with her, buy some lettuce or something. She's in there eating doughnuts for lunch.'

'Oh. So I shouldn't've been walking the dog…'

'Nah, I didn't mean that. She appreciates it. I didn't mean you shouldn't help her. She looks forward to you coming. You're good company. But, well, we could do more. We need to think about it.'

They sat and ate, while Sol returned to his bowl for another big drink.

'What's more, I'm gonna need some help with her wiring. She wants me to rig up interior lights for her wardrobe, so that they come on when she opens the wardrobe door. Dead posh. Glad she can't see *my* clothes storage!'

194

'But you can't do electrics?'

'Right.'

'But Josh can?'

'Aye. He's so good with everything electrical they call him The Wire. He liked that. It's how he started to introduce himself. *Hi. You can call me The Wire.*' He stuck out his hand in mock greeting, before taking another bite of his roll. 'What's up? You okay? You've gone pale.'

Beth's heart was thudding. 'Yeah. I'm okay. It's just that...' How could she explain this? 'It's just that once, when I'd not had Sol for very long, I was walking him beside the canal. It was very late, and I met this guy...'

'You shouldn't walk beside the canal in the evening, at least not after dark. You don't know what sort of types hang out there.'

'No. I mean, yes. You're right. It had been raining, and Sol was restless, so I took him a walk.'

'You should just let him out into the back garden when that happens. He probably just needed a pee, what with the rain an' all...'

'Yes.' How to go on? 'You're right, I mean about who you might meet. But I think there were some guys taking shelter under the bridge. The rain had been very heavy. I think they were... homeless. One of them was under a tree nearby. He made me jump.'

'What did he do?' Jem looked all set to punch whoever might threaten Beth. It made her smile.

'No, it's okay. He didn't do anything. Just warned me to be careful. But, the thing is, he called himself The Wire.'

Jem gasped. 'What did he look like? Did he look like me?'

'It was dark and wet. His hair was long and soaked,

195

sticking to his face. Couldn't see the colour of it. Couldn't see much at all, really, except that he was very thin.' She didn't add that she had run away and driven off as fast as she could, but at Jem's insistence she did explain, as well as she could remember, where she had met him.

'But what were you doing there? Why didn't you just walk down the street, or round the block, or summat, since it was so late an' dark?'

Beth sat for a moment, watching Sol, his paws twitching, possibly dreaming of chasing rabbits on Arthur's Seat. 'Remember I told you I'd had a period of depression? Well, I was having lots of trouble sleeping, and it seemed to help, being in the car, driving around and walking.' She couldn't look at him, but he said no more, and after a moment, he put his arm round her shoulder and gave her a quick squeeze. Then he carried on eating.

After a few minutes he said, 'I was just wondering, would you be able to take me – to go with me – to the spot, see if we could find Josh? I mean, you could stay in the car if you don't want to meet him again – yet.'

Beth still didn't say anything – couldn't think of anything to say.

'He's not – Josh isn't – I mean, he wouldn't hurt you or anything. His bark is worse than his bite. He was always such a cocky little tyke. Always had to have the last word.'

'Yeah. I mean, no.' What *did* she mean? She was embarrassed. That's what she meant. How could she tell Jem that his brother had summed her up with uncanny accuracy after a mere two-minute encounter in the most unlikely of circumstances? But the strange thing was, and she only realised this now as she recalled that meeting, that Sol hadn't growled or barked, hadn't backed off. He had just stood

196

looking at the dripping being who had so unnerved Beth by the canal. Sol, in his wisdom, hadn't been afraid.

'Yes. Okay. We'll go and see if we can track him down.'

They left as it was getting dark. Beth parked in roughly the same place as before in the supermarket car park. They took Sol, who looked a bit surprised at being put on a leash. But Beth felt better knowing he was within reach, and he was generally a very acquiescent dog. Beth recognised the spot beside the canal – the very tree – where The Wire had been leaning when he stopped her and introduced himself. There was no one there now, and Jem looked disappointed.

'See that bridge,' Beth said, pointing, 'with a kind of tunnel underneath? There was a guy sheltering there. I think Josh knew him. Let's try.'

When they arrived, she found herself hanging back, her courage failing her. 'Jem,' she pulled his sleeve, 'don't actually *go* under the bridge. It's… it's very dark under there. You wouldn't be able to see anyone anyway.'

Jem stopped and gave her arm a squeeze, then stepped forward until he was just outside the bridge. 'Hiya. Anyone there?' His voice was echoey and unnatural.

'Aye, well that'll depend who ye are and who ye'll be wanting,' replied the slow gruff voice that Beth remembered.

Beside her, Jem stiffened. 'My name's Jeremy, and I'm looking for my brother Josh… The Wire.'

'Aye, and will he be looking for you too, like?'

'Well, I don't know… probably not, but I really want to find him…'

'Ah, so ye really want to find him, is it?'

'It's hopeless. He's not here,' Beth whispered, trying to pull Jem away.

'Please sir,' Jem began again, 'if you could just tell me...'

'Come in here then laddie, show yersel'. Ye've no need tae be feart.'

Jem looked round at Beth. She recalled that Scottie's voice held no threat. In fact, if this was Scottie's permanent abode, he had far more reason to be afraid of intruders like them than they had to fear him. She gripped Jem's arm with one hand, and tightened her hold on Sol's leash with the other, and they edged forward together until they stood in the mouth of the tunnel, leaning away from the dark wall and towards the glinting canal.

Beth heard the same shuffle and wheezing sigh, and the gruff low voice said, 'Aye, it's true. Ye do indeed look like him. Like young Josh, The Wire.

They waited. Sol snuffled around their feet, straining on the leash towards the voice. 'So...' Jem said at last, 'do you know where we could find him?'

A loud voice from behind them boomed into the tunnel: 'That would depend why you want to find him!' Jem turned suddenly and Beth let go of his arm. Sol barked sharply, the sound amplified by the tunnel, and tugged on the leash.

'Sol!' Beth tried to change hands with the leash as the dog strained forward. Jem was saying something, someone was laughing and the leash was caught round her ankles. Lifting one foot high, trying to free herself, she stepped backwards, felt her foot losing its grip on the damp canal bank and, as if in slow motion, she slid ignominiously into the dark, sluggish water.

The cold took her breath away. Shocked and terror-stricken, she tried to shout out, but her mouth filled with dirty water and her hair tangled across her face, threatening to choke her. Eyes tight shut, she thrashed about with her arms, and felt the weight of her clothes pulling her under. Water filled her ears and all sounds were muffled apart from the whooshing and splashing of the canal and Sol's strangled barking. All she had learned in swimming lessons deserted her, and she didn't know which way was up. But then, Jem was in the water beside her, holding her, lifting her, thrusting her towards the bank where a helping hand stretched down to pull her out.

Dripping, shivering and sobbing, with Sol whimpering and trying to lick her face, Beth crouched under the bridge while Jem climbed out.

'So, my big brother's found himself a pretty girlfriend who's definitely a land-lubber.'

'Josh! That was your fault! You don't change, brother. Why do you have to go around shocking people? Why can't you just…'

'Well, well, well! If it isn't Elizabeth!' The Wire exclaimed. 'I've told you before, Elizabeth, this isn't your place. Go home, where you belong.'

Anger stanched Beth's tears abruptly, and she searched for a crisp retort. But Jem said sharply, 'Josh, I would've liked to say how nice it is to see you again, and to ask you how you're farin', but I can see you havnae made any progress towards being acceptable in society.'

'That would depend on your definition of progress, brother. If you mean joining the status quo, entering the rat race, owing money to a bent landlord who refuses to treat the damp seeping through the walls, paying taxes so the government can join the arms race, then no, I havnae.'

'Gie' us a break, Josh,' Jem said with a sigh. 'Me and Beth, we'd like to talk to you. Beth would like to get to know the real guy behind the defences...'

Beth wasn't at all sure she would, but Jem was being patient and reasonable, and that, at least, impressed her. But she was also freezing and soaked, and she couldn't see where this conversation was going.

'But the main reason,' Jem continued, 'is that we'd like to offer you a job. A paid job.'

'What, buy myself some respectable gear, treat Scottie to a hot meal, go to the cinema...?' His tone was mocking, but Jem was not put off.

'Whatever. Aye, an' use your training. It's a wiring job. In a private house. Lighting an' that. But we're cold and wet, thanks to you, so we're off just now. But if you're interested, meet us in the entrance to the supermarket tomorrow at six and, who knows, we might even buy you a sandwich and a coffee.' Without waiting for a reply, he put an arm round Beth's shoulders and steered her towards the car park.

'You okay?' he asked, finally, as they got into the car.

'Yes. Thanks. But you're wet too. Sorry...'

'Funny thing is, the canal's only about waist deep just there.'

Now Beth looked at him properly. His jeans were soaked but his shirt wasn't. It must be true.

'So I...'

'So you wouldn't have drowned!'

Now Beth felt stupid and ashamed, and even more embarrassed than before. 'It was just the surprise, the shock, and I've always hated water, even though I learned how to swim. Jem, I'm so sorry.'

'Don't be. It gave me chance to be chivalrous, and Josh chance to pull you out!'

Beth gasped. 'He pulled me out?'

'Aye. Like I told you, Josh's bark is worse than his bite. When Mum and Dad split up, he took it hard. He was still young – he's four years younger than me – and when Mum took up with a new bloke, he couldn't hack it. His chief method of defence is attack. Chip on his shoulder as big as a house. Dad asked me to look out for him, so I've tried, but, as you saw, it isnae easy. Now, you okay to drive?'

So Beth dropped him outside his mother's house and drove back to Arthur's View where she braced herself for questions from Heather. But there was a pinprick of light at the end of the tunnel – no, more than that. There was a dawning realisation that life could be good, that she didn't long for it to end, that she hadn't wanted to surrender to the water's pull. Now she had Heather and Gregor. There was Jem and the possibility of work. Penny Tyler was a friend who needed and appreciated her. Sol depended on her. The future was – not rosy – but at least possible. Very possible.

Beth

Edinburgh

September 2012

Beth crept in through the back door, hoping to get changed before being seen, but Heather was sitting at the kitchen table with her laptop open.

'Hi Bethie. I've found a website you should see. Hey, you're drenched! What happened?'

'We were walking by the canal and I lost my footing.'

'You poor thing! Go and have a shower, then come and look at this.'

'What is it?'

'Go and warm up. I need you to concentrate.'

So Beth did so, grateful to avoid an embarrassing admission. When she returned, Heather showed her a new business start-up website. 'If you and Jem are going to earn *real* money, you need to have your business on a proper legal basis,' she told Beth.

'Our business? I wouldn't really call it a business. Not yet, anyway. And in any case, it's Jem that's been doing the work, not me.'

'But who's been walking the dogs, and taking Mrs Squires to the shops and preparing healthy meals with her, and sorting her garden, visiting her and her shut-in elderly friends, and cooking for Penny Tyler's sister's eightieth and treating Jem's cut finger?'

'Yeah, but anyone could do that,' Beth said.

'Maybe, but you're the one who did.'

'But it's just helping. Getting requests to lend a

helping hand.'

'Yes, and the number of requests is increasing, and anyway, you said Jem would like to move to Edinburgh and work here,' Heather persisted.

'Yes, that's true.'

'And if you ever have to ask someone else to do jobs that you and Jem aren't qualified to do, you'd need insurance and all that.'

Beth glanced at Mount Hood on the fridge and sighed. 'You're right. And I was going to tell you, we're already going to ask someone else. Jem called it *outsourcing*.'

'There you are, you see,' Heather said with a note of triumph.

'But the person we're going to ask is Jem's brother, Josh.' Reluctantly she gave a truncated account of both her encounters with Josh and watched Heather's expression change from horror and fear to disbelief and indignation.

'Doesn't exactly sound like a *team player*.'

'No, but he's all we have at the moment. Jem says he's well qualified and he needs work. He needs to be – well – settled. Jem's worried about him.'

'I'm not surprised.'

'I guess Jem would need the legal side if he left his job in Penicuik. I expect his boss Callum does that side of things for him at the moment.'

'Well, look at the website. See what you think. And get Jem to look as well.' She tilted the screen towards Beth, who began to read and experience a growing excitement. It was certainly a possibility.

Heather

Edinburgh

September 2012

Heather let herself in the back door, threw her jacket on to a kitchen chair and put the kettle on. No dogs. Pa must be out on the hill with them. It had been a long day. On occasions when Marjorie was absent, the workload seemed to double.

She heard the click of the side gate and a sudden burst of raised voices. She went back outside to find Beth and Jem coming from the shed. There was another guy with them, a skinny guy with shoulder-length unkempt hair. Jem's brother? He was holding forth about something he didn't agree with. After what Beth had said, Heather was on her mettle.

'Oh, hi Heather,' Beth said. 'You just home? We only came back for some of Jem's tools.'

Jem nodded a greeting and lifted his work bag by way of explanation, then added, 'Heather, this is my brother Josh.'

Okay, act normal. She stepped forward and held out her hand. 'Hi Josh.' Josh nodded but didn't shake her hand.

Ah, so that's how he's going to play it.

Heather asked, 'Cuppa tea anyone?'

'Yes please…' Beth began. They trooped into the kitchen.

'So this is the wee lassie that suggested the business course?' Josh asked Jem.

'So this is the wee laddie that might join you?' Heather asked Beth.

Then she turned to Josh. 'You should check out the business website. It looks like…'

'It looks like you're wanting us to join the status quo, to pay our taxes, to kow-tow to the establishment. Like you in your uniform.'

'Josh…' Jem warned.

Keep cool. She responded, 'Uniforms are utilitarian. This is merely a type of clothing that allows freedom of movement, that is clean and unlikely to transmit germs, and is easy to launder,' Heather countered.

'Launder! Swallowed a dictionary, didye?'

Heather glanced at Jem. He was clearly embarrassed, but Beth – was that the hint of a smile? Heather looked back at Josh. What a wee upstart. She told him, 'I know that you studied, too, and must've chewed on a few dictionaries of your own. I guess you've digested ACB, conduit, alligator…'

'So now you've joined the rat race you want me and Jem to join it, too. And Elizabeth. You'll aim to climb the job ladder, work for a bigger better practice, meet a rich guy, buy a house, have 2.4 kids, buy them posh bikes and the latest in electronic gaming equipment without the slightest inkling of how the other half live, or of…'

'So you would advocate insufficient nutrition…' she looked pointedly at his skinny frame, 'negligent personal hygiene and a refusal to accept responsibility as a Scottish citizen, and instead, eventually, become a drain on the NHS, a self-confessed belligerent drop-out with an axe to grind that is big enough to chop up the chip that's on your shoulder.'

At last Jem's face betrayed the hint of a smile. He was edging nearer to Beth.

'Nice little pad you've got here,' Josh said, leaning with exaggerated nonchalance against the wall, and looking round the kitchen scornfully. 'Comfortably settled in middle class suburbia with not so much as a how-d'ye-do to a world where displaced people have no chance of feathering their own nest because of wars and fighting and political unrest, where we're selling arms to Saudi Arabia and...'

'Josh, she used to...'

'...where a young Syrian guy set himself on fire because the president is a dictator, and where...'

'Tunisian,' Heather said, beginning to enjoy herself.

'What?'

'Mohamed Bouazizi. The guy who set himself alight. He wasn't Syrian. He was Tunisian.'

'Yeah. He was protesting against the government, against the dictatorship that kept putting the taxes up...'

Jem whispered something to Beth.

Heather interrupted, 'He was protesting because he couldn't get a street vendor's license, about the injustice of the system against unemployment.'

'Whatever.' Josh was frowning fiercely.

Why the deliberate effort to be aggressive?

'He started that occupation of Taksim Square,' Josh continued, 'until they threw out the president...'

'Tahrir Square. Taksim Square is in Istanbul. It was inaugurated in 1928 after the formation of the Republic of Turkey in 1923. Tahrir Square is in Cairo. It means Liberation. It celebrated liberation from British occupation in 1919.' There was a giggle threatening, somewhere around her diaphragm. Jem was laughing now.

'But that president – Nasser – he was...'

'Moubarak.'

'What?'

Beth was grinning broadly. Heather tried to keep a straight face.

Jem began, 'If yous could jump down off your soap boxes long enough to make us a cuppa tea…?'

'Cuppa tea?' Josh said, 'That'd be good.' He turned to Heather. 'Hi. I'm Josh. They call me The Wire. Pleased to meet you.' He held out his hand to shake. 'Pardon my germs.'

Heather looked at his hand. It was perfectly clean. She shook it and laughed aloud. 'So what was all that about?'

'Ach, I just like to know how the land lies, like to size up the opposition.'

'But no one's opposing you!'

'What about all that stuff about germs and taxes and not contributing to society?'

Jem and Beth, now laughing openly, moved in to stand between Heather and Josh. Jem pulled out a chair at the kitchen table. 'Here, Mate. Sit down.'

'There's some flapjack in the cupboard,' Beth told Heather. 'I'll put some on a plate.'

'Right. And what were you two giggling about?'

Beth looked at Jem, who supplied, 'Irresistible force meets immovable object, or some such saying. You've met your match, bro!'

Heather grinned.

'So what's this about doing a business start-up course?' Josh asked.

'It was Heather who found the website,' Beth said, 'but Jem and I thought it would be a good idea to set our work on a firm legal footing.'

'Right. I'm in,' Josh said, sipping his tea noisily. 'Here!

Yous didn't go ahead without me, didye?'

Beth

Edinburgh

September 2012

Beth and Jem sat together at the kitchen table at Arthur's View. They heard Heather's car pull up in the front drive, then her key in the lock. Beth called, 'Come in Heather, it's open.'

Heather went in unzipping her jacket. Shrugging it off, she leaned over Beth's shoulder to look at her laptop. 'Hi. What're you two doing?'

'Welcome home, the worker!' Jem said, grinning. 'Busy day?'

'You could say so. One slipped disc, one stiff neck, one frozen shoulder, two recovering colles fractures…'

'*Two?*'

'Yep. Two different elderly ladies – and it's not even icy weather yet! But what are you two working on?'

'Our business plan. We have a helper –'

'A *counsellor*,' Jem interrupted.

'Yeah. He's called a counsellor, Kieron. He said we have to draw up a business plan.'

'A business plan? What does that entail?'

'A lot of work! But we enjoyed the session, didn't we, Jem? Kieron was great – really motivating. We have to itemise the kinds of work we can undertake…'

'…and he pointed out the difference, like, between what we'd be *willing* to do and what we'd be *qualified* to do.'

'Willing,' Heather repeated, 'like dog-walking and baking as opposed to joinery and plumbing.'

'Yes,' Beth said, 'anyone can walk dogs, but baking – I'm booked to go on a food hygiene course! It's not directly linked to the business start-up, but Kieron said it would be useful.'

'But we cannae just charge random amounts for jobs, like. We have to *guess*…'

'…estimate…'

'Yeah. Estimate what each job's worth.'

'We have to research what other companies charge – for labour, for resources…'

'We've to choose a name…'

'…and produce a business card…'

'…and come up with an advertising programme…'

'I reckon you're not going to need that,' Heather said. 'Word of mouth has done that job for you up to now.'

'Aye, that it has. And we dinnae want to get swamped too early.'

'Right,' Beth said. 'If Penny Tyler and her community continue to promote us the way they've been doing, we'll be in work for years!' Suddenly she realised the import of what she was saying and breathed in sharply, but it felt all right. She felt no sad regret at the loss of medical training.

'The next session with Kieron's gonna be finance,' Jem said. 'Accounts, insurance – personal liability and public liability – like if I drill a hole in the wrong place…'

'But we've made a start,' Beth said, 'and we've got a name: High Fives! What d'you think?' She and Jem gave one another a high five as she said it, and dissolved into companionable laughter.

'It's great!' Heather said. 'Really. A great name. Much more sparky than Helping Hands. But it says what you want to say.' They looked back at the laptop.

'What was that?' Heather said suddenly. She went to look out of the kitchen window. 'I think... I think there's someone in the shed. Pa keeps all his tools in there. He must've forgotten to lock it. But it's broad daylight...' Instinctively she looked at Jem. So much for feminism and equality.

As if on cue, Jem got up and went to the back door. He looked round the room. 'Have you got anything to...?' He didn't finish the sentence, but Heather was thinking baseball bats. Too much TV. She and Beth got up and followed him.

Outside the shed, they paused. There was definitely someone in there. Jem's hand reached slowly for the door handle then, just as in the American cop shows, he flung open the door. A gardening fork clattered to the floor.

'Josh!' All three of them gasped with surprise and relief. And indignation.

'Josh, whatever are you doing here? You can't just...' Heather began.

'Hello gorgeous,' he said, grinning. 'Just rigging up a light in here. Pitch black at night. Cannae see a thing.'

'But Pa... But we don't use the shed at night.'

'But there's no electricity in the shed,' Jem said.

'Aye, but this is a battery lamp. Ye just pull this cord – see – but dinnae forget to switch it off or ye'll kill the battery.' He was fixing the lamp on the shed wall, just inside the door.

'But... but where did you get the money for...' Heather bit her tongue. She didn't want to know, just in case.

Josh turned a little-boy-innocent face to her and said, 'Your Mrs Squires – she doesnae pay wi' sweeties.'

Jem was nodding. Beth stepped forward. 'But we

should reimburse you –' She giggled. 'Pay you back. How much did…?'

'Aye, well, we'll see about that later,' Josh said. 'Now, yous go back inside and let me get on with it.'

Back in the kitchen, the three of them sat, stunned. Eventually Jem began, 'Sorry – my brother – he's such a loose canon. But he – he's got a heart. He just doesnae know how to –'

'Pa's been cursing that shed for years,' Heather admitted. 'Sometimes he needs something from it at night, and he has to take a torch, and it's awkward –'

'Aye, well our Josh says he does want to fit in, an' he's been doing various jobs for us already, like at Mrs Squires' place, but he's still living rough.'

'Can't he stay with your mum? Or your dad?' Heather asked.

'Heather!' Beth scolded. She'd explained about Jem's and Josh's parents and their situations. But an idea so momentous suddenly crossed her mind that she gasped and felt quite shaky.

'Beth! You've gone pale. 'What's up?' Heather was staring at her. Beth cursed her own skin. She had great mastery over verbal expression, Gregor often said so, but blushes and pallor – who could control those?'

She glanced at the Mount Hood picture. Such transparency. 'Well,' she began, 'there's a house. Our house. My house. It's sitting empty all this time.'

Heather's eyes widened. 'Scuse us a minute,' she said to Jem, and pulled Beth into the hall, closing the kitchen door behind them.

'Are you suggesting that Jem and his crazy brother live in *your* house?' she hissed.

'Well, I've been thinking for a while how illogical it is to have it standing empty.'

'But Jem and *Josh*...?'

'He's really okay. It's all bluff.'

'I know, but it's pretty antisocial bluff.'

'You gave him as good as you got, that first time he came here. Put him in his place. Called his bluff.'

'Yeah, but that's me. And I happened to know about that stuff he was spouting, about the Middle East. But you, Beth, you're not very... I mean, I'm not sure if you could...'

'I know. I'm not like you. I don't react like you, or think quickly like you, but actually...' Beth paused. How to explain what she was beginning to understand, without sounding superior?

'He's dealing with stuff. We all are. And we all deal with it in different ways. Marian helped you deal with yours, and I wouldn't have been able to deal with mine at all, without you and your pa!' She gave Heather a hug. Pulling away, she added, 'They would look after the house. They've been trained, the two of them, to build, not destroy. And they're very clean. They do a great job of clearing up after they've finished. You ought to see them at work...'

'Okay, I'm persuaded.' She took hold of Beth by the shoulders and looked hard at her. 'And that's why I admire you, Bethie. I respect you hugely. That's why you are exactly the right person to give high fives. To *help people*.'

'That phrase.'

'Yes!' Heather was grinning. 'Yes. It's you. It's what you do.'

Respect, she'd said, not pity. That spark of life within Beth, almost eclipsed among the ashes surrounding her, had begun at last to glow. For a while, now, Beth was beginning to understand how things were. She was trusting herself, not embarrassing herself, not creating in other people a sense of obligation. That flickering flame was able to withstand a little cold wind. She knew she was naïve, gullible, that she'd had no opportunity to become street-wise in the way Heather meant it, but she believed she might, in time, be able to offer light and warmth for others.

She hugged Heather again. 'C'mon. Let's go back in.'

Jem looked up from one to the other of them.

'Sorry, Jem,' Beth said. 'We were talking about the house. My house. Seems silly to let it sit empty, while you and Josh...'

'Now hang on, Beth, that sounds...' Jem began.

'Sounds like a plan,' Heather interrupted. 'Better ask Pa. He'll know if there's legal stuff and so on. Sounds great, at least for the time being...'

Gregor

Edinburgh

October 2012

Gregor looks up. A librarian with a stack of files under her arm moves noiselessly to a shelf labelled *News Archives: June to September 1982*, near to the table where Gregor is studying. He is only peripherally aware of the librarian. The archives are immense and comprehensive, but riveting to Gregor. This research has yielded information surpassing his dearest hopes and dreams.

Gomersall. A surname. Apparently, if spelt with only one *l*, it's a village in West Yorkshire, setting for one of the Bronte novels. Names can easily change spelling: look at Thomson and Thompson, D'Arby, Derby and Darby, Whyte and White. In any case, it's still an unusual name, especially in Scotland. Yet Beth says she was born in Edinburgh. She has never claimed a Yorkshire heritage. Mind you, Heather's Cairo friend, Mrs Braithwaite – Margaret? Miriam? – probably hasn't claimed Cumbrian ancestry, either. Gregor has always been fascinated by the way British surnames have evolved, from appearance, like Redhead, or Longfellow, nationality – take French or Scott, or even jobs, like Thatcher... As for himself, he is proud to be the bearer of two truly Scottish names. But he has to accept that not everyone shares his passion for enquiry.

Back to Gomersall. He hasn't been able to grasp that Beth could be so rootless, so alone. He has accepted the deaths of both her parents – harsh, unequivocal facts. Any support from her father's brother Bob and family has been disappointingly absent. Beth has long since lost contact with her mother's family: any remaining relatives on that side cut all ties after her mother died. Beth fears they blamed her father. Which might be justified, after all. That has to be consigned to the unknown and unknowable.

Yet names and family trees have always fascinated Gregor. Heather has called him a bloodhound, rootling out anything of interest, intrigue or doubt, like trained sniffer dogs at the airport, or those forensic scientists in the TV detective dramas.

One of his favourite television programmes has always been *Who do you think you are?* Celebrities from fields of entertainment, news presentation, academia – you name it – have been astounded, delighted or ashamed to find royalty, heroes, even murderers among their ancestors. They have met relatives of whom they were totally unaware, whose nationalities were different from their own, whose social status was unfamiliar. They have learned of jobs or walks of life they would never have considered.

But Beth – how is it that she has shown no curiosity about her forebears? Of course, just surviving has been all-encompassing in her young life, and an interest in medicine stems from a scientific study background rather than history or biography. Of course, not many people share his sniffer dog mentality.

He's delighted to witness Beth's slow but sure recovery, her renewed health and energy and her growing enthusiasm for the embryonic business. Jem is proving himself. He's reliable, affable, friendly. There's no blossoming romance there, more's the pity. But it's early days. Heather has been a staunch friend for Beth. It seems to be reciprocal, and he thanks his lucky stars that Beth has

216

brought Heather back into his life. He's very happy to have two daughters!

And now, if the results of his research are not leading him astray, he could have unearthed a world-shattering piece of news archive. Excitement and nerves, and his inability to differentiate between the two, make him determined to keep his hopes and suspicions to himself until he has some certainty – some *evidence*.

Heather

Edinburgh

October 2012

Sitting alone at the kitchen table, Heather opened up her email. There was one from Ryan.

Hi beautiful!

How are you doing? How's the job? Your pa? Your lodger?
At last it's a bit cooler here – such a relief, but I'm sure you could do with some warm sun after your Northern Hemisphere so-called summer season. The political situation has calmed, too, and even our embassy has cooled its usual strong recommendation to stay away!

So why don't you come for a visit? There are lots of people here who would love to see you. Andrea has returned to class after a summer break. Rosa has got engaged to an Egyptian guy! Lots of people tried to warn her off, but I've met him – Ayman, her fiancé – and he's great, and totally devoted to Rosa. Her Arabic has improved no end, too. I don't know about mine!

Come for a visit. I mean it! Come and cheer me up, keep me company, warm my heart with your lilting Scottish accent and your warm smile. I miss you, and I'd love for us to have time together, time to chat face to face, time to think about whatever the future might hold…

Heather's heart was hammering. This email was different from Ryan's usual chatty style. She always enjoyed his rambling about the open-air rock and jazz concerts at the Sawy Culture Wheel, evenings out at Al Azhar Park with students from the American University or that Saturday afternoon when a bunch of them had taken over a hotel's roof-top swimming pool and introduced the Egyptian staff to water polo. But this email was in an entirely different league. More personal. More heartfelt. Ryan wasn't one to wear his heart on his sleeve or to write anything slushy. This was real.

So how did she feel about it? About Ryan? Of course, it wasn't the first time she had asked herself, but now it was more urgent, more important. Friendship with Ryan was no longer just a pleasant extra, a daydream when life felt a bit empty. He was thinking along similar lines.

'You're even quieter than usual, hen,' Marjorie remarked as Heather sipped a quick instant coffee between patients. 'What's going on in that pretty head? It's a bloke! Must be, to make you blush like that!' Heather wasn't aware of blushing, but neither could she come up with a quick denial, so she just laughed.

'Who's the lucky guy?' Marjorie persisted.

'Well, he might just be a good friend, nothing more.'

'Only *might*?'

Marjorie was serious now. Heather trusted her. She knew Marjorie was only asking out of interest and concern. No way would she mock or tease. Maybe she had become aware of those lunch break conversations that centred around spouses and children.

'In Cairo there was this guy Ryan...'

'The American who was so helpful after your other bloke was killed?'

'Yes. I didn't realise I'd...'

'No, you didn't labour the point, hen. I've got a memory for these things, ye ken. You're a good lass, and we all just want you to be happy.'

Heather marvelled at the notion of her love life – indeed any part of her life – being in the public arena, and the realisation that she was part of a team, and the team cared.

'Yeah, that's him. He's still there. His Arabic must be pretty good now, though he denies it. We've been emailing on and off all this time. He's suggested I go for a visit.'

'Back to Cairo?'

'Yeah.'

'How would you feel about that, after, you know, and with all the shenanigans in the Middle East?'

'He says the political situation's calmer now.'

'But after what happened to your last bloke…'

'Tony. Yeah. But, you know, Tony and I were never that close. He was a friend, and in Cairo it's important to have a friend to go places with. Especially if you're a girl.' The misunderstanding with Tony's parents flooded over her again.

'Well, you and this Ryan must share a common background, being in Cairo during the uprising, an' all, and wanting to learn Arabic, too. It's important to have aims and goals in common. What's he learning Arabic for, anyway?'

'He's not quite sure yet. Wants to do something diplomatic. The US Foreign Office or something.'

'If he's got nothing set in concrete yet, this is the time to get in there and influence him, hen. From what you said, I'd imagine he's the listening, caring type. It's what you want in a man. Now take my Barry for example. He's…'

The staff room door opened and a colleague leaned in

briefly to inform Heather that her next patient had arrived.

'Off you go, lass,' Marjorie said.

Heather wanted Beth's opinion. When it came to anything approaching romance, Beth would be dispassionate, objective and clinically honest.

'You've mentioned him quite often. Whatever you've said about him has been good. He's kind and thoughtful. It looks like he hasn't been going out with anyone else since you've been back here. He's been waiting for you!'

That was something Heather hadn't considered.

'You haven't been out with anyone over here, either,' Beth continued. 'He's American – a different culture, if that quote about *two nations divided by a common language* is true - but you're both up for adapting to a new culture – to Egypt, I mean, - and you're both keen to learn Arabic.'

'Would you go out with someone from another culture, Bethie? Would you *live* in another culture?'

'Probably not. Not such a different one as Egypt, anyway. But we're talking about you, not me.'

Beth was such a closed book. Heather sighed. Anyway, she was right. They were talking about her and Ryan. 'You wouldn't... I mean... would you *mind* if I went for a couple of weeks? Left you in the lurch?'

'You mean with that ogre, your father?' Beth was really grinning now.

'No!' Heather felt herself blushing. 'No, I didn't mean that. I trust him now. Really. Anyway, he seems quite engrossed in his latest piece of research, whatever that is. I don't think he'd even miss me for a week or so. No, I mean, High Fives is well underway now and you don't need my little bit of input.'

'You've been a huge help,' Beth countered, 'but you should go. Of course I don't mind. How could I go wrong with all these competent guys around me?' She smiled. Her confidence had grown exponentially. 'Anyway, you won't be gone for ever. At least...'

'No, course I won't. I just might be a bit clearer, that's all. And there are lots of people I'd like to see again, not just Ryan. There's Andrea and Rosa, and I'd like to meet her fiancé, and of course I'd love to see Marian again.'

'Go then. What's to stop you? Go! You need to find out if there's any *chemistry*.'

Pa had never been a great fan of heat or beach resorts. Arthur's Seat was his idea of paradise but he was surprisingly encouraging. 'Go for it, love. Egypt hasn't been in the headlines for weeks now. Anyway, as you've pointed out, the country needs tourists.'

'I'm afraid I wouldn't be much help to the Egyptian economy!'

'But you'd give those waiters at the restaurants in Sharm El Sheikh something to do to stave off their boredom! It would be great if you could get a few days real R and R down there. Beth spends her days with Jem and Josh, she knows she's safe and welcome here. There's nothing to hold you back.'

'Yeah. She's doing okay, isn't she?'

'More than okay, I'd say.'

'Like that story, that bird that came alive from a fire...'

'A phoenix rising from the ashes. She's fine. It's your chance. Go for it, love.'

Ryan had written that the language school always took a break at the beginning of November, and hotel rooms in Sharm were going for a song. The thought of a couple of days of warm sun, sand, peace and quiet was very attractive. So the email was written, the ticket booked and the nervous, exciting countdown began.

Heather

Egypt

November 2012

Ryan was easy to spot in the arrivals hall, a head taller than many men, and his was certainly a lighter head than most. Blond, almost. The Egyptian summer had bleached his golden hair. As he made his way through the crowds towards her, she fought the natural reaction to hug him. She remembered that life-restoring hug in her flat the morning after Tony died, the gentle, sensitive company and good advice in those desperate days that followed, the relief and gratitude when he had taken responsibility but not overridden her choices. She had felt so comfortable with him then. Initially there had been no guilt about crying or not crying, laughing, chatting, remaining silent, eating a special lunch with him or sleeping all afternoon on his sofa. But now she remembered to respect the restrictive culture, and hoped he would, too.

He welcomed her with a warm smile and a light touch on her shoulder. He picked up her suitcase easily, and she followed him as he weaved his way to the exit. It was a relief to stand back while he negotiated with the taxi driver, then to hunker down in the grubby back seat and watch the familiar route through the outskirts of Heliopolis to Zamalek. She refused to cringe at the speed and unpredictability of the traffic, but instead to marvel at the unrivalled skill of the drivers.

Once inside Ryan's familiar flat, they made up for their lack of hugs at the airport. Martin had moved out, but

Ryan's new flatmate, Manuel, stood up to shake her hand once they finally disengaged. 'You are very welcome. At last I meet this beautiful lady, this lady who fills Ryan's thoughts day and night!'

'Belt up, you Spanish idiot!' Ryan said, punching him good-humouredly on the shoulder. 'Get on the phone to Otlob and order us some koshari.' He handed his mobile to Manuel, who placed their dinner order efficiently in fluent Arabic. Delivery was equally efficient, and conversation flowed easily as they sat in Ryan's sitting room, their plates of hot, greasy, comforting food balanced on their laps.

Heather was glad that Ryan had arranged for her to sleep at Marian's home. Not only did it give her chance to catch up with Marian, but where Ryan was concerned, the stakes were higher now. Previously, she'd have been happy to spend the night as well as the afternoon on the sofa in Ryan and Martin's flat. Only respect for Egyptian cultural convention had stopped her. But it was different now. Besides, she admitted to herself, Marian's pad was luxurious and made for genuine rest and relaxation, and Marian herself was as friendly, stimulating and hospitable as ever.

Heather preferred to wander round familiar haunts in Zamalek in the morning, while Ryan was in class, and in the afternoon the two of them walked into the city centre, past the Maspiro building, venue for so many disputes against the media and journalists' input during the uprising, and past the police headquarters, still a stark empty, burned-out shell.

It wasn't until the second day that Heather expressed a desire to go to Tahrir. 'Are you sure, honey?' Ryan asked. 'You don't have to go so soon, or even at all, if it brings back horrific memories.'

Glossing over the 'honey' endearment, Heather insisted she *did* want to go, to exorcise some demons, perhaps, or simply to remind herself what it looked like empty of campers, and to see whether the paving stones had been replaced, or the street vendors relocated.

'So how did it feel?' Marian asked later. 'How does Cairo feel, generally? Is everything as you expected?'

They were curled up on adjacent sofas in Marian's art gallery of a sitting room, drinking hot chocolate. 'It's only recently become hot chocolate season,' Marian had explained. 'I love it, but when the temperature outside is in the thirties, let alone forties, you just don't fancy it, somehow.'

'Cairo is great,' Heather said warmly. 'I did wonder how I would feel. I mean, after the tear gas episode, and all you hear on the BBC, and of course Tahrir and Tony. There have been moments when I thought I must be totally mental even to consider coming back here, having once escaped! But the crazy traffic, which doesn't obey any of the rules but works anyway, the energy and buzz, and those cheeky little kids that call out *Hello, how arrre you? What's yourrr name?*'

Marian was smiling in recognition.

'It gets under your skin, you know? But in a nice way. There's an open friendliness in the street. People smile and seem to be interested in you. I know it's because we're foreign and therefore odd! But when you're away from it, you miss it. I love Scotland, too, of course. My parents are there, and my flat and job, and my new friends, but it's tame compared with Cairo.' Marian was nodding. 'I'm so glad I came.'

'So you're off to Sharm for a day or two?'

'Yes. Ryan has booked air tickets and a hotel for three nights.'

'Have you been there before?'

'No. Went to St Katherine's Monastery and climbed to the top of Sinai – *before* all the upheaval, but I haven't been any further south.'

'It has a different feel. There's an old village area, pretty and characterful in an oldy-worldy sort of way, but the resort is very relaxing. You can sit on the beach or by the pool in your bikini and no one stares at you. The sea is pale turquoise, and the fish! You wouldn't believe the tropical fish! They look artificial – those brilliant colours – pink with yellow spots – like something out of a Disney cartoon, but they're *real!* Can you snorkel?'

'I've never tried, but I'd like to have a go. I'm a confident swimmer. Ryan says you can hire the equipment.'

'Yes, you can. Watch out for the coral. It's beautiful, but if you catch your feet or your knees on it, it'll rip your flesh to shreds.' She pulled her skirt above her knee to reveal a scar, white now, but jagged.

Heather grimaced.

'It's difficult to judge depth when you're snorkelling.'

'Yeah. Thanks for the warning.' Heather looked down and took some sips of her chocolate. When she looked up again, Marian was watching her.

'And Heather? As for the other thing – take it slowly. From what you've said, I'd infer that there's more at stake with Ryan now. You don't have to make any hasty decisions. It's true that you're not a teenager any more, but your life is still ahead of you. Don't rush into anything.'

Heather nodded. Parental advice was easier to take

from Marian than from either parent. Maybe Marian had made mistakes in the past – hadn't everyone? But Heather didn't know about Marian's mistakes. Her parents' mistakes were glaringly obvious.

She slept well, and packed some of her things in a small bag borrowed from Marian, and left the rest in Marian's guest room.

Sharm El Sheikh kept its promises. The sky was unreservedly blue, the gentle November warmth caressed their skin, the sea and the fish were just as Marian had described them.

At Heather's request, Ryan had booked single rooms for the two of them, and she loved him for it. He was proving to be the perfect gentleman. He deferred to her every preference, he was sensitive and he listened. Heather remembered what Marjorie had said, and smiled.

'I have one request,' he said with uncharacteristic diffidence. She looked up, surprised. 'Could we turn our phones off? Let's give this holiday our undivided attention.' Heather complied willingly. The clinic would carry on fine without her. Pa, Beth, Jem and The Wire would look out for each other. Marian and Manuel knew where they were. There was nothing to tie them down.

They unpacked briefly, then went for a swim, deciding to leave snorkelling until the following day. There was a wooden jetty – a walkway – from the beach to the point where the land suddenly shelved and real swimming or snorkelling could begin. But Heather and Ryan chose, instead, to wade out the hundred metres or so among the Disney cartoon fish, where the water was tepid and crystal clear. They held hands and laughed at the fish that came to look at their feet, then swooshed away, their curiosity satisfied. Then the jetty ended in a platform, the water was suddenly unfathomable and instantly colder, and they launched themselves beyond the platform for a brisk swim. Shivering after a few minutes, they agreed to walk back through the shallow water, and the lowering sun soon warmed their skin and dried their swimsuits.

After a quick shower they ambled along the beach and watched the setting sun sink rapidly into the sea. 'I always forget how quickly the sun sets here,' Heather said.

'Yep. There's virtually no dusk.'

'In Scotland in the middle of summer, it's light until at least ten o'clock, then dusk goes on and on. In fact, it never really gets properly dark. Then it's light again by about four.'

'Land of the midnight sun.'

'That usually means somewhere in Scandinavia – Norway or Finland or somewhere in the Arctic Circle…' She caught his slow smile and was embarrassed. 'Of course, you know that.' He carried his vast general knowledge lightly. 'But Scotland in summer is good enough.'

'You love it, huh?'

Heather paused. Was this a loaded question? Did he want to know whether she was willing to leave her homeland? She'd already faced this question once, when she decided to go to Egypt and learn Arabic. But no, at that time, she hadn't thought about missing Scotland, just about leaving the morass of her parents' miseries, and of aiming to make her own fresh start. Besides, Egypt was new, then, and exotic.

They were standing still, watching the spot where the sun had been. His arm round her shoulders made her feel secure, protected. He was tall, broad-shouldered, safe. He turned her small chin towards him with his big hand, and his questing kiss absolved her from answering.

Dinner was buffet style, but the choice was almost overwhelming. They decided to try a little of everything. There were plenty of beef, lamb and chicken dishes, and varieties of fish that Heather had never heard of. There were wonderfully colourful salads and cooked vegetables and dozens of sauces. Heather only drew the line at squid. 'What, you don't like squid?' Ryan teased, feigning shock and disappointment. He laughed hard when she voiced her fear of those tentacles fixing on her tongue.

It was a perfect end to a perfect day, and after dinner Heather said she'd like to stroll along the beach in the moonlight. She wanted to avoid the two of them being together in one of their rooms at the end of the evening. What was wrong with her? He was tall, attractive, generous, caring and yes! - they *did* speak the same language. She giggled momentarily, and he looked down at her questioningly. She looked away and nestled into his side.

A sudden memory came to her, of Beth's father's slippers, partially hidden under an armchair in the sitting room at Beth's house. They were familiar, worn, comfortable and empty.

Heather

Sharm El Sheikh

November 2012

The following morning, after a buffet breakfast of a thousand choices out on the terrace, Ryan and Heather went snorkelling. Careful to leave valuables in their rooms, they walked along the beach to the hut from which they hired snorkels and masks, then left their towels, flip-flops and T-shirts in a heap on the sand. They decided against hiring wet suits. The water was no colder than the North Sea during a Scottish heat wave.

They swam together, never too far from the wooden platform, while Heather got the hang of using the snorkel. Due to the political unrest and the out-of-season chill of the water, they had the entire ocean to themselves. An undreamed-of fairytale realm of colours, textures and secret life lay underneath them. From time to time they returned to the knee-deep water to squint into the brilliant blue sky and allow the sun to warm them, before returning to the silent, constantly changing wonderworld around the coral.

At last, sated by beauty and incredulity, they returned the equipment and lay on the sand, eyes closed against the brightness, soaking up the warmth. Heather dropped off to sleep, and when she next opened her eyes, she was under the shade of a beach umbrella. Ryan was propped up on one elbow, looking at her. 'Didn't want that fair Scottish skin to burn,' he said.

'Thanks. But my skin's a quarter Portuguese. My mother's father was from Lisbon. It's my father who has to dive into the shade as soon as the temperature nears twenty!'

'So that explains your Mediterranean look.' He bent over to kiss her lips lightly. 'You hungry?'

'Starving.'

'We can eat at that beach café. We'd better steer clear of the salad, but as long as we have something cooked, we'll avoid the bugs. I'll run up to the hotel and get some money.'

While he was gone, Heather stood up, brushed off some of the sand and went to stand in the shallow water. Again she marvelled at the crystal clear sea and the exquisite colours. Music was playing unobtrusively at the beach café, but apart from that it was quiet and peaceful. There was no honking of car horns, no exuberant greeting or sudden angry eruption, no signs, really that they were in Egypt.

Holiday romances are notoriously unreal and unreliable. But this wasn't a holiday romance. This was a friendship – a relationship? – that had stood firm through the worst – even because of the worst. She and Ryan had remained faithful within this friendship for over a year. Heather had told him about Beth, about the new business and her part in it. She'd explained how her father, eventually exonerated after a high school student's attempt at blackmail, had decided he liked research and writing, and had taken early retirement.

Ryan told her how his mother had been diagnosed with breast cancer, how his little sister had failed an all-important exam and had slid into depression and how he was undecided about his future career. This was no flash-in-the-pan, nor love at first sight. This should be mature, wise, informed decision time.

Heather looked up. A tiny wispy cloud had covered the sun, but it left as soon as it had arrived. Ryan was returning at a jog. His golden skin took the sun easily. He didn't seem to go red or blotchy the way some fair-haired people did. She left the water and went to join him. 'What are you grinning for?'

'There was some middle-aged guy at reception. I guess he was British. He was over-dressed – jeans with an ironed crease, long-sleeved shirt and leather shoes. He was quite agitated.'

'So you reckon he was British, eh?' Heather said with mock disgust. 'You mean he wasn't some American bum with a baseball cap, psychedelic Bermuda shorts and three cameras slung around his neck?'

'Touché! Now come and choose your fodder.'

They settled under the beach umbrella with pitta breads stuffed with shredded spicy beef, and with tubs of tahini and hummus between them, while the warmth, the peace and the beauty stretched out all around them.

'Thank you,' she said suddenly.

'What for?'

'You know.'

'No I don't. Tell me.'

'For everything. For arranging this holiday. For sticking by me. For being such a good friend. For...'

'Madam! Miss McLuskie...' A smart uniformed receptionist from the hotel was walking briskly across the sand towards them. 'Please to come. There is someone in hotel who wish to see you. Please to come.'

'What, now? Who?' Heather demanded.

'Man, from England. Please to come.'

Ryan and Heather hastily pulled T-shirts over their swimsuits and gathered up towels and the remains of their lunch. The receptionist was already walking back to the hotel.

'Must be a mistake,' Heather said, though her heart was already beating too fast and she was sweating lightly.

Perched uncomfortably on the edge of an armchair in reception was an unmistakable figure. 'It's the guy I saw earlier, the British guy,' Ryan said.

Heather stood still, rigid and incredulous.

'What's the matter?' Ryan took her hand and spoke quietly.

She pulled her hand away. 'It's my father!' she spat.

'Heather, darling! I've been trying to reach you...' Pa got up instantly, his arms outstretched in greeting and moved towards her.

She took a step backwards. 'What the hell are you doing here? What gives you the right to track me down, to dog my steps? I'm twenty-five, Pa, not a child, not a teenager. You agreed to my coming, encouraged me, even. How on earth did you find me? How *dare* you come and ruin my holiday!' Her voice was rising and Ryan put a firm hand on her shoulder and steered her back outside, away from the mystified stares of the receptionists and of a young couple crossing the foyer. Her father dropped his arms to his sides and followed Ryan and Heather outside.

'What's the matter?' she fumed. 'Don't you trust me? You're a fine one to judge trust! Why didn't you try to stop me coming, if that's how you feel? You were all for it. You even mentioned me visiting Sharm. What did you think I was going to do? Spend every day in a museum? Research the history of the revolution? You didn't even...'

'Shh, Heather. It's okay, honey. Just take a breath for a moment.' Ryan stepped towards Gregor. 'Good afternoon, sir. I'm Ryan Jefferson. Pleased to meet you, though sorry about...' He waved a hand vaguely towards Heather and the foyer. 'Maybe we could sit down together in the hotel bar? Can I buy you a beer?'

'Thank you. That would be welcome. It's warmer than I thought. I reckoned that in November...'

'Didn't do your homework, Pa!' Heather muttered, not looking at him. 'We're a long way south, remember?'

They were the only people in the bar. Ryan bought beers for himself and her father, and a fruit juice for her. She opened her mouth to remonstrate - she'd have liked a white wine – but her anger, already beginning to defuse, was not directed towards Ryan. The room was comfortably air-conditioned. They settled in armchairs, Ryan with his hand on the arm of Heather's chair, without actually touching her.

'I've been trying to reach you,' Pa said. 'Tried your mobile for two days. Knew you were in Sharm. I tracked down Marian from the Embassy, and she told me the name of the hotel. Just arrived here early this afternoon...'

'I can see that,' Heather said.

Now Ryan touched her arm briefly. 'Is everything all right, sir?' he asked. 'Back home...'

'Thanks, son. Yes, all fine. It's just that...'

'What's happened, Pa? Is it Beth? Is she... Has she...?'

'She's fine, love. Hunky dory. She and Jem and The Wire – business is booming.'

Heather's thumping heart, and see-sawing anger and anxiety were taking their toll. Suddenly she felt exhausted. She sighed, and in a voice that was almost a whisper, she asked, 'Then what are you doing here, Pa?'

Her father took a long draught and leaned forward in his chair.

Gregor

Sharm El Sheikh

November 2012

Gregor takes a deep breath, drinks from his rather bland but welcome beer and stalls for time. He should have anticipated such an outburst from his little Mediterranean fireball. So she hasn't quite forgiven him. Her anger towards him, and her anxiety about life in general and Beth in particular, are still lurking just below the surface. And as for this polite, deferential, handsome American, he seems too good to be true.

'I'm really sorry to take you both by surprise. And yes, I recognise that I'm overdressed, but I remembered your comments about cultural sensitivity, sweetheart, so I thought shorts would be a bit informal. Didn't realise that resorts were so non-conforming. When I manage to check in to a room I'll change into a lighter shirt.'

He needs to gain a hearing, but first he'll aim to sweep away the debris of triviality and misunderstanding and inject a little humour or at least a lighter touch. 'Seems you've found yourselves a bit of paradise here – a wee slice of Shangri La. Excellent choice.'

He clears his throat. 'I have no intention of raining on your parade, or being an uninvited extra, but there's an idea I need to run by both of you.' He drains his glass gratefully. Heather is still glowering at him, sitting rigidly and ignoring Ryan's proximity. He must have embarrassed her immeasurably, but what could he do? Ryan's expression is open, and Gregor construes him as curious but cautious.

He addresses his first comment to Ryan. 'I imagine Heather has told you about her friend Beth Gomersall and the terrible problems she's been through.'

Ryan nods.

'I think this trip is a much-needed break for Heather after an anxious time of trying to shore up Beth and help her to face her various tragedies...'

'I understand that you've had a considerable hand in helping, too, sir.'

'Gregor, please.'

'Yes sir – Gregor.'

'Has she also told you that I'm a historian?' From Ryan's hastily concealed smile, Gregor infers that the word *boring* has not escaped the telling. 'I'm passionate about history. It teaches us so much about human nature – psychology, sociology and religion, about inherited cultural expectations, about education, criminal activity, the judicial system, as well as...'

'Pa *please!*' Heather scowls, but Ryan is grinning and Gregor returns his smile. At last there's the reluctant ghost of amusement from Heather.

'I'm particularly interested in family trees. I've delved into ours quite a bit, and into Heather's mother's Portuguese background – fascinating.'

'*Pa!*'

Gregor drops his tone of voice. 'Recently, I've been researching Beth's family tree.' He has all of Heather's attention now. 'It wasn't difficult to make a start. Gomersall is an unusual name, after all, and she said she was born in Edinburgh. I just couldn't quite believe that she has no relatives except this aunt, uncle and cousin currently in Australia.'

'And does she?' Heather is leaning forward, digging her nails into the arms of the chair.

'Not does, but did.'

Heather leans back, disappointed, and says dully, 'Well, we know her mother died and that her maternal grandparents broke off contact because they blamed Beth's dad for the car accident. They lost their only daughter, after all.'

Gregor clears his throat and prepares to deliver his earth-shattering news. 'Her family tree was much easier to trace than I imagined. The events are much more recent. If I'd been sure, I'd have told you earlier, before you came. Thing is, she also had twin brothers, Ashley and Aidan. They were born four years before Beth was. When Beth was a baby the family came on holiday here, to Sharm. There was a motor boat accident. Aidan's body was washed up some ten miles away down the coast, but Ashley's was never discovered.'

Heather has gone very pale, now, despite the tan. At last she reaches for Ryan's willing hand. 'How do you know?' she demands. 'Does Beth know? Why didn't she tell us?'

'I imagine Beth has no idea. She was less than a year old, and from what we've gathered from her, her family wasn't one to divulge secrets or feelings easily, if at all. I started off with the council's record of births, marriages and deaths. I didn't have to go very far, because this is current generation stuff. Once I found out about Aidan's death in Egypt, I went to newspaper archives. I reckoned a story like that would have made it into the local rag, if not the nationals: *Scottish family in Egyptian boat accident!*'

'And was it?'

'Yes. But stories like that are quickly brushed aside when the next heart-wrenching account comes along. And as for local reporting, a child's life isn't regarded in quite the same way in Egypt, especially here, so far from the capital.'

Ryan looks offended. 'Ah, sir – Gregor – the people here hold great value in…'

'No, I don't mean to be disparaging at all. It's just that Egypt is a big place, the police force back then was small and under-resourced, and one foreign child is naturally the concern of foreigners, not local people. Besides, the nuclear family isn't regarded in the same way here. Responsibility is shared. Children are easily adopted by any relative or even random family. Africans and Arabs will often use the word *brother* when they really mean second-cousin-once-removed, but families here are much more extended, especially in the villages. You've heard that saying *It takes a village to bring up a child*.' Ryan nods but Heather is staring at Gregor, her expression unreadable.

'But if Ashley was still alive, Beth's parents would surely have searched and searched until they found him. Like Madeleine McCann's parents.'

Gregor waits for a beat, and Heather answers her own question. 'They never found her.'

'Madeleine who?' Ryan looks from Heather to Gregor.

'In 2007 a three-year-old British girl disappeared from a holiday apartment in Portugal,' Gregor explains. 'Her parents and hundreds of police and well-wishers mounted a multi-million pound search that went on for years, but no one turned up anything at all. They don't know whether she was kidnapped, murdered, or whatever.'

'In Portugal?'

'Aye. Europe. In a well-known holiday destination.'

'But this is a well-known holiday destination,' Heather objected.

'Not so much back then. They were staying just a bit off the beaten track, a bit south of here.'

'Ras Mohammed?' Ryan asks.

'Not quite that far, but remember this was almost twenty years ago, and everything was a bit less sophisticated. Even Sharm wasn't known then as it is now.'

'But where does that leave us, Pa? There's nothing we can do about it.' At last Heather is on side.

'Well, we could do worse than take a drive down to Ras Umm Saeed, wander round the village a bit, chat to the locals.'

'Chat to the locals? *Pa!* What do you think this is? A Rose Street pub on a Saturday night?' Heather's decibels have risen again, but this time Ryan steps in.

'Sure thing. I'm up for that.' He looks sideways at Heather. 'Besides, I'd welcome some Arabic practice! I'm in Level 5 now, you know.' She grins. 'All right, brain box. You can do the chatting. Let's do it.'

Heather

Sharm El Sheikh

November 2012

Ryan arranged with one of the hotel receptionists for a taxi for the following day. They resisted the allure of the coral and made an early start along less frequented roads towards local fishing villages. At a distance, the first village was picturesque – poor but with a relaxed, centuries-old pace of life. Ryan got out of the car to ask a local fisherman about motor boats. Yellowing gap-toothed grin met brilliant-white American smile. With much ardent gesticulating the Egyptian advised him to try the resorts. When he began to explain that they didn't want a ride, but to find out if anyone remembered a motor boat accident some years ago, he drew a total blank.

Ryan got back into the car. 'Nada, I'm afraid. Niente. Reckon he was disappointed that we didn't just want to enjoy what his country has to offer. He may have been a fisherman, but he knows Egypt subsists on tourism.'

The same conversation was repeated in village after village all along the coast. They stopped twice for drinks and snacks, but Heather began to jiggle with impatience and inactivity and Pa complained briefly that his long legs were stiff. In the late afternoon they decided to call it a day and return to the hotel. The return journey, on a faster main road, was mercifully shorter.

'What do y'all want to do tomorrow?' Ryan asked after their evening meal. 'We could keep trying or…'

Heather sighed. She and Pa looked at each other.

What was he thinking? He'd come all this way. Hell, *she'd* come all this way - for a holiday. A potentially life-changing holiday. Which was more important, to discover whether Beth had a brother, or to find out whether Ryan was her future? In the light of either possibility, the discomfort of another day of dusty, boring road travel paled into insignificance.

'What do you reckon, Pa? Keep trying, at least for one more day?'

He leaned forward and planted a kiss on the top of her head. A good decision, then.

'Could you bear it, Ryan? One more day?'

'Yep, of course. No problem. It'll give me more good Arabic conversation, after all.'

How kind, how positive he was. She loved him for it.

'Well, I don't know about you two young people, but I'm tired. I'm going to retire early. See you at breakfast. Eight o'clock?'

How tactful. 'Goodnight Pa.'

'Goodnight sir – Gregor.'

Ryan went to the desk to book a car for the next day. Later they strolled along the beach. The moon was low and almost full. Silvery reflections played on gently lapping waves. Amazing how life could be transformed in a matter of months. Her pa was a good man after all. Not perfect, but good enough.

Beth, sweet Beth, had emerged from the abyss, made friends and started a business, brother or no brother. And Ryan – he must be the kindest, most helpful, understanding, patient guy she could ever wish to meet. And she believed he was hers – for the taking. So why did that conversation with

Beth about chemistry mar her waking hours and plague what should have been her sleeping hours?

Breakfast was a strained affair. The taxi company had sent a different driver – an ill-humoured one. Maybe he'd been warned by his colleague about their strange, apparently fruitless requests.

They arrived at yesterday's stopping point quickly, due to the fast road, and then began again the trail from coastal village to village, but this time, at Ryan's suggestion, they all got out of the car at each place and ordered glasses of tea at a roadside tea shop. 'Relationships always score over enquiries here. We're not fixing on interrogating the locals, just on being friendly.'

In most villages, fishing boats were tied up to rocks or trees along the shore, but the third village boasted something of a harbour, with a crumbling jetty. The smell of sea salt and fish mingled with strong Arabic coffee.

The three of them settled unhurriedly at a café table and resumed their roles of relaxed tourists with time to spare and an interest in local history. Ryan talked with the elderly waiter about the fishing industry, the tragedy of the country's political situation, the beauty of the scenery.

Heather could at least follow, if not join in. She looked round. At a neighbouring table two old men wearing traditional cotton galabeyas were passing the time of day with a game of backgammon.

Three young jeans-clad locals, laughing over something on a mobile phone, looked up and came over to join them. 'Hello. Welcome in Egypt. Where you from?'

'Amreeka,' Ryan replied, pointing to himself, and they

nodded, 'and Scotlanda.' This seemed to arouse more interest. All three turned their attention to herself and pa.

'You like Egypt?'

'Oh yes,' they chorused, and Heather added, 'Gameel awy. *Very beautiful.*'

The young men's English was soon exhausted, so Ryan continued in Arabic as they grinned and nodded. Occasionally there was a brief burst of laughter, and sometimes they clapped once with delight. At first Heather could follow most of the conversation, but eventually she lost the thread. Pa's eyes glazed over.

Suddenly the young guys became serious. Real discussion replaced banter. The two older men stopped their game. One of them hissed something to the young men. The old waiter called to the proprietor of a small vegetable stall between the harbour and the road. A quick incomprehensible interchange followed. Heather willed herself to remember vocabulary, expressions, even the non-verbal signals she'd learned.

The older men turned their chairs, and Ryan moved his own chair to make a space for them to join them. One of them growled something at the waiter. The young guys glanced anxiously at one another.

Heather's neck prickled. She was, of course, the only female, but there was something more, something that made it difficult to look casual.

Pa was alert again, glancing from speaker to speaker. 'What's going on?' he murmured to Heather.

'Dinnae ken,' she whispered back.

'Keep smiling,' Ryan told them. 'I think something's going on.'

Heather and Pa sipped their glasses of tea. The driver

leaned against the café wall for a smoke. His posture was relaxed, but his eyes were alight with curiosity.

Ryan's smile was forced. He was leaning forward in his chair. Heather caught occasional crucial words – boat – accident – foreign family. The conversation became faster, more urgent, the words less intelligible. She tried to stop her knee jiggling.

Finally she caught Ryan's eye. He leaned back and grinned. His warm presence, jovial manner and American accent began to thaw the strained atmosphere. He drew out his wallet again. This time he took out not money, but photos – four photos, which he distributed to the men.

'This is my home,' he explained in Arabic that Heather could understand. She caught a glimpse of the pictures – American streets with Cadillacs, the Statue of Liberty, the White House and a Hollywood film set.

The men were delighted, and good humour returned in full measure. With many greetings, hand-shaking and toothy grins the Egyptians wished them well, the three of them took their leave while their driver stubbed out his cigarette and they all returned to the car. 'Homeland pictures,' Ryan murmured to Heather as they got in. 'It's an ice-breaker they taught us at the language school. First time I've been able to use it!'

'Fein? *Where?'* the driver asked.

'Meshi, meshi. Al atoul. *Straight on,'* Ryan indicated, waving his hand. Once the café was out of sight, Ryan asked the driver to pull over under the shade of a clump of trees growing beside the road. 'One moment, please.'

He got out of the car and signalled Heather and Pa to do the same. A distant call to prayer reached them on a breeze that rattled the date palms.

Ryan took a deep breath. 'Well! That sure produced more than I expected. More than I could even have hoped.'

'What? *What!*' Heather squeaked.

'They said that there was a young guy who was brought up in a neighbouring village. You'll have noticed the first guys looked to be in their mid-twenties. They remembered there was a boy who was whiter – lighter-skinned than most of them. You know how, generally, the further south you go in Egypt, the darker the people's skins?'

'Yeah.'

'Well, there was a guy – they called him a *whitey* - who was very clever at school. They said he looked like he was from Cairo – black hair but light skin. His name was Ashraf Daoud.'

'Ashraf… Ashley,' Heather whispered.

'Right! But in Arabic, the name Ashraf Daoud is about as common as – as – Andrew Davies. They said that in school his English was much better than theirs – though of course I told them how good theirs was!' Heather nodded impatiently. 'Then he went to study medicine somewhere in Scotland. Did you notice that they knew the word Scotland?'

'Yes. I sort of thought that was unusual, especially in a village. Even in Cairo they didn't always know it. Sometimes people used to ask if it was somewhere in England!'

Pa snorted.

'Don't take the hump, Pa. It happens.'

But he stood up straighter. 'Could've been Edinburgh. There's an excellent school of medicine and they do train overseas students.'

'But what about his family? Did he have brothers and sisters? Were they white, too?'

'The young guys didn't talk about that. I asked if they

had any memory of a boat accident about twenty years ago. Of course, those younger guys would've been too young to remember, but the older two said something to them that I couldn't catch – like, warnin' them off, or something. There was some sort of undercurrent.'

Heather shivered. 'Yeah. I could feel it.'

'But every coastal community has boating accidents,' Pa observed.

'Yes, but you'd think they would've remembered one where a foreign family was involved,' Heather objected.

'Yeah. Well, whatever – they weren't divulging anything about that. Also, the name Daoud – David – is a Coptic Christian name, and all those guys were Muslims, so they hadn't naturally mingled with the Daoud family very much. I was working hard to keep the atmosphere friendly. They didn't like my prying. There's a world of difference between sociable interest and vested curiosity. I was having to act a part.'

'And you did it brilliantly,' Heather said, giving him a quick peck.

'I wonder,' Pa said, 'whether we could try to track down the family?'

'Hmm. I'll put it to the driver,' Ryan said. 'But I'll have to explain a bit to him about why and who and so forth.' So they returned to the car, and in measured Arabic, he launched into a truncated version of their quest.

The driver was scowling. His reply didn't sound positive. 'He says he doesn't know the area,' Ryan explained, 'and I think he's also a bit wary of trying to track down a Christian family for a car load of crazy foreigners. He assumes we're Christians, too, and he'd be the only Muslim.'

'What's he worried about?' Pa asked, frowning.

'Oh, Pa, you should understand this from a long-term historical perspective. And with the recent political upheavals everything's more edgy.'

But it must have been hard for Pa, not understanding any Arabic at all, and after all, it was *his* quest.

'Yeah,' Ryan agreed. 'Anything may seem like a veiled threat, sir. They expect foreigners just to want to sit on the beach or snorkel.'

They seemed to have reached an impasse. 'I'm starving,' Heather said. 'Ryan, will you ask the driver if he knows a good restaurant?' Heather glanced at her watch. Four o'clock. Egyptian lunchtime.

The driver cheered up and pulled out back on to the road. The restaurant he chose was clearly one that set its cap at foreigners. The dining area was outside, behind the restaurant building, enclosed by lovely hibiscus and bougainvillea hedges. An appetising smell of fried kofta with cumin wafted from the kitchen. The waiters spoke passable English, the tables were already laid with clean white cloths, glasses and cutlery, while a little waterfall splashed merrily from a picturesque artificial rock formation in the middle of the terrace.

'I've got an idea,' Heather announced once the meal was finished and they waited for coffee. 'Marjorie's daughter – you know, my colleague, Marjorie, at the clinic, well, her daughter works in admin at the University. Maybe she could look up the records of international students who studied in the medical school about, say, six or seven years ago? It's not like we're looking for John Smith. Or – or Andrew Davies.' She grinned at Ryan. 'A foreign name might be easier to find.'

'It sure is worth a try,' Ryan conceded. 'Anyway, I think we've done as much as we can here and we're all a bit weary. Can you snorkel, Gregor?'

Heather looked at Pa with interest.

'Certainly.'

'Pa! You've never been snorkelling!'

'Sweetheart, your ma and I went snorkelling in Eilat before you were even a good idea!'

Heather

Cairo

November 2012

Back at the resort, Pa and Ryan went snorkelling, but Heather, with mounting excitement, preferred to start texting and trying to phone first Marjorie, then Marjorie's daughter. The calls were expensive, but more fruitful than she dared imagine. She took a hurried shower and went to seek out Pa and Ryan in the bar before their evening meal. They were relaxed and apparently enjoying each other's company. Should she delay interrupting them? But she couldn't contain her excitement and burst in on their conversation. 'There *was* a guy called Ashraf Daoud who studied Medicine at Edinburgh!'

Pa leapt up and gave her a hug, before pulling up a chair for her to join them. 'And?' he said.

'He returned to Egypt after qualifying.'

'Ah. So where does that leave us? Egypt's a big place.'

'Not so big,' Ryan said, scratching his stubble thoughtfully. 'He'll have gone to work in one of the main Cairo hospitals to gain some experience, even if he aims to end up in Upper Egypt. I guess we could visit those and find out who's on the staff roll.'

'Well, I seem to remember you two were booked to fly back to Cairo tomorrow anyway, and I've got an open ticket, so we'd better do it. We can't give up at this stage, especially when the trail's still hot.'

'She's... she must be a quite some girl, this Beth,' Ryan observed. Heather looked at him. He was staring thoughtfully into his empty glass. She was suddenly struck by a searing guilt. She and her father had completely sabotaged this trip, which was meant to be a quiet, possibly romantic one for her and Ryan, just the two of them together. He had been unreservedly polite and friendly to her pa, he had acted as their guide and interpreter, he hadn't baulked at their change of plans, their enthusiasm or dogged determination. But what was Beth to him? Nothing.

'Oh, Ryan, I'm so sorry,' Heather said, mortified. She took his hand and pressed her lips to it. 'She *is* quite some girl! She's special. She has become like a sister to me, and I think we both...' she glanced at Pa, '... feel kind of responsible for her because she just doesn't have anyone else. And if we could discover that she *does* have someone else... if she *does* have a brother who's living...'

'Have y'all thought about how they both might react? I mean, neither of them had any idea, if what you believe is right, and they're living in different continents. He has a firm job and her business is just getting established. How's it all gonna work out? If it's true?'

The final evening buffet was a subdued affair. Heather's excitement had turned to turmoil. She looked at all those exquisite buffet dishes, the salads and the desserts, and felt queasy. She tried not to mention Beth during the meal, but only to talk about subjects that pertained to Ryan – his language learning, his home town, his family. She steered the conversation on to Pa's research, Ryan's interest in international affairs, and his possible career trajectory. She remembered the photos on Ryan's fridge and asked after his sister and brother. She noticed he was tactfully avoiding the

251

family topic on her side. He'd remembered her parents were divorced. But the conversation was stilted: polite, measured, neutral.

Back in Cairo, Ryan offered accommodation at his apartment for Gregor. 'I'll sleep on the sofa,' he said. 'You can have my room.' But Gregor insisted on booking into a simple hotel in Zamalek, while Heather returned to Marian's and recounted the whole saga.

The three of them agreed to meet up the next morning and take a taxi to one of the hospitals. But during the night, that dreadful, familiar Egyptian complaint, the griping stomach cramps, followed by a long time spent in the bathroom, overtook Heather. *Pharaoh's revenge,* they used to call it. Hour by painful hour the interminable night crawled by, until at last Heather heard Marian moving about, and indulged in her sympathy and her ministrations of weak black tea and tried and trusted medication. Her worst fear was that Ryan and Pa had it as well, though she recalled that she had eaten a different meal from them on the plane. A quick phone call put her mind at rest, and her gratitude and admiration for Ryan moved up yet another notch when he insisted on trekking round hospitals with her father while she stayed in bed and recovered.

Full of apologies, Marian said she had an appointment to keep, but she made Heather some plain toast before she went, and left her a supply of water, tea in a flask and a phone number.

Alone in the flat, Heather succumbed to a few tears of weakness and disappointment, before pulling herself together enough to shower and put some clothes on.

She knew that Pa and Ryan were due to start at the Anglo-American Hospital, because it was nearby. 'No luck at A-A,' Ryan's first text read. 'Continuing to Dar El-Fouad. Hope u feel btr.' She was, indeed, a little better, but yesterday's excitement had morphed into today's terror that, after all this raised hope, her pa's expensive trip, and hers and Ryan's aborted one, there may be no pot of gold at the end of the rainbow. Dar El-Fouad was in Sixth of October City – an expanding suburb and a long taxi ride. She tried to talk herself down from her self-made pinnacle of breathless expectation and settle to an infinity of waiting.

She went to the window and watched the five-ways junction, ingesting and disgorging vehicles. It was unwise to stop at red lights in Cairo. The car behind would bump into you, or at least honk with incredulity. There was no such thing as rush hour in the city traffic. At any hour of the day there could be gridlock. Rushing was impossible. Cars, buses, trucks and vans nudged, insinuated, crept and finally, mercilessly, gained a few metres on their neighbours.

The city was like a child who had delved, willy-nilly, into the dressing-up chest: its antique cloak was rich, dusty but bejewelled with the shimmering achievements of its regal past. Its brown leather moccasins were worn and weary, but its head gear, its arrogant crown, demanded subservience. This is not Africa, not the Middle East: this is Egypt, Mother of the Earth.

Heather opened a bag of crisps and ate a few. She drank some more tea and flicked through a couple of Marian's books. Finally she closed her eyes and slept on the sofa.

When she woke up, it was already dusk. She checked her phone: no further texts. She switched on the television news: President Morsi had announced authority over the courts, thereby removing any accountability of his own. His reasoning? – the courts were full of Moubarak appointees. *A brazen power-grab,* the journalists called it.

Israel had killed a Hamas commander in an attack in Gaza, and Lady Gaga had topped the UK charts again. At last, with profound gratitude, Heather heard Marian's key in the door.

'Look who I found wandering the street!' Marian greeted her, and was closely followed by Ryan and Pa. A few more tears of relief and weakness ensued, and while Marian busied herself producing first cold drinks, then tea and cookies, Ryan and Pa collapsed, hot and tired, on to the sofa.

Despite their exhaustion, there was an optimistic buoyancy. 'C'mon then, tell!' she insisted.

'The trail is indeed still hot,' Pa said. 'In fact, I think we can claim a successful day's work.'

'We started at the Anglo-American hospital,' Ryan began. 'There was a Sudanese receptionist who looked up staff records, both current and going back a few years, but she couldn't find Ashraf Daoud.'

'They were friendly and helpful,' Pa interrupted. 'I see what you mean about relationships coming first. They were certainly willing to chat.'

'So we took another taxi to Dar El-Fouad. That was a different experience. Like gettin' blood out of a stone.'

'But it might just have been that we arrived on a busy day.'

'Yeah. There had been a car accident.'

'But in the end, they said they didn't know any Ashraf Daoud on the staff at present,' Pa finished.

'So we went on to Qasr Al Aini,' Ryan continued.

'And there...' he paused, as if for dramatic effect, and grinned at Heather, who pounced on him and pretended to shake his broad shoulders.

'Ryan, pleeease!'

'And there we reckon we struck gold. There was a doctor called Ashraf Daoud. They paged him from reception and asked us to wait a while.'

'Can you imagine?' Pa added, 'Suppose we'd interrupted a busy doctor on his rounds, with a wild goose chase!'

'But he came eventually, very curious to know what we wanted. We must've looked odd – two white foreigners, not sick or injured – demanding to speak to a random Egyptian doctor! But he wasn't random. Sure enough, he's paler skinned than most Egyptians. He has thick dark hair, but he has kind of blue eyes! He *does* come from the Sharm El Sheikh area and he *did* train in Edinburgh.' Ryan sat back with a kind of satisfaction.

'But what about his family in Sharm? What about his childhood?' Heather insisted.

'Interestingly, he couldn't remember his very early childhood,' Pa said. 'He said he has four older sisters. His parents aren't very wealthy, but very proud of him. He won a scholarship to study in Edinburgh. He said he loved the city, but Egypt is his home, even though he doesn't get back down south to see his family very often.'

'So... where do we go from here?' Heather asked.

'Doctor Ashraf couldn't stay with us for long. He was on duty, and there were lots of admissions. *But...* he's off duty tomorrow at 6 o'clock, so we're meeting him for dinner.'

'Six in the *evening*?' Heather said stupidly.

'*Dinner*, sweetheart,' Pa said with a smile.

'But I can't wait that long!' Heather wailed.

'I ... I ought to go back to language class tomorrow,' Ryan said quietly.

'But you can join us for dinner,' Heather insisted.

'You don't really need me. Dr Ashraf speaks excellent English, and you'll have no problem finding a taxi into town.'

'But Ryan, I came here to... well, there were lots of places and people I wanted to see... but I came to see *you*...' Heather leaned into him and squeezed his arm.

'Yeah, it's been great,' Ryan said quietly, and the past tense was not lost on Heather.

Marian reappeared and read the atmosphere. 'A bit more rest for you, young lady,' she said. Pa and Ryan agreed to leave, stopping briefly for a sandwich on their way, while Marian offered to make scrambled egg for herself and Heather.

As soon as they had left, Heather's tears began again in earnest. 'Why can't I be friendly with a guy without hurting him?' she sobbed. 'First Tony, now Ryan.' Marian handed her tissues, and they sat for a while.

'I don't think you can put *those* two in the same category. I know you feel guilty about Tony, but he was his own man, even if he was a bit of a lad. From what you've told me, I don't think you could ever have tamed him in a way that would've been satisfactory to both of you. It was good for each of you to have a companion here in Cairo, but you'd have been incompatible long-term. As for Ryan...'

Heather stopped crying to hear what Marian had to say about Ryan. She had felt very secure having Ryan, Marian and Pa in the same room together. If Beth had been there, the circle would have been almost complete, but then there was Jem, and his brother, and Marjorie, and Ma, and suddenly Heather felt overwhelmed. So many good people were part of her life, and what contribution was she making to any of them?

'As for Ryan?' she prompted.

Marian paused a moment, then said, 'Ryan is a very good man. He's extremely kind and thoughtful, he's generous and unselfish. He's a bit indecisive career-wise at the moment, but he'll get there. But...'

'But what?'

'How would you feel about becoming middle-aged and growing old with him?'

Heather was silent. How to phrase this answer? It wasn't a surprise question. She'd thought about it many times. That's what this trip had been about. It was so much more than catching up with old friends. It went well beyond reminiscing about language learning in Cairo, or about a romantic break in a beach resort. She'd had a lovely time. Ryan's loving care had certainly not gone unnoticed or unappreciated. But...

'When I'm with Ryan,' she began slowly, 'I'm already old.' The tears flowed again, then, and Marian held her for a long time until finally she leaned back, blew her nose and murmured, 'Sorry, I always seem to be abusing your hospitality.'

'Nonsense,' Marian said brusquely. 'That's what I'm here for – to be useful when needed.'

'My ma – in Edinburgh – she's great, but she's kind of busy just now.'

'Yes,' Marian paused. 'And my daughter in the US, she's kind of busy right now.'

'I guess she was never as demanding as me,' Heather said with a wry smile.

'Don't you believe it!' Marian snorted, and went off to make scrambled eggs.

Gregor

Cairo

November 2012

The six o'clock deadline is hours away, so to minimize the interminable wait, Gregor suggests that he and Heather find somewhere to go - something to do - that's not too taxing. After her stomach upset she isn't yet up to sight-seeing, and he himself has little heart for it after yesterday's chaotic taxi tour of the crazy city. But he follows Ryan's suggestion of going to the Zamalek Marriott.

He tries half-heartedly to persuade Ryan to take a day off language class and accompany them – Ryan's Arabic is obviously pretty good already – but he senses that a corner has been turned, so he doesn't insist. He wonders if his own presence has skewed the trip irrevocably. But he couldn't pass up the opportunity of following his hunch while Heather and Ryan were in Sharm. He couldn't have continued his research without their help. Anyway, a rock-solid relationship should be able to weather a change of plans. There are more important things in life than a change of plans.

The Marriott Hotel proves to be a wonderful oasis of calm, beauty and shimmering cleanliness in the middle of the buzzing metropolis. There is no need to be a resident in order to enjoy the facilities. They merely have to put their bags and themselves through the security check as if for the airport, and they can enjoy the manicured lawns and flower beds, the shops, the coffee point or the restaurant.

The building is beautiful and feeds Gregor's insatiable

hunger for history. The original part was a palace to house the guests for the Suez Canal inauguration celebrations in 1869. It saw receptions, parties and the wedding of King Farouk and Queen Nariman. The architect was Egyptian, but a German designer was responsible for the interior – even the furniture and drapes. Gregor sighs with appreciation.

'Did you know the wife of Napoleon III stayed here?' he asks Heather, reading from one of the plaques.

'No, but I know the first performance of *Aida* took place here.'

'The Verdi opera?'

'Yes. I saw it – not here, of course – at the Opera House. With Tony. He said opera wasn't normally his scene but he enjoyed it. It was brilliant. Breathtaking.'

Tony. The young man who died. Most of Heather's time here is still a closed book.

The palace murals depict traditional village scenes, but it's the ceilings that capture their attention – exquisitely carved and painted. Gregor and Heather wander around until their necks are stiff, admiring the décor. Then they move outside, squinting in the bright sun, and stroll around the gardens like characters from *Mansfield Park*, ruminating on what it would be like actually to *stay* at the Marriott. Heather would like to sit down, so they choose a café table outside overlooking the swimming pool, and an obsequious waiter comes to take their order.

A couple of swimmers are in the pool now. Heather is watching them. 'You know,' she begins, 'it used to be such a joy – an oasis in the desert, literally – to go for a swim on Saturdays.'

'You went swimming here?'

'No, not here. It costs a fortune to swim here. But

there are other hotels with pools, many of them with roof top pools, where you can buy a day ticket, and you feel like you're far away from the madding crowd. Tony and I used to go sometimes. You could buy a cheap lunch and sit beside the pool. It was...' She tails off. It's that closed book again.

Their coffees arrive and they sink into the unaccustomed lap of luxury for a while.

'So, how's it going, sweetheart?' Gregor ventures after a while. He knows he's taking a risk. Is Ryan the *significant other?* Is an American son-in-law on the cards? Is Heather furious with him for interrupting the trip? Maybe it's too soon to put the question.

After a long pause and a measured sip of coffee, Heather replies, 'I know I sometimes mock your passion for history, Pa, but I'm probably about to eat humble pie and admit that it can pay off.' This isn't what he meant, but he doesn't pursue the Ryan line. 'Of course,' she adds, 'if it turns out that this Ashraf is nothing to do with Beth, I might decide you're up the creek without a paddle after all, but we'll wait and see. I cannae let myself quite believe we've found a relative for Beth – a brother even! However is she gonna take the news? She might hate him! And us. She might never forgive us for meddling. But it's certainly worth a try.'

Up to now Gregor has been buoyed by the chase, his mind filled with excited anticipation that couldn't be any less than Howard Carter's on the brink of discovering Tutankhamun's tomb, or Philippa Langley's, with an invincible hunch that the bones of Richard III lay under a car park in Leicester. But Heather's realism is beginning to temper the schoolboy enthusiasm that has been sending adrenalin coursing through him. Her misgivings are niggling at him.

Even if Beth *is* pleased to find she has a brother – even if she *isn't* horrified by their meddling – what then? She lives and works in Edinburgh. He lives and works in Cairo. Beth has never been to Cairo and, as far as Gregor can tell, has no desire or intention even to visit. Ashraf trained in Edinburgh, but that's finished now he's qualified, and none of them has money to splash often on plane tickets. His heart is thudding at the enormity of what they've done – of what *he's* instigated – of what they might be going to find.

Silently, they watch the swimmers.

Eventually she continues, 'It makes you appreciate privileges, you know? Little things, like a good night's sleep if you can get one, a clean restaurant, a relaxing Saturday, email that works.' They are both silent. They haven't discussed Gregor's emails – the ones she didn't reply to. Did she read them? He's convinced that she now believes that he didn't *behave inappropriately* – the very phrase makes him shudder – towards any high school girl, but does she understand anything about the agony of those days? Of being mistrusted by everyone who meant anything to him? Of trying to justify himself to family, friends, colleagues, students, members of the history forum who heard that he was taking *gardening leave*? Perish the thought.

'You okay, Pa?'

'Yes, pet. Finished your coffee? Shall we make a move?'

'Yep. Pa...?' she pauses, 'what are we actually going to say to this doctor?'

Gregor chuckles. 'You're going to ask him in your best Arabic if he's ever watched *Who do you think you are?* on television.'

'But Pa, they don't have those programmes here...'

It's just a lame joke, and she thumps his shoulder.

'Well, it seems to me that passing on greetings, cementing relationships and drinking coffee are great Egyptian pastimes...' She's nodding. 'So we'll capitalise on those, and see where the conversation leads us.'

'You're getting pretty good at reading the culture,' she admits.

'I've got a good teacher.' He grins, and can't help feeling complimented, despite the grandmother-sucking-eggs aspect. He's still so thirsty for her approval. How pathetic.

They take another tour of the hotel garden before emerging again into the city's hurry and noise, its dust and exhaust fumes. Heather's Arabic is not too rusty to take them by taxi into the city centre to Filfila. She reckons it's a good restaurant for introducing visitors to Egyptian food in a friendly, authentic environment, and it's central and easy to find.

'He's Egyptian, Pa, so...'

'We can expect African timing? The westerners have the watches, but the Africans have the time?' He loves that cliché.

She nods and grins. 'You know why that happens, don't you?'

'Tell me.'

'Relationships are more important than timetables, or than business meetings bent on making money. So if you bump into a relative or friend on your way to a scheduled meeting, you have to stop and greet them, and enquire after all their family members and so on.'

'We could take some of that on board,' he says, then regrets that his comment might be misconstrued. Ah, the egg shells, the eggs shells.

'Are you sure you'll recognise him, Pa? He might be looking for Ryan.'

'Yes. Anyway, he'll be looking for a couple of foreigners. We're easy enough to spot.'

They order soft drinks and try to enjoy the ambience. The tables are made of chunks of tree trunks, smoothed and polished to a fine sheen, but making for irregular shaped seating. There are creeping plants decorating the walls. There's a big tank of tropical fish. 'Not quite as dramatic as the fish at Sharm,' Gregor comments.

But Heather isn't looking at the fish. She's very pale, or perhaps it's the subdued lighting. 'Are you okay, pet?' He follows her gaze. There are two young men walking towards them.

'Ashraf? Mohamed?' Heather asks.

'Heather? Friend of Tony?'

Non-plussed, Gregor stands and offers his hand to shake. 'Dr Ashraf,' he begins, 'thank you for coming. This is my daughter, Heather.' Suddenly he feels out of place. There is something going on here, and he isn't part of it.

Ashraf shakes hands with Gregor. 'Mr Gregor, it's good to see you again. This is my colleague, Mohamed. He works at the hospital with me.' More hand-shaking, but Heather looks like she needs to sit down.

'Heather? Sweetheart?'

'Pa, these are the two doctors who were in the Square – in Tahrir – when Tony was killed. They looked after him. Well, me actually.'

'When Tony was killed?' Gregor hears himself echoing her stupidly. So they've met before? But that doesn't alter the reason why they're meeting now. He pulls himself together. 'Please, take a seat. What would you like to drink?' They sit down and Gregor looks around for a waiter.

The three young people are staring at each other incredulously. Finally, Heather begins an abbreviated account to the two young men of the hours, days and weeks that followed Tony's death, filling in Gregor's own patchy picture with big brush strokes. Dr Mohamed is just sitting back smiling and sipping his cola, but Ashraf is leaning forward, listening intently. He and Heather haven't taken their eyes off each other.

At last, Heather's story is complete, and Ashraf, now the Egyptian host, suggests they order dinner. There is small talk about the coral and tropical fish in Sharm while they are served hummus, babaganoush and koshari. Heather breaks off little pieces of pitta bread and dips them in the hummus. Ashraf, too, eats minimally, but Mohamed is tucking in enthusiastically and Gregor himself is quite hungry. Finally, over coffee, he embarks on the spiel that has circled inside his head for days.

'The thing is, you see, I'm a historian. I'm particularly fascinated by family trees, ancestry, that kind of thing. We have a friend back in Edinburgh, Beth, Elizabeth Gomersall. That's quite an unusual name in Scotland. Makes it easier to research. Anyway, Beth has had some problems.' No need to go into detail. 'It seems her family came on holiday to Sharm El Sheikh when she was very small, just a baby, and that there was an accident. The family were taking a motor boat ride and the boat capsized.'

'And Beth? She was hurt?' Mohamed interrupts. 'Those boats, they are not very...'

But Ashraf is riveted by his account – he comes from the Sharm area, after all – and Heather is watching keenly for his reaction.

Gregor continues, 'It seems Beth wasn't hurt. Of course, she wouldn't remember anything about it because she was too young. But my family tree research shows that...' Here Gregor pauses. How can he convey the next piece of earth-shattering information with its possibility of life-changing import? '... that there were twin boys, Beth's brothers, in the boat with them. One brother was drowned. His body was recovered further down the coast. But the other body never turned up, and we wondered, we wondered...'

'We wondered if you could remember anything about that motor boat accident from when you lived in the Sharm area as a boy,' Heather finishes for him. He breathes a sigh of relief. She has cleverly diffused the urgency. Gregor takes a sip of coffee. His racing heart is slowing now that the ball is in Ashraf's court.

Ashraf is frowning, thinking hard. Finally he asks, 'Do you have names for these brothers?'

'Yes, they were Aidan and... and Ashley.'

'Ha! Like my name! Ashraf.' They share a smile. Gregor's tension defuses a little. He has been so focused on Ashraf and Heather that he has been ignoring Mohamed. Why is Mohamed there, anyway? For moral support? Out of cultural convention? Or curiosity? Now he says something urgently in Arabic to Ashraf, who looks shocked, and says nothing for a long moment.

'His childhood,' Mohamed begins finally, 'was in a village near Sharm, but he doesn't...'

'It's okay Mohamed,' Ashraf stops him and turns to Gregor. 'I don't remember anything when I was really small,' he says. 'My mama and baba are simple people, very kind, very hard-working, very proud of me.' Now he smiles, embarrassed. 'My sisters, they are all married. I have seven nephews and nieces. My sisters all went to school, but they are not very... they didn't receive much education. The education of girls wasn't important to our family. But they married good men who work hard and give the family a good – how do you say – a good livelihood. They are not rich, of course,' he laughs briefly, 'but they have enough to eat, they have running water in their homes, they are clean...'

Mohamed interrupts again in Arabic, and Ashraf nods slowly. He picks up his coffee cup thoughtfully, but doesn't drink. 'When I was at school, I was different from the other students. At first I thought it was just because I have sisters but no brothers – that I was not used to being with boys. But I found it very easy to learn English, much easier than other boys, and studying was no problem for me. My parents were very proud, but also – I don't know – maybe embarrassed. They wanted their son to... to blend in and be one of the young men of the village.

'At high school in the village I had a lot of problems. The other students avoided me because they said I was too clever and too white! It was like racial prejudice among my own kind!' Gregor compares Ashraf's skin with Mohamed's. It's true that Ashraf's is a little paler, but the more noticeable feature is his eyes – his blue eyes. 'I was transferred to another high school in Sharm itself, one with a better reputation. I was nominated for a scholarship to study medicine, and I won. So, when I was eighteen I went to Edinburgh and studied to become a doctor – and you know the rest.'

'But there is more!' Mohamed objects. 'There is more

to tell you.' He turns to Ashraf and says in English now, 'You must tell the whole story.' Now he speaks to Gregor. 'I come here today because Ashraf – he tell me a little about your visit to the hospital. How it is strange – how his childhood is like a jig-saw puzzle with missing pieces. I want that he tell you.'

Ashraf takes a deep breath and resumes his story. 'In the village, eventually, my parents were ostr... how you say... people did not accept them willingly.'

'Ostracised?'

'Yes. Ostracised. My sisters had a lot of friends in the village. They told me the people didn't like that I was different. They are wonderful, my sisters, I love them all. But my father stopped drinking coffee and playing backgammon with the men in the café, and my mother stayed in the house all the time. So, after a few years, the family moved to a different village.'

'But,' Mohamed adds, 'his family is Christian, and most of that village is Muslim. So his family pretends to be Muslim, too. His father goes to the mosque every Friday, but...' He looks at Ashraf.

'But they are Christian, really. So we are still not completely accepted in the village, and it is my fault.' He runs his hand over his face. 'I love my family, and I send money to them every week, but I do not see them very often. Sometimes I think... I think is better if I stay away.'

Gregor is touched by this tale of rejection, but so many questions remain unanswered. Suddenly, Heather sits up straight and leans forward. 'Ashraf,' she asks, 'can you swim?'

Why this non-sequitur? 'What...?' Gregor begins.

Ashraf looks equally shocked. 'Well, in fact, I can't. I

am ashamed to say it. I was brought up near the sea, but I did not learn to swim. The other boys swam among the fishes around the coral. They didn't have snorkels, like the tourists. They just learned to hold their breath a long time, you know? There were not swimming lessons. The boys – somehow, they just learned. But they had a lot of fun, and I... I always felt frightened of the water.' He laughs, embarrassed. 'So when I was a little older I always made the excuse that I had to study, or that I didn't like swimming, but I think the boys despised me.' He sits back, then adds, 'Why you ask?'

Heather's eyes are shining, and a high colour has replaced her earlier pallor. 'It may be nothing, but I was just remembering how Beth is terrified of water. Her father made her have swimming lessons, so she *can* swim, but she never chooses to, and she never wants to go on boat rides.'

Gregor pauses and makes the connection, belatedly, between fear of water and a boat accident. Heather is a step ahead. Finally he pursues another line. 'Who do you look more like, Ashraf, your mother or your father?'

'Neither very much. My sisters all look like our father – eyes like this,' he pulls his eyes a little at the edges, 'and a chin like this!' He sticks his chin out so that his lower teeth overlap his upper ones. 'We didn't have orthodontists in the village,' he adds apologetically. 'But my mama, she has black eyes, dark skin and she's short and round! Very – how you say – cuddly!'

A lull falls upon the group. What now? No one has voiced the question, acknowledged the unspoken possibility that Beth and Ashraf are related. Gregor looks round. The unimaginable has become imagined. Mohamed is thoughtful and serious. Heather is flushed and hopeful, but Ashraf –

Ashraf is pale and his eyes have taken on a hunted look. He puts his coffee down, undrunk, and he's staring at his hands on the table. His long elegant fingers are working, never still. Suddenly, he asks, 'Her name? What you say is her name?'

'Beth. Beth Gomersall. Elizabeth.'

He lapses into silence again.

They become aware of conversation and laughter at other tables, of the bustling of waiters, the arrival of food and drink orders, aromas of spicy beef, or warm sweet rice, of strong coffee, of life being lived around them, while the four of them remain in a state of suspended animation.

'Gentle!' Ashraf whispers. 'Be gentle with the baby! My mama used to say, but...' He covers his face with his hands. His shoulders are rigid.

Mohamed, alert now, speaks to Ashraf quietly. 'Beraha! I also. My mama say *Beraha*, when I play with my baby brother. But she tell you in English, or in Arabic?'

Ashraf sounds out the two expressions. 'Beraha! Be gentle!' Then shocked, he adds, 'Be gentle with Baby Lizzy!'

'Lizzy!' Heather gasps. 'That's what...' She doesn't finish, and a delayed realisation washes over Gregor like a tidal wave: Ashraf, if he *is* Ashley, is about to find, not only that he has a younger sister, but that he has lost a brother, mother and father. This young man is of an age to be his own son. What can he say to help him?

Mohamed speaks to Ashraf again in Arabic, then turns to Gregor. 'He always say, he not remember when he very small. But I – I remember when my big brother, he take me on his bicycle, in the basket in front – my mother very angry*! He only a baby! He only two!* she say. *You want to kill him?* But my brother, he laugh. He say, *Mohamed safe. I good cycle rider.* So our mama hit him round the head with a towel and tell him not be cheeky. And many more memories I have, some good, some bad. Then my family move to Cairo when I only four years old and I go to good school, study medicine in Cairo University. I met Ashraf in Tahrir during the Thawra – the revolution. He always say, he not remember no early childhood.'

Mohamed pauses, then adds darkly, 'Families that have only daughters always want sons. Maybe that was good chance for them.'

Heather leans forward and reaches a hand towards Ashraf, stopping short of touching his arm. 'Ashraf, what are you thinking?' she asks gently.

He lifts his head slowly and cups his hand around his chin. 'I'm thinking, Who am I? Is my life a lie? I know what you want to ask: am I this brother? Did I have a brother who died? And Beth's parents…?'

'I'm so sorry, Ashraf. They died.'

'They died in the boat accident?'

'No, it was later.'

'But my baba and mama in Sharm…'

Time to step in. 'They love you, son,' Gregor says. 'Nothing changes that. And I've been told that Egyptian families are not like our western nuclear families. They're generous - much more willing to take in an extra child – a cousin, an orphan, someone who needs them. If they found you alone on a beach…'

'But I need to know,' Ashraf says now. 'I must know, but not offend my parents. And if…'

'DNA,' Heather interrupts. 'Take a DNA test. We'll get Beth to take one as well.' She sits up very straight. 'At home, among my paramedic colleagues, I'm sure I could find out about a clinic that would do a DNA test. Could you…'

He reads her mind. 'I will do a mouth swab and send it to you by taxi before you leave Cairo.'

'But we'll not raise Beth's hopes too early,' Gregor adds, recognising instantly that impossibility.

'And anyway, maybe she will not like me!' Ashraf says with a sheepish grin.

'I don't think there is any danger of that!' Heather laughs, and, contrary to all she's been telling Gregor about cultural convention, puts a hand on his arm. Ashraf covers her hand with his own in a very western way, and smiles.

Heather
Cairo
November 2012

Back in Marian's comfortable guest room, Heather had listened while the late night sounds of conversation, laughter and ubiquitous car horns gave way to the early morning sounds of delivery trucks and a different kind of muted communication before she finally slept. In a moment, it seemed, her thoughts, plans and aims, her entire world view had changed. She told herself repeatedly not to be so melodramatic. She and Pa had fulfilled their aims – his aims - had done what they had intended to do. They had met Ashraf, and it seemed very possible that Pa's meticulous research had paid off. She could hardly remember seeing him so excited, though the years had taught him restraint. His generation, it seemed, didn't leap up and punch the air, didn't shout Hallelujah or dance a jig. Maybe some would hit the champagne, but that wasn't Pa's style. True, he had been proud when she graduated, delighted when his papers were published in his favourite history magazine, but exhilarated? Nope. Instead, she realised, the memories she had taken with her to Cairo, initially, had been of his loneliness after the divorce, his anxiety that she was leaving at all, his shame at the need to take gardening leave. Those happy memories of picnics on the beach, races up Arthur's Seat or McDonald's Happy Meals were buried somewhere under the constant effort to forget.

But last night she had recognised that fire in his eyes, the zeal of the quest, the satisfaction of a job well done, but something more – and she felt it herself – the gut-wrenching yearning to uncover good news for Beth. And why? She had been a stranger to them both. She had stumbled across them – Heather smiled under the bedclothes at the unintended pun – had entered their lives at the same point and something about her extreme vulnerability, yet steely, if misplaced, determination to overcome her difficulties alone, had made both her and Pa long to disprove the hopelessness of her situation.

Thousands, maybe millions of people were in exactly that situation – alone, homeless, aimless. The world was overflowing with displaced people, refugees, mothers, fathers, brothers, sisters who were injured, sick, bereaved, rejected. Every news bulletin left Heather wrung out with the injustice of the world, and her own inability to make any difference where it really mattered.

Maybe that was why Beth was so important. *She* mattered, and Heather *could* make a difference. Was that all their friendship boiled down to – assuaging Heather's own guilt? She turned over again, her bedclothes and thoughts in an impossible tangle.

And what about Ryan? What about herself and Ryan? She called to mind his sandy hair, his open, friendly face, his big capable hands. He was kind, considerate, good-looking, protective, hard-working. He was good for her. Suddenly aware of thinking Pa's thoughts in Pa's words, she sat up abruptly, hot and flustered. She could hear the reasoning in Pa's tone of voice: he'll look after you, he'll always put you first, he'll be faithful and caring.

Heather got out of bed and went to the window. Most of the street lights were out now and she could make out a few stars despite the light and dust pollution. She allowed her mind to replay that meeting, that Romeo and Juliet encounter, when Ashraf had walked in and recognised her, then that heart-rending moment when he realised what they were suggesting, his head in his hands, those long, graceful fingers gripping the curly dark hair, then when she put her hand on his arm and he didn't withdraw, the frisson she had felt at the touch of his own hand. What had he been feeling?

Sweat prickled Heather, despite the cool of the early hours. She moved to open the window, but checked herself. Mosquitoes were less common in November, but even then, it only took one to destroy any possibility of sleep. She drew the chair up to the window and leant her forehead against the cool glass. Tomorrow, a decision would have to be made. Tomorrow must be today already! There was a tell-tale pink glow in the sky above the eastern buildings. She had come to Cairo wondering – expecting – hoping? that Ryan was the one. That she and Ryan would – what? Fall in love? Want to spend the rest of their lives together? Or just have a good holiday?

How far had she allowed herself to plan? An American boyfriend, an American husband, would be exotic. She'd be taken to meet his family. She thought back to those photos on his fridge, the healthy, smiling blond siblings with their American teeth, their endearing habit of saying 'Ma'am' and 'Sir', their open-hearted hospitality. She'd also thought about distance. Where would they live? Which grandparents would their children get to know and love? Children? What was she thinking! Ryan hadn't even proposed. Was he even planning to? How presumptuous. Instead, she fixed her thoughts on Ryan, on his warm affection, snuggling up by a glowing fireside on a winter's evening. Fireworks? No, just rosy embers.

Why hadn't she met a good Scottish guy, whose background and upbringing she would understand, whose parents, she thought ruefully, would probably also be divorced? They would have seen the same films, studied the same syllabus at school. They'd laugh at the same old, well-worn Scottish jokes.

But Ashraf lingered at the fringe of her thinking all the time. Exotic? More like problematic. Recognising him in that restaurant had triggered something, some neural spasm registering alertness. In any average day, especially in Cairo, you can lock eyes with dozens of people. Why should this particular interlocking be any different? But it was.

Her heart lurched as she thought what Ashraf had to do as a result of Pa's research. She imagined those adoptive parents, except that there had been no adoption. That couple, Mama and Baba, whom Ashraf loved, respected and provided for, had kidnapped him, had stolen him, had deprived Beth's parents of bringing up their son, of letting Beth have the life-long company of a brother. Heather was angry, but she hadn't even met those people. She wouldn't be able to communicate with them adequately, her Arabic had become so poor and rusty.

No, she told herself. Concentrate on Ashraf. Well, that wasn't difficult. She returned to Marian's word - chemistry! Yes, that was it. Chemistry. That hot-wired moment, when the atmosphere had crackled and sent electric messages of recognition and something else across the airwaves of the restaurant while others, even Pa, had remained oblivious. Now she was being ridiculous. She got back into bed and the warmth of the covers lulled her to a late sleep, just as Marian got up to make her early morning tea.

It was well after nine when Marian knocked briefly on Heather's door and came in with a cup of tea. She opened the curtains a little and Heather squinted at the bright sunlight. 'Come on, sleeping beauty, rise and shine. Ryan and your dad will be here soon.'

Heather groaned and turned away from the light.

'Another bad night?' Marian asked. Heather grunted.

'Paracetamol?'

'Mmm, please.'

By the time Marian reappeared with a couple of tablets and a glass of water, Heather had managed to open her eyes and sit up. 'You know what you said about chemistry...?'

'Yes?' Pause. 'With Ryan?' Pause. 'I'm guessing there isn't any.'

'Yeah.' Heather took the glass of water from Marian and downed the first tablet. 'What'm I going to do, Marian?'

'Well, let's see. You're going to take the other tablet, drink your tea, have a shower and get some clothes on, and if you haven't gained any colour by then, you're going to use a bit of blusher. Then you're going to come and meet Ryan and tell him what happened yesterday.'

Heather smiled. 'You're right. It's not fair to ask you.'

Marian returned the smile and left, closing the bedroom door behind her. But Heather remembered that undeniable chemistry when Ashraf had covered her hand on his arm.

Pa and Ryan arrived together, having met on the way to

Marian's. What they had talked about as they walked? Ryan seemed different, somehow, more reserved, no longer the expansive host. Marian, as always, provided coffee and tray bakes, and the four of them chatted inconsequentially for a few minutes, then Marian said she had things to do, and left the three of them in the sitting room.

'So, pet, are you going to tell him about yesterday, or am I?'

'Your turn. It was your initiative,' Heather said, and sat back to sip her restorative coffee and to study the expressions of both of them while Pa recounted their day.

After a few minutes Heather was able to listen objectively, and it was an eye-opener as she witnessed Pa's account, and observed their man-to-man conversation. She might as well not have been there. Pa told how Beth had stepped into his life, how he and Heather together had adopted her into their family and helped her set up a business. It had been such a gift to find Beth's family tree so easily, in contrast to the nerve-racking roller-coaster ride trying to track down her brother.

From Ryan, she heard how the Egyptian revolution had changed the ambitions of so many young Egyptian men and women, how they were so full of hope, while the older generation had become disillusioned, convinced that change was no longer possible, that a mere comfortable lifestyle would never be within their grasp, and how the events of Tahrir had, in some cases, driven a wedge between parents and offspring.

He recognised Ashraf's position as the son, the only son of his family, and the expectations and responsibilities that engendered, issues that had failed to impact Heather up to now. He spoke of his own career uncertainties, his sympathies for Egypt, but of a heightened awareness of his foreignness, his lack of belonging. This was a less familiar Ryan: the holiday persona and the everyday persona were not quite the same. But she and Ryan hadn't met on holiday. Far from it. He had risen to the occasion when she needed him, and what had she done for him? Nichts. Rien. He was looking down, his shoulders drooped, his gentle hands motionless on the chair. Finally, as if dragging himself back to the situation in hand, Ryan said 'So where does that leave him? And the two of you?' His glance took Heather into the question.

'He's going to send us a DNA swab, and we're aiming to ask Beth to do the same,' Heather told him.

'What are you going to tell her?'

'We'll have to lay our cards on the table,' Pa said. 'Anyway, there's been enough deception on both sides. We've resolved to do everything above board now. In broad daylight.'

Ryan looked at his watch. 'I've got a class this afternoon…'

'It's only twelve thirty,' Heather interrupted. 'Let's get a sandwich at Beano's. Um, Pa, do you…'

'Got to get a couple of things, er, books from that shop you showed me, Ryan, a few postcards…' The three of them grinned nervously at each other, their subterfuge so blatant. 'Okay, so you two need to have lunch without me, just the two of you. Maybe Marian and I…'

'Permission to laugh out loud, sir?' Ryan asked, and some of his comfortable glow had returned. So they did, and with calls of thanks to Marian, he and Heather left Pa to collect up cups and plates.

Heather

Edinburgh

December 2012

Heather loved to have a window seat in a plane. She peered excitedly at the recognisable places as Edinburgh came into view. 'Look, Pa, there's Arthur's Seat. I bet we could see home if the clouds would disperse a bit. Look, the bridges – the Forth Bridge and the road bridge.' The typical Edinburgh breezy weather blew the 747 until it felt like a model aeroplane. 'Woah! A roller coaster ride!' Heather leaned back in her seat to give Pa a clear view, but when she turned to look at him, he was quite pale, his eyes fixed forward. 'You okay, Pa?'

'Not so keen on flying these days. Out of the habit, I guess.' The plane finally bumped down and came to rest. 'Ah, terra firma. The firmer the firma, the less the terror,' Pa muttered, smiling weakly. For Heather, flying was the thrill that both introduced and then capped the adventure. She loved everything about it: the incredible views, the choice of films, the little neatly packaged meals and the unending wonder of modern travel. Funny, despite her fear of heights and slight claustrophobia, she loved flying. Planes were different. All or nothing.

A misty breeze met them as they stepped on to the tarmac. 'Aha, the haar!' Pa said, breathing in the chilly damp air.

Heather shivered, and thought of Egypt's 360 days annually of guaranteed sunshine. She remembered Ryan saying 'We don't need rain. We've got the Nile. As long as no one pulls the plug, we're sorted.'

Martin had replied, 'And as long as no country in the south builds a damn or redirects it!'

'Penny for them?' Pa asked, as they waited by the conveyor belt for their luggage.

'Oh, they're worth much more than that,' she smiled, 'but what are we going to say to Beth? And how? And when?'

'Well, on the basis of brushing nothing under the carpet, I reckon we should tell her everything we know, as soon as we can.'

'But what if it all comes to nothing? What if it's a storm in a teacup? We'll be building up her hopes then letting her down with an awful crash.'

'She's been an only child all her life. She might need some time to try the idea for size, so she has maximum adjustment time if we *are* right. Anyway, remember we need a DNA test.'

'I've always fancied the idea of secretly taking a glass that she has drunk from, or an apple core…'

'You watch too many American detective dramas. No, we need to do this by the book.' He reached forward to heave Heather's suitcase from the conveyor belt. 'My goodness! Whatever have you got in here?'

Having retrieved both cases, they made their way to the bus stop. Heather pulled her light jacket round her. Pa put his arm round her shoulder and pulled her close. 'Should've accepted Beth's offer to collect us from the airport.'

'What? She offered, and you refused?' Heather squeaked, pulling away to look at his face. 'Why?'

He pulled her back again. 'Didn't know whether the

flight would be delayed. Didn't know how we'd be feeling. Couldn't predict the situation...'

'No kidding!' She decided not to philosophise about life, but instead, snuggled in to his proffered warmth.

Nero's rapturous welcome began as soon as Pa's key was in the front door. Beth had left a note on the kitchen table: *Welcome home! Hope your flight was good. Casserole in the oven – please switch on at 180 degrees. Am at Mrs Tyler's with Sol. Back around 7. Beth*

True to her word, Beth was back just before seven o'clock. She and Sol burst in with a gust of cold November air and a round of enthusiastic hugs. 'Welcome home! How was your trip? Nero missed you.'

'But what about you?' Heather asked mischievously.

'Course I did,' Beth said, giving her another hug. She turned to Pa. 'Did your research go well, Gregor?' Then she directed her question to Heather. 'Good holiday?' She raised her eyebrows meaningfully.

'Excellent,' Heather said. 'Seeing Ryan again was great. He and I will always be good friends.'

This statement hung in the air for a moment, then Heather turned to her father. 'Pa?'

'Yes, on both counts,' Pa replied. 'So glad you've prepared a meal for us all. We've got so much news to share, we're all going to need fortification.'

'Pa's been a dark horse,' Heather said. 'I'm the only one around here who's played it straight. But we've made a resolution, no more secrets. Right?'

It took the whole of main course and dessert for Heather to tell of her times with old friends in Cairo, students and teachers from the language school, then Marian and finally, Ryan. 'He's a fantastic person. He's so warm and caring. He was just the friend I needed when Tony was killed, and he gave me a wonderful holiday. His Arabic is so good now, we didn't have any problems with taxis or shops or bookings.' She enthused at length about snorkelling and the countryside around Sharm. 'He thought of everything and I felt so safe travelling with him.' She looked at Beth. More later, her look said.

'Then I turned up,' Pa interrupted fortuitously. He was more sensitive than she had given him credit for. 'And the next bit concerns you, Beth, and that's where I've been less than strictly honest.'

Heather was watching Beth closely as Pa spoke. She watched her colouring change from flushed to white, and flushed again. Even Pa was blushing. But he was explaining gently, so gently, how he found the name Gomersall unusual and interesting, how he couldn't quite believe she had no relatives other than Paul and his parents and how he'd begun, then followed up, his research. Heather knew, in Beth's place, she'd have been jumping up and down, firing questions, objecting loudly. But not Beth. True to form, she accepted the information stolidly, silently, almost without blinking.

As Pa explained the taxi ride around the outskirts of Sharm, searching for Ashraf's village, Beth's lips parted, and she began to breathe fast and shallowly. He recounted meeting Ashraf and Mohamed in the restaurant, and Mohamed's quiet insistence that led Ashraf to believe their story was plausible.

Heather told of her own incredulity that they were the two doctors attending in the make-shift clinic when Tony was killed.

There had been a brief flurry of tears when Beth took in that Ashraf was a doctor. 'So Dad would've had his medic in the family, after all,' she said wistfully. And finally, 'So, where do we go from here?'

'We need you to take a DNA test. Could you do that?'

'Well, I suppose so, but...'

'I'm sure I could find a clinic if I ask around at work.'

'But...'

'But what, Beth?' Pa asked.

'Well, it sounds so impossible.'

Heather stepped in. 'Do you think it's impossible, Beth? Do you think me and Pa are coming from cloud cuckoo land?'

There was a pause, and Heather saw Pa's wisdom in giving Beth as much time as possible to adjust her thinking, in case it turned out to be true.

'Beth, are you sure you don't have *any* memory of little brothers?'

'Pa, she was a *baby*! She wouldn't remember anything from that age!'

'But didn't your parents refer to the boys *at all*?'

'I was only six when Mum died, and even before that she was unconscious for a long time.'

'But how could your father say *nothing* all that time? Didn't you grow up with toys that used to be theirs, for example?'

'Toys...'

'What about photos? Weren't there any family photos of when you were a baby? Every family...'

284

'Photos!' Beth exclaimed, standing up so suddenly that her chair toppled over.

'What? You have family photos?'

'Marc Ravello – the lawyer, remember? He said Dad had left Mum's photo album for me in a box under the stairs.'

'With photos of you as a baby?'

Gregor picked up the chair and Beth sat down again slowly, resting her elbows on the table, her head in her hands. 'I didn't look.'

'You didn't look, Bethie?' Heather squeaked. 'How could you not look?'

'Heather!' Pa warned.

'I found the album, but I only looked at the first page.'

Gregor
Edinburgh
December 2012

Why should it take all three of them to go back to Beth's house and collect the album? Gregor sighs. How will he ever understand the female psyche? But he grudgingly accepts the role of a mere male, and drives the two girls in his car. In the dank December drizzle the house has a sad, neglected look, previously disguised by the July sun. The cold, damp, undisturbed air in the hall seeps inside his jacket. Beth seems to want to stand in the doorway, with the front door ajar. In fact, she's standing more outside than in. At her suggestion they've brought a torch. There's no light in the cupboard under the stairs - surely it would have been a simple job to rig one up - but it's not his place to ask.

'So what am I looking for, Beth?'

'I… I threw the album back in, and didn't look where it landed. Can't even remember whether I put it back in the box. But it must be somewhere behind the…'

He crawls into the space, with Heather holding the torch, shining it over his shoulder. He suppresses a shudder. All this stuff is so old. This cupboard has been untouched for years, not just five or six months. There's a pile of National Geographical magazines. The top one is dated 2003. Is that the oldest or the newest? Are they even piled chronologically? He gropes behind heaps of nameless stuff, carrier bags full of what might be old clothes, a couple of folding garden chairs, some metal tools.

Gregor has never been keen on spiders, but chivalry

has always necessitated dealing with them. Don't think about them. His hand finds a book-sized box. He opens it and takes out an album with a shiny cover.

'Think I've got it! Is this it?' He reverses out and straightens up with the album in one hand. He wipes off the dust with the other. One corner is battered.

'Yes.' Beth sounds relieved and she is already backing out of the front door.

'Okay. Let's take it back home,' Gregor says. He holds the book out, but Beth doesn't take it from him, as if it might be diseased. She gets into the car without a backward glance, leaving Heather to lock up the house.

Back home in the warm sitting room, the two dogs are sharing the hearth rug amicably. The girls sit together on the sofa, while Gregor takes a moment to wash his hands and put the kettle on. He and Heather are longing to open the album, brimming with anticipation, but buttoning their lips. This is Beth's moment, but she is prolonging the agony beyond all reasonable tolerance.

'Beth…' he begins.

'Sorry,' she says, shaking herself a little. 'The first photo is of my mum and dad, probably before I was born, and they look so happy, and then I was born and everything got worse and worse, and it wasn't my fault, but I felt they were loading it all on to me – or at least, Dad was - so I got angry and threw the book back in the cupboard.' But the album remains closed on her lap.

'Well,' Heather says at last, 'please can we see?'

Egg shells. In years gone by, Gregor would have sighed *women!* But his vested interest in what this album might show extends beyond Beth to his daughter and his historical research, to say nothing of the time, effort and money invested in the Sharm trip. Is he being selfish? Couldn't they just get on with it? He perches on the arm of the sofa and looks over Beth's shoulder.

Slowly, she opens the album at the first page. There is the smiling young couple. Gregor tries to see a family likeness, but they are both simply dark-haired, slim and tanned. Beth is trembling. Heather grips her arm. 'It's okay, Bethie. It doesn't change anything. It might just make the next step clearer. Let's play detectives!'

A small smile, and at last Beth turns the page, and the next page, and the next.

Wedding day, and the sun obliges. Can you gild the lily? She, the loveliest bride, he the proudest bridegroom. The photo is not an official one, but amateur and poignant, oblique, capturing a private joke shared by the couple, an enquiring glance from the best man, giggles from the two pink-silk-clad bridesmaids. The lady in the feathery hat must be Beth's granny. And that other couple, the ones with a baby, are they Uncle Bob and Aunt Nessa?

Holidays on the beach, stripy towels and a flask of tea; holidays in a tent, camping gas and billie can; holidays in the mountains, wind-tousled hair. In a coffee shop, sedate and relaxed; in a rowing boat on a lake amid heather-clad hills; glamorous at a party; formal at a presentation; sight-seeing at the Forth Bridge, Edinburgh Castle, Glen Coe, the Eiffel Tower...

Skater jeans and wide belts, pedal-pushers and white trainers. Abba satin trousers and thigh-high boots. Long hair, short hair, beard, moustache, ubiquitous denim jackets.

Beth gasps. 'That's Mum! Mummy with a baby...

'Dad with a baby...
'Mummy and Dad with a baby each...
'Mummy with a baby on each arm...'

The photos are ordinary – normal. It could be any one of a million families, doing ordinary things...
Parents together, each with a little dark-haired boy.
Toddlers in nappies sitting on the lawn.
Toddlers in dungarees on a picnic rug.
Toddlers toddling hand-in-hand.
Naked toddlers on the beach.
Little boys on tricycles.
Little boys on swings.
Batman suits, Robin Hood outfits, Superman cloaks, football strips...

But it's extraordinary, abnormal. It's evidence. It's Beth's life handed back to her, a jigsaw puzzle with all the pieces in place.

Beth isn't blinking, her blue eyes round with – what? Amazement? Delight? Incredulity? Beth has always been so enclosed, so hard to read. True, she's been opening out a bit with the High Fives business and Jem's friendship - even the banter between Heather and Josh – it has all been prising open that pretty clam shell. But now...

'Look!' she exclaims, barely above a whisper. 'It's Paul! It's the twin boys with Paul! But why didn't he say? Why didn't I know? He must've remembered them... Why?'

Heather turned the next page. There was Beth's mother with a baby. 'It's you, Bethie. The baby's you!'

Beth stares at the picture. 'But I look just the same as...'

'...the same as Ashley and Aidan. Your brothers.'

Beth turns the next page. It's a family photo – all five of them – Mum, Dad, Aidan, Ashley and Beth. The adults are smiling, one boy is laughing, the other scowling, the baby is trying to reach for something outside the picture.

'Wonder which one is Ashley?' Heather says, peering.

Beth lays the book down on her lap. 'They look – we look –' so happy. So... so normal.'

Beth

Edinburgh

December 2012

Habits were formed, and could be broken. The Internet was a habit, an addiction, for some people. It was the first thing they did each morning and the last thing each night. But Beth had broken the habit. Part of building the wall had been protecting herself from painful news. She didn't want to hear about bombs in the Middle East, fatal car crashes or school shootings. Survival was hard enough without those. Uncle Bob and Aunty Nessa were not available, so she had given up emailing, given up even switching on her laptop or phone. True, for the first few days after taking up residence in her car, she had charged her appliances in a library, and had nervously checked to see if she was missed. But communicating her life-shattering news to anyone – high school friends, university class-mates, anyone – had been a bridge too far.

When she had met Heather and Gregor, communication with them had been enough – even too taxing some days – so she had no need for the Net. She'd had a couple of phone calls and texts with Heather from Egypt, and some arrangements with Penny or Jem, but the Net was a broken habit and she didn't miss it.

So what had prompted her to check her email after such a gap? There were the usual adverts from drug companies – a medical student's lot – and some very old timetable changes for last term's lectures, but there, only five days old, unread, was one from Paul. Did he know about

Dad? Had he written reams of platitudinous sympathy? No, not Paul. Maybe he had lots of new friends and was very busy. Perhaps he had met a nice girl and got engaged.

Open the email. Think positively. Congratulate him.

Hi Beth,

How goes it? How was the end of term? Do you feel like a doctor yet? Yeah, I know, there are still years to go. Did you enjoy dissection? I used to imagine girls would get squeamish over it, but not you. You used to press me for details of dissecting frogs! Disgusting girl!

Sorry for being out of touch. Been on a walkabout with Mum and Dad. It was a great time. They're back home now. Have they been in contact? They'll have some ace photos. Go round and see them. Fact is, I lost my mobile. It's somewhere at the bottom of Lake Alexandrina. Went on a boat trip and dropped it over the side. I know...silly boy! So I lost your number, but here I am at last. Please email your mobile number to me. Back at work now, and missing the great outdoors and, if I'm honest, family and British friends. Aussies are great for matches and barbecues, but sometimes I crave that Scottish accent – you know?

It'll be your Christmas break soon. Are you and Uncle James doing anything special? Pleeease get Uncle James to get in touch with Mum and Dad. This silly non-communication has gone on long enough. I'm seriously thinking of coming home for Christmas, but I couldn't bear it if they insist on this ridiculous embargo.

Anyway, forgive my silence, and get in touch soon.

Lotsaluv,

Paul

So he didn't know.

Beth sat for a long time, thinking, or rather, blanking. Part of her wanted to rush into the hall, to call upstairs to Heather, to tell her... But this was a private moment. She needed to savour it, to decide how to react. She tried to order her thoughts, to get her wayward ducks in a row.

Dear Paul,
I have some very sad news to tell you.

Delete. Too blunt. Try again.

Dear Paul,
Obviously you haven't heard the news from this end, and I'm sorry to have to be the bearer of bad news, but, the fact is...

Delete. Too flowery. Try again.

Dear Paul,
It was great to hear from you at last.

Delete. At last...? Too condemnatory. Try again.

Dear Paul,
Great to hear from you. Glad you had such a good time with your folks on your walkabout. Sorry to hear about your phone. My number is...

Maybe she should just give her number and ask him to call her. Tell him she had some important news.

Dear Paul,
Great to hear from you, but sorry about your mobile. Silly boy! My number...

He might think *she* had got engaged. No chance.

How could she word such a piece of news? Spoken words were not like emails. They couldn't be deleted or retrieved. No. Better to email the news and then go and visit Uncle Bob and Aunty Nessa. Whatever their feud with Dad had been, or his with them, it wasn't hers. There was no reason for enmity as far as she was concerned. Nessa had always been such a good friend. She could have been like a mum if Dad hadn't withdrawn from family so comprehensively.

Dear Paul,

Great to hear from you. Glad to hear you had a good time with your folks. Yes, I'll definitely go and see them. In fact, I tried to visit in the summer.

It would be really wonderful to see you at Christmas. Do come over. There'll be plenty of Scottish accents!

There is some awful news that I have to share with you. Dad had a terrible accident … Lies. Delete. *Dad passed away…*delete passed away…*is no longer with us…* delete. *Dad hanged himself…* Delete. *Dad took his own life…* Delete.

Dad died in June. I tried to contact your folks but they had already left. Saw your neighbour. Had a hard time – obviously, but everyone was very kind… Delete. She hadn't given anyone a chance. Had hidden behind the wall, refused Marc Ravello's hospitality, hadn't contacted friends or colleagues.

Had a hard time, obviously, but made some new friends – Heather and her dad Gregor. I'm staying with them just now near Arthur's Seat. I have a dog, too, but that's another story.

But there's more news. Gregor's a historian. He did some research on our family tree. I used to have twin brothers. They must have been about your age. I've seen a photo with them with another boy that looks like you. Don't you remember? There was a motorboat accident, and one of them was drowned, but the body of the other one was never found. Gregor even wonders whether he might still be living.

Once she had made a start, the dam was breached and news flowed. She paused, read and reread what she had written, and finally signed off.

There's so much news at this end, and at yours, too, I'm sure. Do come home for Christmas and meet Gregor and Heather, and my dog.
Love,
Beth

Love, Beth.

Such a brief greeting. She wanted to write *lots of love*, or, *missing you…* or *special greetings…* or *love to my dearest and bestest and only cousin…* and she began to giggle maniacally.

The door to the hall opened. 'Hi Beth? You okay? What are you laughing at?' Heather was looking round, as if she expected someone else was in the room. Maybe he was. Paul had become so real to Beth while she was writing, it was as if he were right there, instead of the other side of the world. In an instant her eyes welled up.

'Fine, Heather. Really. Had an email from Paul.'

'About time! What's he been playing at? Your only relative…'

'Get off your high horse! He'd been on a kind of safari, and he lost his phone, but now he says he might be home for Christmas.'

'Oh, that would be good! Or would it bring

everything back to you?'

'It would be great. I've just emailed him – briefly – but there's so much more to tell him. Obviously. And I'd love you to meet him.'

'Did you tell him…?'

'I told him Dad had died but I didn't say how. I told him I might have a brother and I told him I'm living with you.'

'It's possible he knows about the boat accident.'

Beth thought about that.

'He must remember your brothers. He was about the same age, wasn't he?'

'But if he remembers, why have we never spoken about it?' Something caught at Beth's throat. 'He has always been my… my sort-of best friend. It was always such fun when he was around. Was he deceiving me all this time?'

'But he's been away in Australia for quite a while?'

'Yeah. Years. It all started with his gap year. He said he wanted to get away. To spread his wings a little. He was only eighteen, but he enjoyed being away.' There was that lump in her throat again. 'But he used to email me. Told me about the sheep farm. I told him about applying to medical school. Told him about Dad changing jobs and everything. He said I should take a gap year, too. Even invited me to go to Australia and see for myself.'

'There you are, you see!'

'But Dad seemed to need me. Couldn't go so far from home. Dundee was enough to be away and independent but to get home for weekends.'

'I just wonder…' Heather pulled out a chair at the table and sat down opposite Beth and her laptop. She picked up a coaster and turned it over and over. Beth waited. 'I just wonder whether the disagreement between your dad and Aunty Nessa had something to do with your family story. Something about Ashley and Aidan.'

'But how could it be? Nobody even ever mentioned Ashley and Aidan. Bob and Nessa weren't even there in Sharm El Sheikh.'

'I know.'

Their silence magnified the ticking clock, the hiss of the boiler responding to its thermostat, occasional cars passing in the street.

Eventually, Sol hauled himself up from reclining under the table, and pushed his nose into Beth's knee. 'Time for a walk soon,' she told him.

'But not before a cup of tea,' Heather said, getting up and reaching for the kettle.

'Ah, the British panacea.'

'Blame Pa,' Heather said.

'I thought his was coffee?'

'Did I hear coffee?' Gregor said, bursting in the back door. 'It's raining cats and dogs. I think Nero and Sol might have to be content with a tour of the back garden tonight.' He took off his waterproof and shook it lightly over the sink. Then he looked from one to the other of them. 'Everything all right in here? It feels like there's something in the air.'

'Beth had an email from Paul.'

Gregor's face lit up, but before he had chance to reply, there was a *ping* and Beth gasped, 'He's replied. Already.' This time she didn't hesitate before opening the email.

Gregor stood stock still, eyes wide, but Heather sucked in her breath, her knee jiggling.

Beth took in Paul's reply silently.

Dearest Lizzy,

I am SO sorry. How awful for you. I wish I could be there with you right now. Wish I HAD been there. But here's the next best thing: I've booked a flight. Never mind waiting till Christmas. I'm coming straight away. I will email Mum and Dad with your news – and mine about the flight – but I'd love to see you before they do. I'm due in Edinburgh at 3.40pm on Wednesday. Any chance you could meet me at the airport?

Best love,
Paul

'He's coming,' Beth whispered, before turning the laptop so that Heather and Gregor could read.

'Oh Bethie! That's SO good!' Heather leapt up to hug her. 'Of course you'll meet him at the airport! He'll be wrecked. It's a twenty-four hour flight, apart from jet lag.'

'Oh, he'll manage. He's young and fit, I presume!' said Gregor.

'Lizzy?' Heather said. 'That was what Ashraf said. Why does he call you Lizzy?'

'It was my dad's name for me when I was very little. He used to call me Fizzy Lizzy. But he told me Mum had chosen my name. She wanted to call me Elizabeth all the time, but Elizabeth Gomersall's a bit of a mouthful. So I became Beth. I used to like being Lizzy.'

She turned the laptop back towards her. 'It must be early morning there. It's probably warm and sunny.' She glanced towards the rain-spattered black kitchen window. 'Wonder if he remembers Scottish weather? Funny to think he must've been on the computer at the exact moment I emailed him.'

'He sounds like a decisive young man,' Gregor

declared. 'I'm really looking forward to meeting him – and his parents at last. Hope they won't think I'm...'

'They'll think only the best, Uncle Gregor, just as I do!' Beth said with a grin and got up to hug him.

Beth

Edinburgh Airport
December 2012

Both Heather and Gregor, individually, had offered to accompany Beth to the airport, but she had declined. This was something she wanted to do alone. But now, waiting at International Arrivals, with one eye on the electronic board that announced *landed* and the other on the swing doors that disgorged travellers, she was shaking with nerves. Would she recognise him? Of course, he used to post photos on Facebook, but it was a long time since she'd used it. Would he even recognise her? She didn't think she had changed much. Maybe she was a bit thinner, and her hair was longer, but otherwise…

Another posse of passengers was arriving, some exhausted, some excited, some inadequately dressed for a Scottish winter. Most were looking around, hawk-eyed. They were greeted with waves, hugs, shouts, shy smiles, formal hand-shakes. How would she greet Paul?

And there he was!

Easily recognisable, the same old Paul, but now with a full beard, a tan and tousled light hair, and she was enveloped in a hug that made up for all the weeks, all the months of crippling loneliness, and she was laughing with joy and relief.

'You're taller!' she gasped.

'You're more beautiful!' he said.

'Don't be daft! Where do you want to go? Should I drive you straight home, or would you like to meet Gregor and Heather? They're dying to meet you.'

He put one arm round Beth's shoulders and pulled his suitcase with the other. 'Let's get out of everyone's way.' He steered her away from the milling, chattering, meeting, greeting crowd. 'What I'd really like...' he paused and looked around. 'What I'd really like is to go to that coffee shop,' he indicated with his chin, 'and talk to *you* before I meet anyone else.'

'But you must be exhausted. Don't you want to go home and sleep first?'

'Managed to sleep on the plane a bit. Anyway, I'm a seasoned flier these days, you know.' He beamed and his eyes crinkled. Beth relaxed.

'Okay.' She wanted nothing more than to sit and talk with him, even though her news was so awful. At least, since he was family, there was so much she *didn't* have to explain. So much that he already knew. Oh, how she had missed that comfortable feeling of knowing and being known, like old jeans that had moulded to your shape.

They took a table in a corner and Beth insisted on getting coffees. 'I'm the one with the currency, after all!'

When she returned, he had shrugged off his jacket and Beth could see he'd grown strong and lean. He sat comfortably, with his legs stretched out under the table, but as she put the coffees down he sat up and leaned forward eagerly. 'There's something I want to say before we begin,' he said.

'Okay,' she said.

Here it comes – his engagement. Maybe he's already married. She glanced at his left hand. No ring. But she was psyched up to congratulate him warmly. To welcome another cousin into the family, such as it was.

'This family,' he began with a sigh, 'is not renowned for its transparent integrity. Nor even its solidarity. I wouldn't call it lies, but certainly the truth has been pretty economical. Deception, you might call it.' She waited. 'So I want us to agree on something.'

She nodded. Anything.

'That we'll be honest with each other. That we won't hold back anything bad, or even good! That we'll be willing to admit what we don't like, don't understand – whatever!'

Like Gregor's postcard. She smiled. 'Sure thing. You're on.'

He reached across the table for her hand and squeezed it momentarily.

'Okay. So. You emailed about twin brothers. I remember them. Ashley and Aidan. The 'A's. Used to play with them before you were even born. The boys and your mum and dad used to come and play in our garden. We lived in Balerno then. Big garden. Mum used to say *the 'A's are coming over* - and we'd have a great old game. I loved it, because I didn't have any brothers to play with, and they were about the same age as me. There was an apple tree we used to climb, and a space behind the garden shed where we made a den. Then you were born and your brothers loved you because you were small and cute and pretty, and I suppose I felt a bit jealous. Asked Mum if I could have a baby sister!'

Beth's heart thumped. Brothers. Her brothers had loved her.

'Then, when you were a few months, just crawling, I think, or maybe you'd taken a few steps - can't remember the timing exactly – you all went on that disastrous holiday to Egypt, and came back without the 'A's. It was like a nightmare that went on and on. I remember Mum telling me not to mention the boys whenever you and your parents came round, because it upset your mum so much. Then she said your mum had forbidden your dad or anyone else to mention them, and had given away all their toys. I remember feeling indignant and disappointed. I said to Mum *They could've given them to me!* Oh boy, did I get a ticking off for that. *Selfish, uncaring child...*' So I never dared tell her or anyone that I felt you were all mine, then, that I didn't have to share you with anyone.' He looked away, colouring beneath his beard.

Beth gasped, now, and racked her brain to try to remember something – anything – that might have been a clue. Nothing. And as for belonging just to Paul – rockets were firing off in her head, catherine wheels whizzing round, scattering colour and threatening an avalanche of exhilaration and turmoil.

He looked back at her. 'I suppose your mum was suffering from post-traumatic stress or something, but the real problem was your dad, for going along with her request. Sorry – I shouldn't say that.' Again he took her hand for a moment. 'But we agreed on honesty?'

She nodded.

'If only your dad had insisted that she went to the doc, got counselling or something. Then at some point around that time Granny began to lose the plot – became very forgetful – d'you remember?'

'Yes. Dad didn't want us to visit her. Or, didn't want *me* to visit. Used to go while I was at school.'

'Yeah. Know why that was?'

'He said he didn't think it was any fun for me to visit a poorly old lady.'

'Well I reckon it was because he didn't want her to let slip about the 'A's. She might've blown his cover. And of course before that there was the car crash, and then your mum....'

'Yeah.'

They paused. The coffee machine hissed, and customers came and went. A waitress bustled around them, wiping the next table and removing their own empty cups. Beth thought she had become inured to bad news. But this wasn't wholly bad. This was... different. A revelation. Now she had a hundred questions but none that she could frame. But facing them with Paul right beside her was like night turned to day, a rosy glow in a black void.

Paul stretched and rubbed his face. 'Want a bun or something?'

Beth nodded. She wasn't hungry, but she was desperate to prolong the conversation. 'I'll get it,' she said. 'Scone and jam?'

'On second thoughts, I'd rather have a beef wrap. The plane meals were okay, but...'

Beth bought snacks and juice, and the conversation seemed to drift up to a more superficial level, like a warm-down after strenuous exercise. They chatted about his flight and the films he had watched, but Beth felt tense, eager to dig deeper. It was like playing pass the parcel. As they unwrapped layer after layer the truth was beginning to take shape, but this was Paul's story. Must be patient.

He gathered up the last crumbs with a moistened finger and drained his juice. 'When your mum was injured, your dad blamed himself. I think he blamed himself for the boat accident, too.'

'Had he been driving the boat?'

'No, but my mum said he was the one who wanted to go on the trip. Your mum had said you and the boys were too young to appreciate it. But he'd insisted. Then, of course, he'd been driving the car when your mum was injured.'

'Had he been drinking?'

'My parents had always wondered about that. Your dad never drank heavily, but he enjoyed a glass of wine with his meal – two if he was out with friends. Maybe just enough to slow his reactions.'

'He never drank at all after that. Wouldn't let me even try an alcoholic drink.'

'How did you manage in freshers' week at uni?'

'With difficulty! Well, I didn't miss it, of course, because I had never drunk, but I felt a bit daft. Sometimes I accepted a glass of wine, then just pretended to sip it. But I never told Dad.'

'Then your dad got more and more depressed and more paranoid about anyone mentioning the boys. After they died, your mum wanted to *make a new start* – Mum thinks they had even talked about having another baby, after you. After your mum died, your dad believed he was respecting her wishes. My mum was cross with him. She thought he was totally out of order to keep you in the dark. She was constantly on edge and so uptight about letting something slip.'

'But what if she had? Why the cover-up, the deceit, the secrets?'

'My folks thought that he was so entrenched in trying to please your mum, trying to redeem himself, as it were, that he was almost *living* the lie, never mind telling it. And you had to live with him, after all. If Mum had destroyed your confidence in your only parent, we'd all've been up a gumtree.' He leaned forward, closer to her. 'They may all have been misguided, but they wanted the best for you. They really did.'

Beth looked away and tried to take in all this information. 'Anyway,' she began, 'there's something I haven't told you. Something you haven't asked.'

'I know. About this crazy idea that one of the boys didn't drown?'

'Yes, but...' Beth had been careful to mention that very briefly in the email, in case it turned out to be a mistake. Sometimes, when she thought about it, it seemed like a fairly tale, yet Gregor had made that trip to Egypt specially, and now she wanted it to be true as much for his sake as for her own.

'Well yes, but that's a whole other story. No, I was meaning...'

'I haven't asked what happened. How did your dad die? Was it another accident? Or was he sick? Cancer? A heart attack? Must've been very sudden...'

So Beth interrupted and told him the whole story of Marc Ravello, and leaving university, and the way she, too, had failed to ask pertinent questions, though in her case, it was wrong suppositions. She cried a little, when she spoke about the banisters, and he leaned across the table to give her a peck on the cheek. But she was becoming adept, these days, at allowing herself a few tears, but then controlling them, and feeling better for both the tears and the control. Heather assured her it was progress. She told Paul about the house and how she couldn't face it, but at that point Paul broke into her monologue.

'That doesn't sound like our Lizzy.'

'What doesn't?'

'Unable to face something. You used to be passionate about discovering things. You were ambitious. You wanted to do medical research and *push back the frontiers of science.*'

'I said *that?*' Beth felt herself blushing. 'Sounds like a line from *Star Trek*: *to boldly go...*' They shared a laugh.

'Sure. You used to be so enthusiastic. About everything. You had opinions, like, even about visiting your mum in hospital and then Gran.'

'But I felt so guilty, when I looked back, about how I *didn't* want to visit Mum. How Dad used to go alone and leave me with Gran.'

'You were a small child, but you just wanted to go and sit on her bed and chat to her, but your dad was so wound up about everything, even at that stage, that he wouldn't let... wouldn't just let you be *you.*'

'But you were only...'

'I know, I was only eight or nine, but I noticed, and I used to hear Mum and Dad going on about it.'

Beth considered this, remembered how, later, her mother had become a taboo topic of conversation, how Dad had said she mustn't upset herself by dwelling on her mum's situation, or the accident, then finally, of course, her death.

'But I wasn't the one trying to avoid getting upset,' she said, as if Paul had been party to her thoughts. 'It was *him*. He was protecting *himself!*'

Paul was watching her intently. She remembered those frank blue-grey eyes. 'He held himself in a straight-jacket, Lizzy, and he restricted you as well. He changed, and gradually he made you change, too. It was your dad who used to call you Fizzy Lizzy, but your mum thought that name was too frilly.'

'Frilly?'

'Yes. You told me that was the word she used. And later you told me you'd read your mum's old copy of *Little Women* and you didn't like the character called Beth because she was such a tear-jerker – sweet but not at all feisty.'

'Did I really say *that?*'

She began, vaguely, to recall the various conversations, to feel the determination, the energy, the motivation that used to be hers, but most of all, she was astounded that Paul should have remembered. She took his hand for a moment, then, embarrassed, she released it and fiddled with the salt pot on the table.

After a moment she continued the account of how she had met Gregor, then Heather, and how they had invited her to stay with them. The only bit she left out was how she had lived in her car for a couple of weeks. And the wall. And hospital. That could all come later. She didn't want him to think she was totally loopy.

'So you're not planning to go back to uni?'

'Not any time soon. The dean has offered me a place next year if I want it. But…'

'But it was really your dad's idea, wasn't it? You becoming a doctor, I mean. My mum used to get hopping mad about it. Used to say he was brain-washing you.'

'Brain-washing me? But I did enjoy the study. You know how I liked dissection, then worried that I must be a bit weird!' She pulled a face and they both grinned.

'I used to reckon you'd be a good surgeon – all scalpel but no bedside chat.'

'But my heart wasn't in it, you know, and when Dad was gone there didn't seem any point. Apart from anything else.' For a moment she experienced again that earthquake of instability, life's free-fall with its endless empty horizon. But here she was, with friends, a home, a business and – yes – a family.

There was a natural pause. Beth shook her head a little and they both gazed around them. 'Still peckish?' she asked him. She went to buy a bar of chocolate, which they shared, square by square, while she told him about High Fives and Jem and The Wire. 'So we are *an emerging new business*. We've got a logo, a website, paper fliers for adverts and two and two halves employees!'

'Two and two halves?'

'Yeah. Jem and I are the two. Heather is one of the halves – she helps when she can, evenings and weekends, and The Wire is the other half – he turns up when the muse takes him! But he's getting better.'

'Yes, well. I'd like to meet them all.' He yawned and rubbed his face again. His fingers in his beard made an unfamiliar rasping sound. 'What's the time, anyway?'

It was almost eight. They had been there nearly four hours, talking and remembering, and there was still so much to say and ask. 'C'mon, I'll drive you home, and after you've slept and confronted your jet-lag we can talk some more. I haven't heard anything about your job, and not much about your walkabout.'

'There's plenty of that, and lots of pics once I've dug out my camera. Anyway, there's still that huge mystery – that one of your brothers might not have died?'

'I know, but I think I'll need Heather and Gregor there to help to tell it. It's their story after all. And I've been a bit nervous about seeing your folks again after so long, but now that you've explained...'

'Oh, they're longing to see you again, and they're *mortified* that they weren't around when you needed them.

Anyway, there's more family news on our side, too.'

Oh no. So here it comes. He really *is* engaged. Knowing she couldn't bear any more suspense, Beth plunged straight in. 'Tell me! You've won the lottery! You've got engaged! You've got a pet kangaroo!' The more ridiculous she could make the suggestions, the more easily she'd be able to hide her reaction. Was it so wrong, after all this time, to want to have her only cousin to herself just for a short while?

'No, none of the above. You're not anywhere close, though the kangaroo's a nice idea. Anyway, it's really my mum's news, so maybe I'll let her tell it.'

He refused to be drawn, so Beth drove him home to his parents' house. He yawned a lot more and didn't object when Beth said she'd rather postpone her reunion with his parents for a day or two, at least until he was rested. So she dropped him outside the house and drove back to Arthur's View and another long newsy explanation. But it was different now. Paul's memory of herself and her family had revised her own. Her parents weren't quite as she remembered them, but, best of all, she herself was not the failure that she had branded herself. The protective wall, the weeks in her car, the hospital episode – were just that – an episode. That chapter in her life no longer defined her. It was just the sling on her arm before the plaster cast enabled healing, the bandage around the wound, before sutures repaired the gash.

A welcome rush of warm air embraced her as she opened the front door. The dogs bounded to greet her, Christmas music was playing in the sitting room and the enticing smell of fried chicken lured her into the kitchen. Heather was at the table, reading something on her laptop.

'Hi Beth! How did it go?' Heather jumped up to hug her. 'What's Paul like? Did you recognise him? Is he exhausted? When do we get to meet him? We saved you some dinner. Are you hungry?'

'Ravenous,' she said, hanging her coat up in the hall and taking a seat at the kitchen table.

Heather

Edinburgh
December 2012

Heather put a plate of chicken and pasta in front of Beth.

Pa came in from his desk in a corner of the sitting room. 'Had a good day, Beth? Paul arrived okay?' Beth nodded through a mouthful of pasta.

'How's his jet lag? I expect it's just kicking in right now!'

'He'll be wanting his breakfast at supper time, or his bed at breakfast time, more like,' Heather added. 'Pa, are you going to tell her, or will I?'

'Tell me what?'

'We got the DNA results,' Pa said.

Beth gasped. 'And?'

'It's a match. He's your brother.'

'Pa!' Heather shrieked.

'What?'

'How could you deliver such world-shattering information in a mere dozen words?' Her own instincts were to build up a story with all the tension of opening the email, and wondering, hoping, yearning... all those whoops of joy and tears of relief when they read the news, all the hopes built up on Beth's behalf, transferred into longings and questions of her own.

Pa had the grace to look a bit sheepish.

Heather looked at Beth. Would that super-controlled alabaster complexion ever soften into lines betraying what she was thinking and feeling? But Beth's face, initially drained of colour, turned suddenly pink and a few tears welled up and splashed over. She brushed them away, smiling.

'Oh, I don't know what to say,' she exclaimed, laying down her fork. 'Thank you. Thank you for making the effort, Gregor... for having the notion in the first place to look up my family tree... for everything...' She waved her hand around the room. 'For taking me on board!'

'We emailed Ashraf.' Heather continued. 'He's going home to Sharm for Christmas, and then he says he's going to try to come over.'

'Over here? Ashraf's coming here?'

'Yes. You'll want to meet him as soon as possible, and of course he wants to meet you,' Gregor said. 'He's more of a seasoned traveller than you are, I mean, it's easier for him to travel. It wouldn't be suitable for you to travel to Egypt alone, and Heather and I have only just got back. He'll aim to come in January.'

'He'll be able to see the photo album – himself as a toddler and you, and Paul!' Heather said.

She felt Pa's hand on her shoulder. 'I think we should hold back on the photos, at least at first. Let him get used to the folk he *has* got before he takes to heart those he's lost.'

'He's got an aunt, uncle and cousin, as well as a sister,' Beth said slowly.

'Aren't you excited, Bethie?'

'She *is* excited, pet. Just because she doesn't squeak and holler and dance on the table like you...'

'Pa! I do *not* squeak and holler and...' But Pa and Beth were laughing so hard that Heather's indignation popped like a bubble and she joined in.

'We're delighted for you, Beth,' Pa said then. 'Ashraf

is a great guy, and we know you'll like him.'

'But will he like me?'

'Funny. That's exactly what *he* said.'

Beth

Edinburgh

Christmas Day 2012

From the back seat of the car, Beth looked out at the driving sleet. So much for a white Christmas. Corelli's Christmas Concerto was playing on Radio 3.

'Can't wait to meet this famous aunt and uncle and see Paul in situ,' Heather said.

'Very kind of them to invite us,' Gregor added.

Beth looked at the backs of their generous heads. Of course, it was logical that they should all have Christmas day at Bob and Nessa's. It absolved her from having to make the difficult choice – actual family, or Heather and Gregor.

But Beth was nervous. Despite a letter of sympathy, written by Bob but also signed by Nessa, she still hadn't seen them since Paul's arrival almost a week ago. A few good walks with Paul, ending in country pubs or coffee shops, had been wonderful and had appeased her impatience a little. His parents, he said, both had fluey colds.

They made a dash from car to front door, then came the round of exclamations, introductions, handshakes and hugs.

'Come in, come in!' Bob urged, 'It's so good to meet you and to be able to thank you for looking after our girl.' Beth didn't feel at all like their girl, but she said nothing as they all filtered through to the sitting room for mulled wine and mince pies.

It was all there – the tree, bedecked with red and gold – cards clipped on to satin ribbons – mistletoe above the dining room door - the proverbial pile of tastefully-wrapped gifts under the tree. There was the elegant candlestick that used to be Granny's, in another life, when they'd played charades, pulled crackers and worn silly paper hats.

'So glad to meet you at last...'
'History? Ah, never my strongest suit!'
'Egypt in the revolution? Must've been scary!'
'Barbies on the beach on Christmas Day? You'll be missing *that*, eh Paul?'
'So what d'you think the Queen will say?'
'The Olympics, of course...'
'...and the Diamond Jubilee celebrations.'
'All that rain...'
'The Duke caught pneumonia after that, you know...'
'Not surprised at his age.'
'And what about Whitney Houston?'
'Poor thing, and what a loss.'
'Neil Armstrong, too. Now *there's* a piece of history for you, Gregor!'

'Delicious, Nessa. Thank you so much. This turkey is really tender...'
'How d'you get the roast potatoes so crispy?'
'...fruit salad if you prefer. Not everyone likes Christmas pud!'
'Cheese and crackers, anyone?'
'No thanks, couldn't possibly.'
'Me neither. I'm stuffed.'

Beth was taking tiny morsels of pudding on to her spoon.

Normally, she loved this rich winter treat, but today she couldn't get it down. Her throat kept closing up. Paul was looking at her but she couldn't meet his gaze. As the day had approached, she'd wondered how she would cope with all the sympathy, regrets and condolences her family would offer. She'd done her own grieving. How would she square their shock and sadness with her own determination to move on now?

Instead, she was appalled by the superficiality, the heedlessness, the apparent insouciance of all she had been through – without them. Her father had hardly been mentioned. *They were mortified,* Paul had said. Her dad had been Bob's brother, after all, Nessa's brother-in-law, Paul's uncle. Paul had said Nessa wanted to talk to her. To impart some vital piece of news. What did he mean?

At last she looked up from her dish, but Paul was looking at his mother.

Bob stood up. 'Let's repair to the sitting room. We can toast the Queen with our coffee. Put the kettle on, Paul, there's a good lad.' Bob led Gregor and Heather through, but as Beth rose to leave the table, Nessa put a hand on her arm.

'My dear, sweet girl,' she began, then enveloped Beth in a hug which made up for everything, a hug like – like – the hug at Granny's funeral. Nessa held Beth for what seemed like minutes, and when eventually she pulled away, Beth saw she was crying. Beth herself cried then, tears of gratitude, tears that expressed mutual understanding better than words ever could.

Nessa pulled a tissue from her sleeve and blew her nose. 'I wanted to get this –' she waved a hand at the detritus on the table '- out of the way first.'

'It was wonderful, thank you...'

But Nessa shook her head dismissively. 'Truth is, I wasn't *so* surprised when I heard about your dad, I mean, about how he...'

Beth nodded.

'I guess his life had been a downward slide ever since that Egyptian holiday. But, you see, the deception started well before that.'

'My brothers...'

'No! Even before that.' Nessa paused and sighed. The national anthem was playing on the television in the sitting room. Paul was hovering near the kitchen doorway.

Nessa took a deep breath and sat up straighter. 'Your mum and dad married before Bob and I did. Your mum was very correct, very elegant, poised... well, beautiful. You only need to look in the mirror!' She smiled. 'Your mum and dad met as students. She bowled him over - so intelligent, so organised, perfect really. Sickening!' She laughed briefly. 'Anyway, he worshipped the ground she walked on. I think he thought she was too good to be true. He couldn't believe she would choose *him!* So he was treading carefully, lest his bubble should burst. Then Bob and I met.'

She sat back, crossed and uncrossed her legs and smoothed her skirt.

Beth forced herself to breathe normally.

'See, I was pregnant before Bob and I were married.'

'But that's not so very...'

Nessa sat bolt upright. 'No, I mean... Before I met Bob. Well, not *met* actually...'

The flush from Nessa's neck had reached her cheeks. Reaching out to take her aunt's hand, Beth had never felt so adult in her life.

'Fact is, Paul is not your Uncle Bob's. I had a fling - a

one-night-stand - with a guy whom Bob and I knew. I already liked Bob. We were about to get together. When we started going out, I discovered I was pregnant. Bob was so good to me. I'd been drunk that night. He said we all make mistakes. He was *so* kind...'

Nessa shed more tears, then, but hurried on. 'We announced our engagement, but your mum disapproved. Said your dad should tell his brother not to have anything to do with *soiled goods*. But we went ahead and got married. Then I had Paul. Bob always loved Paul as his son, but your dad – well, he was caught between his brother and his gorgeous wife.'

'But Granny...?'

'Your granny was lovely, such a peacemaker. Can you imagine it? She loved both her sons so much, but their wives had this dreadful thing going, disapproving, being no more than civil to each other. And of course Granny took Paul on board and loved him as her own grandson. No problem there.'

A sound from the kitchen. Paul was still there. Surely he could hear all this.

'Then there was that car accident when your mum was so badly injured. His loyalty to your mum grew out of all proportion. Almost as if, by taking on board all she ever wanted or aimed for, he could bring her back. His animosity towards Bob grew, too, and Bob became very defensive. It made family times more of a trial than a joy. So we sort of tried to avoid each other. Paul used to get angry. Said he couldn't wait to escape the family *atmosphere*.' Nessa brushed away a few more tears. 'Then at Granny's funeral...'

'Yes. I remember. Dad and Uncle Bob were annoyed that we had left the two of them together to look after the guests.'

'Yes. Of course, that was the tip of the iceberg. They hid the worst of it from you. You were only...'

'Fifteen.'

'Yes.'

'Mum...' Paul stepped into view and leaned against the door frame.

'Yes love, I'm getting there.'

'Paul didn't know – all these years – he didn't know that Bob was not his dad. It was part of Bob's defiance. I think he wanted to prove to your mum and dad that we were just as much a family as you five were.'

Beth was seeing Uncle Bob in a new light. His brashness, his teasing, his lack of warmth – they were all a cover-up. She knew all about cover-ups. Now her heart ached for him.

Aunty Nessa continued, 'I think p'raps Bob thought, after your mum... that he and your dad would become closer. Brothers again. But it seemed to work the other way. Then last week, when he heard about your dad from Paul...'

'I tried to get in touch...'

'Yes, I know, pet. I'm so sorry...'

In the doorway, Paul cleared his throat. 'Lizzy, we're not blood relatives...'

As the implications of this fact dawned on Beth, Paul stood, straight and tall, under the mistletoe, his eyebrows raised in enquiry and invitation. Her own rose in reply.

Beth

Edinburgh
January 2013

'Hi Aunty Nessa, it's me, Beth.' She was clutching her phone hard. 'He's coming, Nessa! Ashraf's coming!'

There was a brief pause, then a gasp. 'Oh, Lizzy, I'm *so* glad. Then you'll know for certain...'

'But we do know. The DNA...'

'Yes, of course. But I mean, when you see him, when *we* see him, 'cos you were only a baby...' She took a breath. 'When?'

'Next Friday. The third.'

'How wonderful! He'll be here for his birthday, then.'

Beth paused and shifted her phone to the other ear. 'His birthday?'

'Yes love. The fourth. January the fourth.'

'How do you... how do you know that?'

'Oh, I always remembered the 'A's' birthday. They were due on Bob's birthday, you see.'

'The twenty-fourth?'

'Yes. But they were early, of course, being twins. But I guess that's why I've always remembered.'

Beth paused again. 'But – d'you think he knows? I mean, knows when his birthday is?'

It was Nessa's turn to pause.

'Are you still there?'

'Yes pet. I guess you're right. If he didn't even know who his parents were, how would he know his birthday?'

'I wonder when he celebrates his birthday? Or if he

celebrates it?'

'Well, we'd better give him a birthday he'll never forget. A birthday to make up for all the others...'

Waiting at the airport again had all the import of the previous occasion. Recognising Paul had turned out to be easy, and reconnecting with him, a joy. But this was altogether different. Never mind recognising Ashraf – she hadn't even met him! At least, not for twenty years. But now she had Paul with her.

And Gregor, who already knew Ashraf.

And Heather, who not only knew him, but who had confessed to that elusive chemistry and who, she knew, was reining herself in with extreme difficulty, for Beth's sake and her own.

'There he is,' Gregor said calmly at last, and he and Paul, by agreement, stepped forward to greet him, while Heather gripped Beth's elbow and jiggled up and down, and Beth held her breath, stiff with apprehension. He was tall, like Dad, and – well – Egyptian-looking, though Beth didn't know any Egyptians. It must be the tan, the wavy dark hair and a certain, more formal style of dressing. Hungrily, she took in his face, taut yet supple, with startling blue eyes, the firm, strong eyebrows, the blue-black stubble, a slight smile, wavering between curiosity and apprehension.

Paul had taken Ashraf's suitcase, and Gregor was ushering him towards her and Heather. Heather's excited tension was infectious, and Beth felt her features freeze in a stupid, artificial smile.

'Beth? You are Beth?' He looked at her, blinking his long lashes once or twice, exuding sparkles of handsomeness.

Hot and breathless, she held out her hand to shake.

'In Egypt, we greet our sisters like this,' Ashraf said, and kissed her on each cheek.

'And how about friends?' Heather asked cheekily, absolving Beth from having to say anything.

'For friends who are as dear as sisters – yes!' Ashraf said, grinning. He kissed Heather similarly.

Sisters. Beth's heart was pounding with relief and excitement. So he had taken the relationship on board. She was his sister. He was her brother. How did adult brothers and sisters interact? Of course, every family was as different as the individuals within it.

Then Gregor was there, his arm reassuringly around her shoulder. 'Come on, Beth, everyone. Paul, you take Ashraf and Beth, and Heather and I will go in my car.'

The first few signs of spring may have sprung in Beth's life, but the weather outside the airport continued its winter pageant. Litter hurtled clumsily by in the grip of an icy wind that made them all gasp and shrink. Beth felt stupidly responsible. The grey cobbled streets, so much a fibre of her very being, the early dusk in a day in which daylight had hardly arrived, the gaunt silhouettes of Edinburgh's cityscape – what did they convey to an Egyptian whose sun always shone, whose sea was iridescently blue, whose city was vibrant with traffic and pedestrians all year round?

Back at Arthur's View, Gregor cranked up the heating. 'You'll be feeling chilly, son. Egypt – and hospitals – they're much warmer than Edinburgh in January.'

'Actually, Cairo flats are not so warm in January, Pa.

They're built to keep cool, not warm. But at least the winter's very short.'

Nero and Sol, having welcomed everyone exuberantly, settled nose to tail in front of the radiator. Ashraf was disconcerted. 'It's okay,' Heather assured him, 'they're both perfectly domesticated. They're friendly and clean and they don't bite. But I know Egyptians find it strange that we keep our dogs in the house. I guess everything's strange.'

To Beth, the dear house was comfortingly familiar. The Christmas decorations were slightly droopy now, but with that glorious lingering smell of cinnamon and oranges. Heather pulled the red velvet curtains against the encroaching black night.

'But remember I studied here,' Ashraf said. 'I even remembered some of the landmarks as we drove here – the castle, snow on the Pentland Hills. It would be interesting to see the university again. Beth, you have studied medicine?'

'Only for a year.'

'Here in Edinburgh?'

'No, in Dundee.'

'Ah. Is far?'

'No, only about an hour's drive. It was convenient for...' Beth stumbled. How much did he know about her mum and dad – *their* mum and dad? How much, exactly, had Gregor and Heather told him? She looked helplessly towards them.

'Ashraf, son, there's a picture I'd like to show you,' Gregor said, and strode quickly into the kitchen, returning with the Mount Hood postcard.

'Ah. So beautiful. It is in Scotland?'

'No, America. But we're taking it as our motto: see

how the scene is reflected so exactly in the lake? Nothing's blurred or hidden? It allows no secrets. Everything is revealed.'

Ashraf nodded.

'We'd love to hear how it went with your parents. You visited them over Christmas?'

'Yes. It was a little cold, even in Sharm El Sheikh! But it is easier to get holiday time from the hospital. Only Christians want time off work at this season.'

That was a new idea. Beth turned it over.

'My sisters – they all visited with their families. All the children – it was fun - a happy time. But I told them about you,' he nodded towards Gregor, ' about you, and about the DNA result. They did not understand so easily!' He chuckled. 'You know – they are not doctors, not...' He stroked his chin. 'My oldest sister, Hiba, she remembered.'

'She remembered what?' Heather squeaked. Gregor frowned at her impatience.

'She remembered that when she was small, she had no brother, only three little sisters. She remembered when the younger two were born. Then, suddenly, there was a brother! But my parents, they were frightened. They thought I would be angry. They feared there would be some... some law of prohibition. But they have always been so... so...'

Everyone waited, determined not to interrupt, but to allow Ashraf to tell his story in his way and in his time. Paul put his empty coffee mug on the table and stretched out his legs comfortably, but his expression was one of joyous wonder, and he never took his eyes off Ashraf.

Ashraf twisted his long elegant fingers together. 'My baba, he told me what happened. He was on the beach, walking and smoking. Mama didn't like him to smoke around the little girls. He saw something. He thought it was old clothes, washed up by the sea.'

Beth thought of the photos Heather had shown her. She tried to picture the beach on the Sinai Peninsula as Heather had described it, and how she and Ryan had left their clothes in a heap on the sand when they went swimming.

'He thought it was just clothes, but it was me!'

Ashraf spread his beautiful doctor's hands in an expression of surprise. 'He picked me up and found I was still alive, still breathing. He rushed home with me, and he and Mama looked after me. They thought I must be a gift from God – the son they had always hoped for.'

Beth ached with the joy of that village family, felt the initial incredulity, then the welcoming acceptance. A boy to love and care for at last!

'Of course, they thought I was Egyptian. Hiba remembers that I couldn't speak. Baba thought it was due to the sea and the shock. Or maybe I was late to learn to speak. Perhaps I tried to tell them my name, because they assumed I said Ashraf, a common Egyptian name. I believe they had no idea, then, that they were doing anything wrong. Perhaps they were not.'

They sat in silence, allowing this news to sink in, until eventually Paul said, 'How did they react to the news of Beth? That you had a little sister still living?'

Ashraf took a long time to answer, while Beth's stomach churned with fear and uncertainty. She was his sister, but would his family reject her? Was she an inconvenience, at best, or worse, a threat?

'Family history is very important to my people. It's an oral history, the stories of their grandfathers and great grandfathers, from generation to generation. I think that, perhaps, they had always known something like this would happen. Even God's gifts are not without consequences.'

'But, but… didn't they realise there must have been a grieving family somewhere? A family that lost their child?' Heather was indignant.

Ashraf was silent again. Then, 'I really do not think that idea reached them. But when I told them about Aidan, my… my twin brother, they wept. Mama especially. And when they heard about Beth,' He turned to Beth, then, and she felt herself blushing. Heather bounced along the sofa to sit close to her, and held her hand. 'When Mama and my sisters heard about the baby sister and her mama and baba, they all wept. Even Baba wept.'

Now Beth was weeping, too, weeping for the grief of the loving family who had been so good to Ashraf, but well aware of the upheaval that her very existence had brought upon these people. 'Ashraf, I'm so sorry,' she murmured. 'I never wanted to hurt your – your parents.' But now she had a brother, nothing on earth could take him from her.

'If anyone has upset the status quo here, it's me,' Gregor said. 'But once we discover the truth, I feel we're morally obliged to reveal it. Anyway, Ashraf, you could tell them that they haven't lost a son, but gained a daughter!'

Ashraf took Beth's hand, now, and said, 'Please don't cry little sister. One day, I hope you can meet Mama and Baba. I know you will love them. And of course, they will love you too.'

'But I won't be able to understand them, or speak to them.'

'I will teach you. Arabic is an easy language!'

'Don't you believe a word of it, Bethie,' Heather

exploded. 'It's impossible. But you'll have him to translate for you.' A look passed between Heather and Ashraf, then, and Beth felt the warmth of an enclosed circle.

'Ashraf,' Gregor began, 'when's your birthday?'

Startled, Ashraf thought for a moment. 'At home we don't celebrate birthdays very much, but I believe mine is in June. June the sixth. Why you ask?'

'Ah!' Gregor, Beth's rock, was suddenly pale.

'What, Pa?' Heather had noticed, too.

'The date of the accident,' Gregor explained. 'That must have been the day you were found. The day they rescued you.'

There was a sudden hush. This assumption sank in slowly. Then Paul said, 'Actually, Ashraf, you were born on the fourth of January. My mum and dad – your aunt and uncle – remember it well.'

'My aunt and uncle. Of course. I wish to see them soon.'

'You will! Tomorrow!' said Heather, leaping up and dancing around Ashraf's armchair. 'We're going to take you out for a birthday treat and you'll meet them tomorrow!'

Beth

Edinburgh
January 4, 2013

'You don't need me today,' Gregor protested. 'This is a family thing – your family.'

'But none of this would be happening at all without you, Gregor,' Beth protested, and so they all planned to meet up in the National Gallery, where they could sit and enjoy coffee in a warm environment and get through initial introductions.

Beth's renegade heart was turning somersaults, and no amount of rational thinking would lay it to rest. The tectonic plates of her life had recently slid into new, unrecognisable shapes. Now her thoughts skittered from soaring hope to crushing anxiety. How would Nessa and Bob react to Ashraf? Despite the positive DNA result – the faceless objective reality of that unimaginable truth – she wanted her relatives to meet. To reunite. Only the firm, deep foundations of warm flesh and blood could sustain her through life's unpredictable earthquakes.

The windows of the coffee shop looked straight out into Princes Street Gardens where the Christmas fair and German Market were in full swing. Gregor was watching the woolly-hatted holiday crowds, their faces rosy with winter air and mulled wine. Heather was sitting close to Ashraf, chatting animatedly. Beth's eyes were glued to the entrance, waiting for Nessa, Bob and Paul.

And there they were!

As soon as Nessa spotted Ashraf, she ran to hug him

and held him for a long moment, but it was Bob who then clasped Ashraf fervently, wet-eyed, and kept his arm around his nephew's shoulders for minutes, while Gregor went off to buy coffees and Paul encouraged everyone to sit down.

Unwittingly holding her breath, Beth watched her newly-acquired family. Nessa was staring at Ashraf. 'Yes, Ashley, it's definitely you! Look.' She fished a photo out of her handbag. 'That's you, holding Beth, and there's our Paul. You and he would be about four. You'd had your birthday but Paul hadn't had his yet – his comes in April – and that's... that's your brother, Aidan.'

Ashraf studied the photo closely. Beth longed for a better look, but this was a seminal moment, and even Heather was holding back. When Ashraf finally handed the photo to Beth, Heather took her arm and leaned in. There they were, the four little children, posed on Aunty Nessa's sofa: Ashraf in the middle, awkwardly holding a dark-haired baby. Aidan was on his left, grinning at the camera, and sandy-haired Paul was on his right, looking at the baby.

'The baby,' Beth gasped. 'Is that baby really...?'

'Yes, it's you, girl!' Bob assured her. 'Prettiest little thing you ever saw!' Astonished, Beth looked from the photo to Bob, who was beaming. He had changed so much since Christmas, since Nessa's revelation. Or maybe it was just Beth's perception that had changed.

'How do you know,' Ashraf began, 'how can you be sure that I am the boy holding the baby, and that it is not my brother?'

Nessa smiled. 'Aidan's hair would never lie down. Abigail – your mum – she used to wet it and stick it down and complain about it. She liked things just so. But yours was always perfect.'

Beth, Heather and Ashraf peered at the photo again. Sure enough, Aidan's hair was sticking up in a comical quiff.

The coffees arrived, and Nessa held her cup with one hand, and Ashraf's hand with the other. 'There's so much,' she began, her chin quivering, 'so much to catch up on, but...'

'It doesn't matter, Mum,' Paul put in. 'He's here now. We're all here now.'

Nessa nodded and sniffed, but didn't let go of Ashraf's hand.

Emotion had left Beth feeling drained, and she drank her coffee greedily.

'Come on, let's see what the Christmas market has to offer,' Bob urged eventually. Beth would have happily remained for hours, watching her family interact, but they zipped up their jackets, donned hats and scarves and the seven-strong cohort stepped out into the cold where they exclaimed, wondered, laughed and sampled everything on offer. Every time Ashraf commented on something that caught his eye, one of them bought it for him.

'But my birthday is not so important...' he began, embarrassed.

'Oh yes it is,' they chorused in pantomime mode, until he was loaded with German cheese, a Hungarian painted candle-holder, a Peruvian knitted hat, an Italian leather wallet and finally, at Gregor's insistence, a tartan scarf.

'You cannae come to Scotland, son, and not get a Scottish gift!'

They toasted him in mulled wine, plied him with burger and waffles and took a hundred photos.

They stopped at the temporary ice rink in Princes Street Gardens. 'Ashraf, can you skate?' Heather asked.

Ashraf looked on with disbelief.

'Not much ice in Egypt,' Paul said wryly.

'Never mind, I can't skate, either, and I come from Edinburgh!' Beth remonstrated.

'Well I can,' said Heather, 'and so can Pa. C'mon, we'll take you. You cannae come to Scotland and not try skating!'

So, with Pa on one arm and Heather on the other, first Ashraf, then Beth, were towed along, ankles wobbling uncomfortably on hired skates, while Paul struck out confidently and Bob and Nessa cheered from the edge. Ashraf's attempts were admirable, and the others declared him a natural, but Beth's efforts were so suffused with giggles that her legs were weak and her knees buckled often until they all left the ice, rolling with laughter.

The low, early afternoon sun dipped behind the castle and the whole market and fairground was plunged into shadow and an early dusk. The lights were already on in the big high street stores that flanked Princes Street and on the Christmas tree below the castle, while the gathering twilight enhanced the multi-coloured lights of the fairground itself.

'I guess we'd get the sunset from up there!' Beth stood below the Ferris wheel, gazing up at those gently moving carriages.

'You can't come to the Christmas market...' Paul began.

'...and not go on the Ferris Wheel!' Heather laughed.

'My treat,' Gregor declared. 'How many tickets should I get?'

'I'm not so good at heights,' Heather confessed, 'but I couldn't bear to miss out.'

'Do not worry,' Ashraf said with solemn formality. 'I will care for you.'

Heather blushed and giggled, but she sat very close to Ashraf as they climbed into the compartment with Beth and Paul. The wheel turned slowly, and the four looked down to see Nessa, Bob and Gregor laughing companionably.

'Your dad...' Beth began to Paul.

'...I know. He's a changed man, isn't he? He always loved the 'A's. His own flesh and blood, in a way that I'm not.'

Beth took his hand. But he continued, 'Ashraf, you've brought your Uncle Bob back to life.'

'Then I am very happy.'

'And as for Beth...' Paul continued.

'Yeah!' Heather said. 'Transformed!' She and Paul exchanged grins.

'Uncle Bob calls you Ashley,' Beth said, trying to divert attention away from herself. 'I guess it's hard for them to adapt. You need a neutral name – one that fits in both Egypt and Scotland. Do you have a middle name?' Then, 'Silly question! I'm sorry...'

'Actually, he does.' Paul said. 'Ashley James.'

Beth gasped. 'He was named after Dad!'

'Yes. And Aidan was Aidan Lindsay.'

'Mum's maiden name!'

'Ashley James Gomersall, meet Ashraf Daoud!' Heather giggled.

From forty metres above Princes Street, questions of names, business, house sale, jobs, careers and all the seemingly insurmountable drawbacks of geographical locations, disappeared like the vapour from the German wiener stall. No longer could they smell fried onions, coffee or mulled wine. Up there, the air was crisp and sparkling, clean as a new start. Against the backdrop of other people's longings and lies, deceit and despair, Beth's life had taken unprecedented turns, but the constant sun, insouciant, dipped majestically behind The Castle Mound and the city's characteristic skyline stood proud against the navy blue sky.

15013201R10185

Printed in Great Britain
by Amazon